Leaden Skies

Books by Ann Parker

Silver Lies
Iron Ties
Leaden Skies

Leaden Skies

Ann Parker

Poisoned Pen Press

Poisoned
Pen
Press

Poisoned Pen Press
6962 E. First Ave., Ste. 103
Scottsdale, AZ 85251
www.poisonedpenpress.com
info@poisonedpenpress.com

Printed in the United States of America

In memoriam
Donald L. Parker
1921–2006
and
Corinne C. Parker
1924–2006

Requiescant in pace

Acknowledgments

Well, where to start. At the beginning, of course, and that means family. Bill, Ian, and Devyn, it's only with your love and understanding that I manage to move from the first word of the first draft to the final word of the polished story. To all my sibs and relatives in Colorado and elsewhere, thanks for being there, cheering me on, giving me places to stay, people to talk to, and the warmth and laughs that are part of being a tribe.

And there are friends, as well, whose support ranks right up there with family. I owe particular and special thanks to Camille Minichino (aka Margaret Grace) and Dick Rufer, who invited me to "stake a claim" in their guest bedroom for several "writer's retreat" weekends. Those retreats helped me blast through to THE END. Thanks, Camille, for your friendship and brain-storming (and chocolate!) through the years, and Dick, for your humor and excellent 24/7 technical advice and support.

Experts who lowered me a ladder when I dug holes too deep to climb out of include Dr. Doug Lyle, M.D., Janice Fox from the Lake County Public Library, Kathleen Antrim, Dani Greer, Colleen Casey, and the librarians at my local Livermore Public Library. I'm also indebted to the Colorado Historical Society and the Denver Public Library for their wonderful resources and staff. I want to thank Katie Walter, who, years ago, got me thinking about fire insurance maps, map makers, and striders as a possible anchor for a story, and Mary Reed and Eric Mayer who showered me with mapping/surveying links, information, and encouragement. A tip of the hat goes to the awesome ya-hoo groups for Women Writing the West, carmelsloop, BIW, Weapons_Info....I'm sure I'm missing some, but believe me, I am grateful for all the helping hands folks have offered in the real and virtual worlds. Any and all errors are mine.

Thanks to my critiquers who kept me from wandering too far afield, doubling back, and/or getting lost in the wilderness of words: Camille Minichino, Penny Warner, Kathleen Antrim, Colleen Casey, Mike Cooper, Margaret Dumas, Janet Finsilver, Dani Greer (and her virtual red pen!), Claire Johnson, Rena Leith, Staci McLaughlin, Corinne Davis, Carole Price, Gordon Yano, and Janice Fox. And a special thanks to Jane Staehle for thorough ARC proofing.

The people of Leadville deserve special mention and their very own paragraph. I'm forever indebted to Bob and Carol Elder, who shared George Elder's letters with me; Hillery and Bruce McAllister, who showed me around Western Hardware's base-ment; and *Herald Democrat* editor Marcia Martinek, who toured me through the newspaper's collection of old presses. Carol Hill and the folks of The Book Mine, and Nancy McCain and staff of Lake County Public Library deserve a special round of applause. Also, a special thank you goes to Paul Copper, who spent a good chunk of an evening a couple of years ago talking with me about Leadville's mythical tunnels (which existed once, everyone agrees) and times "long past."

To Kate Reed, my webmistress, thank you for keeping me anchored in cyberspace. ☺

To the real Jim Kavanagh, you finally get to "cash in" on a role in this book. Thanks for being so patient.

Last but far from least, the Silver Queen Saloon would not have seen the light of day once (much less three times, so far) if not for the amazing folks at Poisoned Pen Press: the extra-ordinary editor (TEE) Barbara Peters, publisher Rob Rosenwald, associate publisher Jessica Tribble, and all the other Press-ers—Marilyn, Nan, Geetha, Annette, and my cover designer Marsha. Thank you, all, for making my dream come true.

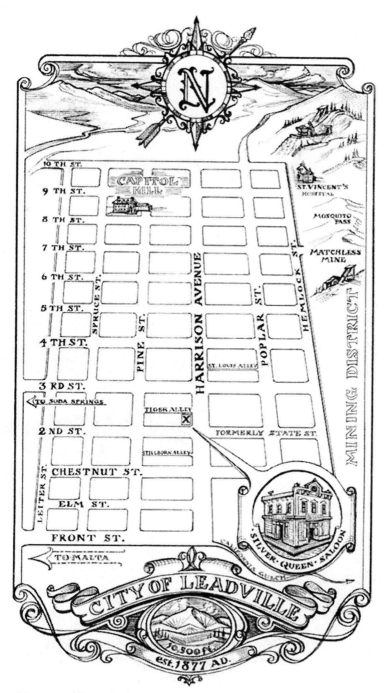

Map created by *Michael Greer, Greer Studios*

Chapter One

"And lead us not into temptation,
but deliver us from evil..."

—Matthew 6:13

July 22, 1880

When the summer storm arrived late that afternoon, it was hailed as a blessing. Damp splots the size of half-eagle gold coins pocked hats and shawls, sent small dust explosions puffing up from dirt streets ground to dust beneath boots and wagon wheels, and tempted small children to stand with faces upturned, tongues thrust out to catch the drops.

Many who lined Leadville's overheated streets, hoping for a glimpse of Ulysses S. Grant arriving for his five-day visit, had been there since sunrise. They welcomed the rain, the cool wind that accompanied it. But after the thunder passed and the drenching continued, hour after hour, the thousands packing the avenues began to curse the clouds and their liquid gift.

Damp crawled up trouser pants and wicked up the hems of long skirts and petticoats. Drops trickled off hat brims to wilt celluloid and lace collars and chill the backs of necks. Streets, which had produced clouds of dust mere hours ago despite the best efforts of "squirt wagons," now flowed mud.

"He's coming. Just left Malta."

The whisper moved through the crowds like a gathering wind. Ears strained to hear the faintest of train whistles over the murmur of voices, the snort of horses, the shouted directions of those preparing the parade route from the point of disembarkment to the hotel where "Unconditional Surrender" Grant and his party would stay.

Still, not everyone's attention focused on the impending arrival. In the red-light district of Leadville's State Street, rain conferred anonymity while darkness stilled the voice of conscience. Behind the heavy damask curtains of a three-story brick fortress on the corner of State and Pine, another world beckoned.

Mapmaker Cecil Farnesworth tipped his head back to examine the front of the substantial building. Rain dripped off the brim of his hat, mingling with the drops that fell from the sky and slapped his face. With a long intake of breath, Cecil stepped up on the porch, out of the rain. He removed his hat and, clutching it over his heart like a shield, knocked on the door of the whorehouse.

Chapter Two

Cecil was sure that, by stepping foot inside the house of prostitution on State Street, he had consigned his soul to purgatory, or worse.

Forgiveness, he feared, would be very long in coming.

Right then, though, it didn't matter. He'd come back to see her, the woman with the dark eyes who reminded him of Rachel. He wasn't going to do anything...sinful. He just wanted to talk to her. Hear her voice. See if she sounded like Rachel.

But the visit wasn't going the way he'd pictured it.

After surrendering his hat and heavily soaked overcoat to the silent doorman, he'd allowed himself to be escorted into the drawing room by the woman called Molly. She was all sharp angles—nose, chin, elbows, and wrists. Jutting collarbones created a topographical ridge above a flat, freckled expanse bordered by lace. Not to his taste.

There was no sign of Miss Flo, the woman who ran the place. Flo, as he remembered her, was pleasant, blond, soft, and warm. At least, she'd felt soft and warm, the last time he'd been around. At that preliminary visit, she'd greeted him as if he were an old friend, even before he'd introduced himself and his purpose. She hadn't turned him away as he'd feared she would, but had hugged his arm close to her side, said "Call me Miss Flo, honey," and shown him around the upper floors while keeping up a cheerful line of chatter. He remembered that she'd worn a green dress of silky fabric with fancy trimmings on the back and a low neckline. A diamond necklace—at least, he thought they might be diamonds—had glittered in the light of coal oil lamps throwing back the shadows of the early summer evening. Everything she wore looked expensive. And she'd been so kind. He couldn't remember the last time a woman had not treated him with the most neutral courtesy or, worse, with disdain.

Now, here he was, days later, sitting in the parlor room.

He'd refused the champagne, but been talked into buying a single, high-priced glass of wine. (Another sin he would never have the courage to confess. He'd not touched anything stronger than the weakest of beers in his entire forty-two years of life.) Cecil looked around at the room's appointments. Thick rugs, inlaid wood ceiling, crystal chandelier, silver candlesticks, rich velvet curtains, burnished piano. He wondered, briefly, how it was possible to make enough money at…well, this kind of business…to afford such things. Too, there were the dresses that most of the women wore, all sewn from luxurious materials that shimmered in the candlelight as they shifted and moved about. And he remembered Miss Flo's diamond necklace…maybe it was a gift from an admirer?

He would never have been able to buy that sort of thing for his Rachel on his salary from the Johnson Map Company. Even if events had proceeded to the point where such expensive items were a necessity.

With an inward cringe, he remembered his last walk with Rachel that spring day. Their last day together. How he'd felt as they walked along, side by side, Rachel chattering about her sister's upcoming nuptials. He'd felt young again—she always made him feel that way, his Rachel did—and that life, like the season, was full of possibilities and hope for the future. And then, when he'd asked her hand in marriage, granted, somewhat on impulse and without asking her father for his blessings first, how she had stopped in her tracks. Turned to him, strands of shining black hair escaped from her bonnet and lying along her cheekbones, blue eyes wide, beloved face slack-jawed. Not, it had finally dawned on him, with hoped-for happiness, but with an emotion that looked more like shock. A look, he thought in retrospect, which might have even been tinged with repulsion. That afternoon now seemed so far away. Like Rachel. Half a year and hundreds of miles away from Leadville, Colorado.

Thinking of Rachel, he almost left the brothel right then.

Still, he remained seated in the parlor room, the only man there among—he counted quickly—six women. The horsehair in the sofa pricked through his trousers into the backs of his legs, much as the memory of Rachel's face had pricked his conscience as he'd hesitated on the boardwalk in the rain before summoning enough courage to knock on the door.

But this visit was definitely *not* proceeding as he'd hoped.

The woman with hair and eyes like Rachel, the woman who, incongruously enough, glowed with purity and youth just like his Rachel, sat on the Turkish couch in the corner, twirling a strand of dark hair around one finger. She, like the rest, was dressed up fancy, not wearing the loose garment he'd glimpsed her in when Miss Flo had taken him around the upper stories and he'd made his notes and measurements.

She was watching him.

As were all the women in the room.

The girl with the gray teeth sat across from him. She stared hardest of all. Her face was not unpleasant, structurally speaking. But, she's so young, he thought. Younger than Rachel's almost eighteen years. Too young to be here. Full-bodied, she wore a purple, satiny sort of dressing gown dotted with what might be flowers and butterflies. He wasn't certain about this, as he was trying hard not to stare back at her. She looked as if she hadn't had time to dress properly before Molly brought him into the room. The top three closures of her gown—complicated corded oblong buttons of a vaguely Oriental nature—were undone. White skin teased him through the deep open V as she leaned forward to refill his glass.

The woman's dark, musky scent washed over him, as she remarked, "Another drink, another dollar, Mister Mapmaker.

It's Angelica wine, all the way from California. My favorite too, 'cause it's so sweet."

He had to stop drinking so quickly, he hadn't realized he'd drained the first glass.

The red painted lips parted in a smile. He had an even better view of those teeth as she said, "Guess everyone else's off, hoping to catch a look-see at the first train t' town and Mister Grant. 'Cept for you. Flo's still out there, drumming up business for us all. Did she send you here, Mister Mapmaker? What's your name, anyhow? We can't just keep calling you Mister Mapmaker."

He couldn't remember her name, although she'd told him when she'd handed him the wine glass a few minutes ago. After all, it wasn't her he wanted to talk to. But here she sat, simpering and smiling, the tip of her tongue darting out to touch her upper lip.

Her smile didn't reach her eyes. The way she stared at him made him feel like a rabbit trapped by a hungry cougar.

He cleared his throat and sat up straight, reminding himself that he was taller by a head and a half, much, much older, and had masculine strength on his side. There was nothing to fear. What could she, a mere slip of a girl, do to him, after all?

"I'm a surveyor, not a mapmaker, actually," said Cecil, gripping the wine stem tighter and wondering why he'd listened to the demon that had urged him to turn off the sidewalk to enter this house of ill repute. "I'm in town surveying buildings for the Johnson Map Company. Identifying features of interest to insurers. Type of frame, floor, roof. Pipes." He realized that he was babbling, but the words kept coming. "The number of stories. Placement of doors, windows, the size of the rooms."

He glanced at the Rachel-like girl to see if she was listening. Her wonderful eyes were half-closed, as if lulled by his voice. "It's important," he cleared his throat, "important for the insurers to have all the details. So as surveyors, or striders as we're sometimes called, we're tasked to make a thorough examination."

"That so." The slash of a smile widened. Those gray teeth seemed to take up her whole face. Her sly eyes, a muddy brown color, slid to the other women lounging about the room, sending a message he couldn't interpret. "You want to examine *this?*"

She tugged the half-unbuttoned wrapper aside, exposing one breast.

A wave of tittering flooded the room. Heat rushed up, strangled his breathing, and mottled his face. He shrank back against the sofa. The breast seemed to stare at him. *Eye of the Devil.*

Her wicked grin broadened. She closed the robe, looped a single button, then set one slipper-shod foot on the ottoman between them. "With the proper coin, you can inspect all you want. Of course, if you're looking for a fire, I'm supposin' you'll be wanting to take a poke in the cellar."

She hiked her skirt hem above her knee, providing enough of a view for him to realize she wore nothing underneath. Nothing, that is, but garters holding up red-and-gold embroidered stockings.

The skirt dropped. "The peep show was free. You want to measure the cellar with your rod, mapmaker, it'll cost. How much depends on whether you're using the front door or the back."

She thinks I want to…

Cecil's hand twitched. Wine spilled on his lap in a cold amber splash. He jumped to his feet, setting down the half-empty wine glass with an unsteady hand. "You've misunderstood my intentions. I, I just wanted to talk."

The woman shrieked with laughter. Most of the others snickered or belatedly hid smiles behind ornate fans. All but the one with Rachel's eyes, who just watched, stone-faced, twirling her hair.

Cecil fled the parlor, pushed past the doorman, who made no attempt to stop him, and stumbled out, crashing full-on into a waterproof-swathed figure mounting the front stairs. The person's gloved hand shot out and clutched his arm.

"Watch where you're going!" The sharpness in the feminine voice softened in shocked recognition. "Mr. Farnesworth? Is that you?"

He looked up, aghast, at Miss Flo, her concerned face out-lined inside the loose hood. The parlor house madam's rain-slicked coat blew open in a gust of wind, revealing a sparkly ensemble of patriotic red, white, and blue.

He tore away and fled, the woman's shrieks reverberating in his mind, chasing him into the anonymous crowds of State Street.

<><><>

Flo swept into the drawing room, tugging off her wet gloves, a frown hovering dangerously between her eyebrows. "I was almost knocked down by the mapmaker on the steps. What happened?" She looked around, her displeasure visibly deepening. "I've spent the last hour getting soaked, ruining my shoes, trying to round up business in this lousy weather…" Her gaze stopped on Molly. "Has he been the only customer?"

Molly, gathering up empty glasses, nodded without looking at Flo.

"Our only customer, and you all scared him away?"

Dead silence. The women shifted in their chairs, smooth-ing fabric over their laps, licking their lips, examining their fingernails.

Lizzie snorted. "He was only looking, not buying. Said he came here to *talk*, f'god's sake."

Flo focused on the woman in the wrapper. "Lizzie, is this your doing?"

Lizzie raised one shoulder in a shrug. The wrapper slid down, revealing a bare collarbone.

Flo slapped her gloves down on the end table. Wet silk met wood, sounding like a hand smacking skin. "Lizzie! I've had enough of your antics. He might've changed his mind if you'd given him more time and liquor."

Lizzie smirked. "Oh, we gave him *plenty* of liquor."

One of the other women in the room spoke up. "Miss Flo, he might come back later. While Lizzie was tartin' around, he was making eyes at Zelda." She jerked her head toward the young woman lounging on the corner sofa.

Flo raised one pencil-thin, calculating eyebrow, glanced at the young woman still curled on the couch, then turned her gaze back at Lizzie. "This is a high-class parlor house, Lizzie. Remember that."

Lizzie bared her teeth. "Yes, *ma'am*."

"No drinking. No drugs. No potions for female complaints. No laudanum. I have a reputation to uphold. The gentlemen expect quality, and quality is what we deliver. No sloppy whores, drunk and weeping, or worse. That's how we can charge more than any other place on State Street. That's what's going to allow us to charge even more when we move up-town."

"Flo's sold her soul to the Devil so's we could move up-town to screw all the qual-i-ty gentlemen," Lizzie said in a drunken sing-song.

All the women froze.

Flo swung around to her. "What did you say?"

Lizzie shrugged, a smirk curling her mouth.

Flo walked over to her, put two fingers under her chin and pressed upward, forcing the girl to meet her gaze. "Don't cross me, Lizzie. Remember who's in charge here." The words carried a soft, dangerous charge.

Lizzie yanked away. "Why don't you tell us, Flo. Who *is* in charge?"

A knocking on the front door interrupted further discourse. The squeak of hinges reached the parlor room, along with the low rush of men's voices. The women stirred, like aspen leaves fluttering in the high mountain breeze, their lassitude vanishing.

With a last glare at Lizzie, Flo snarled, "Why do I even bother with you! I shelter you. Feed you. Buy you the best, most up-to-date outfits....And what are you doing wearing *my* dressing gown? Go take it off and put on one of your own. Now!"

Flo hurried from the room, her voice shifting to a cheerful trill as she approached the entryway. "Gentlemen! Good evening! Has the train arrived yet? No? Coming in to escape this dreadful rain, then? Well, you've come to the right place. Let Danny take your coats and hats, and I'll escort you into the parlor where it's warm and pleasant and the girls are waiting. We'll get hot toddies set up all around, unless you'd prefer champagne or wine. We have the loveliest selection, shipped in from California. And the girls are just dying for some company."

Lizzie leaned forward and snatched up Cecil's abandoned glass. Then she sat back, wiggling her bottom into the plush velvet seat. She lazily crossed her feet on the ottoman before tipping the glass back and, with a defiant glance around the room at the other women, drained the last of the wine.

Chapter Three

Cecil paused on the boardwalk, pulled his handkerchief from his waistcoat pocket, and wiped sweat and rain from his face. It was a July night, but here, ten thousand feet up in the Rocky Mountains, the cold froze the moisture to his skin. It was only when an icy breeze whispered through his hair that he realized he'd left his hat at the bordello.

For a moment, standing on the slick and weather-warped boards, jostled on all sides by passersby, he wasn't sure what direction he faced. How strange, for him. He prided himself on his sense of direction, always able to pick out north, no matter if he stood in a coal cellar or the middle of a windowless factory floor.

He squeezed his eyes shut, blocking out the sights of State Street—the dance halls, saloons, hotels. But he couldn't shut out the sounds or smells. Male voices clashed in argument and drunken laughter. The oompahs and blats from brass bands outside dance halls and saloons competed to lure in customers. Smoke from thousands of wood- and coal-burning stoves mixed with sulphur fumes from the smelters and the wet heavy scents of mud, manure, unwashed men, and wet wood. Over it all, like a light blessing from the hand of God, lay the clarifying smell of rain.

After the debacle back home with Rachel, he'd let his supervisor know that he would accept the first assignment available out West, no matter where. Leadville had been a challenge he'd taken gladly. At first, all had gone well. He had been able to push his personal woes aside, be the professional strider that would make the company nod with approval. He met the local officials, explained his business, then dutifully went from building to building and explained his business again and again to owners and managers. Some were accepting, some wary, others downright hostile. He took notes in painstaking details, not to be hurried. Each night in his cramped hotel room, he carefully drew up his diagrams and forwarded his sheets once a week to the home office. The work had filled his days and nights, kept the darkness that was his failure with Rachel at bay.

But all that changed when he first knocked on the door of the brick brothel on the corner of Second and Spruce. Miss Flo had been more welcoming than most. She'd listened intently to his explanations, examined his credentials, and then, with a brilliant smile, hooked an arm through his, and gave him a personal tour of the building. The woman who looked like Rachel had passed him on the second floor, glancing at him once. With that single glance, something inside him faltered. His moral determination melted.

Chills, not all from the cold and wet, racked him. "I can't go back there," he whispered through chattering teeth. "God give me strength." He pulled his jacket closer around himself.

A violent jostling, followed by some creative cursing from the man who'd knocked into him, nearly sent Cecil off the boards and into the muddy river that served as the street.

Cecil clapped his hand to his jacket pocket and almost swore out loud in return. His hat was not the only thing he'd left at that cursed brothel. His firearm, which the doorman had insisted he check, also waited for him.

He remembered the words of warning from one of Leadville's city fathers: *Only a fool goes about at night unarmed.*

At that moment, someone across the street shouted, "Train's down by California Gulch! They saw the light!"

It was as if someone had opened the floodgates. People streamed across the street toward Cecil, heading toward Third Street. He was caught up in their sheer numbers, dragged along with the current, unable to stand fast against the unending flow.

As he neared Third, he saw bonfires lining the sides of the road, police standing at intervals with local militia, straining to keep pedestrians, carts, and riders on horseback from surging onto the road where General Grant would pass by. He halted, in the middle of the cross street, behind the human barriers, unable to move in any direction. The deep mud sucked slowly at his boots. Mire oozed in over his boot-tops, began to attack his gartered stockings with cold intent.

He caught a glimpse of the shining black hulk of the locomotive, now stopped at the foot of Third. Spots of light from the bonfires set the wet black bulk agleam, steam from the smokestack rising through the rain. It looked nearly alive as it disgorged small figures, one after another. The iron horse, he thought. *A carnivorous horse* whispered back a voice from deep inside. He started shivering again.

A compact, gray figure appeared on the platform, hat in hand.

The crowd surged forward, and cheers rose from a thousand throats.

The General, he realized. Ulysses S. Grant. Civil War hero and past president.

As if in confirmation, the massive engine emitted an ear-splitting shriek.

A commotion to one side drew his attention.

Two pistol shots cracked.

People nearby screamed, squeezing back. Police broke ranks, converged on a shadow figure yelling above the wash of cheers, "Butcher! He was nothin' but a butcher for Mr. Lincoln's War!"

The police wrestled the would-be avenger of the South to the ground, but not before a last gunshot rang out.

A constriction and jolt transmitted through the mob and slammed into Cecil. At the same time, a thunderous *crack* sounded, not a block away. The blue and red of fireworks lit the frenzied multitudes.

Cecil stumbled sideways, off-balance, crashed into the person next to him, and collapsed to one knee. A commotion behind him. More screams. He couldn't tell if they were made in anger, fear, or warning.

With one hand in the mud to steady himself, Cecil twisted around. A rearing horse plunged down, hooves flashing, missing his face by the merest breadth. His heart, his breathing, froze.

More commotion and warning shouts came from those who had been quicker to evade the terrified horse than he. The rider slid from the saddle and knocked Cecil aside, all the while saying urgently to the horse, "Easy, easy, Lucy girl. Whoa!"

Cecil's supporting hand slipped, his elbow and left side landing in the mud, while the rider fought to keep the horse from rearing again. With the horse finally under control, reins gripped taut in one hand, the rider hooked a shrinking Cecil under one arm and hauled him to his feet.

Cecil blinked, inches away from the ashen face of the rider. Smooth, sharp features were branded with fear, anger, and something else. The phrase "exhaustion of the soul" popped into Cecil's numb mind from somewhere.

Cecil watched, as if from a distance, as the rider's mouth opened. He fully expected a stream of curses to emerge, accompanied by a blow or a knife to the gut.

An undignified end seemed imminent.

Automatic words surfaced, wrapped around his mind, as familiar and smooth as the worn beads of his childhood: *O my God, I am heartily sorry for having offended thee—*

Instead, the mouth croaked:

"Jesus! I almost killed you!"

It took a moment for the fact to penetrate his numbed senses that the voice belonged to a woman. Details pricked through the fog of misery and self-loathing that enveloped him: She was dressed, absurdly enough, in men's attire. Tall, about his height. Her face, illuminated by the stark light of a nearby bonfire, held none of the feminine softness he so admired in his Rachel's face. Instead, high cheekbones echoed overall angular planes. Eyes cut through him with a gaze sharp as the knife he'd been expecting. Dark, unaccountably short hair hung loose, plastered to her cheeks. Her mouth tightened, thinned out by anger or perhaps worry. The grip on his arm shook as if with palsy.

Someone seized his other arm.

"Are you injured?" A masculine voice, too close, almost at his ear.

Cecil shrank from the concern in the tone. He didn't deserve it, this compassion.

The gentleman addressed the rider. "He doesn't appear hurt, Mrs. Stannert. Mostly shaken. Those shots, it's a good thing the police were nearby. I wouldn't be surprised if there's more mayhem in store. For certain, that fellow isn't the only one plotting against Grant. In any case, we should take this gentleman somewhere where he can recover. Perhaps to your saloon."

His mind tried to wrap around what he was hearing: *A woman. Dressed as a man. Who works in a saloon. What manner of woman is this?*

She spoke rapidly, with intensity. "It will take forever to get up State to the saloon in this crowd. We can't cross Third until the procession passes. I don't know. He looks like he's not altogether right in the head. Can he walk, do you think? Can you walk?" This last was directed at him. Without waiting for a response, she continued to her cohort, "Should we put him on one of the horses? Turn him over to the police for safekeeping? What do you think, Reverend?"

Cecil blinked. Confused. *Reverend?*

The man's somber dark garb, mellifluous words, the professional sympathy—now, it all made sense. The reverend hemmed and said to the strange woman, "Perhaps I should take him to the church. Or the mission. It's not far from here. Someplace quiet until he recovers."

The situation suddenly came clear to him.

A man of the cloth. And—

Another she-devil from State Street.

His strength returned. His feet came unstuck from the mud. He ripped from their holds and bolted, pushing his way through the crowd, heading toward Harrison, the main street of town. Rain pelted his face, ice-cold needles driving into his flesh.

He stopped only when he reached the cross street that would lead him to the brothel.

I can't go back. I shouldn't. Not now. I should go to the hotel. Get my hat and gun tomorrow. Or buy new ones.

Even as these possibilities crowded his mind, he was moving toward State Street, shaking, every nerve screaming for release, sweat soaking his undergarments and seeping into his outer clothes to mingle with the mud and rain. He pushed against the tide of humanity pouring in the opposite direction, all moving as one to greet the incoming train.

Chapter Four

"My God," Inez Stannert whispered. "Oh, my God."

The sweat, which had coursed down her back as she'd fought to bring her horse Lucy under control, was now an icy sheet on her skin. Her fingertips tingled inside her gloves from the force at which the older man had twisted away. "I almost. Almost." Her throat closed up.

She couldn't say it.

I almost killed him.

Inez closed her eyes, blocking out the night and the shimmering rain made visible by the bonfires.

A hand found hers. Reverend Sands' fingers tightened on her own, a warm presence.

Inez opened her eyes and turned to Sands' gaze.

She sensed that the reverend was peering at her, even though his face was cast into darkness under his soggy, wide-brimmed hat. His voice wrapped her chilled soul like a blanket, soothing, offering comfort. "The man, just now, he'll be all right. We helped him get to his feet, and he ran away. He lives because of your quick thinking."

He drew her close, in a brief hug. Inez allowed herself to relax into the familiar yet furtive embrace, stolen, as it was, in tight quarters and within the possible observance and subsequent disapproval of surrounding strangers. Inez and the reverend were shielded from eyes in one direction by her horse Lucy's proximate bulk and from eyes in the other direction by a sea of backs and general disinterest. Any possible spectators had turned away, no longer entertained, now that the show of near death was over. Instead they all strained forward on tiptoe, attempting to catch a glimpse of Grant and his entourage, to hear the distant voices of Leadville's city fathers delivering their initial greetings.

Sands let her go. Inez, pushing unwelcome events into the past, looked to the train and saw that most of the arrivals and welcoming party had mounted into carriages, wagons, and other conveyances. Lucy huffed, a weary breath that expanded and collapsed beneath the saddle cinch. Inez stroked Lucy's wet and matted mane. "Soon, Lucy. Soon," she murmured. "I'll get you to a stable where you can rest."

The procession on Third jerked into motion. Inez tightened her hold on Lucy's reins to keep her from responding to the crowd that was backing up against them, squeezing away from the streets. Mounted police and military companies passed by first. Colorado state cavalry were followed by a drum corps, infantry, a band, and the battalion veteran corps.

An open-topped barouche, drawn by four black horses and nearly invisible beneath red-white-and-blue decorations, came abreast. Figures waving from the seats. A beard-rimmed square face, just visible beneath a hat.

"Is that General Grant?" she asked.

Reverend Sands nodded.

As neighboring spectators pressed around her, jostling for a better view, Inez held fast to Lucy's reins and prayed that there were no more men intent on violence. Waiting. Men waiting for the right moment.

Grant's carriage passed up the street. More vehicles followed, occupants shrouded in wet weather wear and hidden under umbrellas. The city's hook and ladder company was next, followed by volunteer fire companies and trailed by the town's prominent citizenry in carriages.

As soon as the last of the mounted police went by, the people lining the road flooded into their wake.

Inez turned to Sands. "What is the parade route?"

"Spruce to Chestnut, then Harrison to the Clarendon Hotel. Grant is supposed to speak briefly there."

Inez nodded. "Going up State Street would be best. It probably won't be as crowded."

They crossed Third, walking their horses, and proceeded toward State. The bonfires, which had illuminated the path of the parade, receded, leaving them to travel in the dark as quickly as they dared. Bone-deep weariness tugged at Inez.

They squeezed their horses onto the hitching bar by the State Street entrance of the Silver Queen Saloon. Even though there was little room amongst the twitching, wet beasts of burden, the saloon seemed unusually quiet. Inez gazed at the lamplight pouring from the windows. She bet that her business partner, Abe Jackson, waited within, even though every other soul in the city seemed to be jostling for position out on Harrison for a view of the procession. *Probably not a single customer with belly to the bar. But perhaps that will work to our advantage right now.*

She turned to Reverend Sands. "I've no desire to stand shoulder to shoulder to the crowds out here. We'd have an excellent view of the procession and speeches from the rooftop of the Silver Queen. Interested?"

He smiled, and pushed the door open, holding it for her.

Inez walked in, noticing that indeed, the place was deserted, except for Abe and their bartender, Sol Isaacs. Both stood by the half-open main Harrison Street entrance, watching the crowds on the boardwalk. Both had tucked their thumbs into their apron bands. They looked, Inez thought, like disparate bookends—Abe carved from ebony, Sol from ivory.

The two men swung around in unison as Inez and the reverend approached. Abe's brow, etched with worry, smoothed out; his concern visibly fell away.

"Mrs. Stannert, you're a sight for sore eyes," said Abe, by way of greeting. "Me 'n Sol here were gonna close up the saloon and grab some lanterns, and come look for you."

"I'm all right, Mr. Jackson." Inez moved toward him, hands held up, a gesture meant to allay his fears. "I'm sorry to have caused you such anxiety. We came back as quickly as we could, but we weren't able to get through the streets until now. As you see, we're back, and none the worse for wear."

At least, on the surface.

She added, "There was a bit of trouble on Third. Someone in the crowd took a potshot at General Grant. The police were on him right away. I don't think anyone in the parade even noticed, what with all the fireworks and confusion."

Abe crossed his arms, grim. "None of us need that sort of thing. Those folk, if'n they don't like Grant bein' here, they oughta just crawl back under whatever rock they came out from."

"Agreed. But there's naught we can do now except be aware. It's just another reminder that we need to be extra-vigilant these next few days while Grant and his visitors are in town."

She lightened her tone to deflect the questions brimming behind Abe's troubled gaze. "I thought we could catch a glimpse of Grant from the rooftop, hear the speeches. The crowds will not let the general disappear into the hotel without a few words from him I'm certain. And the mayor is not about to let his prepared remarks go to waste, no matter whether it's nine in the evening or two in the morning.

"Abe, Sol, why don't you lock the doors and meet us on the roof?" Inez reached behind the bar and extracted the little-used key to the rooftop and a lamp while Abe and Sol barred the doors.

The group headed up the stairs to the second floor of the saloon and proceeded down the hallway, lit only by a pool of light cast by the lamp Inez had handed to Sol. A door to one side led to the saloon's office and Inez's private rooms; another, further down, to the now deserted gaming room. At the end of the hall, they stopped. Inez inserted and turned the key in a lock that seemed to be part of the wall. A door, unframed and built to look like part of the wall, gave a discontented creak as she pushed it open. The abbreviated staircase that greeted them was more ladder than stairway. The same key unlocked a trapdoor at the top, allowing the group to emerge, one at a time, out onto the flat rooftop of the Silver Queen. They all stepped around the puddles dotting the roof and headed toward the edge for a better view of the main street of Harrison.

Inez ventured closer to the edge of the rooftop, bringing Harrison into view. Leadville's entire population, over thirty thousand souls, seemed squeezed along the boardwalks. From above, the mob looked like a strange species of plant, the tops moving and oscillating, wet and glistening. The noise of the crowd was backed by the roar of minute guns, and the explosions of fireworks and small arms. Colored bonfires stained the long procession green, blue, red. A speaker's platform had been erected in front of the Clarendon Hotel. A grandstand adjoined, heavy with people.

Mounted police had forced a passage through the crowd for the carriages, now halted by the hotel. Inez thought she recognized the editor of the *Evening Chronicle* among the figures on the grandstand. He was arguing with the procession's grand marshal, who had disembarked from the first carriage and was now pointing at the speaker's podium and jabbing at the editor's chest with an emphatic forefinger.

Standing by the pressman was a tall, lanky familiar figure. Inez squinted, certain that, yes, it was Jed Elliston, editor of *The Independent*, taking the *Chronicle* man's side and adding his own gesticulations to the argument. The grand marshal leaned over the grandstand, beckoning to the policemen below. The men in blue lumbered up the stairs and herded the members of the local press off the platform, just as the crowd began chanting, more or less in unison, "General Grant!"

The former president had exited the carriage along with others of his entourage. He turned to either side, shaking the swarm of hands thrust out at him. Two local lawmen, accompanied by what appeared to be a private bodyguard, tried in vain to clear a path for the visitors.

The honored guests were escorted, foot by foot, to the stands, police shoving the way clear. As Grant mounted the stairs at one end of the stand, Inez noted the pressmen were returning, storming the stairs at the other, with Elliston leading the pack. The parade marshal headed them off, accompanied by the private guard. An apparent order to quit the premises ignored, the bodyguard collared Elliston and threw the newsman from the stand. Elliston disappeared, arms milling, into the crowd awash with the red light of the colored fires.

A commotion in the other direction, barely overriding the sounds from Harrison, caught Inez's attention. She turned her back on the proceedings to look west, toward Colorado's highest peaks, now invisible behind the night, the low-lying clouds, and, closer in, a strange glowing light.

Inez crossed the rooftop, curiosity shadowed by a growing foreboding. At the far end of the roof, she could no longer fool herself about the origin of the flickering glow and the attendant smell.

She stared down at the evolving chaos in Leadville's red-light district, figures like small, black cutouts dashing hither and thither in the unnatural light. It felt as if a hand closed over her throat.

"Mrs. Stannert." Abe had followed and now stood beside her. "Is that—?"

His voice unfroze her mind and her stance. She turned to Abe, hardly able to see him, his dark skin and eyes blending into the night. "A fire. On State Street. And the fire companies are trapped in the procession!"

Chapter Five

The light drizzle kissing her face was no match for the intensity of a conflagration, Inez knew. It was impossible to tell how far down the block the fire was, but that hardly mattered. Five buildings, ten, they would all be consumed if the fire could not be brought under control. And quickly.

Without the fire companies able to reach us, we're on our own. A knife of fear slid beneath her breastbone and pricked her heart. For just a moment, she imagined a scene in her mind's eye, as clear as if it were spread out before her: The entire north side of State Street, licked in flames. Her saloon, the roof beneath her feet, the mahogany bar, plank floors, imported carpets, her personal papers and clothes, everything consumed. Nothing left but ashes and glowing embers. The insatiable fire marching up Harrison, the screaming crowds, unable to escape, crushed by their own weight.

She was already moving, without even thinking, toward the trapdoor in the roof. Reverend Sands caught up with her before she'd taken half a dozen steps.

"Inez!" His words overrode the roar on Harrison, now punctuated by with alarmed shouts on State. "You'd best head home."

Abe and Sol hurried past her, heading down the steep trapdoor stairs in such quick succession that Sol nearly stepped on Abe's hat.

Inez turned to the reverend. "We've no time to argue about this."

She started down the stairs just in time to hear Abe shout, "Mrs. Stannert! We're headed up the alley, just so's you know. We're takin' the stew kettle and wash-up pails."

At the bottom of the stairs, she turned and addressed the reverend's descending shoes.

"I can help as much as Abe. The Silver Queen is mine as well."

She flew down the second story stairs to the saloon's ground floor and darted into the kitchen, ignoring the reverend's shouts for her to stop.

Grabbing an empty dishpan, Inez hurtled through the back door and into the alley, pulling out her pocket revolver as she did so.

Usually, the alley was a dark, foreboding place. A place where murder, robbery, and garroting plagued those who moved too slowly and without a firearm or lantern.

Tonight was different.

It was a strange, inverted world. Dark, where light lay in the daytime. Murky, full of smoke where the shadows usually curled. The alley was a bedlam, figures running in all directions, carrying pails, buckets, dishpans, anything that would hold water.

And the mud.

It sucked at her worn riding boots, threatening to pull them right off her feet. She curled her toes to hold the boots on, and slogged forward, anxious to move faster. The crowd grew thicker the closer she approached the fire at the end of the block. Finally, she hit upon an organized line of men. A water cart had been pulled nearby; men were filling an odd assortment of containers as fast as they could, passing them along by hand. Inez paused, the wash pan dangling from her hand, forgotten.

Frisco Flo's parlor house, the last structure on the block, was ablaze with flames that were not the fires of lust or biblical righteousness. So far, the conflagration seemed confined to the back rooms tacked onto the building proper—at least, that was where the flickering lights licked out the alley door and one observable window.

The mere sight of fire curling around the corners of the doorframe, lapping at the porch, sent a fresh sweat of fear coursing down Inez's back. This, on a street where most of the structures—from single-room cribs to two-story saloons—were frame-built, hissed and crackled of disaster.

Shouts from ahead. Smoke roiled out the brothel's back door. She discerned through the smoke that there was more than one bucket brigade. Three, four more, snaked off toward Pine Street, while another squeezed in the narrow passageway between Flo's and the saloon next door.

The rain increased in force, as if the Almighty had finally taken pity on them and brought Nature to their side in the fight. Hoots and huzzahs burst from smoke-roughened throats as the fire dimmed under the onslaught of the volunteers and the sudden downpour.

The back door of the neighboring saloon flew open, crashing against the half-timbered rear wall. The proprietor, Frank Lynch, appeared first, identifiable by his fiercely polished bald pate and impressive shoulder span. He stared at the burning brothel, shook his head, and said, "Holy Mary, Mother of Jesus." Then stepped aside.

Additional half-shadowed figures appeared. A thunder of wood barrels rolled down the back steps. The kegs landed with a sudden squish into the churned-up mud of the alley, sending a spray of muck over everyone within splashing distance.

A crack of thunder and a flash of white light accompanied Lynch's roared pronouncement: "I was going to return this watered-down piss-poor bellywash, but this is for certain a far better use for it. If this ditchwater doesn't douse that bonfire from the Devil, nothing will! Haul it down and put it out, boys. The better brew will be on the house for all gentlemen and ladies that show a coat of soot on their faces for their efforts!"

A general cheer sounded. Someone bumped Inez's arm and shoved a full pail of water roughly into her hand. She dropped the empty wash pan in her haste to grab the pail, and turned automatically, thrusting the sloshing pail out to the next shadowy figure in line.

A warm hand closed in a vise grip over her ungloved fingers, staying her grasp on the pail handle.

She looked up. Reverend Sands, still covering her hand, moved closer until the smooth wool of his black overcoat brushed her arm. The warmth passed through her hand, up her arm, beating back the cold terror that the fire had inspired.

The weight of the pail lifted from her. "This is no place for you, Mrs. Stannert. It's a madhouse on the streets and worse back here."

Before she could argue, he grabbed her arm and pulled her out of the line.

She splashed back a step, alley ooze splattering her already sodden trousers. Where it soaked through, her skin felt as ice.

A shout sounded perilously close by. Four men, the first kegs wrestled up to their shoulders, staggered past Inez and Sands. They zigzagged toward Flo's, nearly trampling the firefighting volunteers who were passing buckets, pails, jugs, spittoons, and other assorted odd containers of water toward the battlefront. The line dissolved to make way for the keg carriers.

"My livelihood is at stake." She attempted to rip her arm from his grasp, which tightened like a snare. "Should the fire get out of control, it's not just Flo and Lynch who stand to lose everything."

Another four men burst out of the saloon, carrying still more barrels. Sands pulled her further away from the chaos into the quiet backwater of a narrow passageway between Lynch's saloon and the neighboring whiskey mill. "There are plenty to help already. It's a miracle no one has been trampled yet." Pressure increased on her elbow. She was certain that marks would remain in the morning. "I'll walk you home. It isn't safe here. This is no place for a woman."

Inez barked a short laugh. "As if anyone will recognize me in this get-up. And besides, if this is no place for a woman, you should go tell them." She waved to the back of Flo's building. Near the front of the battle line, flickering light revealed a hand-ful of Flo's women, feminine distractions muffled by donated overcoats. Flo herself was at the fore, her platinum locks disheveled, skirts looped up to her plump knees. The boarders added their high-pitched squeals, screams, and curses to the chaos as they passed chamberpots and pails. Flo, on the other hand, worked silently. Inez caught an expression of grim determination on her soot-stained face, completely unlike her usual cheerful, vaguely silly demeanor.

Sands eased his grip. "That's exactly what I'm going to do, once I see you're headed back to safety."

It was her turn to suddenly seize his arm. "Look!"

It was unnecessary for her to point.

The first barrel of beer had arrived at the back of the brothel. The carriers gave a heave-ho and threw it through the back door, onto the dying flames. A quick flare, the fire damped, and smoke and steam roiled out.

Hurrahs ensued. Flo's girls began jumping up and down, clapping their hands. The tingle of burnt hops with a nip of alcohol wafted through the air, mixing with the scent of charred timber.

Another keg was hefted and brought to the fire in much the same way, quickly followed by a third. Flames died to a blood-red glow. Firefighting lines dissolved. Volunteers and gawkers surged toward the fading fire. The illumination dimmed, but Inez could clearly see a couple of men had apparently decided to take advantage of the sudden air of celebration, and grabbed at two of the angels of the night, intent on capturing a kiss or perhaps something more.

The demimonde, however, weren't about to take this lying down. They screamed, kicked, shoved their assailants away. Flo whirled around, raised an object—perhaps, Inez thought, a spittoon—and began whaling away at the men. The crowd pushed closer as smoke obliterated the scene.

Sands muttered an oath that Inez suspected would have caused the women of the church's social committee to swoon. "Wait here. Don't move." He released his hold on her and began to work his way through the crowds toward the melee.

A figure across the alley wavered out of the gloom and into the uncertain light, plunging through heavy mud in Inez's direction. Inez turned, gripping a pail and wondering if it would be useful as a weapon or if she would need to pull her gun from her pocket.

"Ha!" A very young woman, dressed in what appeared to be only a soiled white wrapper, and not well wrapped at that, lurched further forward. "Slimy bastard! Thought we'd turn tail and run, did ya? Ha!" She hoisted an object aloft. Subdued light glinted, reflected. Inez tensed, until she realized the woman held a bottle. The woman seemed completely unaware of Inez, gazing instead at the brothel. Inez decided it was probably best not to draw attention to herself and eased away, around the corner.

The woman continued talking to herself, waggling the bottle as if scolding an invisible companion: "Told ya, Flo. You're playin' with fire, and lookit what he did. That son of a bitch."

She tipped the bottle up. The wrapper flapped open. A vertical slice of skin revealed that she wore nothing beneath.

Inez heard a gasp.

She turned and with a start recognized the middle-aged man she'd inadvertently knocked down and almost trampled earlier that evening. He had apparently just come around the far corner of the whiskey mill and stood there, hatless, coatless. His hands opened and closed in a convulsive manner on his jacket lapels. He was staring at the fire.

No. Inez realized he was staring at the half-dressed woman, horror and fascination warring across his face. Perhaps sensing that he was being watched, he turned his head, catching Inez's gaze with his own. His eyes widened. Recognition flared, and something else, some furtive emotion, twisted his features. It took a moment for her to identify it.

Guilt.

"What're *you* starin' at?"

Startled, Inez whirled and caught the woman glaring at her. "Never seen a tit before?" She squelched forward a step, waving the bottle like a sword. "A-ha! You...got...company!"

She pointed the bottle at the older man. "I know you. Prick. Couldn't keep your eyes off…"

Inez turned to see how he was taking this calumny.

He was gone.

The woman continued to harangue as if he was still there. "Come sniffin' aroun'. Ha! Attics. I'll bet! Doors. Think you can stop me? Wait'll Flo hears…"

The back door to the saloon slammed open again, cutting off her crazy rant. The subdued glow from interior lamps spilled out, painted the rain as a delicate scratch of lines in the air. The woman shrank away, convulsively gripped the front of the robe with one hand, clutching it closed, bringing the curtain down on the show.

The door darkened as four more men and another keg came through and thundered off the plank landing. The men floundered momentarily in the mud before gaining their footing and heading toward the back of the brothel. Lynch stepped out onto the plank landing, wiping his hands on the rag hanging off his apron. His attention swerved from the keg brigade to the woman swaying in the mud-splattered robe, half visible in the shadows of the alleyway.

"Lizzie, Lizzie." His previously loud voice was now soft. Affection, rough from disuse, colored his words. "What're you doing out here? Like this? Come inside, warm up by the stove 'til Flo can fetch you. Come along, dearie, that's a girl."

He stepped down the porch steps and gingerly into the liquefied alley, the surface pocking with intense raindrops. "You're going to catch your death out here dressed in nothing but a wee gown like that." He advanced, hand outstretched.

Lizzie reared back.

Watching the scene unfold from the shadows, Inez saw the whites of her eyes, desperate, like those of a wild animal scenting the hunter.

Lizzie pitched her bottle at him.

Despite Lizzie's inebriated state, her aim could not be faulted. If Lynch had not thrown up an arm, the bottle would likely have hit him in the forehead. Instead it hit his forearm, and fell into the ooze at his feet.

"Bastard!" she shrieked. "I'll *bet* you'd like me over there. Warm up by the fire. Catch my death. Wouldn't *you* like that. Not bloody likely!"

With an alacrity that Inez would not have believed possible from someone who had drained a bottle of—Inez glanced at the label, face up and barely visible in the mud—Angelica wine, Lizzie tore up the alley toward the Silver Queen, robe hiked high, mud-splattered white calves flashing, like a besmirched ghost fleeing in and out of the gloom.

Lynch took two steps as if to follow and then spotted Inez, who had moved out of the shadows.

He stopped, shook his head. "Drunk. And crazy, too. Poor soul. Don't know why Flo keeps her on."

He seemed to straighten, inflate his chest. "Never let it be said that Frank Lynch wasn't a man to extend a helping hand, even to those more sinning than sinned against."

Smoke obscured the alley. Inez was seized by a fit of coughing.

"Ah, good," Lynch said, somewhere behind the screen of smoke. "Fire's near out. 'Twas piss-poor beer, that's true, but still, I wasn't lookin' forward to seein' it all go up in smoke." Then louder, "I'm a man to keep my word! Free drinks for those who saved the day and for all the pretty ladies next door!"

The crush of men around the damaged pleasure palace reversed itself and swept toward Lynch's saloon, a jostling of hoarse voices, mud-slathered boots, soaked hats, looking for the promised free drinks. Inez stepped away from the stampede lest it carry her into the saloon. Once the thirsty tide had receded, she squelched forward to Flo's, intent on finding the reverend and assaying the damage to the building up close.

Bobbing lanterns moved through the thick night, their carriers invisible in the pressing dark and murk. The wavering spots, crossing, recrossing, seemingly random in their movement, reminded her of the lightning bugs from her childhood. And like the insects she used to hold, one by one, cupped in her hands, they illuminated little, beyond their own small shapes.

She made out a knot of women, mostly by their white limbs and shifts, stirring nervously in the gloom. High-pitched coughs and crying were threaded by the soothing murmur of Sands' voice. She sloshed closer. By the structure's charred but still miraculously intact back porch, the mud was churned knee-deep from recent turmoil, water, and beer. Sands held one lantern high. Flo stood by, arms crossed tight, holding her elbows. Inez climbed out of the sucking muck in time to hear Reverend Sands say, "You're welcome to use the mission for shelter."

Flo shook her head, face and platinum locks layered black with soot. Tears or sweat had cleared small tracks of white down her cheeks. "Lynch offered me and my girls a couple of rooms upstairs for the night. He's going to move his own whores into the backroom, for now. Danny'll guard the house. He's got orders to shoot first, ask questions later. No one's going to sneak off with the silver or the booze if I have anything to say about it."

She looked at the building. "Danny's checking the rooms. I'm missing two girls." She bit her lip, her upper teeth showing white. "Zelda and Lizzie."

"I saw Lizzie outside Lynch's." Inez stepped into the fragile circle of light. "He was trying to talk her into coming inside."

The lines across Flo's forehead deepened as she raised invisible eyebrows. "Mrs. Stannert? Is that you? Did you come down to help fight the fire? Why, I didn't think you cared."

"I have no desire to see State Street go up in flames. That would be a catastrophe for us all." Inez cleared her throat. Smoke wafting from the gaping back of the building coated her teeth and mouth, tasting bitter. "Your Lizzie seemed sound in limb when I saw her. Although quite intoxicated."

Flo sighed. "Lizzie." The one word was heavy with worry and fatigue. "Well, at least she's with Lynch. We'd better head over there before something happens. I never know, with Lizzie."

"She didn't go inside," Inez said quickly. "Lynch tried to talk her in, but she fled. Ran toward Harrison. She wasn't wearing much."

Flo closed her eyes. "Shit."

"She'll find a place to stay, or she'll come back," Reverend Sands said. "If nothing else, the police will find her, and she'll spend the night in jail."

Flo nodded, eyes still closed.

Soft sobs from the shivering women seemed to pull her from her thoughts.

Her eyes flew open. She was suddenly all business. "I've got to get everyone inside. Zelda, well, she's my newest girl. If she's not inside, she probably went home. She's got family in town. Nothing to be done about it now."

Sands glanced at Inez. "We'll be going then, Mrs. Stannert and I. If you need anything, Mrs. Sweet—"

Flo cocked her head, looking at Inez as if really seeing her for the first time. "Hmmm. Now that you mention it, Reverend… Mrs. Stannert, I'd like to talk with you further. About something that could benefit us both."

"Us?" Inez found the plural pronoun disturbing. She retreated a step, as if physical distance would dispel the grammatical embrace. "I don't see where our interests intersect."

"Besides in keeping State Street from burning to the ground, you mean?" A corner of Flo's mouth quirked up momentarily, then the smile disappeared—a small light blown out with the slightest puff of breath. "Let's just say that it occurs to me that this particular cloud may have a high-grade silver lining. In the morning, but not too early, I promise, I'll send Danny around and find out if you might have a moment to talk. Somewhere away from here. Somewhere discreet. Away from prying eyes and ears."

Without warning, she reached out and gripped Inez's wrist, exposed between glove and half-rolled jacket sleeve. Flo squeezed, then released. As Flo and her girls turned to go, Inez glanced down, almost expecting to see the skin blotched red from the intensity of Flo's grip. Instead, her wrist was encircled with soot, as if she was already manacled to Flo by an as-yet unspecified, dark oath.

Chapter Six

"What was that all about?" Reverend Sands asked Inez.

Inez rubbed her wrist absently. The soot imprint would only be dispelled by a good scrub with soap and water. They were walking slowly up Harrison, from pool to pool of gas light from the street lamps.

They passed the Clarendon, the front of which was now deserted, the grandstands empty. The crowds had dispersed except for numerous late-night revelers who seemed intent on celebrating the arrival of the former president and the first train into the dawn hours.

"Flo's invitation to talk? I have no idea. I suppose if I want to find out, I'll have to meet her." Inez's wrist felt as if the morning sun would find it bruised. "I'm not inclined to follow her dictates, however."

Inez and Reverend Sands strolled side by side. As a concession to her disguise, they forwent walking arm-in-arm. Even so, the sleeve of his coat occasionally brushed hers. When the reverend posed his question to her, Inez was contemplating how the various passersby had no idea of the frisson that jolted through her from that briefest and most accidental contact.

"If she's in search of charity, perhaps the church could help," said Sands.

Inez snorted. "You are one of the most gifted silver-tongued devils I have ever met, but even I have doubts that you could talk the church's board into offering a leg up, so to speak, to the owner of a house of prostitution."

"Let those without sin…" Reverend Sands didn't finish. He didn't need to. Instead, he added, "Flo has been very generous in her contributions to the church in the past. It's not Christian to accept such gifts and turn a blind eye on the givers, no matter what their station or state of their soul."

"Stated like a true politician, Reverend. I think you missed your calling." Inez spoke lightly, trying to stave off the exhaustion that seeped into every corner of her being. She was glad to turn the conversation away from Flo's disturbing proposition. Even though she'd denied knowing what Flo's offer might be, Inez had an inkling that she did indeed know what it concerned. Only a couple of weeks before, Flo had unexpectedly popped up at the back door of Inez's saloon, hinted that she intended to move to a better part of town, and wondered aloud whether Inez might be interested in providing some financial backing.

It would have to be a most profitable deal for me to contemplate entering the flesh trade, even at a distance. Although, as the good reverend said, Flo is a most astute businesswoman. I'd probably add more to my bank account in league with her than I've accumulated through some of my investments in the local mines.

Return had been good until the recent miner's strike in May. From thence forward, it had been a rocky ride, and Inez continued to watch, breath held, as stock prices gyrated up and down, dancing to the tune of East Coast investors and their nervousness over the stability of Leadville's silver future.

She sighed.

The Silver Queen's fortunes are looking up. That's good. But I need something I can call my own. Something that has my name on it, clear and legal. I own a third of the saloon, but only verbally, and those words were spoken long ago, in another life. If the unthinkable happens and my husband returns, I'm not certain those words would mean anything at all.

"Did you mean what you said earlier, about getting a divorce?" Reverend Sands' question seemed almost as though he'd read her mind.

They were at the corner of Harrison and Fourth, preparing to turn the corner and walk the long block to her home. She faced away from him for a moment, away from the lights on Harrison. Fourth Street was dark, quiet, its modest one-story homes, punctuated every once in a while with an ambitious two-story stand against the formidable cold of Leadville's ten-month-long winters.

"Of course I meant it." She turned onto Fourth. Sands followed. "Mark has been gone a year. Over a year. I've had not a word, not a letter, nothing. He could be dead, he could be alive. He loved our son, so much." Her throat closed as she thought about little William, almost two years old and living so far away, back east with her sister, Harmony.

It was the right decision, to send him away. With his lungs, he'd not have lived through another winter up here. And I couldn't leave Leadville then. I still hoped that Mark would return. That there was a reason for his sudden disappearance. An accident. Some unfortunate circumstance. But that was long ago. Now, the time is coming when I will be able to think about leaving. I swore, when I handed William to Harmony, that I would do whatever was necessary to get him back and move somewhere where we could live together. Making a deal with Flo would allow me the wherewithal to do that sooner, rather than later. William may never know his father, but he will know his mother.

She coughed, forcing tears away, and continued, "When I visited the lawyer several weeks ago, he indicated I could sue for divorce on grounds of desertion. That's exactly what I intend to do. And the sooner the better."

The sooner the better.

Despite her verbal assurances to Reverend Sands, a lingering doubt still pulsed, like water seeping from a heated mineral spring in winter.

What if Mark is alive? Not just alive, but here somewhere in Colorado?

There had been indications. Possible sightings. Reported to her second- or third-hand. Not in Leadville, but in Denver. And again, in Central City.

Best to finish the job. I can't claim proper widowhood without proof of his death, but I can end this half-existence with a divorce.

The societal backlash from a divorce was inevitable, but then…

Better a "grass widow" here out West than home back East.

They'd arrived at Inez's small house. She reached for her key and then realized it was back at the Silver Queen. Reverend Sands pulled a small ring of keys from some pocket inside his coat and thumbed through them until he found the one he wanted. He inserted it, the lock clicked, and the door swung open.

She stepped inside, then turned to face him. "Are you coming in?"

His face was invisible, unreadable, cast into shadow under his hat. His figure, no more than a black silhouette, seemed to blend with the pressing darkness of the overcast night, punished by rain.

"Am I invited?"

The slight huskiness of his voice was all the indication she needed that their walk here, together, had served to turn aside his attention from the outside world and its recent troubles. That he was, like her, hoping for comfort and connection in the most human of blessings, the simple touch of skin to skin, breath to breath, heart to heart.

Without a word, she took his hand and gently pulled him inside.

Chapter Seven

Zelda paused outside the two-room shanty on Chicken Hill, her breath visible in the still air, her toes squeezed tight and painful in too-small boots. She checked the precious bundle she'd carried all the way from town. It was still rolled up tight, safe under the shawl. Gripping the shawl close around her face and shoulders with the other hand, she turned to gaze on the eastern horizon, the dark now creased with dawn light. Mosquito Range stood out as a sharp, jagged shape, reminding her of the paper dolls she'd once cut out of dark paper in a childhood that had ended abruptly when her mother died.

Despite the cold, she took a moment to shake out her long skirts, hoping the freezing early morning air would remove some of the smell of sex and smoke that clung to her. Usually, before coming to visit, she always scrubbed up, so Pa wouldn't catch a whiff of all the men she'd passed the nights with.

She rubbed the toe of one button-topped shoe against her calf, balancing precariously on one protesting foot. That cotton stocking would show a gray streak of ash against the red stripes, next time she lifted her skirts. *But soon, maybe I won't have to do that ever again. Leastwise, if I don't want to.*

She tested the front door with a shoulder, knowing how tight it fit against the buckling raw planks of the floor inside. The door, unbarred, released its customary squawk and hiss as it scraped open across the floor. By the cast iron stove, a moth-eaten buffalo robe stirred, animated by an unseen force. A dull metallic gleam, snout-shaped, emerged from beneath the robe.

"It's me," Zelda hissed. "Put the gun away, Zeke. You're no *pistolero*."

There was a dull clunk of metal on wood as the sawed-short shotgun met the floor. A whine emerged next from beneath the robe. "'Tain't no way to talk t' your elders, Miss Zelda."

"You're only elder by nine months, and a whole sight dumber. And watch your mouth and call me by my given name here at home."

"Zelpha, Zelda, it hardly makes a diff'rence. Don't know why you'd pick a whorin' name like Zelda anyways, instead of Posey or something."

Zelda tiptoed over to a rocking chair by the stove and sat down with a sigh, holding the bundle on her lap. "'Cause I wanted somethin' easy to remember. So, everyone still sleepin'?" She hiked up her skirt, slid a buttonhook from its holding place in her garter, and began unfastening the boots.

The robe heaved off. "What yuh think, Zel?" Zeke stood up and stretched, long underwear drooping such that he looked like he had the butt of an old man. "Pa had the better part of a bottle last night, tryin' to drown out the cheers of everyone welcomin' General fuckin' Grant t' town. What Pa didn't drink, Zed did. And your lover boy's sleepin' like a baby. How long's he stayin' here anyways?"

"Long's it's my money that keeps a roof over your miserable head and beef and booze on the table to feed your sorry ass." Zelda threw her shoe at Zeke. It connected firmly with that piece of his anatomy.

Zeke threw a wounded look back at her. "Hey. Zed an' me are workin' too."

"And every penny you make muckin' ore for Silver Mountain Mine goes to the sharps and girls on State Street."

Zeke's nose twitched. "What's that smell? Smells like, I dunno, you burnt your hair or somethin'."

Zelda bent to the other shoe, furiously digging the button loops off the buttons. "Fire at Flo's place."

He scratched. "Thought it was brick or stone."

"Not all of it." One of the loops had gotten twisted and wasn't cooperating. "Back part, the kitchen and mud room, is wood. Anyhow, place filled with smoke so fast, I could hardly breathe. I hardly had time to grab shoes and shawl, and run out." *And got something else, too.* "Leastways I was already dressed. Some of the other girls had nothing on but blankets or shifts. Looked like squaws, standin' outside, all wrapped up. Screamin' and pitchin' fits." She sighed, looking down at the second boot, now unfastened. "Nice shoes. Too bad they ain't my size."

She leaned back, rocked slightly. "When I was walkin' here, I heard some folks talkin'. The city marshal's house got fired up first, they think. Then Flo's. All the firemen were stuck in the parade for Grant, along with the hoses. By the time they got to State Street, marshal's house was gone and two more nearby. Flo's place is pretty much okay, I guess. 'Cept for the back side." She wiggled her toes out of the boot and sighed in relief. "Don't matter, really. Miss Flo's moving uptown pretty soon, to that new place on Fifth."

"That means you'll be makin' more money, then, right? You'll be keepin' company with all them muckety-mucks that got bucks to burn."

"Keep your voice down, Zeke. Don't wake Pa. Anyways, I ain't goin' back." She looked up, daring him to object.

"Zel! You got to! How're we gonna take care of Pa?"

She was tired, itchy, and wanted nothing more than to go in the back, unfold and admire the treasure she had rolled up under the shawl, and then curl up with her beau for a minute. All that just caused her to want to wallop Zeke, just like when they were young ones. Still, she kept her voice low so as to not wake the others in the back room. "You and Zed shoulda thought about that afore you spent all that money you made on the silver strike last winter. Or leastwise you shoulda sent us another letter straightways after the first where you said…Lessee, if I can remember, like the words aren't burned into my brainpan… 'Dear Pa and Zelpha. Come on out to Leadville, Colorad-y, we've struck it rich, we've got twenty thousand dollars, and we're livin' like silver kings'," she sang the last two words. "You shoulda sent another letter quick-on, sayin', 'Dear Pa and Zelpha. On second thought, don't bother comin' out to this place of shit and mud. It snows all-a time and's colder than a witch's tit, even in July. And asides we done drunk up all the money and pissed it back out and if'n you come join us, spendin' every last cent you have to get here, you won't have enough money to get back home and there's no place to live but a raggedy old shanty we done built with our own hands and truth t' tell, dear sister, we were mostly tight and stupid when we put it up and the walls aren't straight and the wood's not cured or cut right—'"

The curtain of canvas that served as a door to the back room pulled back. A voice boomed loud enough to split the roof timbers: "Zelpha, daughter, is that you? Is it the day of worship already?"

"Gotta pee," muttered Zeke, and, clutching the front of his long johns as if to shield his tender parts from Zelda's razor-sharp words, made good his escape out the front door.

Zelda stood and hurried toward the old man, who, bent and shaky, gripped the canvas hanging under the crooked lintel. "'Mornin', Pa. No, it ain't Sunday, but I've come to visit anyways."

She lowered her face to kiss his cheek, paper-thin crinkly skin beneath a skim of white whiskers. The old man caught her arm before she could move away. "What are you doing here? I thought the butcher only gave you Sundays off." He shook her arm, sightless eyes staring past her, his nose twitching. "Daughter, there's the smell of Sodom and Gomorrah about you."

Cursing herself for not stopping at a public well to wet the corner of her shawl and clean up, Zelda settled for a half-truth. "Pa, I'm here because somethin' terrible happened. The place I was workin', that butcher shop in Malta, burnt down last night. And, well, you know how the butcher was lettin' me board in the room overhead? I got out, but was lucky to escape with my life. Everything is gone."

His sunken cheeks seemed to cave in further. "Oh, daughter." Sorrow painted his voice. "What's to happen to us now? But our faith must stay strong. 'A man's heart deviseth his way: but the Lord directeth his steps.' You're a hard worker, daughter, and the Lord will set your foot to further employment. While you search and pray, you stay here. But that young man of yours, it isn't seemly he be under the same roof while you're with us."

"No, Pa," she said quickly. "Reuben's fine for stayin'. He's got nowhere else to go. And I, I've got a place in town. The shopkeeper and his wife. They said they'd let me stay with them. In their house, even, fancy that. You pray for them, Pa. They're good folks with kind hearts. So all I need is one night here. And then, I'll be fine."

The old man nodded once. " 'Every thing that may abide the fire, ye shall make it go through the fire, and it shall be clean.' The Lord's showing his displeasure about the coming of that devil's spawn, Ulysses S. Grant. Blessed be the brave soul who sends him straight to hell and eternal fire and damnation."

"Well, Pa, I suppose you know best about that." She gave him one more peck on the cheek. "Although I heard comin' home that someone tried to do just that with a barkin' iron. The man got pinched by the coppers, an' Grant's still livin' and breathin'. Anyhow, let me get you set down comfortable. Zeke'll get the fire started when he gets back in. I'll get Zed and Reuben goin', or they'll be late for their shift. Then, I'll make up a mess of grits, just the way you like it, like it's Sunday for real."

After settling the old man in the chair by the stove, she hurried to the back room, silent on stocking feet. Two figures lay, inert on the floor, separated from the small space that held her father's bed by another strip of canvas strung across the room on a rope. She prodded one figure impatiently with her toes. "Zed!" she whispered. "Get out!"

"Arr." The figure rolled over, then sat up. A face the mirror image of Zeke's, only considerably more hung-over, stared up at her. "Zel? What're you doin' here? 'S Friday, not Sunday."

"And a workin' day for you, lazy bones." She nudged him again, none too gently. "Git out there and git the fire goin' for Pa. I want to talk to Reuben here."

"Yeah, I know the kind of talkin' you two like t' do," grumbled Zed, scrubbing at his sleep-creased face with a grimy hand.

"Git!"

He got—standing up with a creak and groan that belied his twenty-three years and hobbling out with canvas trousers half on, suspenders snaking along the floor.

As soon as he disappeared into the main room, Zelda pulled out her bundle, unrolled it, and spread it on the bed to admire. Even in the early light, the silk taffeta of the dressing gown gleamed softly. Butterflies and bouquets of flowers embroidered in green and melon silk floss and metallic cord were scattered over the field of purple. She quashed the momentary pang of guilt over snatching up the beautiful wrap from its place on the floor just inside Lizzie's room. Silly twit had gone running outside, dressed in nothing but her shift. Not even any drawers. Not that a whore in the middle of work would necessarily have them close at hand. *It'll look a sight better on me than Lizzie.* Zelda stroked the silk aqua lining, ran a finger over one of the frog closures, and imagined herself wearing the regal Chinese gown, bare feet, nothing underneath but the skin God gave her.

All fired up from her imaginings, Zelda turned from the dressing gown and fell upon the chest of the room's remaining man, who had just rolled over and propped himself on one elbow, rubbing his eyes.

She ran her hands up under his shirt and along his ribs. She stuck her tongue in his ear and, when he squirmed, whispered, "Hey, Reuben, ain't ya happy to see me?"

He jerked his head back and pushed her exploring hands away. "Stop that. Your hands're cold."

Rebuffed, Zelda rocked back on her heels, examining him at arm's length. Reuben's bleary eyes were near hidden behind a tangled greasy curtain of blond hair. His face was pocked with smallpox scars and acne, his features growing into manhood, the boyish qualities disappearing under sharpening cheekbones and lengthening jaw. Swallowing her disappointment at his less-than-romantic greeting, she murmured, "Just thought we'd not waste time."

He wiped his nose on his sleeve. "I ain't gonna do you here in your pa's house." He kept his voice blessedly low, just a whisper.

"Well, we might be findin' it hard to slip away anywhere private for a while. Flo's house is near ruined by the fire on State and anyhow, I quit."

"You quit?" Reuben squinted at her. "No more whorin'?" He sounded hopeful.

"I'm gonna start lookin' for a real job today." She sidestepped the fact that she hadn't actually *told* Flo yet that she'd quit. Time for that later.

Zelda plopped her butt on the floor, feeling the cold of the ground seeping straightways from the dirt below, through the planks, through her thin satin skirt and single silk petticoat to her skin.

"If you're quittin', then let's just run away. I hate bein' below ground." Reuben sounded desperate. "Feels like all that rock's gonna fall on me. It ain't natural. I'm good with horses. I could get a job as a bullwhacker easy, anywhere. Or haulin' ore. I could disguise myself so's no one'd know, grow a beard, dye my hair black."

Zelda ran a hand tenderly down the side of his face, refraining from saying the obvious, that it would take him a long, long time to grow a beard thick and long enough to disguise his sullen rawboned aspect. "We done talked about it, Reuben. I can't leave Pa here, with just my stupid brothers to care for him. And right now, you're safest workin' in the mines, with Zeke and Zed. 'Cause out here, aboveground, they're lookin' for you on account of murder—"

"I didn't kill anyone!" Reuben's whisper threatened to crack with his vehemence. "I wasn't even there!"

"Shhhh, shhhh," she soothed him, rubbing his shoulder and arm, gentle-like, like he was a nervous customer come up to get done for the first time. "I know you didn't kill no one."

Reuben put an arm around her shoulders, pulled her close. "But you're the only one who believes me, Zelda."

Zelda elbowed him away. "Don't call me that name here at home. It's Zel or Zelpha. Pa's only blind, not hard of hearing. And he's not stupid. He'll wonder why you've got my name all garbled up. Now, get up and get going. If you're late for your shift at the Silver Mountain Mine, you'll get fired, sure as shootin'. And you'll never get another job from any of the mines around these parts. See how easy it'll be keepin' a low profile then."

His face fell, and he suddenly looked more like the sixteen-year-old he was than the grown man he tried so hard to be.

Zelda sighed.

She'd originally told him that she was sixteen herself, slicing off those extra seven years as easy as if they were an unwanted blemish on an apple. She'd been playing the part of a young runaway at Flo's. Gentlemen callers seemed to like pretending she was young and innocent.

Or maybe they really thought she was that way.

It didn't matter and she didn't care. The sham allowed Flo to charge a higher price, so they both made more money. Sometimes, with Reuben, Zelda even felt like she *was* sixteen. But other times she was painfully aware of the difference not only in her and Reuben's real ages, but in their responsibilities as well. *If I were really sixteen, I'd say, "You bet!" when Reuben first asked me to run away, and we'd be halfway to California by now.*

She stood up, the cold of the floor transferring from the backs of her thighs to the soles of her stocking feet. "I promised Pa I'd make grits. You'd better get dressed. You've got ten hours mucking ahead, so's you'd best get going. Zed and Zeke won't wait, if you look like you're gonna be late."

"Your brothers are crazy," he muttered, grabbing his trousers and pulling them over his long johns. "They muck all day, come home, drink rotgut, and muck half the night too, so's I hardly get any sleep anyhow."

He glanced toward the corner of the room, at Zelda's trunk from home. Underneath, Zelda knew, the loose floorboards covered a hole that, aided by a ladder, led straight down twenty feet before bottoming out and wandering in a southwesterly direction to an abandoned mine shaft.

"Well, they're hopin' to strike it rich again." She crossed her arms. "Had all that money once, and then…Anyhow, you've heard Zed. He thinks this shanty's sittin' on top of a silver vein, and if they can sneak it out with the owner of that there claim no more the wiser, he'll never miss it anyhow."

The stink of burnt coffee, warmed over, drifted into the room. "Smell's like Zeke's got breakfast ready. You'd best get out there if you're hopin' to have some afore you go."

She looked over at the trunk, thinking of her Sunday best dress, pretty plain, but clean and probably just the ticket for making her look the humble, hard-working, sober young woman she hoped to portray later that day. She moved over to the bed and rolled up the elegant dressing gown, then placed it tenderly in the trunk after pulling out her Sunday dress to let it air. "I gotta clean up once you-all are gone and Pa's had his breakfast. Then I'm gonna put on my Sunday best from home, some new boots I got from Flo's, and go find me a job."

Reuben pulled the suspenders up over his sweat-stained long john top, foregoing a shirt or waistcoat. "What kind of job, Zel?"

She gave him a quick peck on the mouth, then said, "Tell you when I get it." Zelda didn't say that she had a very specific job in mind. A job she'd seen in one of the local newspapers, listed under "Wanted." A job that, after much cogitation, she'd decided she could do as well as any man, given half a chance. *And if they don't want to give me the chance, I'll just have to find a way to change their minds.*

Chapter Eight

Inez leaned forward in her chair, trying to project earnestness, not the desperation she felt. "Yes, I know this seems impulsive, Mr. Casey, and I'm sorry to have dropped by so early and without an appointment, but I'm truly ready to move forward. And I hope you will help me. There's no one else I can turn to in this matter of divorce. At least, no one I trust."

At the word "divorce," William V. Casey, Esquire, had steepled his fingers. Then, as if realizing it lent him a judgmental air, he dropped his hands to the leather-bordered blotter on his desk. Unlike at Inez's previous visit, there was no sunlight captured in his law office this morning. The muted gray of an overcast day filled the room, requiring the lighting of several oil lamps to beat back the uncharacteristic morning gloom. Inez felt as if she were suffocating in a gray land that offered neither absolution nor condemnation, but some indeterminate halfway hell.

She had decided simply to arrive on the lawyer's doorstep that early Friday morning, taking a chance that she could talk her way into his office for a quick consultation before his regularly scheduled appointments. She'd certainly caught him before his usual business hours—Inez had spotted a linen napkin, hastily stuffed in his trouser pocket, as if she'd interrupted his breakfast.

But he'd not complained, and indeed had most graciously ushered her into his office, offered coffee, and then closed the door so they, or rather, she, could talk.

After Inez ran out of apologies and explanations, he waited a moment, and then said, "Mrs. Stannert, of course I'll take your case. I told you that I would at our initial consultation, and I'm a man of my word." He hesitated, then proceeded. "When we met previously, I had the distinct impression—not that my impressions are always correct, granted—that you were going to consider this for a while. In fact, if I'd been a betting man, which generally I'm not, I'd have wagered that you'd not return. Understand, that was just my impression on your leave-taking. As I am to now represent you, I'd like to understand what is the impetus behind your, well, rather abrupt decision to pursue dissolution."

His leather chair squeaked on its swivel as he leaned forward over the desk. One of his perfectly manicured hands slid out over the blotter, then stopped short of the polished walnut surface of the desk, almost as if he was attempting to take her hand by proxy. "Of course, whatever you tell me is covered by attorney-client privilege. Your comments are as safe with me as with a priest in a confessional."

Recalling the rather loose-lipped impulses of several priests in the habit of imbibing too much of the blood of Christ during the weekdays, Inez didn't find his assurance much comfort. *Still, I must give him at least part of my reasoning. It's best if we proceed now, quickly, while the town is caught up with Grant's visit. Perhaps the divorce could become final without fanfare or notice.*

"What's to understand?" Inez twisted the gloves in her lap. "Last week, I considered all you said and my circumstances. My husband has been missing for over a year. When we met, you told me a year sufficed for proceeding on grounds of desertion. Correct?"

Casey nodded.

Somewhat reluctantly, she thought.

She continued. "I truly believe he's dead. When he disappeared, we were making plans to leave Leadville. To sell the business and move to San Francisco. I—we have a small child. William was not even a year old at the time. My husband Mark

Stannert doted on him. There was no reason…no suggestion of any…" She held her breath for a moment, trying to force calm into her shaking hands and curb her fluttering heart where it beat against her corset lining like a panicked moth against a pane of glass.

She let her breath out slowly, and started again. "I can think of no reason why he would simply walk off. Yet, since I cannot prove he is dead, I have no recourse if I wish to get on with my life other than to divorce a ghost. I've lived with this agony long enough. So, how do we start?"

Casey had been studying her closely as she rattled on.

She saw doubt there. He suspected she was holding something back, she knew. Still, how hard would he push her, a frantic woman, who was begging him to take up her cause? *This is what he does for a living. He will surely not throw away this chance for an easy case. There's no one to contest the divorce. No one to object.*

Finally, Casey nodded. Decision reached.

"I have a standard retainer agreement I use," he began matter-of-factly. "It includes the steps involved, what you can expect from me, what I expect from you, and the terms of payment. I can tell you that, if the case is uncontested, which it sounds like you believe it will be, this should be a fairly quick process and relatively inexpensive. I will have the agreement drawn up today and ready for you to sign first thing Monday."

"Monday?" The weekend stretched before her, two days of uncertainty in which anything could happen. "But, I would like to sign you on now. Immediately. If I pay a retainer, could you, perhaps, draw up a simple agreement now and set the wheels in motion today? I will then sign the detailed contract next week when it's ready."

He regarded her. "This is unusual."

"Forgive me, Mr. Casey." She forced a note of apology into her words. "It's just my way. Having made the decision, waiting is nearly unbearable. I will double your retainer, to recompense you for your trouble."

He looked down at his blotter, nudged it so the bottom edge aligned with the edge of his desk. "It's not necessary to double my retainer, Mrs. Stannert." His voice was gentle. "I have been in this business for many years. I understand that the prospect of the dissolution of a marriage is difficult for the parties involved."

Casey reached down to a lower drawer of his vast walnut desk. The small bald spot on the back of his head came into view as he bent to view the drawer's contents. He straightened up and placed two blank sheets of paper on his desk, followed by a pen with a fresh nib, before pulling a crystal inkwell toward him.

"I shall set forth something simple for now, noting that you have retained me as counsel and have paid a retainer." He dipped the pen and wrote a few lines in a decisive slanting script, dating and signing at the bottom, and did the same with the second sheet. He picked up a pewter sand shaker and sprinkled sand on the wet ink, remarking, "Once you sign these, I shall prepare the paperwork for the county sheriff."

"County sheriff?" She frowned. "What is his role in this? I thought we would simply appear before a judge, and it would be done."

Casey smiled. It was meant to be a comforting smile, but all it told Inez was that her assumptions were incorrect.

"Colorado law does allow divorce based on abandonment by one of the spouses. But first, we must conduct 'due diligence.' That means we must use maximum effort and resources to locate your husband and provide him with 'due process,' which means simply 'notice and an opportunity to be heard.' We need to notify your husband that you are filing for divorce, tell him of the court date, and allow him to attend that hearing to provide any explanation he might have for his alleged abandonment."

Inez drew a deep breath. "Very well. How do we proceed?"

Casey said, "The first step is to have the sheriff to serve the divorce papers on your husband. Now, you last saw your husband here in Leadville, is that correct?"

"May of last year, yes." Inez tried to put rumors of Mark's appearances along the Front Range out of her mind.

Casey nodded. "If the sheriff or his designated representative cannot find your husband, then we place a notice in at least three newspapers. A notice in a local paper, the *Leadville Herald* or the *Democrat* would do. Or *The Independent*, if you prefer. At the same time, a notice in one with a larger distribution. One of the Denver papers, for instance."

Cold apprehension nudged her at the mention of Denver. "Why not something in the *Fairplay Flume*? Is a notice in a Denver paper really necessary?"

"I would advise it for two reasons." He leaned back in his chair. It squeaked, almost in sympathetic terror with Inez, as he rocked to and fro. "The Leadville papers are read up and down the Arkansas, into Colorado Springs, and South Park. We'd be treading the same ground with a notice in the *Flume*. Also, didn't you mention last time that your husband might have been sighted in Denver?"

"Last winter." Inez said, cursing herself silently for having mentioned that particular event to Casey and cursing Casey for his good memory. "But nothing was heard after that. It was a very tenuous identification. The person admitted that it was at a distance. Is it truly necessary to reach all the way to Denver? Seems such a waste of time. And money."

"Nevertheless." The squeaking intensified with a last squawk as he quit rocking and leaned forward again, earnestness washing over his round face. "Consider this, Mrs. Stannert. The person who must be persuaded to grant you a divorce is not I—you don't have to convince me of your good faith attempts to find your husband—but the judge to whom we will present your petition for the dissolution of your marriage. If we can say to him that, yes, we made every attempt to find Mr. Stannert in Leadville and in the surrounding territory, and, yes, we made good-faith efforts to locate him—within reasonable means, of course—in the greater Colorado area, including the capital city where he was supposedly last seen…" He spread his hands wide and raised his eyebrows in a gesture of openness. In an attitude that indicated a willingness to hear and a wish to be heard, an attitude of presenting the truth and then being willing to negotiate.

Inez had to admit that, had she been the judge, listening to Casey and his earnest speech, watching him as he walked through the points of her desire to find her husband and her inability, despite all she'd done, to uncover his whereabouts, she'd be nodding and affirming his every word.

"So." His hands retreated to the blotter, bracketing the abbreviated contracts. "It behooves us to do the best we can to be sure that our efforts to find Mr. Stannert extend beyond Leadville, and in a significant way. Not merely in a nearby paper, or in some insignificant, unknown broadsheet that is passed up and down by hand in Ten Mile Canyon."

Casey tipped the sand off the contracts into a wastebasket, picked up the pen, and dipped it in the faceted inkwell. He handed the pen to Inez and turned one sheet to face her. "Mrs. Stannert, if this is the road you wish to take, I'll be your guide, your advocate, and your protector."

Inez gripped the pen so tight her fingers spasmed. Without reading the contract, she signed. Afraid that if she hesitated to read the legal verbiage her courage would flee and she along with it.

Without a word, Casey replaced the sheet with its twin.

She signed the second copy.

Casey stood, went over to a sideboard, opened one of its cupboards, and removed a bottle and two shot glasses. "I know it's early in the day, but I always offer after the signing of a contract. Do you wish—" He held up the bottle, which, even at a distance, she saw held the label of a very fine Scotch.

"I think not, but thank you." She stood, surprised to find that her trembling limbs would hold her erect. "I have other errands to attend to. Thank you for seeing me without an appointment. I do hope I haven't impinged on your schedule."

"Not at all." He placed the glasses and bottle on the desk, extracted an envelope from a drawer, and folded a copy of their contract neatly into thirds before sliding it in. "I shall start the wheels of justice turning. This morning, I shall see what strings I can pull to have the court clerk draw up a summons for Mr. Stannert right away. If we serve the summons inside the county, he has ten days to respond. Outside Lake County but in the district, forty days. I'll see if we can't have the summons limited to the county, given your desire for a quick resolution. Perhaps I can arrange to simultaneously publish the summons in the newspapers, even as the county sheriff is doing his search. If we publish in Leadville and Denver, that might give us leverage for pursuing both avenues simultaneously. An unusual procedure, but not entirely unheard of." He seemed to be talking to himself, preparing his arguments.

His gaze, which had been absently wandering over the legal volumes along the office walls behind Inez, returned to her. His focus sharpened. "It's entirely likely that the county sheriff will pass the task of serving the summons to a deputy, things being as busy as they are right now, with General Grant in town."

"Yes. Thank you. I appreciate your promptness in addressing my circumstances. More than I can possibly express." She gathered her gloves. "My overcoat?"

"In the entryway," he reminded her.

She realized she'd been in such a state on arriving that she had no recollection of removing her coat or hanging her umbrella.

Casey had just gripped the knob to open the door for Inez when the door flew open of its own accord, accompanied by a burst of excited female chatter. "Oh, Willie! I witnessed the most interesting incident while taking my morning constitutional—"

Inez was treated to a view of a purple hat in which a bird with beady black eyes nested. The bird was quite dead and stuffed in the bargain. Then, the hat tipped back, and a pair of brilliant eyes, a startling blue verging on amethyst, speared Inez.

The woman stepped back into the entryway. From her height, Inez would have thought the woman was perhaps a child. Except, her lower limbs were enveloped not in long skirts, but in a reform outfit, complete with purple bloomers and short purple skirt.

"Excuse me," she said with her crisp no-nonsense elocution. "I had no idea. Isn't it early to be having visitors, Mr. Casey?" She then reached past him to Inez, held out a hand, and said briskly, "Allow me to introduce myself. Mrs. Serena Clatchworthy."

Responding automatically to the strange woman's forthright manner, Inez reached for the hand, saying, "Mrs. Stannert."

After a single hearty shake, Mrs. Clatchworthy withdrew her hand adding, as if an afterthought, "Editor, publisher, reporter, and hawker of the *Cloud City Columbia*."

Casey moved between them, blocking Inez from Mrs. Clatchworthy's intent gaze. "Mrs. Stannert is here on a *legal* matter." There was a firm current of warning in his explanation, as if he'd raised a cane within the sight of a child who was pushing the limits of misbehavior.

Serena raised her hands, as if in protest. "Mrs. Stannert, I am the soul of discretion. My business and Mr. Casey's run on separate tracks. Much like our philosophies regarding—"

"Mrs. Stannert was just leaving. Perhaps you might deliver your thoughts on women's suffrage another time," said Casey, not unkindly.

"Well, then. Perhaps I will," Mrs. Clatchworthy said. "A pleasure to meet you, Mrs. Stannert. My brother is the best in the business. You've come to the right man." She retreated across the foyer to a parlor opposite the law office.

Casey ushered Inez over to a walnut hallstand holding Inez's overcoat and umbrella. These items were now balanced on the other side of the center mirror by a furled purple umbrella rimmed with gold fringe, dripping into the umbrella pan. Purple kid gloves were thrown carelessly on the marble inset shelf beneath the mirror.

Inez caught a glimpse of the parlor's interior. Mrs. Clatchworthy, ostensibly warming herself by the painted firescreen, gazed at Inez with intense curiosity. A rocking chair held an open book, face down. Inez imagined the book whining at the mistreatment of its spine, cracked and in distress.

"I'll be back momentarily, Serena." Casey hastily hung Inez's coat over her shoulders, shoved her umbrella into her hand, and walked her out the door. He let himself out as well and closed the door behind them both.

"My apologies, Mrs. Stannert," he began. "Usually my sister's morning constitutional lasts quite a bit longer. It must have been something truly unusual to bring her back so soon." He stopped, his brown eyes taking in Inez's stiff demeanor. "In any case, although we share an abode, I can assure you that Serena—Mrs. Clatchworthy—and my occupations do not intersect. She is completely dedicated to her printing press and her muses and chatters endlessly about work. I do not. She understands and respects the legal code of conduct that I adhere to." He allowed a small smile to crease his face. "All in all, she's quite harmless in her enthusiasms. Most likely, you'll not cross paths again. I just wanted to reassure you that your story and our business remain confidential, as I assured you at the start."

"I'll hold you to that, Mr. Casey," said Inez, recovering her voice.

"Your trust is well placed. Now, I'd better return to the office and prepare the paperwork I spoke of. Good day, Mrs. Stannert."

Chapter Nine

"So, Mrs. Stannert, let's drink to our partnership." Frisco Flo held up a glass that, Inez approvingly noted, did not contain an anemic, watered-down version of whiskey, but, judging from its clarity and dark amber color, appeared to be a bourbon of the first class.

Ignoring the shot glass on her side of the table, Inez pushed the two sets of legal papers toward Flo, along with a pen. "Not until we have your signature next to mine on these papers. A signature with your legal name, I should add. No 'Madam Frisco Flo,' if you please. I'm not about to celebrate handing over hard-earned cash on this deal before all the i's are dotted and the t's crossed. Miss Florence Sweet, isn't it? Or is that an alias as well?"

The silver bracelets on Flo's arm tinkled as she lowered the glass and smiled sweetly. "Why, Mrs. Stannert. Do you really think so little of me that you suspect me of trying to pull the wool over your eyes? Here we are, two of the most successful businesswomen in town. Wealthy by our own efforts, at that. I'd no sooner cheat you than my own sister."

Her smile stayed intact as she picked up the pen and drew the ink bottle to her, dipping the nib. "And actually, Mrs. Stannert, it's *Mrs.* Florence Sweet. Mr. Sweet being departed a long time now."

Inez watched, trying to quell a niggle of misgiving, as Flo dipped the pen and signed twice. Inez was still uncertain what force had propelled her to this particular circumstance. Only a few days earlier, Flo had flounced into the Silver Queen's kitchen, proposing that Inez join her in a "business deal" to move the high-class brothel to a better part of town. "Closer to the mines, the business district, and all that money," was how flo had phrased it. Inez had put the offer aside.

Or so she'd thought.

But in some faraway corner of her mind, a little voice had begun whispering, so faintly Inez had barely noticed it in the wide sweep of events before Grant's arrival. The voice said, *You think you own a portion of the Silver Queen. That was a handshake deal between yourself, your missing husband, and his business partner. So, you want a divorce? What happens when you open this particular Pandora's box? Will anyone believe that you, or Abe, own any part of the business? Suppose the law decides the business belongs to your husband's heir, your son, now living with your sister? Or suppose Mark reappears? You could end up with nothing. You need something of your own. Something "just in case." And what better business in Leadville than one that caters to men's desires and impulses?*

On and on the voice whispered, seductive as a forbidden lover. And then, with her visit to Casey, all those little misgivings flashed over into doubt.

When Flo's doorman had appeared at the Silver Queen shortly after Inez arrived from her meeting with the lawyer, the whispers rose to a crescendo. So, she went. Splashing along in her galoshes, she ignored the chores awaiting her inside the saloon, wondering what deal Flo might offer. Her impulsive decision to accede to Flo's request for a visit paid off. Flo was ready to move out of the State Street building, but she needed cash. Inez wanted the State Street building, but Flo was reluctant to part with it entirely. They haggled. Inez had, in short order, driven what she thought was a very good deal indeed. Their signatures, drying on the duplicate contracts, made her a silent partner, owning a third of Flo's business, in exchange for a stake in the building on State and eventually sole ownership.

"I'd only sell the building to someone I can consider a partner. A person I can trust," she'd explained.

Inez pondered this. "You trust me?"

"Thanks to you, I was able to take over the boarding house and business last winter," Flo pointed out. "You essentially ran the previous madam out of town. I'm grateful for that, even though I know your actions had nothing to do with me. Still, I always thought that we had the same goal—to become independent businesswomen. Am I wrong?"

She was not.

As for the moral implications of being part-owner of a brothel, Inez pushed them aside to ponder at a more convenient time.

"One for you and one for me." Flo slid a copy of the agreement toward Inez. Inez noted that Flo had a hand that would do a schoolmarm proud: the ink showed a careful, controlled pressure on the pen, all the letters even and well-shaped. Even the flourishes looked as if they'd been practiced until perfect.

Flo took her copy and vanished into the back room. When she reappeared, she sat across the table from Inez, brushing her hands together as if to say, "And that is that."

"Are you ready for that drink now?" Flo asked.

Inez picked up the tumbler. Flo raised hers. The glasses clinked sweetly in crystal harmony. A single sip, blooming in sweetness and vanilla, assured Inez that Flo had chosen to honor their partnership with a good bourbon.

"Thank you for coming here," Flo added. "I don't usually conduct business in my own home, but last night's circumstances made it necessary."

With the bourbon's aftertaste lingering in her mouth and the alcohol spreading its heat down her throat, Inez glanced around the small parlor, absentmindedly smoothing her glove in her lap. A glance was all that was needed to take in the sparse furnishings. The ubiquitous warming stove, the table, two straight-backed chairs, a rocking chair by the window. No pictures, no extra furniture, no rugs, only the most basic of curtains to block out light and a lamp to increase it. The room was bare of anything that might make a house a home. Flo's home—little more than a two-room cottage, a block away from her bordello—put Inez in the mind of a hotel room. Easily vacated, with no hint of personality left behind, once the occupant had left.

Flo, wearing a simple maroon gown, fanned herself with a loose sheet of paper. The air stirred her slightly frizzy hair, damp from a recent rinsing and still streaked from the soot of the fire.

"The parlor house reeks of smoke," Flo said conversationally. "But it could be worse. The door to the kitchen was closed at the time, so the damage is concentrated in the back. Still, I didn't think you'd want to meet there. And Lynch's would not have afforded us the privacy we need for this matter. As for coming to your saloon, the last time I paid a business call I was afraid your cook, Mrs. O'Malley, would chase me down Tiger Alley with her broom."

Inez shifted in the chair, thinking of Bridgette O'Malley's propensity for gossip. "Just as well. I prefer that we keep this transaction between us. A private matter."

Flo fluffed her hair absently. "I'm so glad you were amenable to this partnership. I know you've had an eye on my building for a long time, as have many others. I've been approached—oh, I don't know how many times—about selling it. So, you see, we both get what we want here. Once I've moved to Fifth, you can take over the State Street building. We remain partners in both endeavors until you buy me out." She sighed. "I wish we were at the new house now, what with all the visitors in town. Oh well. We'll air the old place out, apply a little perfume, and be ready to open for business tonight." She twiddled her fingers in the air, as if waving good-bye to wishful thinking. "Time's a-wasting, and time is money. Especially in the whoring business. The girls and me are anxious to put last night's dreadful event behind us. We must make hay while the sun shines. Or," she glanced out the window at the drizzle falling from a gray sky, "while it doesn't. So, when can you have the money to me?"

"Just how soon do you plan to move?" Inez countered.

Flo scrunched her nose, calculating. "Today's Friday. We could clear out next Thursday, after Grant leaves, and be ready for business the Friday after."

Inez's eyebrows shot up. "That's very quick indeed."

Flo continued, the old twinkle back in her voice, "I've been preparing for a while now. With what you've promised to me today, along with what I've saved and the investment of a third party, I can finally make my move. Me and the girls will start sorting through the house for what to take with us. As for the new place, once I have the cash from you, it'll take next to no time to sign the papers."

Inez sat up straighter, frowning at the unwelcome news buried in Flo's prattle. "You have another investor? Who?"

Flo smiled again. More indulgently. "I promised you I'd not utter a peep about our business agreement. How could I do any less for my other partner? I'm a woman of my word."

Inez regarded her narrowly. *Who, I wonder, is the third partner. A banker? A businessman or another saloon owner? Lynch, perhaps? I'm not keen on this arrangement.*

Further discussion was cut short by a sudden battering at the door. It sounded as if someone was pounding with two fists.

Flo cut a look, sharp as a razor, at Inez. Inez realized that, without even thinking, she'd leapt to her feet and pulled out her pocket revolver.

The staccato beat was interrupted by a feminine wail, which resolved into the words, "Miss Flo! Oh, Miss Flo!"

Flo's tightened expression relaxed. "One of my girls. Molly. Honestly, they get wound up about the smallest things. Probably one borrowed a necklace and broke it or some such. It was hard getting any sleep at Lynch's last night, and everyone's on edge. But just in case—" Flo extracted a small derringer from a hidden drawer in the table, then moved to the door and opened it.

A woman burst in, nearly tripping in her rush. Her red hair straggled about her shoulders, tears tracked through the face powder. The front of her dress, splattered dark by the rain, was buttoned crooked, leaving a gap displaying a white streak of belly. The disarranged female gave Inez not the slightest glance. She grabbed Flo's sleeve, inarticulate.

"Molly!" Flo's sharp tone served to stop the wordless gibbering.

"M-Miss Flo." Molly rubbed her running nose on one sleeve. "Lizzie. She, she…"

"Jesus Christ." Flo hissed the words with an edge of irritation. "Can't I leave you in charge for a minute without a crisis? What happened? Did Lizzie show up at last? Is she fighting with Lynch's whores? She better not have gotten my girls thrown out on the street. If she's drinking, I'll—"

"No!" Molly twisted Flo's sleeve in her fist. "No! Not, not… Lizzie, she's, she's…Oh shit, Miss Flo. Lizzie's dead! Stone-cold dead!"

Chapter Ten

Flo slapped Molly's face. Hard. The crack of flesh on flesh sounded like a gunshot in the small room. Molly's sobbing abruptly ceased.

"You're lying!" snapped Flo.

Molly's hand flew to her reddening cheek. "I'm not!" She seemed more injured by Flo's disbelief than the actual cuff. "Lizzie's behind the house. In the mudroom. Danny caught that mapmaker with his hands on her throat and her tit. Miss Flo, hurry, Danny's like to kill him!"

Without a backwards glance at Inez or to stop for a hat or coat, Flo hiked up her skirts, showing an indecent length of white calf, and shot out the front door. Molly followed suit.

Thinking of the gun in Flo's hand and the just-signed deal, Inez grabbed her umbrella and hurried out the door, slamming it behind her. She took off for the parlor house as fast as she could without showing more than her boot tops.

The contract with the lawyer lay in her pocket, rubbing against the agreement she'd signed with Flo. Casey's envelope with its sharp corners was a stiff reminder of yet another legal promise made, both of which had surprising and unwelcome addenda appearing after the ink was dry.

Will I come to regret them both?

Chapter Eleven

Inez heard the ruckus long before she saw anything. As she approached the alleyway entrance, women's voices rose and conquered the street noise. A knot of men hovered near the rear of Flo's parlor house, necks craned for a better look. Inez slowed her pace, debating whether to brush on by and gather information later so as not to embroil herself in the sordid dealings of the brothel. *It's too late for that! I've signed an agreement with Flo. My fortunes are tied to hers, for better or worse.*

With a deep breath, she arranged her expression into one of disdainful curiosity and sidled up to the growing crowd.

The scene was not lovely.

The back wall and door of the tacked-on mudroom had vanished into smoke the previous evening along with a sizeable portion of the roof. A more-or-less three-sided, well-charred enclosure remained, open to the sky. One of Flo's women sat on the plank that served as a stair, weeping loudly, fingers twined in brown tresses that all but hid her face. A coalscuttle lay abandoned by her feet. She blubbered, "The stove went out in our room at Lynch's. I j-just wanted to see if there was any coal left in the kitchen."

Flo stood just inside the destroyed mudroom, hand to her breast. The hand with the gun, Inez observed, was hidden in the folds of her dress. Flo sank onto what was left of the floorboards, looking as if she might faint. Her knees hit the damaged flooring, which protested with a loud *crack!* Molly sprang to her side, grabbing Flo's arm lest she fall through. Flo ripped away from Molly's grasp and leaned forward, reaching down into a hole in the flooring, reaching for a bundle of rags.

Inez stepped forward to see better and realized that the bundle wasn't rags, but the body of a woman. A woman dressed in a soiled white wrapper, curled up on her side like an infant, her face obscured by a matted mess of long dark hair.

Up the alleyway, Danny, the brothel's doorman, had some fellow pinned to the ground. Papers were scattered around, wet and torn, mashed into the muck. The feet and legs of the conquered were flailing as the doorman applied unknown pressure to the upper portion of the man's torso.

Inez sensed someone even taller than herself step close behind her, nearly breathing down her neck. She turned to find Jed Elliston, editor, reporter, and owner—if one discounted the fact that his father had shoveled out the money for the business venture—of *The Independent*. She was surprised that he was upright and walking, given his plunge from the grandstand the night before. About the only damage she could ascertain was a knife-thin scrape down one side of his long-nosed, aristocratic face. The mark gave the newspaperman a slightly rakish air.

Eyes pinned to the scene before him, Jed pulled out his ever-present notepad and pencil from beneath his waterproof. Ignoring the small spits of rain that pocked the paper pad, he licked the lead with relish and elbowed his way forward through the crowd. Taking advantage of the vacuum left in his wake, Inez followed.

"Press, 'scuse me, the press, pardon. What's going on?" Jed was now at the front of the throng, near Flo and her women. Inez slid in beside him.

The woman on the step lifted her face. With her hair trailing like snakes, she reminded Inez of a weeping Greek tragedy mask, with a touch of Medusa. "Lizzie's dead!" she wailed. "And that one," she pointed at the prostrate figure on the ground under Danny, "done the deed!"

A gargle exploded from beneath Danny.

Flo's face twisted in fury. "Quit howling, Belle! Go back to Lynch's. Stay with the other girls." She turned to Molly and snapped, "Go get a doctor! She's not dead. She *can't* be!"

Molly jerked as if touched by lightning, stared wide-eyed at Flo, then turned and shoved her way through the crowd, throwing epithets at spectators who moved too slowly.

Jed took advantage of the chaos to climb the step and peer unchallenged into the hole. Inez followed suit, knowing that the curious masses behind her were also pressing forward, jostling to see better what lay under the floor.

Jed shook his head. He glanced at Inez. "Hullo, Mrs. Stannert. I'm no physician, but I'd wager this one's left the world of the living." He commenced his note taking, eyes pinned on the scene before him.

Inez took another step forward, and the deceased came into clear view.

At least, Lizzie certainly looked deceased, bereft of life and movement.

Her face was mottled, either badly bruised, marked by dirt, or both. Flo clutched one unresponsive hand in her own. The woman's dead-white skin made fair-skinned Flo look ruddy by comparison.

"That's Lizzie?" Jed's pencil was poised over the tablet. "Does she have a last name? How long did she work for you, Mrs. Sweet?"

Flo looked up, tears straggling down her face. Then, as if just noticing the one-sided fight in the alley, she struggled to her feet and propelled herself toward Danny and his captive. Inez saw the small nickel-plated derringer flash in her hand as she crouched in the mud beside the victim. Inez, hurrying toward the trio, heard Flo say, "What did you do to her? Tell me!"

The barrel of the small two-shot pistol pressed deep into the soft skin under the older man's jaw. His face was covered in mud; his mustache slimed with blood from what Inez presumed was a broken nose. Danny held him in a chokehold, looking within an inch of breaking his neck. It was clear the fellow lacked breath in his present position to say anything in his defense. Or to confess.

Men pressed Inez on every side. A rough elbow to her side, so sharp she felt it through the protective cage of steel corset stays, caused her to snap, "I *beg* your pardon!"

The transgressor, oblivious, wedged himself in beside her. Inez had to tip her head back to glare at his profile—young, with a dark wisp of a mustache, no detectable beard, dark pools of eyes in a face so pale that she immediately placed him as a tenderfoot from out of town. She gave him the once-over, taking in the elegant stovepipe hat, the expensive cut of his waterproof coat, the fine kid gloves and silver-headed umbrella held high. Not the sort of attire one associated with Leadville's grimy back alleys. From the East Coast, she guessed, or perhaps San Francisco. The rapt eagerness with which he drank in the squalid scene was distinctly off-putting.

"I *never*." Inez considered jabbing him with her umbrella to give him a taste of his own medicine.

"Pardon, ma'am." The apologist wasn't the young upstart, but someone behind her. The speaker squeezed between Inez and her unwelcome neighbor. Her tactile impression was of solidity, a man with muscle on him. Other than that, there was the ubiquitous bowler, rain-soaked, and a carefully curled thick brown mustache.

"Mr. Wesley." He addressed the noisome youngster firmly, but with a certain obsequiousness. "You're expected at the Clarendon. Your mother said that General Grant requested that everyone be ready to leave on time."

Young Wesley gestured impatiently with the umbrella. "Just a moment longer won't make any difference, Kavanagh. You can tell the old girl you did your level best to get me back on time, like the professional minder that you are, but the crowds didn't allow. That's why I provide you with a handsome bonus on top of whatever she pays you. I mean, look at them. Like pigs in the mud." He sounded delighted.

The man named Kavanagh glanced at Inez, his face full of apology and distaste. Whether for the scene or for his employer's behavior was unclear.

"Put him down like a damn dog, Flo!" shouted someone from the crowd. "Danny caught 'im, red-handed. One hand round her neck, other on her boobie. He don't deserve any better than to have his head ventilated for desecratin' poor Lizzie there."

A chorus of "yeahs" and "rights" swirled about Inez. She sensed the mob shifting, pressing in, restless, a living breathing unity, hungry, and eager for blood.

The blast of a whistle echoed off buildings up and down the alley.

"Everyone. Back!" barked a gravelly, hoarse voice, hard, commanding. "Law. Coming through."

Kavanagh inadvertently shouldered Inez as he turned to check the commotion at the rear.

The same voice that had called for blood now said, "Dadgummit. Party's over. It's The Hatchet with reinforcements."

The Hatchet.

Dismay bit the back of Inez's throat.

Somewhere in the rear, the solid *thwut* of a policeman's sap hitting flesh was followed by a yelp.

Kavanagh turned to Wesley. "Mr. Wesley. The police are here. Your mother and the general wait." The politeness was gone, the words, sharp as a whip, were made civil only by being near whisper-level.

Wesley jumped at that, glanced about guiltily, and smoothed his mustache with a gloved hand as if to gain comfort from its presence. "Oh, very well. Guess we shouldn't keep them waiting." His superciliousness sounded off-key, strained.

Kavanagh and Wesley eased away.

The pressure of bodies behind Inez vanished suddenly, and she stepped backwards to regain her balance. A hand closed like a steel band around her arm.

She looked up into the glowering face of The Hatchet: Patrick Ryan, Leadville policeman and duly appointed city collector of fines, fees, and taxes.

The Hatchet was a tall rail of a man. The crease that split the length of his forehead, stopping only at the bridge of his nose, looked as if it had been put there with a hatchet. A sharp nose, curved and long provided another axe-like echo. But his appearance was only part of the genesis of his nickname. The Hatchet had no compunctions about cutting down any fool who dared stand up to him and his authority. A State Street businessman or woman who refused to pay the requisite fees, sometimes several times over, was in danger of experiencing the same fate.

And no one, no one called The Hatchet "Pat," "Paddy," or any other diminutive. It was "Ryan" by those on the force, "Officer Ryan" or "Sir" by all others, and "The Hatchet" when he was out of hearing range.

Inez had taken care to cultivate a neutral relationship with the local law: the city marshal, county marshal, the deputy federal marshal, the ordinary beat police officers, and the local merchants' Protective Patrol deputies, who, to the dismay of the city council, stopped crime more effectively than the city's police force. However, The Hatchet was another matter. As city collector, he had staked out State Street as his own private fiefdom. Given that the city's biggest source of revenue came from fees and fines imposed on prostitution, gambling, and various aspects of the liquor trade, The Hatchet's near constant presence was expected, and dreaded, by most State Street denizens and merchants.

Right now, The Hatchet stared at Inez, suspicion narrowing his dust-colored eyes into slits. He moved her incrementally to the side, out of his path, and released his grip, before continuing his advance on Flo, Danny, and their injured prisoner. Officer Kelly, one of Leadville's finest, trailed in The Hatchet's wake. Inez recognized Kelly by his beacon of red hair and his cheerful demeanor, maintained even when dealing with obnoxious drunks and hysterical dancehall girls. He stopped when The

Hatchet stopped, examined the scene with bemusement, and looked to his partner for direction.

The Hatchet spoke. "What's the trouble here, Flo? Molly was near hysteria, running half-clothed down the street. That kind of thing don't make a good impression on the bigwigs visiting town."

"To hell with them! And to hell with you, too!" shouted Flo, sounding more and more frantic. "I sent for the doctor. Where is he?"

The Hatchet dropped his voice, which still had volume enough to carry into every straining ear in the narrow alleyway. "Too late for the doctor, Flo. I told Molly to get the undertaker. Now give me that pistol." He held out his hand.

She dug the business end of the small revolver further into her victim's neck. He coughed, spraying blood and mud onto the knees of her skirts. "Fuck you, Hatchet."

"Flo, don't make this worse than it is. You're disturbing the peace. Don't add murder to it."

Flo turned on him, teeth bared. The look on her face put Inez in mind of a cornered dog, fear and madness warring in the eyes. "You *dare* take his side!"

She jerked the pistol away from the prone man and toward the city collector. The shot echoed off the boards and bricks of the surrounding buildings.

The Hatchet, untouched, yanked the gun from her before the echoes had died. He gestured Kelly over, who grabbed Flo by the waist and hauled her to her feet, even as she swore and kicked.

The tiny gun disappeared into The Hatchet's pocket as he addressed his partner in a voice loud enough to be heard by the avid crowd. "Add assault on an officer to the list, Officer Kelly." He turned to Danny. It wasn't necessary to say anything to Flo's doorman. He let go of his victim, after first mashing the hapless fellow's face into the mud for good measure, and stepped back.

Hatchet looked at the injured man and said, "Get up."

He got to his knees, coughing, hand covering his nose. Blood dripped between his fingers. Inez got a good view of the top of his head, the thinning brown hair streaked with gray.

"On your feet." The Hatchet hooked an armpit and hauled the battered man upright.

Recognition dawned for Inez as she registered the face beneath the mud and blood.

The man that almost got his head kicked in by Lucy last night. The man I saw behind Lynch's during the fire.

The Hatchet recognized him as well. "Cecil Farnesworth. That's your moniker, right? You're making maps for that fire insurance company back East."

"How, how do you know me?" His voice was faint with pain.

"I know everything that goes on in this part of town and the folks that're doing it. That's my job. And if something's going on that I *don't* know about, I get real testy. I don't like mysteries, like finding you here. So talk quick and don't leave out anything. What're you doin' behind Flo's burnt-up building with your hands all over a dead whore?"

"The damage. To the structure. From last night's fire. I came to see. Also, I need to finish my maps of the building." Cecil dabbed his nose with his sleeve, attempted to straighten his muddy celluloid collar, half torn and hanging from its collar studs. "I've nothing to do with any of this."

His eyes darted toward Lizzie's body, then over the crowd, pausing on Inez. He frowned, as if trying to place her. She thought recognition flitted across his face before he looked away, at the fire-scarred parlor house.

"I was examining the building, then I saw the body. At first, I thought she was unconscious. I was searching for a pulse. That's why my hands were—" He stopped and colored.

Some in the crowd snickered. But most were silent, as rapt as in the presence of a circus performer swallowing a fiery sword or walking a high-wire. Inez found herself mesmerized with the rest. *Is he telling the truth? Will Hatchet believe him? Or is he going to go down in blazes, right here, with us watching?*

Cecil looked at the papers scattered about the alley. "My maps. My notes."

Inez registered a board strapped with loose papers and a broken pencil by the coalscuttle. A page, one end trampled in mud, flapped against the toe of one of her galoshes. She extracted it gingerly with two gloved fingers. A neatly penciled sketch showed boxy shapes and lines, cryptic notations, and odd little symbols.

Flo, still struggling in Officer Kelly's grasp, cried, "You're lying! I heard what happened last night when you came sniffing around. She humiliated you. You hated her!"

Inez could have sworn that the mapmaker blushed, but it was difficult to tell for certain, what with all the filth on his face. He didn't look at the ranting madam, focusing instead on The Hatchet. "I didn't move her or touch her, except to check for a pulse."

The Hatchet nodded once. Noncommittal. "Still bunkin' at the Clairmont?"

"For a few more days."

The Hatchet shook his head. "You stay put 'til we get a handle on this."

"But—"

"No buts. Here in Leadville, we lock up witnesses just to keep 'em around so's they'll be available to testify. I don't know if a crime's been committed here, but a woman's dead."

"She's not dead!" screamed Flo.

The Hatchet squinted upwards, as if Flo's voice had descended from the sullen gray clouds. "Wasn't this one partial to the bottle, or was it the needle? Coroner'll decide what done her in. You can cool your heels in the clink, Flo, until judge sets bail."

"You bastard! None of my girls drink. Or take drugs. How dare you even *suggest*—"

And you." He addressed Cecil. "If you set foot outside the city limits, I'll know. I'll know if you're fixing to board a stagecoach, hop a train, or rent a horse. I'll find you, have you detained in the same cell as Flo here, and tell the jailer to turn his back."

Hatchet turned to Officer Kelly. "Let's go."

As if on cue, Kelly said, "Now, Mrs. Sweet, you stop kicking and I won't hafta drag you down the street, with you making a spectacle of yourself."

Flo's crazed eyes found Inez. "Mrs. Stannert! Help me! Have Danny take Lizzie up to her room. Second floor. Set the girls to watching over her until I get out. Keep her warm. She can't be dead! Don't let that drunk of a coroner touch her with his knife or I swear, I'll take a knife to him myself!"

Chapter Twelve

Inez cursed the Fates that had brought her to this strange pass: Standing behind Flo's parlor house, in the rain, shielding a dead whore from prying eyes. Flo's plea rang in Inez's ears as she waved her umbrella with menace at the crowd of men that simply refused to disperse. "Go! Don't you all have something better to do than gawk? For shame!"

Only a few of the men trickled out of the alley at her reprimands. Finally, Jed pushed his way forward to stand by Inez. He raised his pencil and pad, surveying the malingerers. "Let's see, whom shall I say was at the sordid scene of the discovery of a prostitute's body in Tiger Alley on this rainy morning of Friday, June twenty-third, the day after former President Grant's arrival? Ah, Mr. Sketchley, is that you over there by the rain barrel? Care to comment, sir?"

A mild-looking fellow, who had been stealthily working his way around to obtain a better view, pulled his hat low and exited the alley.

"Mr. Warner, Mr. McClutcheon, won't your wives be interested to read your names in this article. Say, since Mr. Sketchley demurred, would you have a few words I could include, a quote, a man-on-the-street observation?"

The two gentlemen in question melted away, more quickly than snow in a summer rain. Jed cast an eye at the remaining idlers. They hastily withdrew to the mouth of the alley. With a flourish, Jed tucked his pencil and pad into his coat pocket with the air of a cavalier sheathing a rapier.

"Coroner's bound to be here soon," he observed. "So, Mrs. Stannert, since Flo put you in charge, what will you do? Rather strange she'd turn to you, isn't it?"

Inez sighed. "Well, we attend the same church. Although it's been quite a while since she's been to a service." She turned to Danny. "Do you know which room is Lizzie's? Can we go through the back door?"

Danny nodded mutely, then shook his head.

"Barred from the inside?"

Another nod.

Inez sighed again. "Well, if you must carry her through the streets, she should be covered. You'll just attract more unwanted attention otherwise. Be careful with her. Not that I believe she's alive," she hastily added. "Still. Is there something you can wrap her in? A sheet or a blanket?"

Danny nodded and disappeared around the side of the brick building.

"Lord save us," muttered Jed.

Inez puzzled, faced him. "What?"

He was staring down the alley. The object of his attention, approaching them with soldierly intent, was nearly hidden beneath a large purple umbrella rimmed with soggy gold fringe.

Inez caught her breath at the sight just before Jed announced through gritted teeth, "It's Mrs. Clatchworthy." His voice dripped with disdain.

The approaching umbrella tipped back. The bird on top of the purple hat regarded Inez with its ebony glass eyes as if to say, "We meet again."

Mrs. Clatchworthy turned her equally penetrating gaze on Jed first. "Mr. Elliston. I'm not surprised to find you at such a sorry spectacle, no doubt intending to make sport of this poor woman's death." She then looked at Inez blandly, "Well, Mr. Elliston, won't you introduce us?"

"Mrs. Stannert, Mrs. Clatchworthy, and vice versa," grumbled Jed.

"Mrs. Stannert, I don't think we've met," said Mrs. Clatchworthy, with a barely visible wink. "I'm the editor, publisher, reporter, and hawker of the *Cloud City Columbia*." She whipped out a pencil and notepad, identical to Jed's. Balancing the notebook in one hand along with the open umbrella, she poised the pencil above the open page. "Such a tragedy. Are you the proprietress, Mrs. Stannert?"

Inez snapped, "Absolutely not! As Mr. Elliston can attest, the owner is Florence Sweet. Her current residence is the jail. Or at least, that was Officer Ryan's intent when he took her away. He's the city collector as well as a policeman, as you probably know."

"Ah." Mrs. Clatchworthy tilted her head to one side, eyeing Inez in the same beady manner as the bird atop her hat. "Just a passerby, Mrs. Stannert?" She clapped her notebook shut. Both pad and pencil disappeared into her pocket. She advanced up the step and set foot carefully on the blackened floorboards, craning to look around Inez's wavering umbrella. "Poor young woman. Tragedies such as this occur daily. These poor souls are harassed by the police. Imprisoned and fined. Suffer. Die. While the men that bring them shame get off scot-free." She pinned Inez with another penetrating gaze. "Does this seem right to you?"

"Mrs. Clatchworthy," said Jed. "You'll find nothing here worth writing about for that bluestocking rag of yours. Best you run along and investigate the latest literary goings-on."

Inez found her outrage sliding from Mrs. Clatchworthy to Jed.

"Blue?" Mrs. Clatchworthy looked down, plucked at the Turkish-style bloomers to raise one soggy trouser leg an inch above the rim of the muddied boot. "Last I looked, they were purple."

The stockings were indeed purple.

Danny approached, a satin-trimmed peach-colored blanket in his arms, distress marking every step. He moved past Mrs.

Clatchworthy, spread the blanket on the flooring, knelt, and gathered Lizzie out of the hole and into his arms, preparing to place her on the blanket. Lizzie lolled, limp as a rag doll, the flimsy white wrapper parting to expose pale mottled legs. The hand that had been tangled in the long skirt fell loose. Inez bit back an exclamation as an object—small, blue, with a flash of gold—fell from her hand and onto the blanket.

Jed pounced before Inez could stir.

"A-ha!" He held the blue bottle aloft, squinting.

The gold paint, crosshatched on a blue bottle, betrayed the contents in generalities, if not specifics.

He waved the empty glass container at Mrs. Clatchworthy. "So much for your 'poor unfortunate.' Looks like she poisoned herself. Overdosed. No hand but her own was responsible."

Inez snatched the bottle from him. "All we know is that this is a bottle that once held poison. Only the coroner or a doctor can tell us what really happened."

She pocketed the bottle, heard it clink against the barrel of her pocket revolver. Danny placed Lizzie on the blanket, and Inez moved closer. From that intimate distance, Inez finally recognized youth in the slack, unlined features. Lizzie's face was mottled, discolored from bruises, soot, or dirt, Inez couldn't tell which. White crescents showed under nearly closed eyelids. Holding her own breath, Inez leaned close to Lizzie's face, searching for the slightest of exhalations.

Nothing.

She touched, then held the limp hand.

Clammy. Cold as a clod of dirt.

A twinge of melancholy sped through Inez at the contact. She compressed her lips, lay Lizzie's unresponsive hand atop the blanket, and straightened. *I've seen too much of death lately. Why else would I feel anything for this woman. A whore. A stranger.*

"Sisters," whispered Mrs. Clatchworthy.

Startled, Inez almost bumped into the woman journalist, who had moved to stand by Inez and was gazing at Lizzie with a keen, yet sorrowful air.

"We women are all sisters," Mrs. Clatchworthy said with finality. "All oppressed by the men who, in the end, run the world and our lives. Lest we actively choose a different path."

She drew away, raising her umbrella. "I'll see what Mrs. Sweet has to say."

With a swirl of purple and gold, Mrs. Clatchworthy turned and marched toward State Street.

Chapter Thirteen

No sooner had Mrs. Clatchworthy disappeared around one corner than a huffing and puffing Doctor Cramer appeared around the other, accompanied by Molly. A limping scarecrow of a man, Doc made his way up the alley to Jed and Inez, leaning heavily on his cane. He stopped before them and set down his worn medical bag. "Mr. Elliston, Mrs. Stannert. I was heading home from a long night tending to several cases of pneumonia and one breech birth when I was stopped by Mrs. Sweet in the accompaniment of an officer of the law. She was quite hysterical, insisting that there was a woman in desperate need of my professional assistance. And then I bumped into Molly, who said there was a recently deceased woman here and would I please notify the coroner. I decided I'd better come and see the situation for myself."

Doc rubbed a splayed hand over his drooping countenance, as if to awaken dulled senses. Two years ago, Doc had been a mountain of a man with a belly that would have been at home on a captain of industry who regularly indulged in quail, oysters, and fine port. But hard work and high altitude had shaved weight from his physique, leaving him with loose-skinned limbs and jowls befitting of a bloodhound. He bent his gaze to the figure on the blanket.

"At first guess," he said, "I fear Molly is right, and this one is beyond my help." He knelt one knee on the charred flooring, picked up a bone-white wrist, held it for a moment, gently set it down, and equally gently, as if not wishing to disturb a deep sleep, pulled up an eyelid to examine the orb beneath. He blew out one long, tired breath. Doc opened his medical bag and rummaged around, finally extracting a stethoscope.

"Pardon me," he said. Whether the apology was directed to the figure, Jed, Inez, or Molly, it wasn't clear. Inez turned away as he slid the listening instrument beneath the wrapper to position it under one breast.

"Doc?" Molly sounded anxious.

"As I suspected. Too late."

Inez turned back in time to see Doc coil the instrument loosely before setting it back in his bag.

He used his cane to help him rise. "I'd guess exposure to the elements. There was frost on the ground this morning, before the rain picked up again."

"I saw her here in the alley last night, quite drunk," Inez offered.

Doc nodded soberly. "Alcohol, this weather, no proper clothing. That would account for it."

"There's also this." Inez pulled the cobalt-blue bottle from her pocket and handed it to him.

Doc's expression grew graver as he peered at the bottle, then sniffed its rim. "I thought Mrs. Sweet did not allow her women to drink or take drugs. Not even laudanum."

Molly moved up, hands on hips. "That's right. She always said if we drank or became opium eaters, out on the street we'd go."

"What is it, Doc?" Inez asked.

"Tincture of opium. The smell is distinct and lingers in the bottle."

He gazed down at Lizzie. "So young." Then looked somberly up at the three. "I'll talk to Mrs. Sweet and contact the coroner."

"Flo wanted Lizzie laid out in the house. No coroner," Inez said.

Doc retrieved his bag. "Very well."

Inez, watching him picking his way out of the alley, thought his posture more slumped, the set of his shoulders more dejected, than before.

Danny lifted Lizzie, cradled her wrapped form, and began his journey to the front of the brick house. Molly hovered at his elbow, talking in a low and earnest undertone. Inez and Jed followed at some slight distance.

"Is a dead prostitute more newsworthy than the visit of a former president?" Inez asked, somewhat irritated that Jed still trailed along, scribbling frantically.

"Grant's yet to make a public appearance today. Besides, scandal sells. The death of one of State Street's fallen angels draws attention from all sides. From the gentlemen who knew her, and from the proper women who tut-tut and feel superior to her. Good copy. Now, this chap Danny. What's his last name?"

"What makes you think I'd know the names of Flo's hirelings?" Inez inquired coldly.

"Well, you've been here on State Street a long time. You know Flo. I just thought—"

"You can stop thinking right there," snapped Inez, angry that she might have inadvertently tipped her hand in some way.

Danny veered around the corner onto State and approached the front of the parlor house. He mounted the short flight of steps to the front porch and shifted Lizzie's weight to pull keys from his pocket. A muddy, bare foot escaped the confines of the blanket, swinging limply. He unlocked the door and pushed it open. A distinct odor of smoke drifted out. Molly entered first, holding the door for Danny and his burden. As Inez and Jed made to enter, she stepped forward, barring the entrance. "Lizzie's our burden to bear," she said defiantly. "She's not your business anymore."

She shut the door in Inez's face. The latch fell with finality.

Chapter Fourteen

Inez left Jed standing on the State Street boardwalk, disappointed at being locked out of the bordello, and began a rapid return to Flo's house. As she hurried along, clutching her umbrella with a bare hand, she presented her arguments to herself. *I'm going back for my glove. I put it on my lap to sign that blasted contract. Then, Molly came, Flo ran out, I followed and...*

They are my favorite pair.

She could almost picture the orphan glove, lying crumpled under the table in Flo's front room.

But the glove wasn't the only reason she was retracing her steps.

Standing in front of Flo's tiny house, Inez glanced quickly to left and right.

No one.

Inez opened the unlocked door and entered, removing the key from the inside lock. She pocketed it, saying aloud, "The least I can do is lock the door when I leave."

The house was too small to even send back an echo.

As expected, Inez found her glove under the table.

She retrieved it and pulled it on, flexing her fingers to cement the fit, and looked around.

If I were Flo, where would I hide two contracts that I wanted to keep from prying eyes?

There were no places to secrete documents in the simple front room. Inez strolled the perimeter, just to make sure.

All I want to know is who the third party is.

However, if she happened to come across the duplicate copy of her contract with Flo, all the better.

Resolutely, she pushed temptation aside. *A deal is a deal. Even if I didn't have all the facts beforehand.*

Her circuit of the room complete, she headed to the back room, the room Flo had entered, clutching the contract, and exited, empty-handed.

Inez stepped inside and looked around.

This room was even smaller than the one in front. Just big enough for a bed, a rag rug, a petite secretary desk, a washstand, and a small clothespress. The bed was covered with an indigo and white quilt, all geometric triangles and squares, not a frill anywhere.

Inez's gaze wandered to the desktop, which held papers, inkwell and pen, and a cabinet photo. Truth to tell, it was the photo that drew her attention—an image of a baby, swathed in a white gown, held upright by an older man.

Both man and child had something of Flo about the eyes and forehead.

Inez frowned.

Relatives?

She shifted her gaze from the photograph to a capital-laden missive laying close by.

"Dear Father,

I have the Photograph of You and Jane before Me as I write this. How much Jane looks like You! I am enclosing Money for You and Mother and for Janie's Care. Please Do not Fret. My Laundry and Lace-Making Businesses here in Leadville are doing Very Well. I live Comfortable but Frugally, as You taught Us. Please give Little Janie 3 Kisses and tell her They are from her Mother, who misses Her more than all the World—"

The letter, unfinished, ended there.

Inez's heart constricted as if someone had suddenly wrenched her corset strings tight.

Frisco Flo…a mother?

She tried to think back to when she first became aware of Flo Sweet. Back when Flo was simply one of the soiled doves in the house at the end of State, one of the not-so-proper women who attended Inez's church even as the mining camp coalesced into a town. A town that rapidly grew to a city of a size to rival Denver. Twelve, fourteen months ago.

Inez eyed the photograph again, then turned away, feeling guilty, a voyeur. Determined to finish her search, she moved to the bed, lifted the mattress, and knelt awkwardly to peek underneath the simple iron frame. Nothing. Not even a stray pair of shoes or a smear of dust.

The clothespress held only simple dresses and straightforward underthings. Not a flounce or bow in sight, much less a written contract or two.

The washstand was equally disappointing. In the desk drawers, besides writing paper, nibs, and ink bottles, Inez found a packet of letters with a Kansas stamp, bound with a ribbon. Her curiosity over Flo's past dampened by the half-completed letter, Inez let them lie.

With arms akimbo, she cast a final glance around the bedroom. *I've looked everywhere. There are no pictures on the walls to hide a safe. Nothing under the bed, under or in the washstand or the desk. I've looked everywhere—*

Her gaze fell on the rag rug.

—except for one place.

Inez dragged the rug back to expose the floor. A square section of planks revealed cut edges, flat hinges along one side. The opposite side had a cutout, just large enough to set one's fingers in under the boards and pull up. The trapdoor opened soundlessly, hinges well oiled. Below, instead of the expected hidey-hole or modest lockbox was the dull gleam of a serious safe.

"Blast!" Inez sat back on her heels, staring at the impervious metal terminus to her search.

Her first thought: Flo must have had the safe built into the floor of the house.

Her second: Cracking this safe was far beyond her abilities.

Abe could perhaps open it, but I'm no cracksman.

Her explorations, it seemed, would stop here.

Inez replaced the rug, checked that the bedroom was restored, with everything as it was. She glanced toward the photograph and half-finished letter one last time and passed swiftly through the house, locking Flo's front door behind her and pocketing the key.

Chapter Fifteen

"What have I done? And what the hell am I going to do?"

Muttering to herself, Inez unlocked the safe in the upstairs office of the Silver Queen. She crammed the offending legal documents inside, taking care to tuck them way back on an upper shelf where Abe was unlikely to discover them.

As if life hasn't been unsettled enough lately.

With Grant and his many hangers-on in Leadville, it wasn't likely that things would return to normal for the next few days, she mused. Too, plenty of people seemed unhappy about Grant's visit, and an air of unrest hung up and down State Street. Fires. Arson. Death.

Inez shivered, trying to dispel the foreboding that crawled up her spine.

At least, she and Abe would make a fortune in liquor sales, if what she saw when she entered the saloon was any indication There had not been a place to stand at the mahogany bar, unless someone was willing to perch on one of the strategically situated spittoons. The tables were fully occupied as well. The saloon doors—one fronting the proper business district on Harrison Avenue and the other leading to the shadier district on State Street—were in constant motion from customers entering and leaving.

Inez slammed the safe shut, gave the dial a twist, and tugged on the door. Her secrets were safe. For now.

She put her hand in her other pocket, intending to set her Smoot revolver on the desktop, and gasped in dismay as her fingers touched a slender metal shaft.

"Blast!"

Flo's house key.

Back to the safe, spin the dial, open it again. She pulled out the divorce document and dropped the key in the envelope. *I'll get this to her once she's out of jail.*

After re-securing the safe, Inez straightened up and hurried into her private rooms adjoining the office. A change of clothes was definitely in order. She shucked the dress and petticoats, tsking over hems stiff with mud.

Inez turned to her wardrobe, pushing aside walking suits and a somber "Sunday best" polonaise. She settled for a dark blue ensemble and, after dressing, squinted into the mirror and checked her appearance. Her hair continued to grow out, recovering from a near scalping the previous winter when she had parted with her waist-length braid in a determined masquerade. Now, eight months later, it was long enough to twist into a tight knot at the nape of her neck. She leaned forward, noting her complexion.

Too much running about without a proper hat.

Sighing, Inez pushed up her sleeves to expose wrists and a few inches of forearm. She tugged her conservative V-shaped neckline down a little, and ran a hand over the dark-blue bodice, eyeing the light blue piping. *Perhaps not as celebratory a costume as Grant's visit might allow, but I'm not one for dressing up in red, white, and blue like a flag.*

Inez grabbed a folded apron and, with a swish of long skirts, whisked out of her private rooms and the office. The contained roar of masculine conversation lapped at her as she locked the office door behind her and descended the stairs, tying the apron as she went.

She slid behind the bar and approached Abe, who was busy pouring shots. Amongst his customers, Inez recognized three prominent Leadville pen pushers, deep in conversation with a handful of strangers. Probably fellow ink-slingers from out-of-town, she judged, since they had all ordered the same brand of inexpensive whiskey, eschewing the cheaper rotgut or more expensive liquor.

"How are things going?" she asked Abe in an undertone.

"Right fine, Mrs. Stannert." He paused, jingling the journalists' coinage in his hand like a pair of dice. "Sol and me haven't had a chance to draw a breath since we opened." He glanced down the bar to where Sol was mixing a mint julep. "Boy's comin' along right well. Think the next few days'll show us and him whether he's got what it takes for this kind of business."

"Shall I take over here, Mr. Jackson? You could replace Sol at his end so he could help Bridgette with the tables," said Inez.

Their cook looked harried as she rushed from table to table, dispensing bowls of stew and plates of sliced bread.

"Sol could take orders," Inez added, "and Bridgette could handle the kitchen. She's none too happy when she has to deal with the clientele."

As if to prove Inez's point, a man who looked no more than twenty slapped Bridgette's ample derriere as she squeezed between two crowded tables. The gray-haired matron twisted and, with a dexterity born of raising five sons, boxed the offending fellow's ears.

Abe nodded. "Good idea. This keeps up, Bridgette's likely to cut a switch and start thrashin' some of our payin' customers for misbehavin'." He added, glancing at the Harrison Avenue entrance, "Seems like most the good quality from out of town is comin' in through this door anyways. Better you be meetin' and greetin' them than me. They're more likely t' stay around, drinkin', talkin', and preenin', tryin' to impress a good-lookin' woman behind the bar, 'stead of an old bent nigger like me. Let 'em think I'm just one of the hired help." With a parting wink at her, Abe moved down the long length of polished wood, now shining with wet dark rings and puddles of spilled liquids, toward Sol.

Inez took her station and smiled winningly at the journalists. "Are you gentlemen interested in a chaser with that? We have some fine local beer and, of course, Coors from down mountain."

The scribbler from the *Leadville Herald* grinned. "Well, howdy and felicitations, Mrs. Stannert. Quite a show in town! Coors sounds good to me. What about you, boys? Stand you a beer from Golden?" He slid a dollar coin across the counter to Inez. "Keep the change, Mrs. Stannert."

As Inez provided chasers all around, they dove back into their ongoing discussion.

"So, how d'you boys assay Grant's chances?" asked the *Herald* man. "He's got lots of backers here. Darn near made the nomination in Chicago, except for that underhanded business at the end."

A reporter Inez recognized as being from the *Denver Tribune* snorted. "Third term? Not a chance. I'm betting this was his last shot at the presidency. He might've captured it, too, if he'd spoke up, instead of just sitting back and waiting to be anointed, like the Republicans' appointed king."

"I'd sooner risk eternal torture in the bowels of hell than see that spawn of the Devil take a third term!" boomed from beyond the group.

The writers jumped at the voice, which had the timbre of an evocation from heaven itself. Inez identified the conversational interloper and grimaced, irritated. *Preacher Thatcher. How did he get down Chicken Hill on his own?*

The answer manifested in quick order as one of the preacher's twin sons—which one, she couldn't tell—popped up from a back table and hurried over to grab the wavering old fellow's shoulder. "Pa. Come on thisaway. You kin have somma my stew."

Preacher Thatcher turned sightless eyes on his son. "Zechariah. What's wrong with the food your own sister places on the table, bought with the sweat from her own brow, that you spend precious coin on victuals prepared by others?" His voice carried above and beyond the immediate vicinity, as if he spoke from the pulpit.

At least, Inez thought, his speech solved the mystery of which twin it was.

Zeke winced, unseen by his father. "Pa. Only thing Zelpha kin fix that's edible-like is grits. An' I'm tired of grits. C'mon." He tugged on the sleeve of his father's shabby coat, the black so worn and shiny it looked almost green.

Inez crossed her arms. "Zeke, Preacher Thatcher, I do believe it's time for you to take a stroll and enjoy the invigorating nature of this early afternoon air." Inez's tone left no room for argument or debate.

Zeke frowned. "Hell, Pa. You just got us thrown outta the saloon."

"I'd not have come to this den of iniquity if I'd known it was peopled with harlots," said the preacher with dignity.

Inez felt her blood begin to boil darker than coffee on a hot stove. She caught Zeke's gaze with her own and stabbed a finger toward the exit.

Zeke groaned. "Shoulda kept you at the table with a stew spoon in your maw. Or better yet, left you home with cold grits fer dinner and supper. Let's go see Pap Wyman, then. You kin quote scripture and Pap won't mind none."

He hooked the preacher's arm, and, with a last longing look at the half-consumed bowl of stew and his table companions, ushered his father out the Harrison Avenue door.

Inez sidled over to Abe. "Tell Sol that Preacher Thatcher is *persona non grata*. At least until Grant has left town. His sermons are capable of inciting a small riot, and I certainly don't want that here. We should keep an ear out for political talk about Grant or any 'war reminiscences' so those for and those against don't get into a serious row. We've had more than our fair share of such."

Abe, fixing a gin fizz, grunted. "Hard enough to see who's comin' and goin' with this crowd, much less hear what they're sayin'."

A mixed blessing, she had to admit. More folks meant more drinks and more profits. But the variety of people—greenhorns just to town in their fancy duds, prospectors from out of the nearby districts, visitors from who-knew-where staying who-knew-how-long, miners from the consolidated mines, blacksmiths, businessmen, and more—made for a volatile combination. That didn't even include the footpads, pickpockets, and other con men out to pull a bunco on those naïve enough to fall for their tricks with walnut shells and hidden peas, soap bars and hidden coins, marked cards and confederates.

"Barkeep!" The shout jolted Inez from her ruminations and sent her hurrying back to her end of the counter to serve beer to a prospector with bleached out and ancient garments, just in from Ten Mile Canyon. She was vaguely aware of Bridgette, passing by in a whirl, with a fistful of orders.

Next, she heard Bridgette say with delight, "Why, Officer Ryan, fancy seeing you here!"

Chapter Sixteen

Inez froze at the dreaded name.

Sure enough, The Hatchet stood just within their Harrison Avenue entrance, not six feet away. Rain dripped from his waterproof coat into the sawdust scattered in a futile effort to keep mud and wet to a minimum inside the saloon.

He looked at Bridgette, and his face creased into a polite smile.

Inez thought she must be having a delirium.

Then…

He removed his hat. "Mrs. O'Malley."

Bridgette stood before the feared lawman, hands laced together under her chin like a starry-eyed schoolgirl, the orders scrunched into a papery fan. "I've got stew, Officer, just made, and some nice strong coffee."

"Coffee sounds mighty good, if it's not a bother. Do you have any cream?"

"Oh no bother, no bother at all. Cream, yes, yes, delivered fresh this morning. My lands, it's a pleasure to see you. You and the others on the force work so hard. This weekend especially, with General Grant and his missus and all the folk like Lieutenant Governor Tabor and Governor Pitkin come to town."

"Thank you, ma'am." The Hatchet treated Bridgette's discourse with gravity. "We've got our hands full right now. There's some who aren't happy about the general's bein' here. The force's pulled thin. Pockets of trouble, here and there. The hard cases in town are determined to do harm, if they can."

"And then, the fires. Why, and I heard that the city marshal's house went up, poof! Just like that. Poor man. I wonder if he'll stay in town or leave? Are you looking for the firebug?"

"Yes, Mrs. O'Malley, it's a tragedy about the marshal. Not sure what his plans are, and that's a fact. My coffee, ma'am? I've only got a minute here."

"Right away!" Bridgette dashed into the kitchen.

The Hatchet approached Inez. Set his wet cap down in front of the prospector's glass of beer. The prospector took the hint and removed himself and his beer to a position further down the bar.

The Hatchet leaned over the mahogany surface toward Inez. She instinctively stepped back.

"Didn't know you and Flo were friendly," he said.

"Friendly? I'd not say friendly. We both own businesses on State Street. We both pay our fees and fines, excuse me, 'taxes,' as required."

"Then why'd she ask you to take care of that dead girl of hers?"

Before Inez could fabricate a reasonable lie, The Hatchet added, "I'll say this. I'll say this once. Stay away from Flo and her girls. It's a bad business, Mrs. Stannert. Don't get tangled up in it."

"Officer Ryan, your coffee," chirped Bridgette. She was hovering at his elbow, beaming and blushing.

"God bless you, Mrs. O'Malley. There's got to be a special place in heaven for women like you."

Bridgette looked as ecstatic as if blessed by the pope himself.

The Hatchet lifted his cup, the wet sleeve of his coat riding up his arm ever so slightly, pulling the jacket and shirt cuff with it. Inez blinked and bit back an exclamation of surprise. A mass of scarred flesh, long healed, showed at his wrist and disappeared below the cuffs.

Officer Kelly breezed in the State Street door. After a quick look around, he spotted The Hatchet and wove through the crowds to his side. "Sorry t' trouble you, Ryan, but more trouble in Coon Row. Kate Armstead."

The Hatchet nodded. He drained the scalding coffee without so much as a cough or twitch, pulled out an overly large handkerchief from his pocket, and dabbed at the mustache curving around his mouth. With a final cold glance at Inez, he replaced his police cap, smiled and touched his cap at Bridgette, and left with Officer Kelly.

Inez stared at the empty coffee cup before her as if it were poisoned or might burst into flame, then looked up at her cook. "You know The Hatch—um, Officer Ryan?"

She nodded vigorously. "Oh yes, ma'am. He's a member of the parish. I see him at Mass and Rosary regularly."

"Really." The mental picture of The Hatchet on his knees, praying, was unnerving.

"Oh yes, ma'am. And he visits the church every week to light candles for his dear wife—she's not well, you see, doesn't live in Leadville—and his daughter, poor thing, died about age ten, I've been told, barely old enough to take Communion. At least she's with Our Lord."

"Really." Even more mind-boggling was the realization that The Hatchet, one of the most feared men on State Street, was a family man. A husband. A father. *Maybe that's why he's so despicable. Far from home and hearth, some men lose direction, take on a different character, drink too much, become cruel.*

"How do you know all this, Bridgette?"

"Well, ma'am, I keep my ears and eyes open. And between this and that, I put two and two together and get four."

"Ah."

I must remember to be careful what I say when Bridgette's ears and eyes are open and nearby.

"You know Officer Ryan, ma'am?" Bridgette looked expectant.

Perhaps looking to add two more and get six.

"Not well," Inez hedged. "He spends a great deal of time on State Street in his capacity as city collector, of course. And in performing his duties as an officer of the law."

"Oh, and aren't we lucky to have him!" Bridgette gushed. "He's a lovely, lovely man. And I'm not the only one who thinks so. Why, if elections were held tomorrow for city marshal, he'd win, hands down. Now that Marshal Watson's home is gone, well, I wonder if the marshal will stay or leave. And a firebug on the loose! I'm sure that Officer Ryan will find whoever's responsible."

"'Scuse me, Mrs. O'Malley." It was a penitent, hat in hand, looking doleful. "Not t' bother you or none, but I've been awaitin' for my stew awhiles an' I got to get back to the diggings."

"Oh my, here I am chatting away when there's work to be done." Bridgette flashed a guilty smile at Inez and hurried to the kitchen, with a "Right away, young man!" directed to the fellow who was old enough to be her own father.

The Harrison Avenue door swung open on a gust of raucous laughter. A huddle of men in spotless frock coats and fashionable top hats, beards and mustaches gleaming, paused on the threshold.

"What then, Wesley?" said one. "Did the poor chap confess that he'd strangled the parlor lass in a fit of unrequited love?"

Inez squinted at the men, who were not only letting in the rain, blown by gusts outside, but also blocking all entrance and egress. *Wesley. Why does that name sound familiar?* All she could see of the fellow in the middle was a silk stovepipe hat.

"Gustav, recall that I mentioned the madam of the house was straddling him most indecently, skirts hitched up revealing garters of purest silver, the barrel of her pistol plunged into his mouth. Poor fellow couldn't say a word. He was as much in danger of choking to death as to having his brains expelled. It was clearly up to me to bring order to the seamy scene."

Then, Inez remembered.

Flo's. This morning. That young impertinent son-of-a—

"So Wesley, how'd you handle it? Not the sort of thing that you see back in proper old Beantown."

"Well, I couldn't let the poor wretch get his brains blown out without hearing his story first. Frontier justice was about to take place, and it was not clear that he was guilty of anything other than being found at the scene of the crime."

The men finally moved away from the door and toward the bar. Without so much as a by-your-leave, they claim-jumped prime real estate along the brass rail by simply crowding in and spreading out. Displaced patrons, jostled out of the way, turned to the newcomers, and Inez thought she saw more than one with murder in his eye. The storyteller was now fully visible, and Inez confirmed that, yes indeed, he was the "Mr. Wesley" of that very morning, he of the sharp elbows, slight mustache, fine gloves, and silver-headed umbrella.

Inez's hand closed hard on the whiskey bottle she was preparing to put on the backbar. She contemplated whether it would make sense to order them out, give them the cold shoulder, or—

The cut of their cloth convinced her otherwise.

Their pockets were bound to be well-lined. As long as their tastes in liquor followed suit, and they ordered favorably and frequently, it couldn't hurt to let them stay. Too, she was curious to see how far Wesley's story would stray from the road of truth. He had already fairly departed from that particular thoroughfare and was busy forging a tall tale that straggled ever upward, above treeline, into exceedingly rocky and doubtful territory.

"Well, then, Marcus, I strolled up to them, tapped the lady of the house on her milk-white shoulder—the dressing gown having come nearly quite undone you see—and said, 'May I offer some free legal advice, madam? You are standing, or shall I say squatting, before the foremost lawyer of the firm Lawton, Lawton, and Crouse, original of Boston, youngest partner thereof, and, God willing, your future Colorado senator. I have been sent to open a new office in Denver to bring sound and sober legal advice to your rough and uncivilized territory.' She looked up at me, her demeanor changed, she batted blue eyes, no doubt made enormous by overuse of laudanum, and with the poor fellow thrashing around beneath her, said—"

"Welcome to Leadville and the Silver Queen Saloon, gentlemen," Inez allowed her voice to slide into a friendly range. "As they say out here in our rough and uncivilized territory, 'What's your poison?'"

The group looked at her with delight mixed with some alarm. She detected no shred of recognition from Wesley.

"Well, well," interjected one of his companions, who sported a fiercely groomed red mustache of gleaming proportions. "A female mixologist? Something else sadly lacking in Boston and Washington! So, are you one of those infamous pretty waiter-girls we've heard so much about?" He leered, stroking his mustache with the head of his walking stick.

Inez smiled her sweetest smile and said, "Gentlemen. I am the owner of the Silver Queen, the drinking establishment in which you now stand. As such, I'm at your service, ready to fulfill your every desire for liquid libations. But that is the only desire we quench here. Unless you have a hankering for dinner, in which case we serve the best stew and biscuits in town, along with the usual hard-boiled eggs, pickles, etcetera, etcetera. And I assure you, we have such quality spirits that will make you feel at home. We have Spanish wine. French champagne. A choice selection of beers from Milwaukee, Golden, our own fair city, and more. We have bourbon—"

"Have you," Wesley set gloves on the bar, "lemonade, milady?"

The fellow with the red mustache smirked. Another companion coughed into his gloved fist, choking back a laugh.

"Lemonade." Inez crossed her arms and studied Wesley for a hint as to the joke. He was gazing over Inez's shoulder in the backbar mirror at his and his companions' reflections.

"Exactly, my dear gentlewoman," he said. "Braced with some of that fine *spirits frumenti* you mentioned. And crackers and a spoon. If you please."

Deciding to play along, Inez retrieved a tall glass, shoveled shaved ice into it, poured in a quantity of fresh-squeezed lemon juice, and added powdered sugar and water. She tipped in a shot of whiskey and, interpreting the rise of his eyebrows to mean "more," added another. Dipping down to peer beneath the counter, she located a dishpan full of used cups, bowls, and spoons. Inez surreptitiously wiped a spoon clean on her apron, and used it to briskly whisk the now potent lemonade. After placing glass and spoon before Wesley, she retrieved a small plate of crackers for him.

He paid, removed a glove, crumbled the crackers into the glass, and, stirred, creating an intoxicating cracker-mush. Wesley smirked at himself and his companions in the mirror, and said, "I promised the old girl that I'd not drink, on my honor."

"God forbid you sully your honor, Wesley" interjected one of his companions.

Wesley spooned up the concoction with evident delight.

"He'll not fool her," said a voice.

Inez turned to find Wesley's minder from earlier that morning, elbow on the countertop. He gazed at Wesley with an exasperation that Inez associated with mothers of out-of-control children.

"'Her' being whom?" Inez pulled a clean shot glass from under the bar. "And, before you answer, I'm assuming that you are looking for something to clear the morning from your throat, Mister…?" She allowed her voice to lift in a question.

"Pardon." He removed his hat. "Kavanagh. James Kavanagh. At your service, ma'am. 'Her' being Mrs. Wesley, mother of—" he pointed with his chin toward the young man eating his spiked lemonade— "that young jackass."

"Mr. Kavanagh. A pleasure. I'm Mrs. Stannert, owner of this, the Silver Queen." She granted him a professional smile. "Am I correct that you are looking for something a little more straightforward than lemonade you can eat with a spoon?" She nudged the shot glass toward him, bottle ready to pour.

He nudged the glass away. "Tempting, but drinking on the job would get me fired for sure."

"Then you'll have to come back later when you're off duty. And your job would be?" She wasn't sure why she persisted in asking questions when there were plenty of other potential customers, ready to pay, tapping coins impatiently on the mahogany to get her attention.

Kavanagh grinned, displaying a noticeable and not unattractive gap between his upper front teeth. "I have the unenviable task of keeping his nibs, young John Quincy Adams Wesley, out of trouble."

"Out of trouble? That's a tall order. Most young men of his stripe come to Leadville, State Street in particular, looking for trouble of various sorts. I am not at all sure you'll be able to keep him from it." She eyed Wesley again, critically. "John Quincy Adams, is it? Named after 'Old Man Eloquent.' Has his father such high aspirations for him, then, as to become president?"

"Not father, but mother." Kavanagh said. "Being primed for a future in politics. I believe I've heard terms like 'future senator' and 'someday governor' bandied about. Wouldn't be surprised if 'president' wasn't far behind."

"Is that so?" She looked at Kavanagh anew. Of medium height and build, he seemed a man who could take care of himself. Obviously cut a notch or two above the riffraff, yet not high and mighty like the out-of-town gentlemen encircling young Wesley.

A change of suit, and this Kavanagh could blend into any milieu.

Kavanagh glanced into the mirror, seeking out Wesley's image. "Well, since he's here busy telling stories and charming the masses, and I'm here occupying valuable real estate, guess I'll have a lemonade after all, Mrs. Stannert. None of the hard stuff in it, though."

Inez complied, and after accepting his coin, continued, "So, are the Wesleys in Grant's entourage? I don't recall seeing them in Leadville before today."

"Hmmm-mmm. At least, that's the story. More like they're here at the Tabors' and the governor's largesse." Kavanagh cast a longing eye at the backbar and its seductive array of bottles before sipping his lemonade.

Her curiosity increased further at the mention of Leadville's self-made silver baron, now lieutenant governor of Colorado. "Tabor? They know Horace Tabor?"

"Connection's more through the missus than the mister, I gather." He shrugged. "Young Maxcy Tabor knows Wesley. Through some Denver association or other, I think."

She almost snorted. "I imagine it must gall the lieutenant governor to have such a young pup gunning for Congress. Mr. Tabor has made no secret of his own political ambitions in that direction. And, as lieutenant governor and a millionaire, I'd say he's got a head start."

"I suspect you're right about that, ma'am. But the Wesleys aren't slouches in the pocket-change department either. And I'd not want to cross swords with young Wesley's mother. In any case, Tabor and Wesley have been gentlemen all along. No fist fights on the train ride out here. All proper and polite, I gather."

She raised an eyebrow. "You seem to know quite a bit about them. Are the Wesleys so open with their lives?"

He raised the lemonade to her, a modest salute. "I've had plenty of practice being a shadow, and folks don't take much note of what they say in the presence of shadows."

"—And that," announced Wesley. "About sums it up."

"Three cheers for you, Wesley," said his red-mustachioed compatriot. "Seems you ought to buy us all a drink to celebrate your early morning escapade, traipsing about the less desirable parts of town, rescuing the demimonde from the brutal and misguided attentions of the law."

"I can do one better than that," said Wesley. With a flourish, he produced a wallet. His gaze searched out Inez. Upon finding her, he raised his voice and said, "Mistress Barkeep. A round, please, for the house. For all those in this fair establishment ranked top amongst those hundreds arrayed in this most wondrous city in the clouds, which enjoys the heartiest and most honest and hard-working of citizens!"

He had a voice, she thought, that would project well on the stage. Or, out to the Senate galleries. The smile he flashed about the room glittered with warmth, enthusiasm, and an astonishing amount of honest likableness. Not that he needed to exude much charm once he'd declaimed "a round for the house." With those words, he was guaranteed to become the immediate bosom buddy of every man jack in the room.

"Mrs. Stannert!" Abe's voice, sharp and nearly in her ear, shattered her reverie. "If'n you don't mind takin' that fellow's money so's we can see whether he's got the silver to buy afore we pour."

Indeed, the eager crowds jammed forward, empty glasses at the ready.

Inez hastened to Wesley, who fanned a handful of paper money at her as if to bring a breeze to the overheated atmosphere.

She took the bills, blanched at the large denominations, and pulled out the saloon's battered *Heath's Infallible Counterfeit Detector—At Sight* from beneath the counter.

Wesley looked nonplussed.

"Your generosity, sir, is much appreciated by all," said Inez, paging furiously through the slim pocket-sized volume. "It's merely the Silver Queen's policy that, for notes of this size, we need to be sure...." She referred to the steel-etched images on the open page, compared them to the banknotes, then nodded at Abe. He began pulling whiskey bottles from the holding area beneath the backbar.

Armed with a bottle in each hand, Inez commenced pouring into what seemed like a thousand out-thrust glasses, tin and ceramic coffee mugs, and even a stew bowl or two. She, Abe, and Sol lined up the emptied bottles to track the amount thus procured.

One hard-bitten doublejacker, whose customary morose expression was creased in an atypical smile, raised his tin cup to Wesley. "Here's to you, your honor. Should you decide to run, you kin count on my vote."

Wesley beamed. "Excellent! Remember that, old chap, when the next state election comes around. Remember the name of John Quincy Adams Wesley."

The miner said, "And would you be taking the side of the common working man?"

Wesley smoothed his almost invisible mustache. "Let me put it this way. The wealth of the silver barons is most certainly augmented by the efforts of men such as yourself. Every man deserves a living wage."

The miner considered, raised his cup another inch higher in Wesley's direction, then drained it.

Inez blew a loose strand of sweaty hair from her face and stopped pouring, realizing that all the drinkers had been taken care of. She scanned the bottles, pulled Wesley's cash from her apron pocket, deftly separating out what was owed, and extended a twenty-dollar bill. "This is yours. The cost comes to—"

"Keep it, keep it," he waved the bill back to her, shut his wallet, and tucked it away.

She raised her eyebrows. "You're most generous. And this, even though I, as a woman, cannot vote?"

It was meant as a jest. But Wesley jerked as though she'd prodded his private parts with the sharp end of an umbrella, and stared hard at her. He then mustered a smile, and said, "Ah, like all of the fairer, gentler sex, you, milady, wield power over us lowly men vastly superior to that of the vote. Should we give you the vote, I can well imagine a woman president would be next. Thus, women would be leaders not only in the domestic sphere, but the political as well. What should be left for us poor fellows?"

He raised his eyebrows before turning to his companions for confirmation. Several laughed, as if he'd returned her quip with another, finer still. The red-mustachioed one clapped, the sound muffled by his gloves. "Bravo, Wesley. Bravo! You even court the citizens that cannot cast a ballot. Most extraordinary!"

"Ah, but which one of you would not bow down before a fine display of dimples, or a turn of ankle, and promise the moon, or your political allegiance, for one chaste—or not so chaste—kiss?" He turned back to Inez. "Consider it a tip, Madam Barkeep. For the pleasure and the lemonade." He leaned over the bar, closed her fingers around the proffered twenty, and said *sotto voce*,

"I'll be back. I've taken a fancy to your drinking hole, Madam Barkeep, Lady Silver Queen of Leadville."

For twenty, it hurts not to play the flirt to this pipsqueak.

Inez batted her eyes. "Why, thank you Mr. Wesley, you've quite stolen my heart with your passion and your rhetoric. I'll put your money to work by giving half to the Widows and Orphans Society in your name. In this manner, you can be assured that when those little boys become of voting age, they will know your name and praise it." She tucked the bill into the waistband of her apron.

His gaze followed her hand, settling first on her waist, then moving slowly upward, over the curve of her bosom, lingering on her décolletage—that borderland separating cloth from flesh—to finally come to rest on her face. She got the impression that he was seeing her for the first time. That he had turned the viewing glass from himself and focused it on her. His grin widened with approval. At this intimate distance, she noticed his eyes were black throughout, hot and bottomless.

Enough of this. Else he'll be thinking of taking liberties in a country that has no vote.

She stepped away from the bar, fist to waist, and cooled her smile.

Wesley straightened, clapped his hat on, and said to his mates, "Tally-ho! Time to see what else State Street has to offer."

Inez wondered how he'd spin out the scene at her saloon later that day.

Wesley and his cronies departed by the State Street door. A goodly number of others trailed after, perhaps in hopes of a repeat performance at another drinking hole.

Inez glanced down the bar and saw Kavanagh lingering, lemonade nearly gone. She drifted toward him, collecting discarded glasses and plates as she went.

"If you're enjoined to keep him from drinking, it appears you have failed badly. At least, in this round," she said.

Kavanagh took no offense, seeming amused instead. "Mrs. Stannert, I'll tell you a secret. Only because I sense you're a woman who understands the value of a dollar." His eyes flicked to her waistband. "No insult intended."

He fished in his pocket and placed a dime next to the glass. "Lucretia Wesley pays me to keep her son from the saloons, dance halls, and parlor houses, or, if he's not to be dissuaded, to make sure he doesn't raise Cain, and finally, if he does, to cross the palms of any offended parties with silver. But John Quincy Adams Wesley pays me more to look the other way." He winked, adding, "When doting mother and son take their afternoon constitutional, I'll return and sample the wares of your establishment more thoroughly. For now, I'd better check that he's not got himself into some state of affairs that requires my attention." He tipped his hat and smiled, then strolled to the State Street entrance, raincoat over one arm.

Chapter Seventeen

No sooner had Kavanagh reached the door, than it swung open, bringing in the sounds of the street and the smells of rain, wet wood, and liquid earth.

Reverend Sands stepped inside the saloon, hat brim dripping. Rivulets ran off his black waterproof into the sawdust. Each man scrutinized the other, as if sizing up an opponent. The reverend touched his hat, stepped aside. Kavanagh nodded, raised a hand to his bowler, and continued out the door.

Just seeing Reverend Sands step into the room caused Inez's heart to skip a beat. And when his eyes found hers, and he smiled…

She dumped dirty dishes and glasses into the dishpan and hauled the pan out from its hiding place underneath the counter. Taking advantage of the lull, she told Abe and Sol, "I'm taking these to the kitchen," and smiled back at the reverend.

As she rounded the end of the bar, Reverend Sands fell in beside her, relieving her of the pan of crockery.

"No rest for the wicked today?" she murmured.

He looked a question at her.

She paused, her back against the kitchen door. "What I meant was, given your 'late to bed' last night and 'early to rise' this morning, I thought you might be…resting."

"And you, Mrs. Stannert, are sounding remarkably frisky for one who slept no more than myself." He kept his voice low, for her only.

A pleasurable shiver ran through her. She eased back on the passdoor, and it squeaked open. Then briskly, all business, she said, "Thank you so much for carrying the dishes for me, Reverend. May we offer you a cup of coffee?"

Bridgette looked up, in the midst of ferociously dismembering several plucked chickens on the oversized kitchen table. Pleasure washed across her broad face, and she stopped, cleaver in midair, chicken unnecessarily restrained with a hand to its breast. "Well Lord bless us, it's Reverend Sands! And I've got a fresh pot of coffee brewing. Just let me finish here." The cleaver descended, and the neck separated from the body.

The table was littered with drawn and quartered bits of chicken, a slimy pile of innards on one side.

"Actually, I have no time for coffee." Reverend Sands set the dishpan on a chair. He turned to Inez. "I'm just taking a moment on my rounds to propose—"

Bridgette clapped a bloody hand to her bosom. "Heavens above!"

Inez glared at her.

Sands shot Bridgette an amused glance. "Alas, not that kind of proposal, Mrs. O'Malley. This one involves a flurry of invitations that descended upon me." He fished several cards of creamy stock out of his pocket and shuffled through them as if checking that all the cards in a deck were present. "'To Reverend J. B. Sands and Guest: Enclosed are tickets to the public reception and dance for General and Mrs. Ulysses S. Grant on Friday, July twenty-third, eleven in the evening, at City Hall.' That's tonight. And this one, 'To the Honorable Rev. J. B. Sands: The Union Veterans Association of Leadville requests your presence on Saturday, July twenty-fourth, eleven in the evening, at the Clarendon Hotel for a banquet for veterans and friends to honor the former President of the United States and General in Chief of the Union Armies and General of the Potomac…' and so forth. That's tomorrow. Also, I was just notified that the veterans are gathering at five o'clock tomorrow for an informal reception with the general before the banquet. Next, we have an invitation from Doc to join Grant's party and Leadville's luminaries at the track on Sunday, July twenty-fifth. Which theoretically is a day of rest and worship. But apparently not for visiting dignitaries and their hosts." He passed the invitations to Inez, retaining a single sheet of stationery. "Finally, this one. Handwritten. Command presence." He handed it to her.

She read the note aloud with growing amazement. "General and Mrs. Grant are asking you to join them at the Tabor Opera House Monday evening?"

He tapped the note. "Not just myself. A guest as well."

She held out the stack of invitations to him. "Congratulations, Reverend. Your stock in Leadville society is rising faster than that of the Matchless Mine!"

He clasped his hands behind him, without taking back the cards and notes. "My hope is that you will be my companion for these events."

"I'm honored. Truly. But this week, we're so busy. Today was nearly impossible, and that was with three of us working the bar and Bridgette serving and working the kitchen. I can't possibly go."

A strangled sound reminded Inez that Bridgette was still in the room, listening. Inez turned to see Bridgette, hands on hips, bloody cleaver to the side. "Ma'am. You can't say no. He's the PRESIDENT."

"He *was* the president," Inez corrected her.

"Well, that makes him as good as. You *must* go. If you don't, who will the good reverend find to accompany him? Oh, many would like to, but you can't leave him to suffer the simperings and wiles of one of the heathen widows in this town." Bridgette crossed her arms, cleaver still in hand. "I'll get my eldest to help behind the counter for those evenings that you need an extra set of hands. God save us, I don't want him to become a barman, but he's forever after me to ask if you are needing extra help." She chopped down on an unsuspecting chicken, severing a wing. "Even Mr. Jackson would agree, I'm sure."

Inez shuffled through the invitations again, pausing at each. "Tonight's Friday and the public reception. This invitation is very last minute for something of this sort. Well, if Bridgette's Michael is available to help, I will arrange to attend with you. The dance and reception are late. I suspect dawn will be breaking upon the attendees. Saturday evening is out of the question. I have my standing poker game."

"If I'm not wrong, the majority of your players will be at the veterans' banquet," Sands pointed out.

"We'll see, then. I'll say yes to tonight, if Michael can fill in, maybe to Saturday, and yes to the opera on Monday night. Will that suffice?"

"For now." Sands finally took the invitations back. A slight smile crinkled the corners of his eyes.

"Then it's my turn to discuss something with you. Why don't you help me retrieve some liquor. We're low out front." Inez headed for the storage room, adding to Bridgette, "We'll need to get word to Michael at the smelter, see if he could help tonight. If he could be here by eight, that will give Abe time to instruct him and me time to get ready." She turned back to the reverend. "Luckily, I have clothes suitable for a reception upstairs, so you can pick me up here before eleven."

Once inside the room, she lit the hanging lantern. The comforting smell of burning coal oil suffused the air. The lantern glowed, throwing a soft yellow light over the room and its contents. She proceeded to examine the papers hanging on a nail by the door. Notes and lists in her precise writing, Abe's crabbed scrawls, and Sol's careful printing detailed the kegs, bottles, and magnums bought by the crate and wagonload and sold by the glass.

She was aware of Reverend Sands close by. Not touching her in any way. Yet, she felt it: What it was like to be held, wrapped in warmth when they were together. Alone. She cleared her throat, the little cough sounding loud in the close room, and said, "I called on Mr. Casey this morning. I'm starting divorce proceedings immediately. I told him I would pay whatever I must to hurry the process along."

She glanced at him to gauge his reaction.

He nodded. The tender look he gave her filled her heart. She cleared her throat again. "Please, don't think this means—"

"We can talk later," he said gently. "And you can tell me what it *does* mean."

She returned her attention to the inventory list and, using the stub of a pencil attached with a string, made a note. "Over here, if you please." She led him to the whiskey cases, in stacks according to quality. "This one. Can you help me take it up front?"

He hefted the wooden box. Bottles inside clinked. He looked at the contents and remarked, "There were times, Inez, when I could not be so close to liquor without being sorely tempted. And when tempted, I yielded, giving in to the weakness for drink, thinking, as I did, that I was the master. But the truth is, it mastered me. Always, blackness descended on my soul, and I thought that was my life. How it would play out. How I would live, and die. I had no faith then. No faith in myself, in my fellow man, or in God. 'Wherefore let him that thinketh he standeth take heed lest he fall. There hath no temptation taken you but such as is common to man: but God is faithful, who will not suffer you to be tempted above that ye are able; but will with the temptation also make a way to escape, that ye may be able to bear it.'"

He looked up at her and smiled. "Corinthians Ten. Verses eleven to fourteen. When you're with me, Inez, the temptation is gone. Alcohol has no hold on me. Although I will confess, other temptations take its place. But I don't mean to sermonize. Or to make a declaration here, in your storeroom, holding a crate of Old Kentucky." He looked toward the door that led to the kitchen, and a subtle shadow crossed his face. "The fellow who left as I came in. Someone you know?"

"Not at all. His name is James Kavanagh. He's in town with the Wesleys, mother and son. They're with the general's party, I know that much."

Sands nodded. Inez caught a slight frown on his face.

"Is something wrong?" she asked.

Sands looked at her. His eyes—sometimes gray, sometimes blue—were nearly colorless in the lantern light. "I've met the

Wesleys. Saw that fellow, Kavanagh, hanging back by the wall, watching. No one introduced him. I was curious."

She leaned against the wall. "Curious? About what?"

"I've met men like him before."

"What does that mean?"

He shook his head, saying instead, "Do you know anything else about him, besides his name?"

"Well, he's apparently minding young Wesley. Described himself as John Quincy Adam Wesley's 'shadow.' He says he was hired by the mother to keep her son out of trouble up here in Leadville. According to Kavanagh, Mrs. Wesley has plans for her son to enter politics in Denver. Or perhaps Washington." She shrugged.

Reverend Sands regarded her. "Kavanagh was chatty. Wonder why."

"He was just making idle talk while Wesley made a fool of himself and then redeemed himself in the eyes of all Leadville by buying drinks for the house."

"Any chatter was not idle but had a purpose. As I said, I've known men like him."

She tried again. "Like what?"

Sands shook his head again. "Later. Let's get this case to where you need it."

Once they were back in the barroom, Sands slid the case onto a corner of the counter, while Inez went behind. As she reached for the first bottle, the reverend seized her hand, before God and witness. And there were, despite the vacuum left after Wesley's departure, plenty of witnesses.

She flushed, feeling the patrons stare at the sight of a man of God holding a saloon owner's hand. She could feel the heat between them, even through his wet leather glove.

"I'll be back to escort you to the reception at ten." His voice, pitched only to reach her ears, hummed with intensity and promise.

Chapter Eighteen

Zelda stopped on East Third Street, just short of the offices of *The Independent*. She sneaked a sidelong glance at the road, muddy ruts and all, then down at her ill-gotten fancy shoes. She'd kept them clean as best she could while picking her way down Chicken Hill. What with the toe-pinching shoes, her Sunday best—threadbare, but decent—and her ma's Sunday bonnet, Zelda thought she probably looked respectable. Poor, but honest. She moved to face the building and peered at the words painted on the dirt-smudged window.

The Independent
Jedediah Elliston, publisher

—and at the smaller, hand-lettered sign wedged into a dusty corner of the sill:

Typesetter wanted

She took a quick look at the building itself. The offices of *The Independent* occupied a robust log building topped with a tent-like half wall above the door.

She'd thought it'd be grander.

Not that it really mattered.

What mattered was that this Jedediah Elliston take her seriously, that she convince him she could do this job. And she could. She'd lie if she had to, to make him give her a chance.

Well, if I can lie all night long, pitchin' and moanin' for Flo, I figure I can get this Mr. Elliston here to give me a listen.

She tied the bow a little tighter below her chin, hoping that Mr. Elliston hadn't been to Flo's any time lately. Just in case he had, she'd darkened her hair with walnut water and used a fierce brush with a dab of bear grease to subdue the curls. Her hair, now gleaming sable and smooth, was pulled back in a bun tight enough to make her eyebrows ache.

With a deep breath, she opened the door.

Only one person was inside, standing before a table with his back to her. He swung around at the tinkling noise made by the bell above the door. Zelda was relieved that he didn't look familiar. He came over, wiping his hands on a rag. "How can I help you, Miss?"

Miss. Well.

She must look proper enough then.

Zelda said, "I've come about the sign in your window."

"The sign?" He frowned, puzzled.

"About the job. For a typesetter." She held up the page torn from *The Independent*, to remind him of the opening.

His frown deepened.

She kept her expression bland, expectant, thinking he'd be a handsome sort if his mouth wasn't so twisted up, like he'd eaten a lemon straight.

He pulled the piece of newspaper from her outstretched hand. "I posted this under 'Men Wanted.' What makes you think you'd fit the bill?"

She rattled off the short speech she'd practiced on her way down the hill. "I need the job to support my kin up on Chicken Hill. My pa's blind and can't work. My ma's gone, and my brothers, I got twin brothers, they're no help. Too young." *At least when it comes to smarts.* "I can work plenty hard. I don't drink. Don't spit. I won't get all moony on you and go chasin' after a silver claim. You won't regret hirin' me. I promise."

"Have you experience setting type?"

"No, but I learn fast. You show me how to do it once, and I'll remember what you told me. And I'll be to work, every day, on time, if you'll give me a chance."

"How's your spelling?"

"I'm real good at words."

"When you set type, you read letters, words, entire sentences backwards." He stopped at her dumbfounded expression and shook his head, sourness intensifying. "Bah. Hopeless. I'm wasting my time."

"Let me try. I'll work a spell for free. If'n after one day, you don't think I can do the job, then you don't pay and I'll go. You got nothing to lose."

"Nothing but time on a silly goose of a girl," he grumbled.

But she'd noticed that on the words "free" and "don't pay" the prissy old-maid puckered look around his mouth had softened, then disappeared altogether.

"What's your name, Miss?"

"Th—" She stopped and covered her mouth with a delicate cough to give herself time to think. Should she use her real name? "Thomas. Zel Thomas."

He cocked his head and gazed at her a moment, eyes narrowed.

Uh-oh. He knows I'm fibbin'.

"Hands, Miss Thomas," he said abruptly. "Off with those gloves, please."

Holding her breath she peeled off a glove. *Does he know who I am, where I worked? Hope he doesn't try to get fast with me, askin' me to pull his prick t' get the job.*

He seized her freed hand and held it open. "Done much needlework, Miss Thomas? Lace? Embroidery?"

"Some," she said, startled. "My ma used to say I could maybe earn my way with a needle. Why?"

"Nimble fingers required." He dropped her hand. "Okay, Miss Thomas. Here's my decision. If you start now, this very moment, I'll give you the opportunity to learn the typesetter's trade. I need help with tomorrow's issue, *tout suite.* The pressmen are due in tonight, and I'm behind."

Zelda thought she detected a note of panic in his tone.

He then straightened, pulled his slouched shoulders back. "If you prove out today, I'll ask you to come back tomorrow. If tomorrow goes well, I'll pay you at close. Dollar-fifty a day. The first time you're late, or a mistake gets into print, you're fired. I can't afford slip-ups." He stared, as if daring her to turn tail and run.

Instead, she squared her shoulders to match his. "Thank you, Mr. Elliston. You won't be sorry." *A dollar-fifty a day!* She could hardly believe her ears, or her luck. *Not as good as whorin', but a whole lot better than fixin' lace.*

"I've often heard the theory posed that women—some women, in any case—are superior to men in the matter of typesetting. Hard for me to believe that a woman is superior anywhere outside the domestic realm, but I'm an open-minded sort."

He gestured to a coatrack beside a desk overflowing with stacks and crumpled balls of paper. "For your coat and hat."

"I'll keep 'em on, if that's all right," she said, not wanting to reveal her face any more than necessary.

He shrugged. "Suit yourself." He crossed to a row of pegs alongside one of the huge hulking machines and pulled off a canvas apron smeared with ink. "You'll need this, though. Now, for your first lesson." He led her over to a tall set of drawers, and pulled one open. "Type cases here. They come in pairs. The upper case holds capitals, small capitals, fractions, braces, and so on. The lower case holds small letters, points, spaces, quadrats, and the like. Over here is a form, ready to go, with case, type, lead, and furniture."

⟨⟩⟨⟩⟨⟩

Quoin.
　　Composing stick.
　　Leads.
　　Heel nicks.

Widows and orphans.

The words filled her mind like small fish swimming in a stream. More words, the type sizes, bobbed like so much foam on top: Excelsior. Agate. Long Primer.

Her back ached, her fingertips were inky and tender, her eyes watered from looking at all those little letters, and her head felt like it couldn't hold another thing. But, as she stared down at the half-page she'd set—with Mr. Elliston barking and pointing and telling her what to do—her heart felt different. Swelled with pride. She'd done it!

What's more, after fixing a last paragraph so as not to have a lone word sulking by itself on the last line of the page—*a widow-word, that's what it's called*—Mr. Elliston had actually said, "Good job, Miss Thomas." Although he'd uttered the words a touch grumpily, like he didn't really want to, like someone held a pistol at his back.

Then, he'd added, "You seem to have a natural faculty for this kind of work, Miss Thomas."

Now, she wasn't entirely sure about the word "faculty," but it must've meant something good, because he'd actually smiled when he said it.

Pride goeth before a fall.

Her pa's voice whispered in her head. She stroked her hands down the lap of the rough apron, being gentle on her raw fingertips, and silently addressed her father's doom-filled prophecy. *Well, Pa, if'n you don't want for us to starve in this hellhole of a town, you're gonna have to let me have a little pride in what I can do. It'll put food on the table, maybe not as much as whorin' might, but it's a sight better for the soul.*

A strangled clunk of the bell caused her and Jed both to turn toward the door as someone rattled it. An indistinct shadow flitted past the dust-dimmed window, its exact form indistinguishable from other pedestrians.

"What's this?" Jed strode toward the door.

Zelda realized a white space lay on the dark wood floor, like a displaced square of sunlight coming through a small window.

Jed picked up the oversized envelope and turned it over. "Well, it's got my name on it in any case." Pulling out a pocketknife, he slit it open while walking back to the table where he and Zelda had been working side by side. He pulled out several pages, unfolded them, and set them on the table. The top page held a scribbled sentence: *If you think John Quincy Adams Wesley is a friend of the hardworking and voting men of Colorado, read these.*

Jed set the note aside to reveal a letter written on fancy paper, thick and creamy. An engraved heading read "Law Offices of Lawton, Lawton, and Crouse, Boston, San Francisco, and Denver."

The words "personal" and "confidential" were scrawled across the top in a well-versed hand. The salutation—*Dear Mr. Gallagher*—was followed by:

In response to your inquiry, I take it that the question of employees is only a question of private and corporate economy, and individuals or companies have the right to buy labor where they can get it cheapest. We have a treaty with the Chinese government. I am not prepared to say that it should be abrogated, until our great manufacturing and Corporate interests are conserved in the matter of labor—

Apparently a faster reader than she was, Elliston whisked the letter aside with a muttered "Gallagher!"

Zelda thought she heard a note of triumph in his voice. She screwed up her nose, thinking of her brothers. They cursed Gallagher, the absentee owner of the Silver Mountain Mines, daily. She'd never met this man, who was as rich as Horace Tabor, if not more. The old-time girls at Flo's sometimes talked about him in hushed tones, but he'd not been in town for a long while, according to them.

Elliston picked up a second letter, saying, "Same paper, same handwriting, different salutation."

Zelda, peeked over his arm, reading—

My dear Mrs. Clatchworthy,

You needn't worry. Stand assured that I am fully on your side as regards the women's vote. Once elected, I shall work assiduously to make woman in Colorado man's equal partner in all, including property and voting—

Zelda was having trouble reading the rest of the letter because Elliston's hand trembled so. She glanced up at his face. His eyes looked feverish, softer, his face flushed. The tip of his tongue escaped briefly to touch his lips. It was the sort of look she'd seen on faces of younger men who got a glimpse of tit or on older ones who liked to talk about their stock holdings and bank accounts.

"These—" his hands shook— "I'd not trade these for the Matchless Mine, or any silver strike. It's the break I've been waiting for. My bonanza." He gazed at a point high on the wall. "I wonder. Who slid these under the door? Should I verify the information? Check with Wesley? Get his comments? He'll surely deny everything. This is as volatile as giant powder. No, more like nitroglycerine, set to explode in his face, no matter what he says. Who else knows about this, I wonder. Dill at the *Herald*? Robinson at the *Democrat*? Davis at the *Chronicle*? But I have the original letters here. Anything they get would be hearsay. Not that that would stop them."

His unfocused gaze settled on Zelda and sharpened. "There's no time to hesitate. It's either go or no in tonight's edition. Wesley is from Denver by way of San Francisco and Boston. Thinks he can move into town, throw his charm and money around, and get elected, just like that." He snapped his fingers dismissively. "He's just the kind of upstart politician I detest. Slick on the outside, rotten on the inside, and protected by his mother. Oh, she doesn't let any of us near her precious boy. But I've heard him talk from both sides of his mouth, depending on the audience. And I know Mrs. Clatchworthy. This sounds just like her. And Harry Gallagher, after the miners' strike four months ago, I'll bet he's itching to hire cheap labor that won't cause more trouble and make demands. The Celestials would jump at the chance to make half a white man's wages and kiss Gallagher's boots for the opportunity."

"Are there Chinamen in Leadville?" Zelda asked, since he seemed to be talking to her.

He started—*Guess he was talkin' to hisself after all*—then said, "Last one left town in a hurry some time ago. Celestials are not welcome here." He licked his lips again, more nervously this time, then came to a decision. "Well, when Dame Fortune smiles, what can we mortals do but smile back? This will sell a mountain of papers, with all the visitors in town."

Zelda picked up the envelope to give it the eye, not that there was much to see.

"There's somethin' else in here." She pulled out what felt like an oversized playing card, wrapped in paper. She unwrapped it, and a small photograph fell out.

But not just any photograph.

During Elliston's horrified gasp, Zelda had time to observe a number of things about the woman in the image.

First, she hardly wore a thing. *If'n you can even call that bitty gauze drape a thing.*

Second, she was a Celestial. *Kinda pretty, too, but I don't see how she kin be smilin', posed like that. I'd not be smiling, that's for sure!*

Third, and this more of a professional rumination: *How can she bend her legs around like that? Must of been in the circus, maybe.*

Before she could examine the photograph further, Jed snatched it away.

Zelda realized that, as a proper young woman, a proper response was expected from her.

She promptly covered her eyes, as if the lewd image had almost stricken her blind. Behind the dark shield, she contemplated whether she maybe ought to pretend to faint dead away, but the floor was filthy and besides, she wanted to see what Mr. Elliston would do. She peeked through her fingers.

He was giving the picture a look-see, close up and personal. Meanwhile, he gabbled.

"Miss Thomas! I, I don't know what to say. I apologize. Profoundly! I would never have allowed you to touch that envelope had I suspected, had I known…I apologize for having your female sensitivities exposed, uh, what I meant to say is, this carte de visite is obviously something that you should not be…

Well, perhaps I should finish this job myself so as to protect you from further distress."

She hastily dropped her hand. "Mr. Elliston. I was raised on a farm. I'm no shrinking violet. I know about life. Here in Leadville, oft times I am forced—" *forced, that's a good one*—"to walk down State Street, lookin' for my young brothers, who are drawn to that street of sin like, like, moths to eternal flame." *Oh! That's good, too!* "I am shocked, truly, by the sight of that awful picture, but now that it's out of my sight, I shall recover."

She looked down at the paper that had held the card and read aloud: "Found in J.Q.A.W.'s personal effects. Dare him to say diff'rent. He is an unrepentant lover and supporter of the Orientals."

Jed turned the photograph over. "And here on the back, it says—in an illiterate hand, I'll add—'To My John. Come Back. See Soon. Love.'"

He snorted. "Love." He said the word with disgust, then took the cover sheet from Zelda and rewrapped the photograph gingerly as if it were hot to the touch.

He tucked it back in the envelope, set the letters on top, and took in the printer's form holding the front page, finished except for a space left open for an engraving. "We've got to redo this, and fast. Take out the quoin, Miss Thomas—No, not that. The quoin's the metal wedge, there, that locks up the type in the form. I'll work out the headline decks and the lead. When you're done, grab a composing stick, and I'll give you the first line." He turned over a piece of scratch paper and began scribbling.

As early evening slid into darkness, the two worked to reset the front page of *The Independent*. With the headline, the article's lead, and one letter completed and only half of the Clatchworthy note and a brief concluding paragraph to go, Elliston straightened up from his stooped position with a sigh.

He pulled out his pocket watch, clicked it open, and groaned. "The reception for Grant. If I'm going to get there for the reception line, I've got to leave now." He hesitated. His gaze swept over the nearly completed form before coming to rest on Zelda, part doubtful, part hopeful, but with a dash of skepticism.

"I can do it, Mr. Elliston," she said, before he could ask her or change his mind. "I can finish up. All I got to do is set up the stick with the last few lines of the letter and that little paragraph about the card, isn't that right? And then lock it up with the," she pointed at the metal wedge, "I forget what it's called, but I know what it does."

Elliston switched his gaze back to the page and the last empty bit of the form. "You'll need the leads, to put the proper space between the lines."

"I remember."

He worried his lower lip with his top teeth, finally looking square at her. "All right, Miss Thomas. I hope my trust isn't misplaced. I'm counting on you to finish the last few lines. The pressmen'll be by in the next couple of hours. If you'd wait for them, then put Wesley's letters and the envelope in the desk drawer over there." He gestured at the walnut rolltop, nearly hidden under piles of papers and cast off bits of metal and wood print furniture. "Tell the boys to hold off printing the front page for now. I'll be back by one or two in the morning to check it before they run the whole."

"You can count on me."

"I hope so," he said gruffly. He snapped the pocket watch shut, retrieved a proper swallowtail coat and top hat from the coat tree, and unearthed a notepad and pencil from the desk, causing two piles of papers to avalanche into each other. He stuffed pad and pencil into an inner pocket and returned to Zelda.

Her head was bent over the composing stick as she set up the words "Mama sends her regards." She could almost feel his silence. Finally she looked up, afraid that he had changed his mind and was going to tell her to go home, that he'd take care of it. Instead, he pulled two dollars from his pocket and said, "You've earned this, Miss Thomas. See you tomorrow morning. At nine." He touched his hat to her, for all the world like she was a real lady, then left, closing the door with a thud that set the bell clanking.

<>◇<>

Zelda stood back, wiping her sore, ink-stained fingers on a rag and admiring the finished page. It was as perfect as anyone could make it, she was sure. *No widow-words, the lead is all proper, it fits just right.*

After removing her bonnet, she ran one hand cautiously over her hair. It was recovering from the application of bear grease and beginning to regain its natural curl. She picked up the two letters from John Quincy Adams Wesley and the cover note and replaced them in the envelope with the photograph.

And she wondered: Who slid them under the door? And why? *These are sure gonna give this John Wesley feller a world of hurt.* This business of Celestials…she and her pa had seen a Chinaman or two working on railroads as they had made their way to Leadville. It was hard for her to understand why everyone hated them so much. *They're just workin' t' keep from starvin', like everyone else, ain't they?* But there was no ducking the fact that the Chinamen had no friends in these parts. As for women voting—

She snorted, the explosion of derision sounding loud in the empty building and half scaring herself.

I can't see the men allowing such a thing to happen, ever.

And the photograph. Now *that* was interesting. Something she'd not seen before. Zelda wondered if she ought to mention it to Miss Flo, suggest it as a way to drum up business, seeing that Miss Flo was always looking for new ways to bring in customers.

The creak of the door and clank of bell announced a visitor. Not one but two shabby-looking fellows paused on the threshold.

"What's this?" said one.

Zelda grabbed her bonnet off the table, trying to hold the brim with her knuckles so as not to stain it with ink. "You the printers for the paper? Mr. Elliston asked me to stay until you-all arrived."

They stepped into the room, removing their hats. One, with a beard that looked like the moths had gotten into it and done some damage, came over to look at the front page.

"Mr. Elliston said he'd be back by two in the morning," added Zelda, squashing the envelope into the pocket of her coat, thinking she should put it in the desk and hightail out of there. She was anxious to find Flo, tell her that she wasn't going to be working at the house tonight, tomorrow night, nor ever again.

The bearded one looked up at her and said, "Guess J.E.'s gone to see the general, I'll bet. All the muckety-mucks are there tonight." His eyes narrowed. "So, who're you, anyway?"

"I'm the new typesetter," she said proudly.

"Tarnation. Elliston's hired a lady setter? Printer's devil, more like." He and his partner snickered. Zelda glared, not certain whether "printer's devil" was an insult or not, but not liking the sound of it.

The bearded fellow brushed past Zelda on his way to the coatrack, remarking, "Well, Missy, we'll see how long ya last. Be sure t' get your pay right away. Old J.E., he squeezes two bits so tight you'd think he's hopin' they'll pair up and raise themselves a whole family o' pennies." He hung the hat and turned, staring hard at Zelda. "You look kinda familiar, Missy. You been in these parts for a spell? I'd swain I've seen your face afore."

Not liking the direction of the conversation, Zelda started for the door, hastily slinging the bonnet over her hair and tying the ribbons tight beneath her chin. "You-all kin tell Mr. Elliston I'll be back tomorrow. Bright an' early, like he asked."

But right now, I'm gonna go tell Flo: No more workin' on my back. I've got a job that pays for standin' up and usin' my hands in better ways.

Chapter Nineteen

Dressed for Grant's reception, Inez twisted back and forth in her chair in the saloon's upstairs office, twiddling with her fan. Outside the large mullioned window next to her desk, lights from State Street's businesses glimmered, subdued by window glass and reflecting on the puddles and mud in the street. Beyond, in the darkness, were the mountains. There, but hidden, like so much in her life.

She twisted away from the street scene to face the wall that held a small collection of Currier and Ives prints. Having plowed much of the saloon's profits back into the business or savings, she and Abe, by common consent, had given the office only the essentials in furnishings and decoration.

The gaming room boasted handmade rugs from Brussels and paintings in gilt frames. The office, on the other hand, had a braided rag rug, a secondhand loveseat, and inexpensive prints. She focused on two images grouped together. "Trotting Cracks in the Snow" showed horse-drawn sleighs dashing hither and thither. It drove her thoughts to her New York childhood, and to one memory, in particular, of riding in a sleigh with her father at the reins. She was very young. Hard kernels of snow pelted her cheeks; the runners hissed over the snow. She was exhilarated yet frightened by the speed at which they rushed through the freezing air.

Inez shook her head. Seldom were memories of her father good ones. Yet, this one, despite the underlying fear, held echoes of laughter and euphoria.

She fiddled with the tassel on her fan—a concoction of dark wood and lace—as her gaze traveled to the other print. "Prairie Fires of the Great West," while rich in color, struck her now as foreboding, given the current round of arson in town and the still-at-large firebug. The yellow and orange flames of the print leaned in a high wind, dramatic plumes of purple smoke displacing vast prairie skies. The train steamed away from the fire, headlight piercing the dark. Behind, in the vast distance, miniature bison attempted to outrun the flames. It seemed unlikely the herd would escape.

The image that next jumped to mind was of Flo's bordello, the back in flames, the bucket brigade, the disheveled and drunk Lizzie. And the mapmaker, who seemed to appear nearly everywhere she turned. There was something unsettling about him, like a clock overwound, spring not broken, but far too tight.

Was he really just looking around the building this morning? Or did he have something to do with Lizzie's demise? And now, Flo's in jail. And I'm linked to her, by hook or by crook, through that damned contract I signed.

She turned away from the prints and her dark thoughts, glancing at her desktop, unusually clear of papers, bills, and invoices. A long evening glove lay to one side, its many pearl buttons giving a muted gleam, a rich cache on white silk. A single sheet of paper, ink nearly dry, lay centered on the blotter. She hoped Abe would find time to come to the office before the reverend arrived. She had to talk to him about the paper. The sooner the better.

She had told Abe she needed to talk to him about "business." He'd promised to be up as soon as Michael was squared away behind the bar. Michael had appeared promptly at seven, blond hair sleeked back, his fair-skinned face red from a scrubbing. He was attentive, polite, quiet, and, even more important from Inez's point of view, he was the eldest of Bridgette's five boys and knew how to smooth ruffled feathers and head off confrontations.

Despite Bridgette's declarations that her Michael had a great future at the smelter, Inez suspected that he'd jump at a chance to learn the bardog's trade. However, Inez was not certain that she'd want to brave Bridgette's wrath by offering Michael a permanent position.

A knock at the door. "Inez?"

She twisted in the chair to face the door. "Abe, come in."

Her business partner eased the door open and came in, loosening his tie. He stopped just inside the door. "Looks like you're all set for the evenin'. I'd say no man would disavow that you're the handsomest woman in Leadville, Mrs. Stannert."

She smiled thinly. "Thank you. But I find that a bit disconcerting. I'm not trying to attract attention. The fact that Reverend Sands and I are going to be parading around, arm in arm, amongst all of Leadville's populace strikes me as unwise. But how can I demur?"

The calico cat that had been curled up on the loveseat, ignoring Inez, hopped down with a loud *maow* of greeting for Abe. Abe closed the door behind him, scooped up the feline, and sat down on the couch. She settled in on his lap, purring, her claws working on the knees of his worsted trousers. "Well now. I think most of the folks tonight are going to be gawking at Mr. and Mrs. Grant, the governor, and the Tabors. What with all the talk about old Haw Tabor bein' on the outs with his better half, people are gonna be far more interested in those two than who a man of the cloth is escortin' around town."

"I hope you're right. In any case, I'll not call attention to myself by dancing on the tabletops, spitting, or swearing." She smiled half-heartedly.

"There you go." Abe smiled back, teeth flashing in contrast to his dark skin. "So, what's on your mind, Inez? This 'bout Michael? Mebbe hirin' him on? I think he'd be willin'. But Bridgette, now, she'd not be over happy about it. And we can't afford to lose the best biscuit-maker in Leadville."

"I have been thinking about Michael, true. But I wanted to talk to you about something else." She set her fan on the blotter and picked up the paper. "I went to see a lawyer this morning about getting a divorce from Mark."

A small frown creased his forehead. "Go on."

"I can almost read your mind, Abe. You think he's dead. Why should I even bother? But, the truth is, I—*we*—don't know what has happened to him. And I cannot move forward in my life until I settle this. Settle it so I can feel free to consider the future. Now, part of that has to do with making sure we have an agreement, on paper, as to how we view our partnership in the saloon."

Abe didn't respond, but she could have sworn his face had turned from warm living flesh into cold stone.

She continued, determined to have her say. "It simply comes down to this. We wrote nothing down. Nothing. When Mark won the saloon in that poker game, we all shook on it, remember? Three ways, he said. We were all partners, equal, and we'd divide it up equally, just as we did all the other winnings from the past. I've learned this is very suspect from a legal point of view. Even if it was written down that Mark deeded me a third of the business, a judge would probably scoff and dismiss it out of hand. If I only knew for certain that Mark was dead." She sighed. "Well, 'what ifs' are useless. Abe, what we must do is clarify our business relationship, you and I. In writing."

She closed her eyes as a wave of longing washed over her. Not longing for Mark, but for the past. When things were simpler. When it took so little to laugh, to feel alive and free.

"So you get a divorce," said Abe. "I don't see how that changes our business dealin's. We never needed papers afore. Why now?"

She opened her eyes. "It's insurance. Let's say I get a divorce, based on desertion, since we cannot prove Mark's death. We need to have this down in writing, all legal, that this business is ours equally. Half to you, half to me. I don't want anyone taking away what's yours. Or mine, for that matter." She tipped her head up, defiant. "It's going to be complicated enough, what with little William back East. The more straightforward we can make our partnership, the quicker I can take care of this mess."

"And if'n he comes back?"

Inez's eyes narrowed. "You've always maintained Mark met with foul play. That he died, somewhere, somehow."

Abe nodded. "And it's what I believe. But I'd be a fool t' throw down every nickel I have on a blind bet. To speak straight out, I'm not sure that havin' a paper statin' that we divvied up the saloon, half 'n' half, would look so good if it fell into the wrong hands. If Mark's alive, it might look like we just took what was rightfully his. And if'n he's dead? Lordy, I can see someone sayin', hmmm, who stands to win by shootin' this Mr. Stannert in the back and shovin' him down a mine shaft? How about his widow and that nigger she's in business with?"

"It'll not fall into anyone's hands but our own. We'll keep a single copy here, locked in the safe. Abe, I cannot imagine a worse nightmare than having Mark walk through that door, right now, saying, 'Hello, Darlin'.'" She did a dead-on imitation of his Georgia drawl and continued, "Just as if he'd never been gone. If that happens, then, my God, what sort of man did I marry? That he would disappear for more than a year and not contact me during that time? I'm better off without him. I'm done. There's nothing he or anyone else could say to make me return to the marriage."

Abe stared at her soberly. The cat in his lap butted his stilled hand, demanding that he resume petting her. He did. "Well now. Most like we won't see him again." His voice was gentle, as if he attempted to soothe her with words, as he did the cat with his touch. "If'n you feel better havin' my mark on a paper contract, that's fine with me, long's we keep it locked up. Like you said, for insurance. And I got my wife to think of. Should somethin' happen t' me, I want Angel to get my share, for herself and the child."

He moved the cat to the seat cushion and rose, brushing cat hair from his lap.

Inez dipped the pen and held it out to him. She scooted her chair out of his way, small brass wheels screeching. Abe signed the paper without reading her carefully crafted words. Inez took the proffered pen, dipped it again, and signed her own name next to his.

"We're now legal partners," she said softly. "Right down the middle. Equal, all the way."

Abe said, "We always were, Inez."

"Yes, but now no one, even the lawyers, can say different." She rose from the chair with a rustle of silk taffeta and crouched down by the safe on the floor, mindful of her tight corset. She placed the paper in the safe—an offering to the black maw of the iron beast—and pushed the door shut with a clank, closing a door on her past.

A knock on the office door immediately followed, a wooden echo of the metallic closure.

"Mrs. Stannert?" Reverend Sands' voice, muffled by the door.

"Please, Reverend, come in." She stood, smoothed the raspberry-colored satin panel of her dress and reached behind to adjust the complicated waterfall of bows and flounces.

The door opened. The reverend paused on the threshold, hat in hand. "You outshine the stars, Mrs. Stannert."

Inez smiled and retrieved the stray evening glove. "Thank you, Reverend."

Reverend Sands nodded at Abe. "Mr. Jackson."

Abe nodded back. "Reverend." He crossed his arms, the garters black slashes against the white sleeves.

Inez took her evening cloak off the pegs behind the door and handed it to Reverend Sands, allowing him to place it around her shoulders. Ready to leave, she turned to Abe. "Thank you for taking care of everything. I imagine Michael will do well under your tutelage. And you do have Sol to back you up."

"Won't be no problem, Mrs. Stannert. You have a fine time and we'll see you tomorrow."

Inez and the reverend left through the Harrison Street door, Sands opening and holding an umbrella over them both. He steered her over to a waiting landau on the street corner, saying, "Surely you didn't think I'd make you walk the four blocks to City Hall." The driver, dressed for foul weather, hopped off his perch and pulled open the door. Inez gratefully allowed them to help her up, then Reverend Sands eased in beside her and the driver closed the door.

"No, of course not," said Inez. "But I didn't think you'd manage a carriage and driver. I would have thought they had all been spoken for days ago."

"Never underestimate the influence of a man of the cloth. There are those who wager they'll gain a few extra points at Heaven's gates if they can rustle up transportation for a minister."

The carriage lurched forward, wheels churning the mud as the pair of horses strained forward.

"Are you certain you want to walk into such an august gathering with a saloonkeeper on your arm?" she asked. "It's bound to tarnish your image."

He shifted in the seat across from her, his knee pressing briefly against hers. That glancing brush had an immediate electrifying effect on her, an effect that she determinedly ignored.

"Why bring this up now?" His voice was mild. "We've been through it before, and here we are, on the way to the reception. Still, I'll repeat what I've told you many times. I've made my choice, Inez. To stand by your side. Forever, if you'll have me. The ministering, the preaching, there are ways to serve God that do not require that I stand behind a pulpit."

An image of Preacher Thatcher, threadbare jacket, staring, unseeing eyes, beard a-tangle, flashed through her mind. She suppressed a shudder.

The carriage lurched to a stop in front of City Hall. Inez and the reverend disembarked and joined the throngs of well-dressed people waiting patiently in the drizzle to enter.

He tucked Inez's gloved hand under his arm. "Ready to enter the lion's den, Mrs. Stannert? It's time to introduce you properly to Leadville society and the Grants."

Chapter Twenty

Feeling conspicuous walking down State Street at such a dark and devious hour dressed in her ma's bonnet and threadbare coat, Zelda kept her gaze fixed on the warped boards of the wooden walkway and the shoes and boots of the passing men. It was a time of night that no proper woman would be out, much less alone. Zelda tried to ignore the catcalls and whistles. She was afraid that if she looked up, she'd see someone she knew from Flo's. Being so close to the brothel and having to pass by all the hurdy-gurdy of dancehalls, saloons, and questionable boarding houses in that first block, Zelda thought that the odds were good of bumping into a past customer.

How'm I gonna tell Flo? Zelda swallowed nervously.

Flo had always been kind to her. At least, as kind as her kind ever got. And she'd told Zelda, early on, that if Zelda ever found another job and wanted to leave "the sisterhood," she'd give her blessing. Still, Zelda suspected that Flo wasn't going to be happy about losing a girl right now, what with all the bigwigs in town. The night trade was probably jumping.

A faint smell of smoke still lingered about the brick three-story bordello. Zelda knocked, her heart pounding nearly as hard as her knuckles. The door opened. A wash of sound, women's and men's voices, someone playing the piano, streamed around Danny, who blocked egress. Warm, overscented air, with a hint of burnt wood undertones curled out the door to greet her.

"Hey, Danny." Zelda took off her bonnet. Her hair was in full frizz, unchecked by the pomade and encouraged by the damp air. "It's me. Zelda."

"Who's there?" Molly's sharp voice pierced the darkness behind the doorman. He stepped aside and Molly materialized, glimmering in white satin and pink silk, her dark red hair piled high.

Zelda stared. "Molly, you wearin' Flo's new evenin' dress?"

Molly grabbed Zelda's wrist and dragged her inside. "Where've you been?" Her whisper sounded near hysterical. "You're late! And what're those rags you're wearing?"

Zelda jerked away. "These 'rags' are my Sunday best. Where's Flo? I gotta talk to her, right now."

Molly laughed, a short bark. "Well, if you gotta talk to her, you'll have to go down to the jail, 'cause that's where she is."

Zelda's spirits sank. "Jail? What's she doin' there?"

"Shut up. Keep your voice down," Molly hissed. "Follow me."

She disappeared to the back of the house. Zelda followed.

Molly pulled open the door to the ruined kitchen. "We can talk here."

She left the door ajar, allowing light from hallway sconces to penetrate the dank room, and faced Zelda. "You missed all the hullabaloo this morning. Lizzie's dead, and Flo jumped Officer Ryan, the copper that's city collector. So she got thrown in the clink, and I'm in charge. You get some proper clothes on and get into the parlor, now."

Zelda jammed her bonnet back on. "Not me. I got a real job with *The Independent* newspaper, settin' type. They're payin' me good, too. So, you kin tell Flo, I quit."

"You *can't*." Molly gripped Zelda's shoulders so hard pain stabbed up Zelda's neck. Zelda could now see that the pink ball dress—which she had much admired on Flo just a week ago—hung loose on Molly's angular frame. "You're stayin'! At least for the weekend! If you don't, I'll make sure the newspaper finds out you're nothin' but a whore, dressed up in your mama's old Sunday hand-me-downs. How long d'you think you'd keep your fancy job then?"

"You do that, I'll scratch your eyes out!" Zelda considered slapping Molly's face good and proper, but reconsidered at her crazed expression. "Where do you get off bein' all high-falutin' anyway? Flo always said, if I found somethin' better, she'd give me her blessings. You really want her t' know how you made me stay, and how you're wearin' all her things while she was gone?"

"Who knows if she'll ever get out?" Molly sneered. But she stepped away, folding her arms protectively as if to hug the dress to her or keep herself warm. "Okay, listen. I won't tell anyone about your new job and you don't have to screw. But you gotta keep watch over Lizzie so I can put Polly to work." Her small eyes gleamed in the near dark, like a weasel's.

"Keep watch on Lizzie??"

Molly shrugged, impatient. "Keep watch, wake, I dunno. Flo's orders. Flo says Lizzie's not dead. Flo's crazy. Doc Cramer came around and said otherwise, but I know Flo, and I'm not gonna cross her on this. You wanna help Flo out, like she's helped you, then watching Lizzie is the least you can do, if you aren't gonna help with the fucking."

Zelda sighed, thinking maybe she could at least get a little sleep. *Hope she's not all beat up. I won't be able to sleep if she's real beat up.* "Where is she?"

Molly jerked her chin toward the hallway. "Flo's room."

"You put her in Flo's room?"

Molly shrugged. One pink beribboned strap slid off her bony shoulder. "The other rooms are full up."

They moved down the hall, and Molly pulled open a door under the shadow of the grand staircase heading to the second floor.

Polly, who was nodding in the light of a single lamp turned down low, jumped up with a stifled "Shit!" The straight chair she'd been sitting in clattered over onto its side. "Molly, you scared me half to death! Is that Zelda?"

"She's gonna take over here," Molly said briskly, moving into the room. "Straighten up your hair and git back to the parlor."

"Don't know why Flo left you in charge," grumbled Polly, moving to the gilt-edged mirror at the foot of the elegant four-poster bed.

"Because I have more brains that all of you put together, except for the schoolteacher. And she don't know the business. Now, go on, get out."

"Leastways Lizzie isn't snoring, for the first time in her life." Polly swept out of the room without a glance back.

Zelda tiptoed over to the form on the bed, nervous at what she might find. Lizzie lay, looking as if she was nothing more than asleep. Zelda forced herself to touch the hand lying slack on the coverlet.

Cold.

Zelda swallowed. "How'd she die?"

"Dunno." Molly sat on the edge of the bed, staring at Lizzie as if searching for some clue to her demise. "We just found her this morning, lying all curled up in the mudroom. Looking about like this. Well, we cleaned her up some and put her in a shift. Flo wanted that. I think Lizzie just drank herself to death. Or maybe when Flo wasn't looking, it was the laudanum. You know Lizzie."

Zelda picked up the overturned straight chair and said, "I don't have t' sit close to her, do I?"

"Sit wherever you want, as long as you're in the room." Molly watched as Zelda pulled the chair over to the small warming stove in the corner and sat. "Here." She picked up a shawl that Polly had left behind and threw it to Zelda. "It's gonna get cold in here. But no fire. Don't want the body warming up too fast."

Zelda wrapped herself in the shawl, tucking the ends securely beneath her haunches. "Kin I leave a light on?"

Molly shrugged. "Sure. And you'll have to use the pot if you have to piss, because—" She hiked up the long multi-layered skirt of the dress and pulled a key from her garter—"I'm gonna lock the door on you. Don't want some drunken john opening the door by mistake. No one knows Lizzie's here, but you, Polly, me, and Danny."

"So when can I leave?" Even to herself, Zelda sounded plaintive.

"I'll be back before dawn." Molly looked at Lizzie, distaste plain on her face. "I don't know why the hell Flo thinks she's gotta be watched. Doc said she was gone. It's not like she's gonna rise from the dead or something."

Chapter Twenty-one

A symphony of scents washed over Inez as she and Reverend Sands stepped into the closely packed public reception at City Hall. Shy flowery perfumes of rose, carnation, violet, and lavender accompanied the bolder citrus overtones of orange and lemon. All clashed with the astringent bass line of male pomades containing oil of bergamot, mints, ammonia, and more. This olfactory chaos was heightened by the heat created by the crush of people milling about or jostling for position in the receiving line. High windows, opened wide, did little to relieve the temperatures and humidity.

Inez righted the fan hanging from her wrist and began vigorously fanning herself, joining most of the women in the vast room. Reverend Sands kept his hand firmly on her elbow, steering a circuitous path through the crowd as a small orchestra provided a light and lilting musical backdrop for the event. Inez assumed a polite but distant smile, allowing the reverend to decide who to greet and how. She recalled her mother's detailed etiquette guidelines for how far to incline her head at each overture.

Most of their encounters were with church members or Leadville's religious elite. The men, many who frequented the Silver Queen, were uniformly polite if sometimes distant, bowing and acknowledging both the reverend and Inez. The wives, however, were another matter. Women of society, as Inez had observed since her earliest childhood days, were experts at delivering a fatal blow with nothing more than a slight tilt of a fan or the degree of inclination in a nod. So she was prepared for the slightly raised female eyebrows, which spoke more subtly than a verbal utterance of disgust and dismay, the hesitation as finely dressed women debated whether to apply a direct cut to Inez and how to do so without offending the charming and well-liked reverend of a local church. Most of these impasses ended in a draw, with the barest of nods and most frozen of expressions exchanged between Inez and the other ladies.

It was like running the gauntlet. Weapons threatened overhead but did not make contact. Reaching the start of the receiving line was a relief. Inez kept her eyes straight ahead, not wanting to identify all the individuals beforehand, lest she lose courage and determination. *At least Mrs. Grant has no idea who I am nor does Governor Pitkin's wife. As for the Leadville mayor and all the local aristocracy, they will surely be on their best behavior.*

The mayor and wife were first. As Reverend Sands merely introduced her as "Mrs. Stannert," the good woman opposite Inez provided a general smile and friendly nod. Inez allowed her own aloof smile to thaw and returned the acknowledgment in kind. Inez also noted how, on acknowledging Reverend Sands, she lit up discreetly from within, as if a gaslight had been held briefly to her heart. Reverend Sands tended to have that effect on women, from the smallest, shyest girl barely into pinafores to the most elderly of great-grandmothers.

Inez kept her expression neutral and pleasant as she moved up the line to meet the vice president of the Denver & Rio Grande Railroad and his wife. Next, Lieutenant Governor Horace Tabor, one of Leadville's homegrown millionaires, and, Inez was intrigued to see, his wife, Augusta. Mrs. Tabor was well known for eschewing public appearances such as these. Inez thought she'd heard that Augusta seldom left her Denver home these days. Yet, here she was.

Back when Leadville was Oro City and not much more than tents, Augusta had been postmistress and ran her husband's store.

But her position had risen with his fortunes. She was now the wife of Colorado's lieutenant governor, one of the wealthiest men in the United States. Despite the polite smile affixed on Augusta's face, Inez would have laid bets that Augusta would have preferred to be back in the "old days," before Leadville brought such enormous fortune and fame to her husband.

Inez inclined her head murmuring, "Mrs. Tabor," and Augusta did the same with a "Mrs. Stannert." Inez thought a flash of recognition passed over Augusta's face. If so, it was now gone.

More faces and names.

"May I present General and Mrs. Grant."

Inez bowed, thinking that the former president and Civil War hero looked tired. Something about his eyes presaged illness. She recalled that, upon his arrival the previous night, he had attempted to demur from giving a speech, citing a hoarse throat.

The realization that the short, iron-gray man before her had been not only a president of the United States but also hero of the Civil War and engineer of the Confederacy's surrender dazzled Inez in a way that she would not have foreseen. Whereas Ulysses S. Grant struck her as stolid, unmoving, even somewhat stern, Julia Dent Grant's eyes shone, and she nearly twinkled in the reflected glow of celebrity.

Presentations made, still musing about the Grants, Inez automatically moved forward, even as the next introduction was intoned:

"Mrs. Stannert, Mr. Gallagher."

Shock poured through her as an icy waterfall upon bare skin as Inez turned to face a former lover.

It was only years of innate breeding and her mother's stern tutelage in manners of deportment that allowed Inez to keep a calm, polite demeanor.

Harry Gallagher, who had been chatting to the couple who were presented before them, turned to Inez and Reverend Sands. The two men exchanged greetings in the style of men who'd known each other a long time. Harry bowed to Inez, face impassive, as if, Inez reflected bitterly, she held no more meaning for him than a lamppost. Returning his bow with one that skimmed the line between propriety and rejection, Inez resolutely turned to the next introduction.

"Mrs. Lucretia Wesley and John Wesley, Esquire."

So. This is Mr. John Quincy Adam Wesley's most fearsome mother.

Not quite five feet in stature, she seemed nearly invisible standing next to her tall, gregarious offspring. Her dark eyes were mirrors of her son's, but she had a firmness about the mouth that was her own, that hinted of adversities overcome.

A mutual inclination of heads ensued.

Reverend Sands stepped before Mrs. Wesley, preparing a cordial bow. She suddenly grasped his hand, and turned to Inez, saying, "Ah, *you* are the companion of Reverend Sands! He is so well regarded by all. Mr. Gallagher has mentioned him as a valiant comrade in arms during the late War. Mr. Tabor has naught but good to say of his works here in Leadville, and his church. General Grant himself mentioned him favorably on our train trip up to Leadville."

Inez listened in fascination to the list of illustrious folk tripping from Mrs. Wesley's lips. Sands smiled. Inez was intrigued to note that, at least on the surface, Mrs. Wesley seemed immune to his charms.

"Mrs. Wesley, you are too kind with your praise." He slid his hand from her silk-gloved grasp.

Coming back to her manners with a guilty start, Inez turned to the young Mr. Wesley. She caught him staring at Sands with what appeared to be amused fascination. Behind Wesley, Kavanagh stood at a respectful distance with a ghost of a smirk on his face. Catching Inez's eye, he lifted a hand in a sketch of a greeting.

The rest of the receiving line went by in a blur for Inez. No sooner had she and Reverend Sands completed the introductions than Doc came hurrying up as fast as cane and limp would allow in the crowded room. "Reverend! And Mrs. Stannert! So good of you both to attend. Ah, Reverend Sands, this means we have a full complement of the city's ecclesiastical representatives. A good showing from the spiritual side for the general, wouldn't you say?"

Doc beamed as if he were personally responsible for the presence of God's agents at the reception, which could, Inez thought, be the case. Doc had had a major hand in organizing the events for Grant's visit. She suspected that, behind the public faces of the mayor, the governor, all business, political, religious, and military representatives in attendance, Doc stayed busy oiling the machinery, keeping relationships and schedules smooth and untangled. His adoration and respect of Grant was such that it came close to nearly heathen worship, but then, Doc was hardly alone in that. Inez had observed within the saloon and about town that Grant seemed to inspire either great love and respect or great hatred and disdain, but rarely anything in between.

She allowed her rigid smile to relax into the genuine article. Doc grasped her gloved fingers and bowed low over them, as if she were no less than a queen.

"Doctor Cramer, you have done a splendid job, and we know it is all due to your hard work and diligence that General Grant and his wife should have such a splendid reception."

Doc straightened, flushed with pleasure or exertion or perhaps from the blood rushing to his head during the prolonged bow. "Well, m'dear, ah, Mrs. Stannert," he quickly corrected himself. "Our fair city can do no less. We made sure that his first full day here was extraordinary. Extraordinary!" He beamed at Reverend Sands, who gave him an encouraging nod. Thus encouraged, he continued, "Colonel Curry—you know he is head of the committee put together by the Veterans Association—had a carriage awaiting for the general and his party at ten this morning to take them to visit the mines."

He began steering both Inez and Reverend Sands toward the heavily laden reception tables as he talked. "That unseasonable shower *ante meridiem* caused the schedule to slide a bit, but the Grants had ample time to view both Iron and Morning Star mines. Ah, you should have seen the hero of Appomattox at the Iron Mine! He and some of the party dressed to go below ground. In the rubber coat and slouch hat of a miner, he looked like any other underground explorer!"

An usher slid up next to Doc and cleared his throat tentatively. "Excuse me, Doctor Cramer? Colonel Curry wishes to speak with you."

"No doubt another fire to put out. Oh, pardon me, bad choice of words, given last night's arson. Excuse me." Doc bowed again to Inez, and then to Reverend Sands, before hurrying away.

"Our august visitors hardly have a moment to rest, do they?" Inez paused by the punch bowl, with a slight dip of her fan. Sands obligingly retrieved a cup for her. Their gloved hands brushed as he handed her the cup. "That's probably a good thing," she continued, "considering young Wesley's penchant for the bad side of town."

She waited, to see if Sands would respond to this subtle overture. When he didn't she continued, "So, tell me, you spent some time with them today. Is it true that he's being groomed for political greatness? I heard he's got eyes on a seat in Congress. Isn't that what Tabor is angling for? I'd not put money against the Silver King of Colorado. Seems like a losing proposition, unless young Wesley has an ace up his sleeve."

Sands gazed at her, his own crystal cup of punch raised halfway to his mouth. "And where did all this conjecture arise from?"

She shrugged. "Talk at the Silver Queen. Men come. Men drink. Men gossip. Worse than women, actually. I'd say the more they keep young Wesley busy going from mine to mine and touring smelters and such, the better off he'll be. He seems to like roaming the red-light district. A young man's lark, I suppose. But such can be dangerous for those with higher aspirations, or an eagle-eyed mother." She sipped the punch and wrinkled her nose at the too-sweet taste.

Sands leaned forward, and said softly, "Don't underestimate Mrs. Wesley."

"I?" Inez feigned surprise and astonishment. "I've nothing to do with the woman. I'm just voicing what I've heard."

"General Grant!" A birdlike voice rose above the nearby swell of voices. "I understand you support women's higher education, is this so?"

The tumult quieted and heads swiveled to see who was speaking. A diminutive figure swathed in purple satin stood squarely before General Grant.

Chapter Twenty-two

"And in that case," Mrs. Clatchworthy continued, "Do you not think that the next step after supporting higher education for women would be to grant them the right to vote?"

As the crowd grumbled, two Leadville policemen appeared, almost as if they'd been primed for such a disruption. They grabbed Mrs. Clatchworthy's arms and escorted her out with such alacrity that Inez would have bet her purple dancing slippers did not even skim the ground.

Satisfied mutterings moved in a wave throughout the attendees. Inez heard a man behind her say: "Only a fool'd answer in the affirmative. Political suicide, it'd be, to back this folly of women's votes. And Grant's no fool."

Another, quieter voice answered, "Aye, but there are many who'd not be sad to see him hoisted by his own petard. And some who'd hurry him along to that fate."

Inez turned her head, searching out the speakers, but their voices had disappeared into the general murmur. The sea of men in somber black eveningwear gave no hint as to the speaker's identities.

Reverend Sands sighed. "Why am I not surprised. Pardon me, Mrs. Stannert. I want to be sure she is not mishandled nor mistreated. That she has a way home at this hour. I'll return in a moment." He guided Inez to an empty chair, one of many lining the wall, and began pushing his way through the crowd.

Inez, tracking Mrs. Clatchworthy's hasty departure, startled at a light touch on her shoulder. Mrs. Wesley took the empty seat beside her. "May I?"

"Please do." Inez was intrigued to have young Wesley's mother at such close quarters.

The opening notes of a quadrille sounded. Dancers paired up, moved to the center of the floor, and formed squares of four couples.

Mrs. Wesley stared at Inez with a discomfiting intensity. "You know my son."

Taken by surprise, Inez allowed a beat to pass. The music moved swiftly through the violins as she gathered her thoughts. Then: "Pardon me, Mrs. Wesley?"

"Lucretia. Please, Mrs. Stannert, call me Lucretia. I'm well aware of the business you're in. The selling of spirits. The corruption of young men's morals and their souls."

"Mrs. Wesley. I don't see, really, why *my* business is any of *your* business," Inez responded more politely than she felt. "And, as your son is well past the age of majority—"

"He's as ignorant as a child. A boy still in skirts." The fan she snapped open did nothing to hide the tightness about her mouth. "All that he is now, he owes to me."

"Indeed." Inez was intrigued. "And, why are you telling me this?"

"That woman." Lucretia nodded toward the door. "Do you know who she is?"

"Her name is Mrs. Clatchworthy. Our city's suffragist, is my understanding. Runs a small newspaper. Our paths do not intersect."

"Ah, but they do." The intensity had moved from eyes to voice. "She talks of votes for women. True parity with men. What do you think of that?"

Inez hesitated, thinking this was a very odd conversation to be having at a reception for General Grant. And even odder as it was with a woman she didn't know, but had been warned about. She took the neutral path. "I've no particular opinion.

Politics do not concern me, unless talk of such involves a large consumption of spirits at the Silver Queen."

Mrs. Wesley's eyes narrowed. "I have been here but a couple days, but I have my sources. After my son was so unwise as to wander into your *saloon*—" she made the place sound as unsavory as a whorehouse— "I put out inquiries. I was, at first, appalled at what I heard. A woman, whose husband deserted her, in business with her husband's partner. A colored man. This quite goes beyond the pale. But, this is Leadville, not Boston. I then learned that this woman is having a liaison with one of the city's most well-respected ministers."

Inez was speechless.

"No matter." The metronomic fan never missed a beat. "We all have our secrets. It just seemed to me that we might find ourselves with similar goals. And, if so, we might work together, at least for a time, to be sure those goals aren't derailed. But perhaps I was wrong." She began to rise.

Inez tapped Lucretia's arm with her own fan. "Wait! What do you mean, similar goals?"

Lucretia sank back into the chair. "Do you believe women should have the vote?"

"As I said, I haven't an opinion."

"Well, perhaps you should." Those eyes were dark enough to swallow all the light in the room. "As a woman who works hard, supports herself, does it seem fair that a man can simply come and reclaim all that you've done? I'm sure if you think about it, the answer becomes obvious." She leaned forward. "I lived a life like yours. All my work, all the benefit, all the plaudits, went to my husband. Not a bit to me. Then, he found a younger woman." She paused. "Alas, he met with an untimely end. I could have ended up in your place, but for God's will. As it is, my late husband's businesses and most of his wealth have passed on to my dear son."

Lucretia turned her head as if checking her son's whereabouts. Inez noticed that he was standing with the same group of young men he had been with in her saloon. Wesley's mother said softly, almost as if to herself, "I sent him to Boston to get a proper education. Set him on the road to greatness that is sure to come. If—" she turned around to face Inez—"he doesn't misstep."

Just beyond young Wesley stood Horace Tabor with the governor and his own circle of intimates. Inez noticed that Mrs. Tabor had withdrawn and was in conversation with the mayor's wife. In postures of man and wife, Inez sensed a separation far wider and deeper than the mere ten strides that separated them.

Almost as if she knew the direction of Inez's gaze, Mrs. Wesley continued, "Mr. Tabor has great ambitions. Ambitions not shared by his wife. Oh, I've had occasion to chat with Augusta. Her son and mine are of an age and struck up a recent friendship. Augusta and I have much in common. We come from humble beginnings. Our husbands made fortunes in silver—hers, here in Leadville; mine, in Virginia City. Yet, again, all the profits, all the benefits, go to the husband. Is that right, I ask, is that fair, when we put in just as long hours, kept the books, tended the business side as we would our gardens?"

I'm not like that. The thought flashed through Inez's mind, a stubborn denial. *Mark always gave me my separate cut of the profits when we were traveling. I never had to ask or beg for money. He won the Silver Queen in a poker game but split the saloon equally with Abe, his business partner, and me, his partner for life. I'm not like this embittered woman. What she is saying has nothing to do with me.*

"My son," Lucretia said, "has a gift. He draws people to him. He speaks, they listen, and they believe. He can accomplish what I cannot." She seemed to be looking beyond Inez, now, off into a realm far away from the stuffy, noisy, crowded reception hall. "He knows the depths of his father's sins, and the sins of men. He has a name full of destiny. John Quincy Adams, I named him so. It's a prophecy. He will champion our cause in Washington. Mr. Tabor cannot dictate the motion of the stars. My John will rise above him. The stars have said."

Inez had had enough. Enough of the over-sweet punch. Enough of Lucretia Wesley's odd ramblings.

The end of her patience coincided with the quadrille's end and young Wesley's realization of where his mother was and with whom she was talking.

Wesley hastened over as the orchestra struck up the introduction to a waltz.

Inez saw that Jed Elliston was also making his way through the crowd toward them on a direct collision path with Wesley. She had no doubt, given the narrowness of the reporter's glare and the general hungry look about him, that he was after Wesley for some journalistic tidbit or other.

Behind Jed, Kavanagh closed the gap between himself and Jed. Kavanagh's expression suggested that, if he had his way, Jed would not reach Wesley at all.

I need a dance partner. Jed is here, and he will do. And maybe I can find out more about all this business of son and mother.

Inez stood in a rustle of skirts and placed her half-empty cup on the small nearby table. "It's been a pleasure to meet you, Mrs. Wesley. I wish you and your son well. But I've nothing to do with politics. My life is full enough without taking up a lost cause." She smiled to lessen any sting from her words.

Before Mrs. Wesley could respond, her son stopped before them. "Maman." There was a touch of concern behind the filial salutation. The hint of a question. "And Mrs. Stannert, is it not?" He performed a bow and topped it with a charming smile. "Such a pleasure to meet you just now, in the company of Reverend Sands." There was a touch of warning in his voice that telegraphed to Inez: Don't say anything.

"Maman, are you feeling all right? I know it's awfully warm in here."

"Perhaps a touch tired. But it will pass. And this is such an historic moment. The reception. The Grants. The governor. And us here." Mrs. Wesley gazed at her son, years falling away as her face softened and brightened. She reminded Inez of a sunflower turned upwards to the sun.

Wesley smiled down at her indulgently. "In that case, if you feel well enough, may I have this dance? It will be my only chance before the politicians and giants of American industry present insist on having their turns with you on the dance floor."

He held out a hand. She placed her hand in his, and rose.

Inez hastened to Jed, planting herself in his path, between him and the Wesleys. He skidded to a stop before her.

"Why, Mr. Elliston, thank you, I would love to dance with you," said Inez holding out her arms and cocking her head to one side.

"Dance? Mrs. Stannert, if you'll excuse me, I have business with—" His gaze darted over her shoulder.

"John Wesley? Or his mother? Well, as you see, now is not the time to bring it up as the dance is about to begin, and they are engaged. Now, be a good fellow and don't embarrass me. After all, don't I allow you to run a tab as necessary?" Inez closed the distance between them and placed a hand on his shoulder, nearly forcing him to take her other hand in his. She lowered her voice. "I have information for you about the son and mother, and a few questions about them as well."

"Information?" He automatically placed his hand on her waist, his gaze pinned on the Wesleys as though he were afraid they might vanish into thin air.

Kavanagh paused in his trajectory. He then continued, bumping Jed's shoulder with an unapologetic "pardon me," before veering toward the refreshment table. Color flooded Jed's anemic complexion. He made to drop Inez's hand. She increased her grip to a ferocious pressure and murmured, "Don't give him the satisfaction. He's hoping to goad you so you'll be thrown out. Yet again."

The music began in earnest. Inez took a small step forward, forcing Jed to step back. They swung into the rhythm of the dance as Jed grumbled, "I should mash that fellow's head in."

"His name is Kavanagh, and he's only doing what he's been hired to do." Inez was gratified to discover that Jed was not a half bad dancer. In fact, he was quite good.

As they moved about the floor, Jed reversed his gaze to her. "So what was Mrs. Wesley saying to you? Was she trying to talk you into joining the Women's Temperance Union?"

Inez smiled at that. "Well, it was nearly as bad. In my view, anyway. Mrs. Wesley is quite the suffragist. Ah, I'm supposed to call her Lucretia. In any case, Lucretia was weaving a story about her son and how his path was set for politics. She told me that once he became senator, governor, president—the pinnacle of achievement she hoped for was a bit unclear—he would work for women's right to vote."

Jed's grip tightened convulsively, cracking Inez's knuckles.

"Uhng." It was a garbled, half-choked, completely nonsensical response.

Inez looked at him in alarm. "Mr. Elliston. Jed. What's wrong?"

He was gabbling fast, under his breath. Inez caught, "It's true! I didn't doubt, but I wondered. And now, independent corroboration! I can now state, 'a source close to the mother said.'"

"What are you talking about?"

His brown eyes burned with journalistic fervor. "Thank you, Mrs. Stannert. You have given me a great gift! Read tomorrow's newspaper and you'll understand." He whirled her in a tight, joyous circle. "I owe you. I will send every thirsty journalist I know your way for the rest of my days in Leadville."

"Well, you're welcome, although I've no idea what I said to make you jump so. If you really want to thank me, send not the penniless journalists, but the well-heeled investors behind the papers, if there be any." She smiled, to show she was joking, but just. "Now, what can you tell me about Mrs. Wesley and her son? Surely you've done some digging. I'm curious as to where they're from and how they made their fortune."

"Most of my information was picked up from the out-of-town scribes over beer earlier today." Jed led absent-mindedly, his thoughts elsewhere, but he continued readily enough. "In a nutshell, old Mr. Wesley—and he was old, by all accounts, nearly half a century—made it rich in Virginia City silver and married Lucretia Lawson, who was…well, her age varies from fifteen to nineteen. Miss Lawson's occupation at that time varies from runaway turned dancehall girl to daughter of a respectable man fallen on hard times. Anyhow, the Wesley *pater familias* died at sixty-five, having led a long and lusty—oh, pardon me, Mrs. Stannert—life. We'll not go into the latter, but it seems he never lost his taste for dancehall women. Ahem. I'll add, since I know you love a bit of rumor and gossip, that there was some question regarding the nature of his death. But, he was old, she was young, *and* lovely, *and* now very, very wealthy. Or rather, her son was wealthy, which really came down to the same thing in this case. So, mother and son relocated to San Francisco." Jed shrugged.

"We pick up a year or two later, when Mrs. Wesley, with all her charms and her departed husband's money, sends her son, John Quincy Adams Wesley—a truly ridiculous name, there— packing to Boston and the very respectable side of her family. By virtue of said money and Boston connections, J.Q.A.W. slides easily into Yale and subsequently joins a prestigious family law firm. John Wesley is then sent to Denver to establish a new office, and the happily reunited mother and son settle in the lovely city at the foot of the Rockies, where they make quite a splash, society-wise. And politics-wise."

"Thank you. Most interesting. You have also provided me with food for thought. I think we're even, Mr. Elliston."

The orchestra finished with a flourish.

"And thank you, too, sir, for the lovely dance." Inez could see Reverend Sands making his way to her, through the crowd.

Jed bowed over her hand, for once, the gallant. "The pleasure, believe me, Mrs. Stannert, is all mine."

Chapter Twenty-three

Zelda woke with a start.

The lamp, turned down low, guttered. Clouds had cleared, allowing a wash of moonlight to enter through the single window and bathe a swatch of the room. A slash of silver light touched the small hump that was Lizzie's feet under the coverlet and poured across the luxurious rug by Flo's bed.

She heard a crash as the Murphy bed in the room upstairs was pulled down, blocking the door shut for a modicum of privacy. A low murmur of voices, a squeak of boards as weight settled into the mattress, and then a muffled moan. The moan was replaced by the rhythmic squeak-thump, squeak-thump, squeak-thump of the Murphy bed alternately smacking wall and door as a customer proceeded to get his money's worth of pleasure.

Zelda snuggled back into the shawl, which smelled, not unpleasantly, of Flo's signature violet perfume and her distinctive muskiness. She closed her eyes, determined to ignore the sounds of purchased joy, if possible.

An unmuffled snort caused her eyelids to snap open. Zelda straightened up in the chair, looking around, trying to identify where the sound had come from. She stared, in disbelief, as the shrouded feet in the bed twitched.

The sound again.

A definite snore.

Zelda felt as if the spirit part of her was rising straight out of her body from sheer terror. It hung below the ceiling, observing, as her earth-bound body gathered its courage, rose from the chair, and crept toward the bed.

Lizzie's nose, which had been pointed up toward the rafters three stories up, was now angled toward the window. An unmistakable snore bubbled from the presumed-dead woman. Then, some murmured words stumbled out. "Don't, Flo. It's no good."

Zelda shrieked, ran to the door, and wrenched the French hand-painted porcelain doorknob nearly from its mooring before remembering that Molly had locked it from the outside.

She pounded on the panel. "Molly! Someone! Come quick!"

A hasty creaking of floorboards, the unmistakable rasp of key in lock, and the door flew open to reveal Molly and Danny. "What the hell is going on?" whispered Molly harshly. "What're you raising a stink about now?"

"I heard," Zelda pointed a shaking finger at the bed, "I heard Lizzie. She's alive."

Molly's and Danny's faces looked white as masks in the moonlight, dark shadows painted the eyes as empty while silver light glazed the cheekbones.

"She can't be." Molly hastened to the bedside, picked up Lizzie's hand, and let it fall. "She's cold as death itself."

"Look at her! She ain't all stiff. And I, I heard her snore. And, and she talked."

Danny, who had moved to the bed, swung around at her words, slow as a mountain pulled from its mooring, and stared at Zelda.

But it was Molly who spoke.

"You're dreaming, Zelda. It's a nightmare or maybe someone walked across your grave."

"Stop that! I heard her. She was telling Flo to, I dunno, to not do something."

Molly bent toward Lizzie.

Lizzie was mute, as if in defiance.

Molly picked up Lizzie's arm more firmly now, held the wrist, then dropped it. "Shit." She backed away from the bed, addressed Danny. "Go get Doc."

"She's alive!" said Zelda. "I told you!"

"Shut up." Molly said, staying calm. "Danny, go. Fast as you can." She turned to Zelda again. "I'm gonna close the door, lock it again. If something happens, just sit by her. Bring that chair over, and hold her hand. I don't want nothing to happen if… How could she be alive?" Molly's voice was full of wonder and disbelief. She turned to the immobile Danny and made shooing motions. "Go! Go!"

Danny lumbered out, Molly followed him. Zelda ran and grabbed Molly's hand. "Don't go! Don't leave me here alone with her!"

"F' fuck's sake, Zelda!" Molly spoke forcefully. "If she's alive, well, she's in a swoon or…I don't know! We're gonna get Doc here as fast as we can. Just…watch her! I've gotta get the johns outta here and make sure the girls stay in their rooms. I'll be back."

The door slammed in Zelda's face. She heard the key turn and the bolt scrape home.

Shaking, Zelda cowered by the door a while, before finally plucking up her nerve and retreating back into the room. She gripped the chair and tentatively drew it up to the bed. *It's okay. She's alive. I just gotta stay until Doc gets here. I'll tell him, then I'll skedaddle.* Zelda gingerly picked up Lizzie's hand, turned it over to bare the wrist. Zelda swore she could see a pulse beating slowly, under the cold, not-dead skin.

The hand twisted and gripped hers tight.

Zelda's breath stopped.

All seemed frozen, except for the thump of the hard-pressed bed above and other random creaks of floor planks and walls.

Zelda wanted to scream, but no sound passed through her constricted throat, no air entered her fear-frozen lungs.

She raised her eyes from the cold, steel-tight grip on her hand to meet Lizzie's signature half-mad, half-looped gaze. Lizzie's wide-open eyes bored into hers like a miner's drill. The hardened, malice-filled glare wavered. Then, in a slurred, but definitely Lizzie-like way, she rasped, "What the fuck're *you* doin' here?"

Before Zelda could respond, a blackness dropped over her head. A sudden crush banded her chest, slamming her back against the straight-backed chair.

She wrenched away from Lizzie's grasp, clawing at the band, the darkness at her face. The band holding her tight to the chair was an arm, clamped over her breasts, pinning her upper arms, unyielding. The darkness…a damp cloth pressed to her face with a gloved hand…blocked nose and mouth.

She couldn't breathe.

She tore at the gloved hand, her arms tangled in the shawl. Nothing moved that hand. It was as if a statue of stone held her in a timeless grip. She was vaguely aware of Lizzie—screaming? Laughing? The sound seemed far away and faint, far fainter than the heavy breathing of whoever held her to the chair, refusing to grant her the simple life-saving breath she fought for.

The pressure over her face lifted slightly. Zelda took in air in a huge gasp, cloth clinging to nose and face.

The air was sweet. Oh, so sweet. Fruity and sweet.

She was flying. Like an angel.

The creaking above her, the pressure across her chest, the rasping breathing of her assailant, Lizzie's screams, the sweet smell, all, all retreating.…

Chapter Twenty-four

The world returned with the suddenness of a snap, dark shades striped with palest gray.

Zelda blinked, trying to figure out where she was, what had happened, until she realized that she viewed a small slice of the room, from floor level, through a tangle of hair smothering her face. The prickly rug pressed into her cheek.

She rolled her head until her nose was facedown in the pile. It smelled of earth, wet, mold, mud, and things unmentionable. Zelda slowly pushed herself to sitting, and threw up on Flo's carpet—a gush of liquid and not much else.

It was only when she raised a hand to wipe her mouth that she saw, and felt, the dark, sticky sheen that covered it. At first, not entirely clear in her brain, she thought it was printer's ink from the work at *The Independent* that somehow got smeared all over her hands, the front of her dress, the rug.

Her hand brushed her lips.

It wasn't ink.

It was blood.

Zelda threw up a second time, more gag than anything else.

She shakily got to her hands and knees and saw, at eye level, a pale hand hanging over the edge of Flo's bed.

She gripped the overturned chair, pulled her tangled skirts away from her knees, and stood.

"Oh," she said aloud. "Oh. No."

Lizzie lay covered and surrounded by a blackness that soaked the sheets, the coverlet, and the pillow. Her eyes protruded, devoid of sensibility. A dark gash gaped at her throat—a second mouth, laughing up at Zelda.

Zelda stepped back, and her foot trod on something hard, unforeseen. She looked down and saw a knife, equally dark.

The import of her situation struck with the force of a slashing cut across her consciousness.

She whirled around, looking for someone hiding in the shadows, someone who would have placed her in this predicament: covered with Lizzie's blood, alone with the knife that killed her, in a room locked from the outside.

Am I dreaming? Shivering, she grabbed the shawl crumpled in a soiled puddle on the rug. As she pulled it tight around her, something clicked, a rattle of wood.

Her hand ran mechanically over the fuzzy white wool and closed on a string of beads. She pulled. The object tore free of the grasping fibers. It was a small, white necklace—a few large beads separated at regular intervals by smaller ones. A small white cross dangled from the loop, little shiny figure of Jesus spread upon it. The image of death almost made her drop it. Instead, she gripped harder. *It wasn't a dream! Someone was here.*

Tucking the object in her pocket, she moved more confidently to the window. The latch was still in place, the glass intact.

Next, she tried the doorknob. Still locked from the outside, and she with no key. Only now, when she released her grip, the knob was covered with her own handprint, etched in blood. She roughly scrubbed at her hand with the hem of the shawl and cast frantically about the room, ever avoiding the grizzly spectacle of Lizzie's dead and mutilated body on the bed.

It wasn't a ghost! It was someone real, but how…?

She tried to remember the moments before her assailant pinned her to the chair and forced the cloth over her face, and darkness descended. She remembered the bed jolting away above her. Nothing unusual there. The creaking of the settling house. Creaking. Like footsteps tiptoeing across the floor.

It had been behind her, she was pretty sure. She moved to the far wall and tentatively touched the gold striped wallpaper then traced its length with her shaking finger. A painting. A chest of drawers. Another high-backed chair. Flo's washstand. A big old clothespress.

Zelda stopped, then slowly backtracked and narrowed her eyes at the wall between the washstand and the armoire. She touched the thin, vertical line, the small bump of a break in the march of gold striped up and down, from ceiling to floor.

Was it a wallpaper seam, or the thin, almost invisible line of a hidden panel in the wall?

Miss Flo, in cahoots with a panel thief?

A confusion of voices outside the room interrupted her discovery; the turn of the key in the lock was like the rattle of a snake.

Zelda spun around just as the door flew open.

Molly stood, lantern in hand, with Doc Cramer beside her, his stovepipe hat a dead giveaway.

The lantern light threw a ghostly yellow cast over the blood-splashed bed and floor. Molly gasped. The light swung wildly. "Jesus!"

A muffled exclamation from Doc, who moved swiftly to the bed. "What have we here?"

Zelda stood, pinned by the light to the wall. "I didn't do it!" Her voice sounded shaky and unconvincing, even to her. "Someone came into the room. Put a cloth on my face, knocked me out."

"You little bitch!" Molly's lamp swung wildly as she moved into the room. "You always had it in for Lizzie. She was alive when I left her with you. The door was locked. You killed her!"

Zelda, propelled by fear, went to Molly. "I didn't! Someone got into the room, they put something over my face, knocked me out. Then, I woke up. Lizzie was dead!"

Molly stepped back, Zelda's fear reflected on her own face. Zelda realized how crazy that all sounded, with her standing there, covered in Lizzie's blood, the knife on the floor behind her.

"Molly! I'd not kill anyone, ever!"

Molly retreated even further into the hallway. Zelda followed her out, intent on making her listen.

Her arm was grasped from behind, and she heard Doc's voice, usually calm and jovial, now serious and without humor. "Young lady, you best wait with me. Miss Molly, we need to involve an officer of the law and determine what happened here. I will humbly offer my services to the coroner. Perhaps while I detain this young lady, you can—"

The front door opened down the hallway. Zelda felt a puff of cold air on her cheek. Then, she heard the gruff voice of The Hatchet.

Terror tore through her. She had a sudden vision of herself behind bars, her father on the other side, shock, disappointment, disbelief crushing his features.

Zelda violently twisted away with a strength she didn't know she had. The shawl was left behind, dangling in Doc's grasp, shed like an unwanted skin. She shoved at Molly, knocking her against the wall with a crash that rattled the statue of Aphrodite facing Flo's bedroom door.

Zelda gathered handfuls of skirts in both hands and sprinted to the back of the brothel. She hesitated at the back door, knobless and braced with nails pounded into the fire-weakened exterior walls. Using hands and a shoulder, she shoved the door hard. The nails and boards holding the door to the charred exterior had been meant to keep intruders from getting in, not a desperate soul from getting out. The door smashed open, bits of wood spraying.

Zelda raced out through the ruined mudroom and into the pre-dawn alley.

Chapter Twenty-five

Zelda stopped on the threshold of her family's cabin, panting. She pushed on her side, trying to stop the painful stitch pounding beneath the corset and ignore her screaming toes in the too-tight boots. Watching her breath form and melt in the almost freezing air, she tried to bring her disorganized thoughts into some kind of order.

Molly or someone is sure to tell Flo I kilt Lizzie. And Flo'll kill me if'n the police don't get to me first. Why does Flo care so much about her? She's nothing but a whore. It's not like they're kin or anything.

A sinking in the pit of her stomach told her that she was missing something. That for some reason or purpose she couldn't fathom, the whole of God's wrath was going to be visited on her for something she didn't even do. But it didn't matter the whys and wherefores. Zelda knew that she had to find a way out of town. Or, given that it was inching onto daylight, a place to hide for a while until she could figure how to sneak out.

Reuben's always at me about runnin' away and gettin' married. But I don't want to leave Pa here. It'd just be him and the idiot twins.

The thought of her father being at the mercy of her two brothers twisted her guts more painfully than the stitch in her side.

She opened the reluctant door as quietly as she could. The overpowering smell of rotgut liquor hit hard. She tiptoed in and paused by the two snoring, farting lumps by the stove, trying to decide which twin to trust.

She finally settled on Zeke, as he had always been the one, more so than Zed, to being tractable to taking orders and who tended to show more dutiful obedience to their pa.

Zelda leaned down, whispered "Zeke!" and put a quick hand over his mouth. A muffled snort and a quick thrash were her reply. She avoided the swinging arm and whispered, more urgently, "Zeke. It's Zelpha. I'm in big trouble. Now don't you yell none, I'm gonna take my hand away."

The thrashing stilled. She could just make out the gleam of his open eyes in the pre-dawn light. She tentatively removed her hand, and he sat up, whispering, "Zel! What's goin' on?"

She waved away the powerful fumes emanating from him. "One of Flo's girls, Lizzie, got kilt. And they think I did it."

"Hol-y fuck-in'—"

"Shhhh! Lissen, I need somewheres to hide. And I need you t' keep quiet about this. I hope no one comes up here, but please, if they do, don't let 'em question Pa. It'd break his heart if he learnt about me at Flo's."

"Okay, okay, I'll do what I can. What about your lover-boy?"

She thought about Reuben. "I gotta tell him. Jeez, maybe he oughta go with me. If the law comes up here and sees him…"

"Hey, they's gonna be innerested in you, not him."

She bit her lip, not convinced. "Maybe."

"Asides, without you workin', we're gonna need ev'ry cent— his and our'n—to keep us in grits," pointed out Zeke. "Shit! Who's gonna make the grits?"

"Don't worry 'bout that now. Just…where kin I hide?"

"I got the place. The closed-down shaft over yonder. Y'know, the one we're diggin' through. You kin use that rickety ladder, and you got two ways in or out. Here in the shack, or through the shaft."

Zelda frowned. The thought of going underground made her skin crawl. "I don't like closed-in places, Zeke. Asides, how do I get out through the hole in the shack floor if someone comes down the ladder? The entrance is under my trunk, and I'd have t' pound and holler."

"Don't worry. I'll fix it. I'll move your trunk and set a board an' that rug there instead so's you can move it easy. Asides, it's only for a couple days. I'll betcha no one's gonna care 'bout what's-her-name. Liz? I'll go into town and keep an ear out. If I don't hear any business about it, you kin clear town. Mebbe set up a crib in Denver and you kin send us money?" he sounded hopeful.

"That's a ways down the road, Zeke. Just help me hide for now. I don't want Zed knowing about this." She stepped over Zed's unconscious form to reach the tin box that served as their pie safe. Taking a rag from the meager pile of clean cloths, she stifled the small voice of conscience—*who'll do the wash whilst I'm gone?*—wrapped up a few hard-as-rocks biscuits, some cheese and jerked meat, and grabbed the long kitchen knife.

Zeke stopped her. "Here." He thrust his bowie knife into her hand, sheath straps dangling. "Take this pig sticker. You kin use it for the biscuits or if'n there are rats."

She recoiled.

"Naw, just kiddin', Zel. Don't worry. I'll take care of ya." There was a new note of authority in Zeke's whisper, a brotherly tenderness Zelda couldn't recall having heard before.

"Lookee here." Warm wool, redolent of Zeke, settled on her shoulders. "Take my coat. It ain't so cold for me. I'll bring more clothes later. And here's my canteen." He handed her a leather flask. The material felt damp and sticky at the same time to her fingers.

"Let's go, afore the cock crows," he added.

He opened the door. A slice of dawn slid in through the crack.

Hugging food and water to her chest, praying that she'd done the right thing in trusting this brother and that no harm would come to her family as a result of her bad luck, Zelda slipped out the door and followed Zeke.

Chapter Twenty-six

Inez rolled over in bed, yawning, and placed her hands over her eyes, pressing down on the lids. She willed herself to slide back down into slumber. *It's too early.* Beside her, Reverend Sands stirred and flung one arm across her, pulling her close. She allowed herself to snuggle against his shoulder, nose to warm skin. *If only this moment could last forever.*

But of course, it could not.

Sands stirred again. His arm slid away. She heard the hiss of sheets as he slid out from underneath them and the creak of floorboards as he moved about the room, gathering his clothes from the bedpost, the chair, the washbasin. A few minutes later, he sat on the edge of her bed, already dressed in drawers and trousers.

"What's the hurry, Reverend?" Inez reached over to trail one finger down his spine.

"No sermon to deliver, but one to prepare before joining the Grants and their party for this Saturday's tours." He pulled his undervest on. Inez's hand crept beneath the hem. She rested her hand on his back, feeling the muscles stretch and flex as he bent to draw up stockings, pick up a shoe.

"Command performance with the Grants?" she inquired. "And I'd assume that includes Governor Pitkin, the Routts, the Wesleys, the Tabors, and so on? You move in high circles, Reverend. Please pass along my salutations. I'll stand the gentlemen to drinks on the house should any care to amble into the Silver Queen at some time during their visit. Goodness knows,

Doc insisted I buy great quantities of Old Crow in honor of the general's visit. I'll even erect a plaque to commemorate the spot where they stand at the bar." She pulled herself closer to him, curling around him. Her hand circled around and crept down to the front of his trousers. "Speaking of standing erect…"

She heard an intake of breath, held for a moment in deliberation, then released in surrender.

She smiled to herself as a shoe thumped on the rug.

"And there goes my carefully constructed schedule for the morning." He twisted around to face her in the dark. "The spirit moves me to consider delivering an extemporaneous sermon on Sunday. Perhaps you might help me pick a verse to build a homily upon, since this change of plans can be laid directly at your door."

He bent down and kissed her as she put both hands to work undoing the buttons on his dress trousers.

"Hmmm." Inez lifted her throat as his mouth left hers and proceeded along the line of her neck. "I'm not as quick with the Bible as you are, but I've always found the Song of Solomon particularly moving." She slid his trousers off, hooking her fingers to remove his long underwear as well.

"You could start with, 'Let him kiss me with the kisses of his mouth,'" she said.

He complied, pulling Inez up and resting her back against the brass rails of the bedstead. The thin, intervening quilt that separated them slithered down to her lap. "'For thy love is better than wine.'" He whispered the words into her ear.

A convulsive shiver raced over her skin.

He continued, hand tracing the contours of one breast. "'We will be glad and rejoice in thee, we will remember thy love more than wine.'"

"You skipped some," she said, near breathless.

"I'm focusing on my favorite parts."

"Ah. Well. In that case. 'Tell me, O thou whom my soul loveth, where thou feedest, where thou makest thy flock to rest at noon.' And speaking of flocks, lambs and so on, have you…?"

He reached over to the spindle-legged table that served as a bed stand. She heard the crinkle of waxed paper as he extracted a French envelope from its wrappings. She draped her arms around him, pressed herself to his back. It was as if their skin had melded, leaving no boundaries between her flesh and his.

Inez sighed in satisfaction and anticipation as he finished his preparations.

Breaking from her grasp, he turned and gently lay her back down on the featherbed, saying "'O thou fairest among women, go thy way forth by the footsteps of the flock.'"

He settled above her and whispered in her ear: "'Behold, thou art fair, my love; behold, thou art fair.'"

At this point, she could no longer bring to mind much of anything about the Bible, much less the Song.

Finally: "'I found him whom my soul loveth: I held him, and would not let him go.'"

He answered, "'Thou hast ravished my heart.'"

After that, there were no more words.

◇◇◇

"I have a favor to ask of you, my love."

Inez opened one eye. The early morning light pierced her sight like a dagger. She closed it again and rolled to face the opposite direction, the direction of the reverend's voice.

"You mean a favor besides the one I have granted you in letting you keep an extra set of clothes here, and allowing you to leave your evening wear here, so that the good folk of Leadville don't see you strolling home at this hour still dressed for last night's reception?"

"Yes, Inez. A favor in addition to that one." Reverend Sands sounded amused.

She opened her eyes. Once again, he was sitting on the edge of the bed, pulling on his shoes.

"And what favor is that, pray tell, minister of my heart?"

Sands stood, moved to the washstand, poured water from the pitcher into the washbowl. "In addition to preparing my sermon this morning, my plans had included running an errand of mercy."

"Well, you asked for my help with the sermon. I trust that my suggestions and offerings were acceptable?"

He turned and smiled at her. "Very."

It was amazing how that smile could make her feel like the only woman on earth. Eve to his Adam. Until, of course, he smiled at other women. *Jealousy is cruel as the grave: the coals thereof are coals of fire, which hath a most vehement flame.*

"Pardon? Did you say something?" He paused from splashing water on his face and turned toward her quizzically.

"Just thinking aloud, coming up with a closing line for your sermon: 'For love is strong as death.' There you go. Homily completed. So, what is this errand of mercy you'd like me to run?"

He unhooked a towel to dry his face. "I was planning to drop by the jail, give Flo a copy of the Good Book, and deliver some kind words and encouragement. I thought I'd also find out who she's left in charge at her house, see if there's anything the women need after the fire, and encourage them to attend services tomorrow."

Inez rolled her eyes, unseen by the reverend. "Justice Sands. It never ceases to amaze me how you try to draw the blackest sheep into your flock. I know that Flo and the rest used to attend regularly, but that was last winter. Oh, how the town has changed, in just those eight, nine months, and the congregation with it. Consider how the women of the church view me, then multiply that a hundredfold. That is how they'd react if a pack of State Street prostitutes were to come traipsing into the church. Not to mention the consternation it would cause the good husbands who happen to have, shall we say, a certain intimate familiarity with Flo's women."

His face emerged from the towel, expression stubborn. "They are God's children. They have souls, as we all do. For all their trials and tribulations, their use and misuse and abandonment by others, they deserve more of God's—and our—love, attention, and charity, rather than less. They have a greater fight to fight against temptation than any others of the church. We should be providing assistance, not disdain."

Inez threw up a hand to halt the flow of words. "Justice. Reverend J. B. Sands. Please. You do not need to give me a sermon. It's the old biddies of the church you should be preaching to. And I know, if you were to say all this to them, they would gaze into your eyes, get lost in the music of your voice, and when you're done, they'd go off and whisper among themselves, 'Oh, that Reverend Sands, he is so ignorant of the ways of women! It's all right, he hasn't the slightest notion of what he speaks, but his heart is in the right place.' They always find ways to explain away your enthusiastic verbal transgressions, forgive your very generous acts of charity to the misbegotten, blame the saloonkeeper not the minister when you offer your arm."

The last slipped out unplanned. She shook her head, wishing she could take it back.

He stared at her, his countenance hardening. "I follow the path that my life set forth for me. I know the dark side, the low side, the despairing side of humanity. What it's like to walk through the valley of death and despair, believing there is no other way, no other end but a meaningless and final death, with nothing but oblivion beyond. It is the fire that tempered the steel of my life's resolve. This is the work I am here to do—reach out to others who are struggling on that same path."

He flipped the towel onto the towel rod. "I'm sorry, Inez. I don't mean to head down this road right now. I'm only asking this small thing from you, if you please. Go see Flo this morning. Go as a representative of the church. You can give her a Bible from the stack by my desk in the rectory or buy one at Warner's bookstore and tell them to put it on the church's account. It's a token and shows her I…we…care. Be kind to Flo. I understand that Officer Ryan has brought a long list of charges against her. She'll not be released before the end of next week, at the earliest. And she is the one that holds that house together. Who knows who will prey upon the women there while she's gone."

"Enough, enough. I'll do it. I have no grudge against Flo."
*Indeed, her fortunes are intertwined with mine. If her house falls,
I'll fall with her.*

The passing thought tasted bitter. Tasted of regret tinged
with panic. "I'll take her a Bible. Maybe I can even bring her
some decent food. I'll beg a basket from Bridgette. But I won't
tell her whom it's for. I'll simply say I'm off to visit a member of
the church, who's in need of comfort. That will do. She'll fuss
and tsk-tsk, and Flo will be the better for it."

"Thank you." His voice softened. "I didn't mean to lecture
or deliver a sermon. You are my soul, Inez. The light of my life.
'Set me as a seal upon thine heart, as a seal upon thine arm: for
love is strong as death.' Only I'd argue one point at the end: I
believe love is stronger."

Washed and dressed, he kissed her one last time. "You'll be
in my thoughts today. All day, every minute. I'll be by the Silver
Queen at ten-thirty to escort you to the banquet tonight."

Chapter Twenty-seven

Inez stopped before the doors leading to the county jail. She gazed at the brick building, which, although only one story, bore more than a passing architectural resemblance to Flo's brick brothel, and tucked a scented handkerchief up her sleeve for quick retrieval. A small pocket Bible, obtained from Warner's Books, was under one arm. The other carried a covered basket laden with the fluffiest of Bridgette's biscuits, a hunk of butter straight from the cooler and wrapped in waxed paper, and a brimming tin of stew. Inez couldn't figure out how to tell Bridgette that, without a knife, the butter would be useless, most likely melting into a puddle of grease in the overheated and crowded jail.

Inez pushed open the doors and entered, wending her way to the wood addition that held the guardroom and kitchen of the institution. The county jailer, Jake Miller, looked up from his morning paper and coffee, then rose to his feet when Inez brushed through the entryway. "Why, Mrs. Stannert, good morning!"

"Good morning, Mr. Miller. I'm here as a representative of the church to bring a few things to one of your inmates." She placed the book and the basket on the table.

"Smells like Mrs. O'Malley's doings here." He lifted the napkin and inspected the contents of the basket, then replaced the napkin and flipped perfunctorily through the small Bible. "And who's the lucky recipient?"

"Mrs. Sweet."

"Flo?" He raised his bushy eyebrows, then lowered them in a thoughtful frown. "That's right. I remember hearing she's kinda a supporter of Reverend Sands' church and all."

"The good reverend is busy today with the Grant party and asked me to come in his stead. He asked me to visit Mrs. Sweet and find out if there's any aid of a spiritual or material nature we might be able to provide."

"Well, let's go. Parsons' in there with Officer Ryan and some visitors for Flo, so he'll have the keys. We can just pound on the door that leads to the block. Now, 'bout the only thing that Flo needs right now is a ore-car full of silver, what with the fines, charges, and fees The Hatchet's got levied against her. Too bad she doesn't keep her money tucked in a mattress or safe or some such where it's easy to get at. Anyhow, The Hatchet's got such a bee in his bonnet over this, I think he'd make a stink if we let her go anytime afore autumn."

Inez sighed, and picked up her skirts to follow him into the jail proper. As they approached the door to the inner sanctum, it squeaked open and disgorged four people. Miller greeted Assistant Jailer Parsons with "How're the county's guests today?"

Parsons shrugged, holding the door open for the rest of his group to exit. "All enjoyin' their breakfasts. Well, the sane and sober ones are, anyways."

Inez and Miller moved to the side to let the others pass by. Inez identified one of Flo's women, Molly, her formerly wild red hair pinned up and under an elegant hat. The hat, a pale shade of gold, was of a match to her haute couture lilac and gold walking suit. *Business must be good if one of Flo's can buy such an outfit and drag it though the Leadville dust and mud.*

Molly stared straight ahead through reddened eyes, acknowledging neither Inez nor the jailer. Trailing behind her was Flo's doorman and bouncer, Danny. He looked at Inez sorrowfully, as if part of a funeral train. Bringing up the rear was The Hatchet. He stopped to have a muttered word with Parsons, then gave

Inez the once-over, face of stone, before following the others to the exit.

Parsons handed the keys to Miller, who turned to Inez and said, "Be warned, Mrs. Stannert, the smell here ain't pretty. We got a full house plus some right now."

Inez whipped out her handkerchief and pressed it to her nose against the reek.

Miller continued, "Gets so's you can't smell it at all after a while."

Anxious to get her promised task completed, Inez stepped into the jailroom. She paused on the corridor that encircled a large iron cage containing eight cells. As she stepped forward with the jailer, their footsteps clanged on the boiler iron floor. The ringing bounced off the brick walls and added the mutterings and louder vocalizations of the jail population. Flo had a cell to herself, close to the locked door leading into the cage.

Inez stepped up to the bars facing the outside corridor, staring. A worn but serviceable rag rug lined the iron floor, while a satin coverlet and a similarly covered tasseled pillow graced the iron bedstead. A gilt-edged mirror balanced on a washstand that held a porcelain pitcher and washbasin. Embroidered linen runners covered a wood table in the center of the cell.

Flo sat by the table in a high-backed rocking chair, a crumpled paper clenched in her hand. She wore a dark-striped princess polonaise, looking much like a proper woman set to receive visitors in her private parlor. Except for her eyes. Her gaze was locked in a prison of grief, anger, and something else. Fear, Inez decided.

The county jailer surveyed her cell. "Hey, Miz Flo, this is right nice. You've got all the comforts of home here. Nice of Danny and Miss Molly to bring the stuff in for you. And we sure appreciate the donation to the police retirement fund that you-all agreed to make when you are released. Now, here's Mrs. Stannert. She's come from Reverend Sands' church and brought some sustenance for you."

"Sustenance for the body and the soul," said Inez, moving forward with the book and the basket.

"Nah-ah, Mrs. Stannert. I got to be the one to hand these to her." Miller took them from her, unlocked the door to the cage's inner corridor, entered, unlocked Flo's door, and put the book and basket on the table.

Flo didn't even look at the offerings. "Jake, can I please have a moment alone with Mrs. Stannert?"

"Well now, you know an officer of the law has to be present and nearby," said Miller.

Flo looked at him imploringly, tears spilling out of wide blue eyes.

He cleared his throat. "Suppose I could go check the group at the other end of the cage. See if they are done with their breakfast."

"Thank you, Jake." Flo sniffed loudly, applying a lace hanky to eyes and cheeks.

Miller stepped out of her cell, locked it, and then deliberately turned his back on the two women. He strolled down the inner corridor, seemingly oblivious to the shouts and ravings of the inmates in cells to either side. "Hey jailer! When's the judge comin' to town so's I can get outta here?" "Jake! Goddammit, I'm sober now. Tell my wife to come on down and bail me out!"

Flo rose from the rocking chair and came up to the bars, gripping them with both hands. "Mrs. Stannert. I need your help." Her low voice was desperate.

"Reverend Sands asked that I bring you a Bible, and if there's anything the church can do—"

"To hell with the church!" She said this with such vehemence that Inez blinked.

Flo crumpled against the bars. Inez couldn't believe that the woman before her was the same cheerful, slightly scatterbrained prostitute she'd met less than a year ago. Or the practical, business-like madam she'd recently struck a business deal with.

She whispered, as if it hurt to say the words, "Lizzie was killed last night."

"You mean the girl that was found dead yesterday morning behind your house?"

Flo looked up, some of her spirit returning. "She wasn't dead. I knew it! But no one would listen to me, not even Doc." She bit her lip. Then, the words poured out fast and furious. "Molly and Danny were just here. Molly told me. They'd put Lizzie inside, just as I'd asked before The Hatchet hauled me away. The girls were taking turns keeping watch on her. And then, that bitch Zelda slit her throat and sent her to the other side for good."

"What?"

"It's true! Ask Molly. Or Doc! He was there! When they realized Lizzie still had breath in her, Molly sent Danny to fetch Doc and left Zelda alone with Lizzie. Stupid bitch!" she spit out.

Inez stepped back, shocked from the violence of Flo's emotion.

"Molly should have stayed with Lizzie," Flo continued. "She should have never, ever left Zelda alone with her. They didn't get along. I don't know why. Lizzie hated Zelda. Zelda didn't like Lizzie, but she didn't seem the kind to, to…Why would she do that after all I did for her?"

Inez was having trouble following Flo's anguished outpourings.

"Flo, wait. Doc was there?"

Flo nodded. "When Molly unlocked the door, there was Lizzie, throat cut, Zelda with the knife. No one could go in or out. It had to be Zelda." Her voice caught in a sob.

"Flo, I'm sorry. What a tragedy. I don't know what to say."

"Find her," hissed Flo. "Find Zelda and make her pay. Before she gets away. She has a father here in town, an invalid. At least that's what she told me when I agreed to take her on. With me more the fool. She just seemed like any girl, desperate, with no way to make money enough to live on. The law doesn't care about Lizzie. She's only a whore, throat slit by another whore. How…sordid. It's not what the city fathers want Grant and the governor to think of Leadville."

"Flo." Inez tried to break through the firestorm of words, striving for a tone of sympathy and reason. "It's very sad, I agree. Lizzie looked so young. But what good can come of trying to chase this down? Wouldn't it be better to let Lizzie's ugly end go unnoticed and simply give her a decent burial? I'm sure that Reverend Sands would deliver a eulogy, if you want him to. But think, think, if you give in to the desire to pursue this unreasoned fantasy of vengeance, think of what the unwanted publicity will do to your—"

Our.

"—Business. Was Lizzie with you a long time? Even so, surely you can see this makes no sense."

"No! *You* have to see." Flo's hand shot through a gap between bars and gripped Inez's shoulder, drawing her close. Flo whispered savagely, "Lizzie wasn't just some urchin I pulled off the street. Lizzie was my sister. My *little sister!*"

Chapter Twenty-eight

Inez stomped into the saloon in a foul mood. Flo's last words before the jailer wandered back up the block, jangling the keys significantly, had echoed her own fears. "Remember, Mrs. Stannert. You and I, we're riding the same horse. I need to get out of here before the whole cathouse goes to hell. Molly can only handle so much. She's prone to nerves. So many of the girls are. And with all the temptations close to hand. Booze, laudanum, ether, opium. I insist the girls not touch the stuff, but without me around…The Hatchet struck a deal with the judge or someone high up. He said, even if I get the money, I won't get out on bail for weeks. That's too late! Find Zelda today. Tomorrow. Tell me or Danny. I trust Danny; he's been with me forever. Tell one of us, and we'll take it from there."

I wish I'd never agreed to run Justice's "errand of mercy." I wish I'd never signed that agreement. Still, if I can only get through this. Surely SOMEONE at the bordello knows more about Zelda, who her family is, where she might have gone to ground.

In the kitchen, Abe was reading the paper while Bridgette fried up sausages.

"Mrs. Stannert, you seen all the hullabaloo in today's paper?" Abe tapped the front page of *The Independent* with his fork.

Her first thought was that it had to do with Lizzie's death, but she quickly realized that such an event, not all that unusual to begin with, would hardly rate front-page news. "Do you mean the fire two nights ago?"

"Nope. Although that's mentioned along with Grant's arrivin' in town. This is somethin' else, though. Looks like that young fellow, Wesley, has got hisself in a big pickle." Abe creased the paper and handed it over to Inez. "Got the words from some letters here, that he sent t' couple folks in town, sayin' he's all for Chinee immigration and women voting."

Inez grabbed the paper and read. "Interesting," she said softly.

"And why's that?"

"I had a very odd conversation with Wesley's mother at the public reception for Grant last night. Well, it was no conversation, it was more as if she was making a speech to me. She said her son had a bright future in politics and would be backing women's right to vote."

"Well, he'd be standin' pretty much alone if'n he did that," said Abe. "Don't know how the fella'd get elected, as there's no women votin' yet, only men. As for the immigration business, that's enough to get a fellow tarred and feathered in these parts. Suppose the only reason he isn't run out on a rail is that he wrote the letter to Harry Gallagher, and Harry's got a fair bit of pull around the town. No one's gonna cross him, not even over this. Although I wouldn't put it past the Silver Mountain Consolidated miners to get more than a mite upset about it."

She read to the end of the article and said, "Wait. What's this about a lascivious picture showing the charms of a seductress from the Far East? Is Jed making this up? How on earth did he get his hands on all this?"

Abe shrugged. "Guess you'd better ask him for the details."

"No thanks." Inez tossed the paper on the table. "I've enough to deal with at this point. Have you any extra sausages, Bridgette? I'm famished."

"Surely do, ma'am. How did the poor invalid like the biscuits and stew?" Bridgette stabbed two sizzling links with a long and wicked fork and placed them on a plate. "And did you bring back the basket?"

Inez had forgotten all about the invalid story she'd spun for Bridgette. She took the plate and sat across from Abe, giving herself time to think before answering. "She was most thankful and asked me to pass along her gratitude. I forgot the basket. I'll try to pick it up tomorrow."

Abe stretched his legs out, crossed them at the ankles. "Stopped at the post office on my way in. Got a letter for you, Inez." He indicated the cream-colored envelope on top of an already opened stack of invoices. "Looks like your sister's hand."

Inez abandoned the sausages. Using an unsullied cutlery knife, she slit open the envelope carefully and extracted a single sheet. The paper released a small whisper of her sister's lilac perfume as she unfolded it. The smell, combined with the sight of Harmony's handwriting caused Inez's throat to close up.

Harmony. Ten years younger. Calm and considered against Inez's impulsive and stubborn nature. Married well, as their parents wished, and stayed close to home, whereas Inez eloped and left without a backward glance, captivated by the Southern drawl and charms of a charismatic cardsharp and the lure of adventure out West.

Inez sighed.

And Harmony now raises my son. What would I do without her? We know each other's dreams, foibles, and darkest fears. I owe her so much. Who else would have taken in my little William, my life's greatest gift, with such love and compassion?

A second inner voice interrupted: *Were Flo and Lizzie close like this? If Harmony were—God forbid, murdered—how far would I go to find her killer and extract payment?*

Inez knew the answer to that. She'd pursue the murderer through the gates of hell without looking back. Kill him if she could, and hand the Devil her soul with no regrets.

"What's got that murderin' look on your face, Mrs. Stannert?"

Inez started, and looked up. Abe was leaning back in the chair, brown eyes quizzical, one long arm resting on the top rung of the ladder-back chair.

"A stray thought, that's all." She focused her attention back on the letter, scanning through news of her parents, the summerhouse, and the weather. The next sentences swept away the black clouds that had invaded her soul. "Oh! Listen to this. 'My best news I've saved for last. I have made arrangements with my husband for nanny, me, and little William to come to Colorado before the summer is out. I had pointed out that it has been well over a year since I've last seen you, that you are pining for your son, and that circumstances are such that it is far easier for us to come to you than vice versa. And, of course, to leave the busy life of New York for a brief respite at the Colorado and Manitou Springs shall do us good. I have had to promise that we will not, of course, come to Leadville, as my husband has read naught but ill of the violence and turmoil there. I believe he's thinking of the mining strike you wrote of in May? In any case, he refused to share any more information as to his misgivings, as he feels we women are too delicate for knowing much of the rough, violent worlds of men.'"

Inez stopped, aware that she was divulging much more of Harmony's inner thoughts to Abe and particularly Bridgette's avid ears than Harmony would no doubt wish. "Well, and of course, she goes on. In any case, the upshot is, I'll be able to see my sister and son again, come August!"

My sister. My son. She thought of the last cabinet photograph sent by Harmony, earlier that summer. The image showed a child, not a baby but not yet a young boy, still many years of skirts ahead of him. A face still familiar, but rapidly changing into someone she no longer knew. Her heart constricted. "It will be a long month until we meet," she said softly, then refolded the letter and put it back in the envelope.

Bridgette clapped a hand to her broad bosom, beaming. "What wonderful news, ma'am! And just think. You'll be able to take the train nearly all the way to the Springs." Her eyes clouded a bit. "Although the stage might be safer. I've heard terrible things about the trains, ma'am. How they fall right off the tracks in those narrow gorges."

"Piffle," said Inez briskly. "They are as safe as anything else—think of all the stagecoach accidents we read about—and much, much faster."

"Well, you got time to work that out," said Abe. "Right now, we got the piano tuner comin' to bring that old upright back into shape later this afternoon. Just thought I'd remind you 'bout that, so's you can be here when he comes."

"Thank you, Abe. I had forgotten. Too many things going on." She picked up a fork and pushed a sausage around the plate, drawing patterns in the congealing grease. "I'd better go help Sol. He had a lineup at the bar when I came through. It's bound to be a very busy day. A busy weekend."

"Afore you head out there, Mrs. Stannert, I've been thinkin'. About Frisco Flo's place. She was hopin' to move anyhow, last I heard. And now that young gal, Miss Lizzie, some sad business there. Flo's in jail...."

"And?"

"Just mebbe," Abe said. "We're in a position to strike while the iron's hot."

"Meaning?"

"C'mon Inez." He leaned forward, bracketed his empty plate with his elbows. "I know you've had your eye on that piece of property for a long time. Could be, we could swing it now. Talk to Flo, see if we couldn't increase her liquidity a tad and buy the building at a good price. Everybody'd win. She could move to that Fifth Street pleasure palace she's been talkin' about. We could open another place at the other end of the block. What d'you say, partner?"

"Ummm." Inez thought of her secret deal with Flo. The signed contract in the saloon's safe. The kitchen suddenly felt unbearably warm and close.

Sol threw open the door to the kitchen and without preamble said, "Mrs. Stannert. Good. You're here." He glanced nervously over his shoulder. "The Hatchet, uh, Officer Ryan is here. He wants to talk with you, ma'am."

Inez's stomach—sausages and all—did an uneasy lurch. "Tell him I'll be right out."

Bridgette brightened. "Oh, it's Officer Ryan? I had no idea he came here so often. That's what comes of being in the kitchen all the time. Tell him I'll bring him a cup of coffee with cream, the way he likes it, Mr. Isaacs."

Sol nodded and retreated.

Bridgette bustled around, remarking, " Officer Ryan, he's such a hardworking man. He's doing wonders cleaning up State Street from all the sin, may the Lord and all his angels be on his side. I know you and Mr. Jackson grumble about him collecting the taxes, but he's only doing his job. Which is more than can be said for others on the force! I don't know why you dislike him so much."

Inez laid her knife carefully crosswise her plate. *Oh dear. Apparently Abe and I haven't been careful enough about what we say and where we say it. If any of the things we mutter about The Hatchet should get back to him, he could make life very difficult for us. Even more so than he does already.*

She debated how to phrase a caution to Bridgette, but Abe spoke first.

"Well now, Bridgette, just 'cause we get crosswise of Officer Ryan from time to time don't mean he's all bad. I'd not be spreadin' around what Mrs. Stannert and me say in the back rooms, if you catch my drift."

Inez threw a grateful glance at Abe as Bridgette shook the long-handled fork at Abe like she was preparing to attack the Devil himself with one of his own instruments. "Mr. Jackson, I'd never! And besides, none would believe me. Those in a position to know say, when the plate is passed, those twenty-dollar gold pieces come from none other than his own pocket. Why, he's listed in the parish newsletter as one of the seraphim. And that doesn't happen with a penny-in-the-plate-on-Sunday churchgoers. And he's there every Mass. At least, that's what I hear."

Inez shook her head. "How many masses does your church have?"

"There's one every morning at six and two on Sunday. And, there's the Rosary. He's always at the Rosary on Monday nights when I go."

Inez went to the wall of pegs holding a welter of overcoats, hat, aprons, and umbrellas, asking over her shoulder, "Mr. Jackson, please refresh my memory. We *did* pay our fees this month, did we not?"

"On the twentieth, same's always," said Abe. "I handed him the money myself. Want me t' cover your back whilst you're facin' down the law?"

She paused, deliberating. "It might not be a bad idea for you to be nearby. Within earshot. Particularly since you were the one who ponied up for the fee this month."

Abe grinned. A flash of white teeth, slightly feral, against dark brown skin. "Understood, Mrs. Stannert."

Inez tied the apron around her waist and pulled her favorite coffee cup off from a shelf. Bridgette, who was preparing a cup of coffee on the table, jug of cream nearby, jumped forward, enormous enamel coffee pot in hand. "Coffee, ma'am? I was just pouring for Officer Ryan. How full would you like it?" She sounded anxious to make up for her verbal misstep.

"Half will do."

"Only half?" She sounded disappointed.

"For now." Inez held out the cup.

The Devil's own dark brew hissed out the spout.

"Cream, ma'am? I have some right here."

"No thank you, Bridgette. I'll top this off with something a bit more bracing to help me face Officer Ryan and whatever he may want."

Bridgette pursed her lips—her way of showing displeasure when she knew better than to voice it—doctored The Hatchet's coffee, and hurried out the passdoor to the saloon.

Inez sighed. "I had no earthly idea that The Hatchet was a papist. Much less, such a devoted one. Did you, Abe?"

Abe stood and carried his dirty plate to a nearby dishpan. "Nope. But I know plenty of men who found religion at about the same time as they found political ambition. If'n The Hatchet is gunnin' for the city marshal spot next April, he's doin' all the right things, gettin' hisself known in church circles, droppin' big coins in the plate, bein' kind to widows and orphans. Now, if he'd just give us a break on those taxes and fines he seems so eager to collect between fee days, I might just vote for him, too."

Inez snorted. "I'd not elect him for dogcatcher. Even if I could vote. He'd probably tax the poor dogs every time they howled."

Abe held the kitchen door open for her, and she walked out into the main room of the saloon, with all the dignity and poise she could muster.

The Hatchet stood, one foot on the rail, his cup of coffee steaming before him. Bridgette was chattering, hands wandering along the top buttons of her dress, patting her gray hair, done up in a functional bun. Sol jittered around on the other side of the bar, looking nervous as the saloon's cat, which Inez noticed was squeezed into the thinnest of spaces between the out-of-tune upright and the wall.

She slid behind the bar and set her cup of coffee opposite The Hatchet's mug. "Officer Ryan, what may I do for you?"

Hatchet turned to Bridgette and said, "Excuse me, Mrs. O'Malley. I've got business with Mrs. Stannert here. See you tomorrow at late Mass."

"Oh yes." She pinked high on both cheeks. "Well, the Devil loves idle hands so, back to the kitchen I go." She batted her eyes, adding, "I've a multitude of things to do before confession this afternoon," before beaming at him and displaying a missing incisor. "If you'd like more coffee, or some sausages, Officer, just let Mr. Isaacs know and he'll tell me and I'll bring them right out. Bless you, sir."

"Thank you, Mrs. O'Malley. Much obliged." He watched her go back to the kitchen, her ample hips swinging.

He ignored Inez for a beat longer as she drummed her fingers impatiently on the countertop.

Finally, he faced her, leaned over the bar, fist clenched, eyes narrow, jaw jutting forward. His words were completely unexpected. "What was your business with Flo Sweet at the jail this morning?"

Inez turned away to run a finger down a bottle of brandy gracing the backbar, giving herself a moment to collect her thoughts. *I might need more brandy than coffee to get through this conversation.*

She returned to the mahogany and The Hatchet, and poured brandy into her own coffee, remarking, "I went as a representative of our church. Is that a crime?"

"Don't see where any *proper* church is gonna care about the disposition of one of Leadville's most brazen sinners."

"It's exactly these lost souls that need our help most," she retorted. "'O God, the proud are risen against me, and the assemblies of violent men have sought after my soul; and have not set thee before them.'"

His expression was hard as flint. "You'd best not quote the Bible at me, and you'd best stay out of Mrs. Sweet's business. I seem to recollect saying something like this just yesterday. You must have a short memory, Mrs. Stannert." He straightened up. "I've come for the fee for sale of liquor."

"We paid the twentieth. As usual," she said tersely.

"Can't say I recollect such."

"You must have a short memory as well, Officer Ryan."

His fist, resting by the untouched coffee, clenched. Inez got the distinct impression that if she'd been male, she'd now be nursing a bloody nose for her impertinence.

"I'm city collector and an officer of the law. And I'm sayin', you owe for July." Dark violence threaded his voice.

The blatant lie just served to irritate her rather than set her quivering with fear. She glared back, not moving toward the cashbox under the bar.

"Something wrong, Officer?" Abe's calming voice, at her back.

The Hatchet didn't even acknowledge the question. Instead, he turned his back, rested his elbows on the bar, and leisurely surveyed the room. "Seems like there's gambling going on over there."

A small knot of men were playing cards. Another table was engaged in a loud and enthusiastic round of betting as to whether a fly would manage to swim its way out of a tumbler of whisky or whether it would drown.

"Your point being?" Inez asked coldly.

"Gambling's illegal in the state of Colorado," said The Hatchet. "Carries a fine of fifty dollars."

Inez's jaw dropped open. She snapped it shut with such ferocity that for a moment she was afraid she had cracked a tooth. "This is," she searched for a polite phraseology, "absolutely ridiculous. If you were to fine every single person and place involved in gambling in Leadville, you'd have to collect from every man and a goodly number of women."

It was almost as if The Hatchet didn't hear her. He was examining the far end of the room, by the piano. "I understand you staged some theatrical-type entertainment over the past few weekends."

"I believe you were here when one of the afternoon events took place," said Inez.

"I'm suspectin' this wasn't a benevolent performance to help out your church. Guess you owe the city ten dollars a performance. Plus another fifty for sellin' liquor at the same time."

Inez stared. "Are you trying to drive us into ruin? To hell with it! I will not pay!"

Abe set one hand on her shoulder, a warning.

The Hatchet reversed his stance, towering over the bar once more. His pupils mere pinpricks. "Use of obscene language, that's another fifty. And I recollect there's a hundred dollar fine for assemblage of women for purpose of attracting customers to a saloon. You had an actress here for those performances. Add you behind the bar, that's two women. Sounds like an assemblage to me."

Abe's hand pressed down harder on Inez's shoulder, a tactile caution. He guided her to the side, away from the escalating confrontation. "We'll pay the fines and the fees, Officer. You just set down what we owe, an' we'll do what we gotta do to make things legal." Abe slid a piece of paper over to The Hatchet, along with a worn pencil. "Just tote it up, there, Officer Ryan."

The Hatchet scratched out illegible notations, before saying, "I'm letting you two off easy, with a warning. Two hundred fifty will cover it."

"Done," said Abe as Inez gasped. "Miz Stannert, let's go on up and get Officer Ryan here the money we owe."

Abe propelled her up the stairs to the office, pushed Inez inside, and slammed the door behind them. "Don't say a word, Inez. Not a word. Now's not the time to argue with the law. All he needs to do is whisper in the ears of the right people, and we'll be shut down this weekend quicker 'n you can spit and you'll be cooling your heels in the calaboose. And you know how they's prone to forgettin' where they put the keys to the cells when it suits their purpose. You could be there for a long time. A month, more, if'n The Hatchet gets a mind to call in some chips at city hall."

"But, it's outright robbery! It's no different than if he were to pull a gun on us and take the cashbox! Except he's wearing a badge, which somehow makes it all legal."

"Inez, I hear you. Now, you hear me. We stand to make a hell of a lot more'n two hundred fifty this weekend alone, especially since we've decided to stay open on Sunday, this one time. Business keeps goin' like it's goin' the past couple days, we'll have enough to finish up your fancy gamblin' room up here, buy Flo's place, and who knows? Have extra to spare. I'm willing to give The Hatchet his due, and get him out of our way."

"Abe, don't you see? He's punishing us—me—for talking with Flo. What right does he have?"

"He's got all the right that the badge and the uniform give him. And that's plenty right now. Not only is he city collector, he's got most of the city council standin' firm behind him, 'cause he's doin' a bang-up job collectin' fees, fines, and such to fill the city's coffers. That talk that Bridgette was makin', it wasn't just

Irish blarney. It's a real possibility that he could end up bein' marshal come the next election."

Abe spun the dial on the safe, clicked through the combination and opened it. Inez, arms crossed, watched grimly. He counted out two hundred fifty in mixed bills and coinage. "We'll get a receipt for this," he promised as he closed the safe and placed the money in an envelope.

"A lot of good that does," she grumbled. "He just looks right through them when it suits."

Back downstairs, Abe put the envelope on the bar. "Here y'go, Officer. You can count it, and sign off here." He pushed the list of fines and fees so it lay side-by-side with the envelope.

"I'll count it later." The Hatchet scribbled an illegible scrawl on the list and pocketed the envelope inside his vest. He turned to Inez. "Keep your eyes on your own business, Mrs. Stannert. That's my last warning."

Inez deliberately turned her back on him, making a point of rearranging the pyramid of Old Crow bottles on display. She watched in the backbar mirror as The Hatchet headed toward the State Street door.

She grabbed the brandy bottle and slopped more brandy into her coffee cup. "That's a fine way to start the day." It wasn't until she picked up the cup that she realized her hand was shaking. Willing herself to hold it steady, she gulped the coffee, no longer scalding but tepid with alcohol.

"Easy, Mrs. Stannert. Gotta pace yourself this weekend." Abe moved the bottle out of her reach. "There'll be folks who'll pay to have some of that fine brandy. Can't sell it if you drink it all."

Chapter Twenty-nine

Inez was still smoldering over The Hatchet's behavior, Flo's strong-arm tactics, and the now out-of-reach brandy bottle when Doc showed up.

Inez smiled mechanically, not really taking him in except to note that he was limping more than usual. "Hello, Doc. You're here early. Aren't you accompanying Grant and the rest on their excursions to the mines today?" She looked around for Abe, to get him to pull down the bottle of pricey brandy he'd placed up high on a shelf on the wall. "Are you thinking of a nip to get your day started?"

"Just coffee, Mrs. Stannert. Just coffee."

His tone was so abrupt, so bereft of his usual jocular verbal circumlocutions that she stopped trying to get Abe's attention and turned to examine him. Doc's face was always loose in the skin, but today his face sagged even more than usual.

"Rough night?" Inez asked.

He hesitated, then admitted, "Not the usual house calls. In fact," he scrubbed at his face, leaving it looking even more tired and wrinkled, if that were possible, "I didn't sleep a bit after the call to Flo's early this morning. I'm still bothered by certain aspects of the whole incident."

Inez leaned over and set a hand on Doc's sloped shoulder. "Hold on, Doc. I'll get you some coffee and something to eat. Why don't you sit down over there?" She nodded toward an empty table, back by the kitchen, removed from the barroom's noise and commotion.

"Thank you, m'dear. I think I could take a seat. For just a moment."

Inez guided him to the table and went into the kitchen to retrieve a sizable mug of coffee and a plate with three sausages.

She delivered them to Doc and sat across from him, with a fresh cup of coffee of her own. He set his top hat to one side and pulled the sausages toward himself, tucking the proffered napkin into his stand-up collar.

"Thank you. This shall be the first food I've had today. I went from Flo's straight to the coroner's office." He cut up one sausage into precise, vertical slices, neat as a surgeon. "I shall have to head directly over to the Veterans Hall in a bit, make sure things are in order for the reception. Grant and all the veterans, you know. Just all us old War veterans, for a bit of reminiscing. Very informal. Very last minute. You are coming to the banquet afterwards, aren't you?"

"Reverend Sands will be picking me up after the reception."

"Good. Good." He was silent a moment, chewing. "It was a long night. First the public reception at city hall, then this business at Mrs. Sweet's place. No sleep at all. Used to be, I could go for several days on just a nap here and there. Ah well. I hope I might find a chair in a corner and catch forty winks before the veterans gather. With that, the banquet and the inevitable speeches, it could be another long night."

She clutched her cup and prepared to lay her cards on the table. "Doc. I should tell you. I went to the jail this morning. The reverend wanted me to visit Flo, bring her a Bible, words of cheer, and so on. It turns out, Molly—she's running the house in Flo's absence—had just been there. She had delivered the bad news to Flo about Lizzie." Inez took a deep breath, thinking that Flo hadn't exactly said it was a secret, hadn't asked Inez to keep a confidence. "I don't know if you are aware of this, but Lizzie was Flo's sister."

Doc set down the slice of sausage that he'd lifted halfway to his mouth, and lowered his eyes to his plate. For a moment, there was silence between them. He then said, "Thank you, m'dear, for telling me that. I didn't know. However, I wondered about their connection. Flo spent a great deal of time worrying over Lizzie. Asking me questions, looking for advice."

"Advice on what?"

Doc looked up. Hesitated. "Well, she's gone now. And it's certainly nothing new to the poor inhabitants on the line. Flo thought Lizzie was using laudanum, perhaps even eating opium. She was certainly drinking. Flo doesn't allow this sort of behavior, it's a point of pride with her that her women are clean and sober. So, she was desperate when she couldn't trace the source of the suspected drugs or where Lizzie got her liquor. Well, it's easy enough to come by all that and more, as a rule. But Flo runs a very tight house, you know. Flo is kinder to her women than most, and that's admirable, but I did wonder why she took so much time and care with Lizzie in particular. Why she seemed so desperate to help the young woman, who obviously was wrestling with her own demons. Now, it's clear. As I said, thank you, for helping me put the pieces together. I was intending to visit Mrs. Sweet next, to let her know what happened. I'll be better prepared knowing what you've told me about that relationship and about Molly having already delivered the sad news."

Doc tipped the brim of his top hat up off the table, as if to see if any other dark State Street secrets might crawl forth.

"Doc." Inez pushed her cup to one side and leaned forward. "What happened last night? Flo swears up and down that a girl called Zelda killed Lizzie. Apparently, the room was locked, and it was only Lizzie and Zelda in there."

"Yes, I was with Molly when she unlocked the door to Flo's room. Danny, their doorman, had secured my services and brought me there." Doc pulled on his lower lip. "It was a scene of carnage. Lizzie apparently had revived from a deep coma. It was I who had pronounced her dead initially, you know. A mistake I shall carry with me for a very long time. However, once Lizzie revived, someone cut her throat. It was a vicious slice, came close to decapitating her."

Inez winced.

"When we opened the door, the girl Zelda was there." Doc hesitated. "Odd, but I could distinctly smell chloroform. The anesthetic. She kept insisting that she did not kill Lizzie. That there had been a mysterious intruder. Could it have been a hallucination? Could Flo's girls be indulging in a variant of ether frolics? It could be they've turned to that, since laudanum and whiskey are forbidden in the house." He seemed to be talking to himself.

"Ether frolics, I've heard of. But I had no idea that chloroform could be used in such ways."

"Ah, m' dear. Chloroform, ether, opium, chloral hydrate, and even your good brandy and lesser whiskey can be used for good or evil. On the one hand, as a physician, I've had many occasions to bless the anesthetics, opiates, narcotics, morphine, even cheap rotgut, for bringing relief to the patient. And, on the other hand, as long as the world is as it is, with its pain, suffering, and disappointments, a certain percentage of humanity will become beguiled by opium, chloral, and other deadly drugs and develop morbid cravings."

"But chloroform?" She raised her eyebrows.

He nodded. "Good for the surgery and for insomnia, chronic pain, asthma, and chronic cough. Why, I've found it offers a welcome respite to those suffering from miner's consumption, when used properly. I prescribe it, in moderation, as do other physicians. To self-administer takes a steady hand, an iron will, and a thorough understanding of the drug's limitations. It has a pleasant smell, rather like apples, and the sensation it provides has been described as," he harrumphed, "intoxicating. Which leads some to indulge over and over. But the line between sedation and death is a thin one. It is not a drug to trifle with. If Mrs. Sweet's women are playing with such, I must have a serious talk with them." He shook his head. "Still. If Zelda took chloroform to perhaps calm her nerves, took overmuch and became comatose, how did she kill Lizzie? Perhaps she administered the chloroform to Lizzie first. But to kill Lizzie and then take the sedative herself? Any way I look at this, it makes no sense."

"What happened after you unlocked the room and found Zelda?" Inez prompted, trying to steer Doc back to the story and away from his pharmaceutical speculations.

"We prepared to detain her, but, well, she slipped my grasp. She was heading out of the bedroom. I caught hold of her shawl, but she was remarkably fast on her feet and escaped out the back." He tipped his top hat again, releasing the darkness beneath. "Neither I nor Molly were prepared to chase her. I was left holding the shawl. And I tell you, the shawl was bloody, but it held the scent of chloroform. And that is what I cannot understand. There was no vial in the room. No handkerchief used to deliver the vapors to the face, as you might expect if someone were using it for entertainment. So, where did it come from?"

He, released his hat, leaned back in his chair, and stared at Inez. "Zelda is a little thing. Short of stature. She did not appear to me to be the sort who could wield a knife with such strength as to cut deeply with one pass. So, I'm troubled. Troubled by the whole incident. But, this could be no more than an old physician's doubts and cautions catching up with him. Back when I was a young physician, we were embroiled in war. *The* War. There was no time for pondering when the patient lay screaming beneath the saw. There was never enough ether, or chloroform, or whiskey for the tasks at hand. We had to move fast, finish the procedure, and move on to the next."

Doc stopped, then continued, "Lizzie was killing herself by degrees, for whatever reasons. She will most likely not be mourned by any besides Flo."

He glanced down at the remains of the sausages. "Thank you, m'dear. Perhaps I can put it out of mind for now. There is so much more to do today."

He looked at her and smiled, obviously trying to inject some of his old heartiness back into his voice. "We will see you tonight. And," he shook a finger at her playfully, "I warn you.

I'm still maneuvering behind the scenes to bring the general by your establishment for a shot of Old Crow or a hand of cards. Old soldier that he is, I think he would appreciate both of those things, with a good cigar, more than all the full-dress banquets and grand balls put together."

◇◇◇

Shortly after Doc left, Bridgette bustled off to church and confession, promising to return as soon as she could. "It's really important I go today, ma'am, since I'll be working on the Sunday tomorrow and missing Mass. No, no, ma'am, it's one time, I understand, and I really don't mind. But it is a neglect of my Sunday obligation and a sin. I've not missed Sunday Mass in years, so I want to let the good Father know so I can get busy on my penance."

A while later, Sol ushered a cadaverous fellow over to Inez, who was completing negotiations with their liquor wholesaler over an incoming shipment of California wines.

The fellow set his worn leather bag on the bar with a clank. "Mrs. Stannert?"

She smiled. "Mr. Lang! You're here to resuscitate the patient over by the wall? I warn you, this one's not nearly as hearty as my parlor grand at home."

He adjusted his pince-nez. "Some think they'll become rich by finding silver. They should take up the piano tuning profession. The burgeoning interest in the musical arts along with the dry air and extreme changes of temperature keep me busy. I never have a moment's rest, and my bank account thrives."

Inez ushered him over to the upright, commenting, "She's seen better days."

"Let's see what I can do." Lang played various scales and tested the action of the pedals before opening the top of the cabinet and peering inside at the workings. He pulled a variety of tuning hammers, wrenches, and mutes from his bag, and set to work.

An hour later, he approached Inez, who was wiping up a spilled glass of beer. "Mrs. Stannert, why don't you try her now?"

Inez wiped her hands on her apron, slid onto the piano stool, and ran through the scales, testing the piano's range. "Lovely, Mr. Lang. At least, as lovely as she's ever sounded. You are a true artist."

His dour face creased into a rare smile. "More in line of a physician, I'd say. But thank you, Mrs. Stannert."

"Mr. Jackson will pay you," said Inez. "And have a drink on the house."

"Much obliged." He settled his hat and moved to the bar.

Inez tinkled through a bouncy rendition of "In the Evening by the Moonlight." Emboldened by the piano's improvements, she moved into more demanding terrain. The opening chords of Chopin's Waltz Number Seven flowed unbidden from her hands to the keys. She allowed herself to drift on the melody line. But the music insisted, her hands required, that she pay attention. She bent her head to the keyboard, and focused. The music moved slow, faster, faster, then drifted again. All else receded. The voices in the room, the smoke in the air, the hollow hammer of boots on the floor, the opening and closing of the nearby door. The music seduced her, as it always did, with the brilliance of fire, the surety of a flood.

As the last notes died, there was a smattering of applause. A nearby voice said, hesitant, but approving, "Nicely done."

She swung around.

The mapmaker stood there, board and papers clutched to his sack jacket. His eyes shone above his purple, swollen nose. "Chopin Valse Number Seven. Opus Twenty-seven. I particularly enjoyed how you played Part A. Very nice."

She smiled, then stood. "Thank you. Do you play? You sound as if you know something of music."

He hemmed and glanced uneasily around the room in general and back at her. "I have done my share at the keyboard."

"Well then?" She gestured to the stool, the invitation implicit.

After a pause, he placed his board and coiled tapeline on the staircase and approached the stool. He sat. Stood and corrected the height. Sat again. Ran his hands tentatively over the keys.

He had, she noticed, unusually long fingers. After a little wandering, he launched into the same waltz. But with a difference. The waltz snapped with aggression and a very controlled pedal.

She'd never heard the piece, usually rendered romantically, played in such a fashion. When he finished, she applauded, noting, "The counter melody within the arpeggio. Very clever. As was that left-hand variation."

"My own interpretation. I'm surprised I still remember it."

"You have a rare talent, Mr. Farnesworth."

He seemed abashed by her praise. "Once, I thought on being a concert pianist." He looked at the keyboard and said under his breath, "But it is no way to make a living."

"Why, we could use a part-time pianist here. Are you interested?"

He stood hastily. "I haven't played since—" He stopped. Then, at her inquiring silence, finished. "Since my fiancée died."

"I'm so sorry."

A furtive look flitted across his face. "It was a long time ago."

Inez injected a brighter note into her voice. "Well, in any case, Mr. Farnesworth, it's good to see you again. Last I saw you, you were—" She stopped, realizing that in her desire to take the conversation in another direction she may have inadvertently strayed into another mine field.

"—having my face ground into the mud," he finished bitterly. "I had nothing to do with that woman's demise. In fact, the local police told me this morning that I am exonerated of her death. She apparently was still alive yesterday."

He gathered his papers and his tapeline. "I've got to finish the job I was sent to do. Mrs. Stannert, may I see the upstairs?"

◇◇◇

After tapping walls, measuring windows, asking about the construction of the building, and examining the ceilings, Cecil seemed satisfied. "Thank you."

"And have you finished all of State Street now?"

He shook his head, somewhat despairingly. "This block is a warren of shanties back by the alley. Getting access to them, and even to some of the larger buildings, is proving difficult. I still haven't completed my examination of that brick structure, the boarding house at the corner of Pine and State." A grim expression crossed his countenance briefly, like the shadow of a passing cloud. "I've no choice but to complete the job. That's what the Johnson Fire Insurance Company has hired me to do."

He was following Inez down the stairs when Bridgette came in. She looked up at Inez with a broad smile that faded as her eyes widened. Cecil Farnesworth, focused on his notes, glanced at Bridgette, then back down. Inez paused at the bottom of the stairs, watching as Cecil made his way through the saloon to the State Street door, shoulders squared, board clenched to his chest. A strange sputtering sound caused her to turn to Bridgette, who had her gaze glued to the mapmaker's departing back. "Do you know him, Bridgette?"

"Well, not exactly, ma'am. He's a stranger to me. Not someone of the parish." She played with the fringe on her shawl, staring distractedly at the now swinging door. "But, he's of the faith. You see, I saw him. That man. At confession. I recognize the nose, poor fellow. He was before me. And, I don't listen, ma'am, that isn't seemly to listen to another's confession, but he was loud and…he was crying, ma'am. Crying in the confessional. It was the nature of the sound that caught my attention. I don't know what demons haunt his soul, but from the sound of it, I'd say it will take more than a stray confession in a passing town to bring him any lasting peace."

Chapter Thirty

After the dinner rush, Jed showed up, enormous circles under his eyes. He was immediately besieged as he walked in the door.

"Hey! Elliston! Good issue!"

"That bit about that upstart Wesley. How'd you come by that?"

"Sources that wish to remain anonymous," he said mechanically.

"Ya sure scooped the competition. Not a word of this anywhere else."

"Say, what's this about a lewd photograph? You gonna share the details if I buy you a drink?"

Elliston didn't answer. He simply removed his hat and set it with precision on the bar.

Inez noticed that his usually carefully groomed hair was in disarray, as if he'd rushed out of his rooms without more than a desultory combing that morning. An uncharacteristic faint stubble shadowed his usually clean-shaven face. He was but a rumpled shadow of his self on the previous evening at the reception.

"Whiskey, please, Mrs. Stannert."

"What? You're not going to celebrate your good fortune with something a little more substantial?" Inez turned to scan the bottles on the backbar for something better than the usual firewater.

"I'll celebrate later." He scratched his chin, as if suddenly aware of its sandpapery condition. "Say, can I get whatever the daily special is? I've not eaten yet today."

Inez tipped some Old Forester into a glass and looked at Jed with concern. He was the kind of fellow who preferred to take his meals at the finer venues around town—the Saddleback, the Clarendon, or the Clairmont—the better to see and be seen and to pick up high-grade gossip and the latest news.

"Well, Bridgette has a quantity of excellent stew and fresh biscuits. There might be sausages from this morning."

"Sausages sound good." He took the liquor in a gulp and didn't even shudder. Inez waved down Sol, who was doing double-duty as waiter that day, taking orders for comestibles. He scribbled down Jed's order and disappeared into the back with a handful of slips.

Inez leaned on the counter. "Jed. What's wrong?"

At that moment, the door blew open. John Quincy Adams Wesley stormed in, trailed by an avid pack and the unflappable Kavanagh. Wesley stopped, blocking the entrance yet again, looked around, and—

"Coward!" He stalked toward Jed.

His followers fanned out around him, an assemblage that included his usual coterie and a congregation of newspapermen, including, Inez noted, several of Jed's competitors. The pencil-pushers hung back, eyes bright with the eagerness of newshounds scenting a story in the making.

"Here you are. Hiding. I tracked you here after inquiring at your usual haunts. Flushed you from your liar's lair. How dare you, you damned deceiver, teller of false tales, prevaricator, fraudster. My mother is prostrate. Distraught. Due to you and your lies."

Jed visibly pulled himself together, squared his shoulders, and turned. "Mr. Wesley. Good afternoon to you as well. Your complaint being?"

"These, these, damnable lies! Fantasies fabricated from your febrile imagination!" Wesley thrust a crumpled copy of *The Independent* under Jed's nose. The two men were of a size, but

Wesley's commanding presence and palpable anger set him degrees above the newspaperman.

Inez glanced over at Abe, who had taken a station by the shotgun hidden under the bar. He nodded fractionally to her.

Inez turned back. A heated political argument and shouting match was one thing. Should things turn physical, however, that was something else.

Jed was talking, his stubborn won't-give-an-inch streak reasserting itself. "I have my sources. My proof. I stand by my words."

"Proof!" Wesley spat. "What proof? Show it to me!"

"Letters from your own hand," said Jed staunchly. "On your letterhead. The first is addressed to none other than the owner of Silver Mountain Mining, Incorporated, Harry Gallagher. All here know that Harry would jump at the chance to fill his mines with cheap labor, from the Orient or otherwise, and throw honest men trying to support their families out of work. The other letter, again on *your* letterhead, is addressed to Mrs. Clatchworthy, who is the most ardent supporter of this ridiculous movement to gain women's suffrage. A movement nipped in the bud, and rightfully so, by the faithful voters of Colorado a mere three years ago. Granted, women gained school suffrage, but that's hardly the same as—"

"Do. Not. Lecture. Me. About. Politics." Wesley ground out. "You obviously know nothing, nothing, about my beliefs or my political stance. I don't recall you interviewing me or approaching me in any way about my stands on various issues."

"I tried, but your *bodyguard*," Jed threw a meaningful look at the lurking Kavanagh, "has seen fit to check me at every opportunity. Since you refuse to talk to the free press, we must get our facts in other ways. For instance, it's well known that Lucretia Wesley—"

"Keep my mother out of this!" Wesley shouted the words, drowning him out. "Her views are her own and do not necessarily represent mine. She has naught to do with this."

"And naught to do with your unnatural proclivities?" sneered Jed.

Wesley's face paled.

The mob closed in.

Abe brought out the shotgun and set it on the bar with an audible *clunk* that sounded loud in the sudden silence of the saloon.

The passdoor to the kitchen swung open with a loud scrape and squeak. Sol emerged, balancing a tray holding bowls of stew, cups of coffee, and precariously perched plates of sausages and biscuits. He stopped, mid-stride, tray before him like an offering.

Inez interrupted the tense silence, using a tone of almost motherly severity designed to defuse the situation. "Gentlemen. Civilized arguments on politics and differences of journalistic opinion are well and good and welcomed here at the Silver Queen. But I warn you, should this war of words escalate into violence or if we even sense a hint of impending fisticuffs—"

Far from pouring oil onto troubled waters, Inez's words had the verbal effect of tossing a match to a container of kerosene.

"A black eye or broken jaw wouldn't even begin to compensate the injury you've done to my mother's and my honor by printing those lies and blasphemies, you bastard," hissed Wesley. His large dark eyes had a nasty gleam to them now.

Inez noticed the fourth estate scribbling in their notebooks, pencils on paper sounding like the scrabbling claws of rats.

Perhaps Jed heard the noise as well. He took a step forward and said in a steel voice that Inez barely recognized, "Call me a bastard. Call me a son of a bitch, if you wish. But do *not* call me a liar. I have proof. Proof for everything that appears on the front page of today's *Independent* newspaper."

His voice carried to all corners of the room.

Inez winced. *Now's not the time to try to increase your circulation, Jed.*

"Liar!" Wesley shouted. "If you have proof, show me. You have until tomorrow night to produce your 'proof.' I challenge you to meet me at the portion of track where General Grant disembarked. Sunday evening. Six o'clock. Bring your pistol if you wish to defend your nonexistent honor. If you are not there, with your gun or your proof, I will hunt you down and kill you like the dog you are!"

Jed locked eyes with the newsmen in the audience. "Gentlemen. I invite all of you to be present at that time. Where Third Street crosses the Denver and Rio Grande track and becomes the Boulevard. You can examine the letters and the inscribed photograph for yourself, and cast your own votes."

Wesley glared around at the room, gaze murderous. "You should *all* be there to see this sorry specimen of the so-called free press receive his comeuppance or die. He'll be coming with his tail tucked between his legs. He will bring no proof, because there is none." He swung back to Jed. "Who paid you? Which of my enemies paid you to tar me with such blatant corrupt deceits? Whoever they are, they are on the side of those who are working against my goals of bringing political parity to the common man. I shall drag the names of those responsible from you if I must disembowel you in the process."

With that, Wesley cast the crumpled newspaper into a nearby cuspidor, where it floated soaking up the brown oily liquid. He stormed out of the saloon, his entourage following like a shadow at his heels. Kavanagh brought up the rear. Inez saw him unobtrusively reholster his long-barreled revolver under his coat.

A chill prickled her neck.

Kavanagh caught her gaze and lifted his eyebrows as if to say, "Now *that* was a close one."

The door closed with finality on his heels.

Inez released her held breath. Beside her, Abe did the same. A moment later, everyone else stirred. Glasses held at half-mast clinked down on tables. Others were lifted and contents emptied. Chairs shifted back, voices rose in a speculative murmur.

"So how's your aim, Elliston?" called out one wag.

"Good enough."

Inez, standing close by, caught the faintest quiver of fear underlying Jed's enforced bravado.

"I'll give two-to-one odds on our local scribbler here besting that Denver whelp tomorry night!" shouted one of the card players at a back table.

Cries of "Done!" and "I'll take those odds!" were interrupted by proposals offering alternative odds on one side or the other, including: "ten-to-one on young Wesley. I've seen Jed try to shoot!"

Laughter and protests as to supporting one of their own versus the "outsider" erupted.

Inez reached over and tapped Jed's arm. He whirled around. His eyes were as wide as a deer's facing a forest fire bearing down at full speed.

"Mr. Elliston, allow me to offer a round for the house, and to place a private bet on your behalf," she said loud and clear for all to hear.

A general hurrah arose, and patrons raised glasses empty or near so. Abe looked disgruntled.

"Too many free drinks these days," he grumbled.

She leaned over and murmured, "The rotgut is fine. If it's free, they don't care what kind it is."

"Your call, Mrs. Stannert," was his reply. He began pulling bottles of their cheapest out from beneath the backbar. Sol brought a plate of sausages to Jed before grabbing several bottles to fill glasses waving from various tables about the room.

"Mr. Elliston." Inez released his arm and took the sausages hostage. "Please, come up to the office. Let's discuss what odds you think I should favor for this contest between freedom of the press and the overweening ambitions of politicians still wet behind the ears."

She came around the bar, took his arm, and, holding out the sausages as an inducement, dragged him upstairs.

Once in the office, she closed the door for privacy, guided him to the worn velvet loveseat, and pulled out a bottle of her private stash of brandy from its place of honor on her roll-top desk. She poured two glasses and handed one to Jed, who sat staring at the untouched sausages on the plate.

Inez lowered herself into her rolling desk chair, then pulled it forward with a squeak of wheels so she could better gauge his expressions and ascertain when he was telling her the truth and when he was lying.

"Jed. Look at me."

He looked at her. Dejection and panic clear on his face.

"You have the letters and the photograph?"

"As I told you at the reception, they were delivered last night in a single envelope—"

"Do. You. Have. The. Letters?" she emphasized.

He didn't answer.

He didn't have to.

"And this purported image, this lewd carte de visite?"

His shoulders slumped further.

"Jed." She injected a note of urgency into her tone. "What possessed you? It's one thing to make up stories of swells picking silver up off the ground on Capitol Hill on their way to the opera. It's quite another—"

"I had them. Had them all," he said. "I gave them to my typesetter to put in the desk. I had to get to Grant's reception. When I went to the office this morning, they weren't there."

"Well, where is this typesetter of yours? Perhaps he inadvertently took them home. Given the nature of the photograph, I suppose I could understand if he—"

"She! She was a woman."

Inez blinked. "What? Who was a woman?"

"The typesetter." He shoved the plate of sausages off his lap and onto the nearby table, and clasped his hands between his knees. "I'd just hired her. She and I worked together all day yesterday. She was quick to learn, I was patting myself on the back for having found a typesetter I could count on. I even paid her a full day's wages! But then, when the letters and photograph weren't in my desk, and when she didn't show up this morning… Oh hell. Could she have been in on this? Have I been played for a dupe?"

He looked at Inez, agony on his face.

Inez tried to think. "What do you know about her? What's her name? Do you know where she lives? Anything?"

He sighed heavily. "Her last name's Thomas, first name Zel, or some variation of that. She lives with a blind father and a couple of young twin brothers on Chicken Hill. I looked through the city directory. I even went up to Chicken Hill this morning and asked around. There are a fair number of Thomases up there. No luck."

Inez sat back, thinking. "Thomas might not be her real name. Who knows if anything she said is true? It could be, Jed. It could be that you were taken. What kind of a shot are you?"

He closed his eyes. For a moment, with his hands clenched, he looked to be in prayer. He opened his eyes. "Not all that great. A duel? Jesus, he'll kill me. If he doesn't, the publishing fraternity will stick their quills in my heart and finish me off."

He loosened his hands, picked up the brandy snifter, and drained it.

Inez couldn't help but calculate the worth of the brandy he inhaled at such a rapid rate.

He looked at her, desperate. "Mrs. Stannert. Can you help me?"

"Help you? If I can. I've no love for that Wesley. From what his mother said last night, I suspect that at least the letter to Mrs. Clatchworthy you described might express his true stand. Although, who's to say? But he is such a cock-arrogant young whelp."

"I don't think Miss Thomas lied to me," Jed insisted. "She was far too desperate for the job. Too...I don't know, genuine. You'd think a girl who'd been tasked with weaseling her way into the newspaper would do some batting of eyes or flashing a bit of ankle or something. She was straight up with me. Well," he amended, "maybe not when she gave me her name. I asked her and she hesitated a bit. I guess I wondered why at the time. Thought that Thomas might not be real."

Inez closed her eyes in turn.

"Good lord," she said under her breath. "Jed. What a mess you have gotten yourself into. Why didn't you wait to publish

that, that inflammatory article? You could have checked some
sources. Talked with Mrs. Clatchworthy to find out if she even
knows the Wesleys."

"There was no time!" Jed said desperately. "I had to strike
when the iron was hot! I was going to press! I thought I'd corner
Wesley at the reception and ask a few pointed questions, but…
You!" He sat up straight, sudden accusation focused on her. "You
stopped me. Then you told me about what Mrs. Wesley said to
you. And I figured that was good enough. I could let it go. If it
hadn't been for you, I might not be in this mess."

"Oh for…Don't blame this on me. But I'll help you as best
I can." Inez glanced at her lapel watch. "It's three o'clock now.
You've got little more than twenty-four hours before you have
to face young Wesley. This girl can't just disappear off the face
of the earth, and I doubt she can simply walk out of town. I'll
see what I can do about chasing down some information on
Chicken Hill."

*Bridgette might be helpful in that regard. And she'll be in tomor-
row morning early instead of at Mass, thank the Lord.*

Inez continued, "And, there's Mrs. Clatchworthy. Jed, are
you attending the veterans banquet tonight?"

Jed shook his head, slumped on the sofa. "Couldn't cadge
an invitation."

Oh, that's right. He's far too young to be a veteran of the War.

"Well, I'll bet you a dollar to a dime that William Casey, the
lawyer, will be there. He's of the proper age. And, if he's going,
he'll bring his sister. I can't imagine she'd pass up the opportunity
to see Grant and hear all his cronies talk of the 'old days,' even
if she has to promise her brother she'll remain silent as a statue.
So, perhaps I can talk to Mrs. Clatchworthy this evening, see if
she regularly corresponds with the Wesleys. She might be more
forthcoming with me about this than with you, in any case."

There was something else. Something niggling at Inez about
the girl's first name, a debilitated father, twin brothers. *Zelda.
That was the name of the girl who'd killed Lizzie. Zel could be
a diminutive. Though most prostitutes don't use their real names*

or something that close. Still. What else did Flo say about her? I remember an invalid father. Twin brothers. Did she say the father was blind?

Too many demands, too much yammering in her brain. She couldn't focus on it.

Perhaps I should make a trip to Flo's pleasure palace and ask a few questions.

She opened her eyes and looked at Jed, who was watching her as if she was the one and only true Savior.

"What is it, Mrs. Stannert. Did you think of something?"

"I'm not sure. Is there anything else you can tell me about this Miss Thomas? Anything that seemed unusual? Unexpected?"

He frowned, blushed, looked away.

"Ye-e-e-e-s? What is it, Jed?"

He cleared his throat. "That photograph. Odd thing. She said there was something still in the envelope after I pulled the letters. So she took it out, it was wrapped in a piece of paper. She unwrapped it, it fell onto the tabletop, and, well, it knocked my socks off. And I'm no neophyte in the ways of State Street." He stopped.

"Y-e-e-e-e-s?"

"I'm not even going to attempt to describe it to you, Mrs. Stannert. Except for what I said in the paper. But Miss Thomas. She, well, she…"

"What? She fainted dead away?"

"No, not at all. I suppose that's what I found odd. In fact, she went out of her way to assure me that everything was quite all right and that she'd keep plugging along. I was ready to send her home, you see. I thought a proper young woman would have refused to have any more to do with it, right then and there. Not that she acted in any way *im*proper, you understand. She was just rather matter-of-fact, I guess you'd say. Didn't seem nearly as shocked as I felt, I'll tell you that."

Inez nodded without comment. *It's a long shot, but worth pursuing, at least a little further. And Flo's house is far closer than Chicken Hill for a quick trip tonight.*

"So, what do you think, Mrs. Stannert? Think I've been suckered by a lovely confidence woman?"

"I think," said Inez, "that there's no way to know right now. Although it's certainly suspicious. While I'm chasing down a few things here, you should hurry to the stagecoach and railroad ticket offices, before they close. See if someone answering to Miss Thomas' description might have purchased a ticket. I know the manager of the Denver and Rio Grande ticket office. If you get there and it's closed, I'll give you his home address. You can tell him I will forgive his tab at the Silver Queen if he cooperates. And, if you've time, I suggest you take your gun and engage in a little target practice. Because, if all this is for naught, you're either going to have to buy your own ticket out of town or be down by the railroad tracks, pistol at the ready, tomorrow evening at six."

Chapter Thirty-one

Everything seemed to be an immediate need. Everything had to be addressed right now. Like a pot on boil or bread rising in the oven, nothing could wait.

Between Jed and Flo, Inez felt she didn't have time to breathe or even think. And, there was Abe's comment about buying Flo's bordello. Plus the very real press of men seeking to slake their thirst before moving on to other pleasures, whose comings and goings had both Harrison and State saloon doors swinging like metronomes with their steady in, out, in, out. It all made Inez feel that her head was close to bursting.

At about five-thirty, during a supper lull, Inez begged off, telling Abe and Sol that she had some errands for the church and for herself. She waved an empty envelope, which she'd addressed to her sister as an added ruse, and said she'd make a stop at the post office as well.

First stop, Flo's boarding house. Inez pondered how to approach Molly and the others, who were probably as nervous and on edge as cats without Flo's calming and firm hand. Lighting on an inspiration, Inez unearthed her girlhood prayer book, stashed away in her upstairs changing room, and returned to the kitchen to beg yet another basket of biscuits from Bridgette. "Another invalid?" Bridgette inquired, looking up, somewhat harried, from cutting out a slew of piecrusts. Five large cans of cherries stood nearby, at the ready.

"Must be some illness circulating through the congregation," improvised Inez. "Poor woman, she has six, no, seven children. And a couple of nieces staying with her, I think. Husband working shifts as a blacksmith in town and down at the smelter to make ends meet. And you know Reverend Sands, always concerned particularly for the poor and struggling. He's completely taken up with Grant's visit, so—"

Bridgette had already excavated another basket while Inez was talking and was piling in the biscuits and tucking in a jar of jam. She pulled out half of a wheel of cheese and cut a large hunk, then extracted a cold chicken from storage and rearranged the things in the basket to make it fit. "I'd give you some stew, but heavens, ma'am. I can't see you carrying enough for seven souls. But you be sure and let that lovely Reverend Sands know that anytime he needs a bit of sustenance for a Christian soul, he can count on me."

"Thank you, Bridgette. Your generosity is appreciated."

Inez watched Bridgette fly about the kitchen, now fully engaged in plunking pie crusts into a line of waiting pie tins. "Bridgette? Do you know a family by the name of Thomas up on Chicken Hill?"

"Thomas? Ma'am, there are any number of them. There's Evan Thomas, George Thomas, Leroy Thomas—"

"A young woman named Zel...something? Zel Thomas, perhaps?"

"Oh heavens, ma'am. I couldn't say. But I'll try to think on it. There are hundreds of souls on Chicken Hill you know."

"Of course, of course. Just thought I'd ask."

Inez tied bonnet strings beneath her chin, gathered up the basket—*How could Bridgette's lighter-than-air biscuits weigh so much?*—and headed out the back door of the saloon into Tiger Alley. The rains of the past few days had abated on Saturday, and a day of sun had baked an ankle-twisting crust onto the ooze.

By walking gingerly on the crust, Inez was able to get to Harrison without mud up to her ankles. She hurried around the corner of Harrison to State, and walked past her own saloon, head down, hoping none would recognize her.

She certainly didn't look like any of the painted ladies of the red-light district, some of whom were strolling the boards even now, looking to whip up business for later that night. All male attention was focused on them, for which she was grateful. She caught snatches of come-ons as she hurried down the block. "Specialty is nice and slow." "Clean and willing to do anything."

Having reached the front of Flo's imposing brick house, Inez paused to catch her breath. She closed her eyes, forcing herself to think about why she was there.

I need to find out more information about this Zelda. Learn what happened that night. See if I can find anyone who knows more about her. Where she might go when she's not here, for instance. If she had a sweetheart, and whom. If she is, perhaps, the same woman as Jed's typesetter. It would be such a coincidence. The odds aren't good. But then, gamblers know that long odds and coincidences pay off more often than common folk believe.

Inez mounted the stairs slowly, raised a tentative hand, and knocked. It took a long time for someone to finally come to the door.

For all I know, they normally wake up at three in the afternoon and are just now sitting down for their "mid-day" meal. My timing with these biscuits may be just the thing to get me in the door.

Inez felt the rumble through the porch boards as a heavy tread approached. The door swung open to reveal Danny. Stoic, stone-faced Danny. Inez remembered Flo's whisper: *Danny's the only one I trust entirely. He's been with me…it seems like forever! If you need help, talk to him.*

No sooner did these thoughts whisk through Inez's mind than she heard Molly's irritated whine. "Danny, who's there? We're not open for business yet."

The red-haired virago pushed him out of the way. She wrinkled her nose, obviously puzzled. "Mrs. Stannert? What the hell?"

"Good evening," said Inez pleasantly and stepped inside as if she owned the place. *Which in a way, I do.* She pulled off her bonnet, smoothing a couple loose strands of hair back from her face. "Miss Molly, I'm here on behalf of the church and Reverend Sands."

"Yeah, I know the reverend," Molly said with a sneer. "Likes to come and talk to us all. Doesn't lecture about sin and fornication. Just invites us all to 'visit' some Sunday, or come down to the State Street mission. Just like we might drop in for tea or something. So what?"

"Well, the good reverend is, of course, worried about the well-being of you all. I brought a prayer book—"

Molly wrinkled her nose.

"But of course, food for the soul is often no match for…"

Inez peeled back the napkin and brown paper, releasing a warm cloud of steam bearing a smell that came as close to heaven as bakery goods could aspire. Molly's pinched face softened. "I dunno." She wavered.

"As you know," said Inez conversationally, "Flo and I, we are not strangers to each other. I think she would appreciate the fact that you've extended courtesy to our helping hand. Shall I just come with you and leave these with the girls, with the reverend's and the church's blessings? I will be happy to put these biscuits, and the homemade jam, and the cheese and cold chicken in your kitchen. I need to return the basket, or I would just leave it with you and be on my way."

Molly's face grew younger as Inez listed the food items. "Well, if you've no problem bein' in the company of whores," she decided, and beckoned Inez down the hall.

Inez walked past the staircase into a narrow hallway that ran the length of the building. A door tucked under the staircase on the left faced a marble statue of the Greek goddess of love, Aphrodite, on the right. The goddess was clothed in little besides her native beauty, with a stone cloth draped casually, and not particularly helpfully, over one cocked, voluptuous hip. There were paintings on the wall as well. Inez, no stranger to the oils that graced the walls of the better drinking establishments from New Orleans to Kansas City to Denver, nevertheless averted her eyes from the canvases depicting the detailed couplings of nymphs and satyrs, and Leda and the swan.

"This way." Molly veered left into a dining room.

Inez noted a door at the end of the hall. A door leading, no doubt, to the torched section of the bordello.

About ten women of various ages and stages of dress sat around an elegant dining table littered with opened tins. They looked up at Inez in confusion.

Molly announced, "This is Mrs. Stannert. If you don't know her, she runs the Silver Queen, the joint at the other end of the block. She's here from Flo's church."

Inez meanwhile had set the basket on a corner of the table, after pushing back a clatter of empty cans, extracted the bundle of biscuits and peeled back the napkin and brown paper that cradled them. A chorus of soft oooooohhhhhhhhs lifted from the residents—a moan of culinary ecstasy.

"I'm tired of damn oysters," said one lovely with a heart-shaped face. She dropped her fork on the table and reached.

Another woman, who looked no more than eighteen, sniffed loudly. "The smell reminds me of my ma. She used to bake the best biscuits and griddle cakes."

Eager hands reached out, grabbing, tearing, stuffing the still warm bread into painted mouths.

"And, here's some homemade jam," said Inez. "And butter, fresh from market this morning. And some cheese. And a cold chicken. Is there a plate perhaps for the cheese, butter, and chicken?" Three plates, none too clean, were pushed her way.

"I'll be ever so glad when Flo is released from the joint," said another woman. Tall and slim, she had sad doe-like eyes that no doubt broke hearts and pocketbooks throughout the business district. "I'm getting bored of living on canned sardines, tomatoes, and peaches. Flo always made sure we had fresh food. When's she scheduled to post bail?"

Molly shrugged. "When the judge says. Probably not for a week or two, accordin' to Officer Ryan."

"Well, The Hatchet would know and *Molly* knows The Hatchet better'n most," said the lovely pointedly.

"Shut your pie-hole, Blanche," Molly snapped.

Blanche rolled her eyes. "I suppose we'll just have to hold on and pray until Flo gets back."

"I understand there was a death in the house." Inez tried to make her voice sympathetic. "I'm so sorry to hear. As Reverend Sands might say…" She racked her brain for something appropriate, and ended up with, "Why did God promise to bless all men, and purpose to save them? Because, he is infinite in love, goodness and wisdom; and cannot do anything but what is for the good of his creatures." *What else.* "And of course, 'Love is an active principle and can never lie dormant; but is ever actively engaged in doing good to each and all.'"

There was a snicker from somewhere down the table. "Of course love doesn't lie dormant. If we were to just lie there, we'd be out on the street in no time."

Inez felt that she'd done her duty in proffering religion as comfort. "So, what exactly happened? I hear all kinds of rumors at the Silver Queen. Some are saying that if a girl can be killed here at Flo's, it won't be long before a customer will find himself stuck with a knife. That it's a dangerous place to come for entertainment."

Cries of "No! It's not true!" chased about the table.

"It was a grudge," asserted one raven-haired vixen. "Zelda and Lizzie, they always were at it. Claws out, like cats."

"No," said another. "Zel didn't have it out for Lizzie. She just didn't like the way Lizzie kept at her. Hell, I wouldn't like it either. Lizzie could be a vicious bitch."

"Well, why'd she cut her with a knife, then?" questioned a blonde, "and where'd she get that knife? They were alone in Flo's room. Molly'd locked the door. Right, Molly?"

Inez stiffened. *Flo's room? That's right, Doc said something about Lizzie being there as well. Yet, I distinctly remember Flo instructing us to put Lizzie in her own room. Was the switch a matter of convenience?*

She studied Molly for her reaction.

Molly nodded absently, busy buttering one of the biscuits and sucking the melting butter that dripped onto her fingers.

"I didn't think Zelda carried a knife." That was from a mousy-haired woman with a slight overbite.

A chorus of derisive hoots, *pffffffts*, and eye-rolling commenced.

"*Every*one carries a knife," said another. "Don't you? You gotta have that or a gun. And Flo won't let us keep pistols. Even those little cute ones. The ones you can tuck between your titties or tie up high on your leg."

"I don't think Zelda carried a knife," the mouse insisted stubbornly.

"So," the blonde continued, as if the intervening conversation hadn't occurred, "there's no way anyone else could have done the deed. Look, when Doc and Molly opened the door, Zelda shoved them out of the way and ran off, all covered with blood. If she didn't do it, why'd she run?"

"Because, you goose, given the situation, no one would have believed her protestations to the contrary," said Blanche.

"Well then, you tell us, Miss high-n-mighty-once-a-school-teacher. How'd Lizzie die? Who killed her, if not Zelda?"

Blanche shrugged. "I'm not paid to try and fathom that mystery."

Inez listened intently, tapping the edge of the prayer book against her gloved palm. "Where would Zelda go if she were in trouble?" She tried to sound as if she was just wondering aloud.

Answers flowed around her like the babbling of a creek over small stones.

"She'd get out of town, quick. That's what she'd do."

"No, she'd not leave her pa! She said he couldn't see."

"She had a boyfriend. The young buck with long hair? I'll bet they ran off together."

"I still don't think she'd leave her pa," said the dissenter stubbornly. "Besides, Molly, didn't you say she'd been bragging about that she'd got a job in town with a newspaper? That she was leaving the screwing business altogether?"

Inez almost dropped the prayer book, hardly believing her ears or her luck. *Bless Bridgette and her biscuits for greasing the wheels of conversation!*

Molly stirred a finger in the jam pot. "Dunno. Zel, she liked to make things up. Mebbe she just said that. She ain't workin' there now. If she stuck around, she'd be in jail for sure. And believe me, if they put her in with Flo, I'd not bet on Zel seein' mornin' light."

"What did Zelda look like?" asked Inez.

"A pretty little thing," Blanche volunteered. "Very curly dark hair. Lovely skin. No pox or anything. I'd kill for skin like that." She fingered her own pock-marked complexion wistfully. "Brilliant blue eyes. Had a natural figure, on the slight side, but made her look young. Some customers like that. They fool themselves that they're taking a virgin. You play along and it's always good for an extra tip. Plus, they get so excited they can't hold back long."

Knowing laughs and nods at the table followed that remark.

The schoolmarm continued. "Zelda looked fifteen, but she had to be over eighteen. Flo doesn't take in anyone younger."

"Except Lizzie," someone said under her breath.

"Lizzie was a special case," said the schoolmarm. "Flo had a soft spot for her. Otherwise, why bother? If anyone else would have smart-mouthed Flo like Lizzie did, she'd be out in the alley. There was something between the two of them."

Molly, two biscuits in, seemed to come to her senses about the surrounding babble. "That's enough!" she said. "Let the dead rest in peace." She twisted in her chair and hollered toward the hallway, "Danny!"

The giant appeared, a silent solid block in the entry to the dining room. Molly slanted a glance at Inez. "Girls, thank Mrs. Stannert. She's leaving."

A chorus of thank-yous followed.

Inez smiled and inclined her head, wondering what a blessing from a whore would count for in Heaven.

Molly reached for another helping of jam. "Danny, take Mrs. Stannert out, okay?"

He stood aside and let Inez pass. The door to the dining room closed softly behind them, shrouding them in darkness.

Inez spoke quickly. "Danny. You know that Mrs. Sweet and I were talking. We're partners now. She's in trouble, and I'm trying to help. Can you show me the room where Lizzie was killed? It's important."

Danny turned and walked down the hall toward the front door. Inez's heart fell. Then he paused, unmoving, by the statue of the love goddess.

Finally, he turned to the right. Inez saw the glint of a key in the muted light of the hallway. A rasp of key in the lock, and the door beneath the stairs swung open. He moved aside, allowing Inez to enter.

Inez stepped inside, set her basket down by the door, and looked around. She'd expected a scene of grisly blood and gore, but someone had been at the room and cleaned it up. The clean bedclothes were rumpled, as if recently slept in.

Inez shuddered. Who would sleep in this room so soon after the gruesome murder? She forced herself to walk toward the bed. "This is where she died?" The coverlet was rose-colored satin, made for a much narrower bed.

Danny's large bulk materialized beside her. He nodded.

Inez walked the perimeter of the room, not certain what she was looking for. Some clue, perhaps, as to what had happened that night or where Zelda might have gone.

She had her eyes cast to the floor or else she might have missed the four long, parallel scratches in the gleaming waxed floor. She stopped, allowing her gaze to follow where the tracks led. The French-style armoire stood demurely upon clawed feet, four feet down the wall, its three mirrors reflecting blood-red light around the room from the waning sun. Inez looked back at the gold and dark blue striped wallpaper, right above where the tracks began, and frowned. A darker area showed that, indeed, the armoire had once resided there for long enough to shield the wallpaper, after which it either walked on its own or more likely had been dragged down a length of wall.

But why?

Inez looked back at Danny, curious as to how much information he might be willing to impart.

"Did you move this armoire recently? Was it where it is now before Lizzie's death?"

Danny shook his head emphatically. No, and no again.

Curious, Inez walked up to the large piece of furniture, set a shoulder against the side, and pushed experimentally. The armoire ground over the floor more easily than she would have guessed, adding a few more streaks to the once-impeccably polished floor. She opened the main wardrobe door, and frowned again.

Either Flo packed her clothes away or someone has been into her things since she's been gone.

The wardrobe was nearly empty.

Inez closed the door softly, pondering.

She returned to the length of wall where the armoire originally was located, running a hand over the stripes.

Her fingers explored a seam. A seam that appeared to run deeper than a mere panel of wallpaper. She followed the break up and over as it made a ninety-degree turn.

"Danny?" Molly's voice.

Danny made a quick hand movement—*stay*—and left the room, closing the door.

Inez heard his heavy footsteps head toward the dining room. A moment later, the footsteps returned and passed her by. She could hear them again, much muffled, heading up the stairs to the second story.

Inez bit her lip, debating. Sneak out and let herself out the front door or stay where she was until Danny returned?

Suppose the resident of the room comes in while I'm still here? I could hide under the bed if I heard the knob turn, but what if she starts her toilet for the evening and things go from there? I could be trapped, hiding here all night under the bed.

It was more of a chance than she wanted to take.

She opened the door a crack, and listened. All she heard was the chatter of the women in the dining room. She grabbed her basket, slipped out, noiselessly shut the door, and started down the hall.

The massive front door suddenly swung open, flooding the long hall with outside illumination. Stabbed by the light, Inez gasped, clutched the empty basket tighter to herself.

A tall silhouette, crowned by the unmistakable flattop shape of a policeman's cap, stepped over the threshold. With every step he took toward Inez down that long, long hallway, his identity, never a doubt in Inez's mind, became more certain. The Hatchet's slit-eyed gaze never left Inez as he wordlessly bore down on her, every tread ominous. He pulled his sap out of a pocket.

"Pat!" The surprised squeak behind Inez was Molly's.

Inez risked a quick look over her shoulder. Molly stood at the back of the hall by the dining room entry, a cluster of wide-eyed women behind her, like a Greek chorus arranged to chant the closing lines of a tragedy.

Inez turned around to face The Hatchet, and forced her voice to a pleasant register. "Why, Officer Ryan, we meet again."

He closed the distance between them and, without preamble, gripped her upper arm and squeezed, as if prepared to drag her to jail, throw her to the wall, or both.

"I warned you. Twice." The statement came across cold, pointed, dangerous.

Inez held up the basket in one hand, the prayer book in the other and fought the quaver from her voice. "More errands for the church," she said, glad for the props. "With the recent death in the house and with Mrs. Sweet…um…detained, we of the church are always trying to reach out to those less fortunate."

Pounding footsteps came down the stairs faster than Inez could imagine someone of that size moving. A thundering crash at the bottom, as Danny took the last three stairs in one.

Inez could see Danny now, behind The Hatchet and approaching.

The Hatchet's murderous gaze finally left Inez's face. He glanced up at the women behind her, as if just realizing they were there. He turned slightly, maintaining an iron control of Inez's arm as he contemplated Danny, right behind him. Danny, Inez noted with some alarm, held a shotgun crosswise his body.

Hatchet released her arm. Tingling pain flooded down to her fingertips.

"Get out."

He didn't make any pretense of courtesy.

Inez pulled her long skirts close, to avoid touching any part of him, and edged around his unmoving figure, anxious to obey.

Danny had, during this short exchange, retreated as well, and was holding the front door open for her quick exit.

As Inez scooted down the hall, anxious to make good on a rapid departure, she heard Molly say, "Mrs. Stannert! What were you doing still here?" Her voice had slid from surprise to aggressive suspicion.

"Just leaving. I was admiring your works of art."

Wincing to herself at this lame prevarication, Inez nearly dashed out the door and down the steps, pulling the bonnet down low to hide her face.

It wasn't until her shoes hit the boardwalk that she realized The Hatchet had entered the fortified brothel without the doorman present to unlock the door from the inside.

Chapter Thirty-two

She didn't have time to ponder this development long before she was hailed from the saloon next door. "Mrs. Stannert! Ah, the very lady I was hoping to speak to." Lynch was leaning on the open entryway to his saloon, wielding a toothpick among his large, unevenly-spaced teeth.

Still shaking over the encounter with The Hatchet, Inez said stiffly, "Good evening, Mr. Lynch. I'm so sorry, I've no time to chat right now."

"Sure, sure, 'tis a busy time. For us too." His joviality and attempt to draw them together in some common bond, saloon-keep to saloonkeep, rang false. "Won't take a minute. 'Tis business I wish to discuss. Come on in, I've some fine brandy to break out while we palaver. I understand you've an uncommon knowledge of bottled Napoleons."

"Mr. Lynch, I really cannot right now."

His face reddened. He crossed his arms, causing massive shoulders and biceps to bulge. With his bald head, he looked ready to take on an opponent in the ring. "Well then, we'll conduct our business in the street as we stroll along. For this is something that cannot wait."

He glanced back into the bar, roared, "Jack McCarthy! That's right, you! You're in charge. Be back in a shake." And fell in step beside Inez.

"You see, Mrs. Stannert, I'm in negotiations to buy Frisco Flo's building." It was a blunt quick jab to the head.

Inez walked, hands folded over the basket, staring straight ahead at the sea of bobbing hats. *He's lying.* "Well, Mr. Lynch, I wish you all the best in your negotiations."

He laughed, without humor. "No, no, ma'am. You see there's been a complication. A derailment. In what were very very delicate discussions, even from the start. And that complication is you."

A solid punch to the solar plexus.

Inez's breath caught in her throat.

She decided the best way to address this was to take the high road, remind him that she was not only a lady, but what *kind* of a lady. A lady not to be trifled with. The queen of State Street. Holding her head high, she turned toward him with a regal revolve. "Explain yourself, sir. I've no idea what you're talking about. Your to-ings and fro-ings with Mrs. Sweet do not concern me."

Lynch still had the toothpick in his mouth. It worked furiously up and down, like the antenna of a small wiggling insect he was devouring.

Revolted, Inez commenced walking. "I really must be getting back to the Silver Queen. Good day."

Lynch continued to pace her, seemingly untouched by her frosty, dismissive attitude.

"Well then, Mrs. Stannert. I'll take off the kid gloves and tell it to you plainly, since you seem not to be heedin' the finer words I'd been rehearsin' to say over a friendly snifter or two." The lilt of Old Erin was stronger than ever in his voice as his attacks became more direct. "I've seen you and Jackson sneaking 'round these past few days, each of you, walking back and forth, front and alleyway, looking the place over. I mean—Jesus, Mary, and Joseph—I just observed you go in and not half an hour later, come out. So why, Mrs. Stannert, is someone the likes of you spendin' so much time in a cat house?"

They'd reached the State Street door of the Silver Queen. Inez set one gloved hand upon the planks. "Really, Mr. Lynch. I was there on behalf of the church. If you doubt me, ask the girls. They'll tell you I brought food and spiritual comfort."

He snorted and spat to the side. Inez marveled that the toothpick stayed intact through these ejections. "Sure you did, sure you did. And next you'll be telling me that's why you visited Flo in the jail the other day. And surely as I stand here, I saw her talking to you after the fire. You two are in cahoots. So, I thought I'd just let you know, in a friendly, businesslike sort of way…"

Lynch removed the toothpick from his mouth, and pointed it at Inez, a tiny wooden sword.

"Stay away from Flo. Stay away from her girls, and the building. I have friends on the force. Friends that could make your's and Jackson's lives very difficult. If you don't stop, you and your *partner*," said with a sneer, "will find yourselves cryin' in your beers, because that's all you'll have left. "

Having delivered his knockout punch, Lynch replaced the toothpick, wheeled around and walked back down State Street, leaving Inez staring after him, clutching her empty basket.

Chapter Thirty-three

"How'd the church business go?" The question to Inez was delivered absentmindedly, as Abe collected a welter of dirty glasses from the end of the bar.

Inez felt a twinge of guilt as she looked around the frenetic saloon. *I haven't been pulling my weight these past few days* .

Her only comfort was that Bridgette's eldest, Michael, was present, working a second shift at the saloon after a full day at the smelter. With his slicked-down hay-colored hair, ready smile, a bounce in his step as he collected a dishpan of dirty dishes from Abe, and the cheery "Good evening, Mrs. Stannert!" he threw in her direction, it was hard for her to believe he'd just finished eight hours of hard, physical labor.

"Mrs. Stannert." Abe again. He'd paused in his whiskey pouring. Nine glasses were lined up, three abreast, like soldiers in parade formation. "You look like you've seen a ghost."

"It's nothing." *Nothing I can tell you without spilling everything.*

Abe shook his head, obviously not believing her. "Well. Got someone here who's been waitin' for you the past half hour or so. That mapmaker fella. Over there." He pointed with the now empty bottle in the direction of the piano.

Inez stepped away from the crowded bar and saw Cecil, sitting at the piano bench, his inevitable surveyor's board on the keyboard lid. Cup of coffee resting on top of the upright. She felt a pang of annoyance. "What does he want? Did he forget something?"

Abe shrugged. "Guess you'd better ask him. He's not talkin' to me."

He started sliding the shots down the bar, straight into waiting hands.

Inez wended her way through the packed room to the mapmaker. "Mr. Farnesworth. Can I help you?"

He looked up from his survey notes, startled, then stood. "Mrs. Stannert. I'm glad you're here. I almost..." He faltered.

She finished the sentence to herself. *He almost lost his nerve to come here. To wait. This isn't about maps. This is about something else.*

He confirmed her hunch when he added, "Is there someplace private we can talk?"

"Of course. There's the office upstairs, as you well know." She softened the sharpness of the remark with a smile and added, "You measured its dimensions, as you might remember."

Halfway up the stairs, Inez turned to look down and try to signal her intentions to Abe. From that vantage point, she saw a mass of crowns—hats and heads—at the bar, at the tables, filling the spaces in between. A haze of smoke from cigars and pipes covered everything with a light fog. Abe and Sol moved back and forth at their respective ends of the bar, hands moving fast, pouring, collecting money, picking up and replacing bottles on the back bar, tossing dirty glassware into dishpans under the counter, pulling out fresh, wiping up spills. They looked like tin windup toys wound to their fullest tension, set into frenzied motion.

Inez continued up the stairs, unlocked the office, and motioned Cecil inside. She moved around, lighting two of the available lamps, remarking, "You understand, I don't have a lot of time. It's a very busy evening for us."

"I know." He sounded apologetic. Almost sad. "And I'm sorry. But, I didn't know who else to talk to. I'd hoped, given that you seem to be a confidante of Mrs. Sweet's, I could talk to you."

Inez checked herself and stared at Cecil. *How is it that everyone seems to know—or suspect—that Flo and I are in league?*

He addressed his surveyor's board. "I've been doing some soul-searching. I had fallen away from my church and faith. But I am trying hard to find my way back." He sighed. A soft, defeated sound. "In any case, I want to show you something. I'm showing this to you because, well, the woman who died at Mrs. Sweet's place. At first, I was falsely accused. The pain was unbearable. And now, I believe someone else, a young girl named Zelda, has been falsely accused." He looked up, eyes haunted.

Inez sank into her office chair. "For the sake of argument, let's set aside the question as to why you'd think Mrs. Sweet's and my interests intersect and focus on this Zelda. My understanding is that she was found with the body, in a locked room, with the weapon. Locked door, locked windows. It looks pretty damning to me."

"There is another way into the house besides the doors and windows." Cecil smoothed out a paper on the board, and passed it to Inez. It was a sketch, light pencil marks, crosshatching, strange hieroglyphics.

"I can't decipher this. What am I supposed to be looking at?"

"Here—" He pointed to two general shapes, a square and a smaller rectangle. "The square is Mrs. Sweet's building. The rectangle is the building next door. See this?" His pianist's hand traced a faint line connecting one to the other.

"Yes?" said Inez intrigued. "What is it?"

"A tunnel."

Chapter Thirty-four

It felt as though she'd fallen into a hidden mine shaft. "A tunnel? Between Mrs. Sweet's parlor house and Lynch's saloon?"

"Yes." It came out almost as a confession.

"When did you find out about this?"

"Just this afternoon. I went to the saloon and finally gained entrance to some of the rooms. They've been occupied until now. I found the door in the saloon. Partially hidden, but I've seen things like this before, so was alerted."

"This sort of thing is common?"

His mouth twisted. The lines around his eyes made him look suddenly old, older than the streaked gray and brown hair would indicate. "Tunnels abound, Mrs. Stannert. Oh, not so much here in Leadville. I've mapped a few, though. A prominent banker here, for instance, has a tunnel that leads directly from his home to his bank. Handy for bad weather, when the streets are foul. Other tunnels are for more deceitful purposes. Tunnels between hotels or saloons, such as this one, and houses of ill repute. Not uncommon at all."

Inez sat back, fighting a chill of comprehension. *A hidden passage. Lynch would know, and Flo. Who else?*

"Have you identified where the other egress is, where it comes out in Mrs. Sweet's building?" she asked cautiously.

He shook his head, his shoulders slumped. "I had only one opportunity to map the building, before Mrs. Sweet was incarcerated. And then, I only mapped the upper floors, nothing detailed on the main floor. I'd hoped, since you've been in there, that you could tell me the layout of the ground floor. And is there a basement or cellar? A house that substantial, I'd assume a cellar, at least."

"I can help you there." She decided that denial and demurral at this point would be futile and counterproductive. "However, let us, please, keep this between us. There are forces at work here, and if it was someone else's hand at Lizzie's throat, well, I needn't tell you, they would be anxious that no one finds out."

He nodded vigorously.

She slipped the pencil from its loop on the board and pulled a sheet of clean paper from beneath the maps and notes. "The front has a door and parlor to the left. The stairs are straight ahead with a hallway on the right." She sketched quickly. "Down the hallway, there's a door to a sizeable room underneath the stairs that stretches back quite a ways. Past that, a dining room. To the back, the kitchen and mud room, well, you know about those, you were sneaking around when you were caught with Lizzie."

She looked up. He looked chastened. And guilty.

"I'm curious. Were you really just checking for a pulse when Danny and Molly surprised you?"

He reddened.

"Oh, never mind. It's none of my business, and I make no accusations. Believe me, being part of State Street, I've learned to cast a jaundiced eye on so-called sins that hurt none but the sinner."

She turned back to the map. "I've no idea if there's a cellar. But this room," she tapped Flo's boudoir, "is the room where Lizzie died. I was just in there—don't ask why, please—and I spotted a break in the wall. Right about here." She darkened a portion of the wall. "A large armoire had been moved. It had blocked that part of the wall. The break had the shape of a door, at least as far as I could trace it. My examination was cut short by circumstances."

He had pulled out his maps of the two buildings and was looking from them to her sketch, nearly aquiver with excitement. "You say it was a large room? Larger than expected for a private chamber?"

"Oh yes. Most definitely."

"Adjoined to the front parlor?"

"Next to it. Between the front parlor and the dining room." She stopped, beginning to see where his thoughts were heading.

He was speaking quickly. "I'll bet it used to be the second parlor. It's in the right place. Back parlors tend to be less used. In family residences, they're informal, private areas."

"I'm aware of that," she said wryly.

He continued, as if he hadn't heard. "I'll bet this used to be a way for callers to move inconspicuously between the boarding house and the saloon. They could come through the tunnel into the second parlor, unseen, and proceed to the front parlor, the grand staircase, or even take the back staircase to the upper floors, if they were really bent on remaining unnoticed."

"You seem to have a great knowledge of how bawdy houses work," said Inez, then immediately regretted her words when the blood rushed up past his collar again. "Ah, I can add a bit more. The previous owner, who built this," she tapped the brick parlor house, "was also the owner of this." She tapped the saloon. "Mrs. DuBois kept a very upscale, discreet establishment. Like Flo, ah, Mrs. Sweet, only more so, I'd say. I'd not put it past Mrs. DuBois to have had such a secret passage. And once the two establishments had separate ownerships, well, I can imagine Mrs. Sweet would not necessarily want to carry on a clandestine business arrangement of this kind with Mr. Lynch." *But I now see why Lynch is hankering after the whorehouse.*

She sat back. "So, Zelda may have, indeed, been the unfortunate victim in this piece. Aside from Lizzie, that is."

"Do you know where Zelda is?" He sounded so hopeful. So eager. "We could let her know what we've found. We could take this information to the police."

"No!" It was said forcefully, without forethought. Inez softened her tone. "I think we need to pursue this a bit further, just the two of us. Who knows of the tunnel besides Lynch? Is it common knowledge? Certainly any of Flo's women who were part of Mrs. DuBois' house would know of it. If even just one survives from those times, it means that probably *all* of Flo's girls are aware of it by now. Heavens. This may not be as easy as I thought to untangle."

"I can find out." He sounded anxious to help. "I'll go talk to Lynch about it tomorrow. He was voluble. Liked talking about his business, his plans for expansion."

"No doubt," she said dryly. "While you do that, I shall make inquiries into Zelda's whereabouts. No promises," she hastened as his eyes brightened again, "but I'll see if I can't find her, deliver her the possibly good news, and see what she has to say. I am," she pinned him sternly with a gaze, "uncommonly good at ferreting out liars. If I should have a chance to meet her, face to face, and she is lying to me about her involvement—" *or if you are about your intentions*— "I will know. Sooner or later."

His hand closed convulsively on the sketch Inez had drawn. He stood up suddenly. "Thank you, Mrs. Stannert. I knew I came to the right person. Your trust in me is not misplaced."

I hope so. I sincerely hope so.

Chapter Thirty-five

As the clock ticked down the minutes to when she expected Reverend Sands to appear to escort her to the banquet in honor of General Grant, Inez reflected that it felt odd not to be preparing for the usual Saturday night poker game with her suite of gentleman "regulars." But most of them were at the Veterans Hall reception for Grant and would no doubt be at the banquet. Jed Elliston was the only non-veteran in her circle of playing partners, but she suspected he was busy chasing ticket agents after hours and hunting down the particulars of his mystery typesetter.

Inez felt certain, with a natural gambler's instinct for playing a hunch, that the prostitute Zelda and the typesetter Miss Thomas were one and the same. After all, how many women worked for any of the newspapers in town? A writer penning a society column here and there, if even that.

It must be the same woman.

Inez was so certain, she had even sent a willing street urchin out to search for Jed and bring him to the saloon, with the promise of a nickel should the small boy be successful. The urchin returned, so crestfallen in his failure, that Inez had given him a penny for trying.

In the light of her upstairs dressing room, Inez turned this way and that, checking the drape of her green velvet dress and whether the diamonds at her throat overwhelmed those on her earrings or bracelet. She remembered when Mark presented them to her, insisting that she wear them regularly: "We've got the funds, Darlin'. Consider it advertising, shows we're successful, opens the doors to the high-rolling players."

To her, it never made sense, though. Wouldn't a gambler dripping with diamonds be a warning to astute players that they were in the presence of someone who made a living at cards, and opponents beware? Why put yourself up against a professional?

However, this was not her concern tonight. Tonight, she'd be seated at the reverend's side, trying not to yawn through long speeches about the glory days of "The War of the Rebellion" and men's valor in facing down the Southern enemy. Behind it all—the smiles, the inconsequential conversation—she'd be furiously thinking, conjecturing, trying to work out the whys and wherefores of what happened to Zelda and the connections to Jed's precarious predicament.

She reached out a silk-gloved hand and gently touched a cabinet card, propped up on the top shelf of the washstand. She traced the outline of her son, captured on photographic paper and mounted on cardboard. He held his beloved toy from infancy, a stuffed rabbit, now showing definite signs of wear and missing one button eye. She swallowed the lump that rose in her throat unbidden.

Only one more month and she'd see him again.

Her thoughts switched then to a different cabinet card. The photograph in Flo's private residence. An image of a baby, held in a grandfather's arms. A half-finished letter.

A muffled knock brought her out of her reverie.

She exited the dressing room, went into the office, and opened the office door to Abe, who said, "Didn't want t' walk in and interrupt you. You got time to talk?"

"Certainly." She retreated back inside, sat on the edge of her office chair, careful to not smash the satin flounces and bows down the back. She laid her ivory and silver fan on the desk blotter and said, "Actually Abe, since you're here, I have a question for you."

He sat, knees cracking, on the worn loveseat. "Fire away, Inez."

"Does it make sense that a local policeman might have keys to various businesses and so on?"

"Mebbe. Can't say I'd trust any of the law around here with the keys to our joint. We'd be outta liquor by mornin', and a force with a powerful hangover."

"Any reason you can think of for The Hatchet to have keys to Flo's place?"

"The Hatchet?" Abe's gray eyebrows arched. "Well now. I didn't think he and Flo was on speakin' terms after the business a couple days ago. He's the one that pressed charges, right? Mebbe her stand-in thought hirin' him for protection was a good idea 'til Flo gets out. What with the fire an' all. Seems like lettin' the fox in the hen house, but, he is the law. And the city collector at that. Probably could have keys to damn near any building in town, if'n he wants."

"Hmmm." She leaned back, forgetting about the flounces for a moment.

"So, you were visitin' Flo's place? Checkin' out whether we oughta invest? Would make a fine hotel or proper boardin' house, in contrast to the improper ones I know you don't approve of. Mebbe a restaurant on the bottom floor. Could let Bridgette build a kitchen to her own liking. Might have to get her priest in there to sprinkle some holy water around the place or cast out the demons or some such afore she'll set foot over the threshold. But still, I'm not above contributin' some to her church fund or whatever they call it if it'll help. With Bridgette in charge of the macaroni and beans end of things, we could make a killin' in no time."

Inez's face grew uncomfortably warm. "Actually, I was there to extend the church's helping hand to the unfortunate. You know, rescue a few souls. Encourage them to seek out the mission, should they need help."

"Uh-huh." Abe's brown eyes took her in like a cardsharp watching a greenhorn try to bluff out a bad hand.

The uncomfortable silence stretched on. Finally, he sat back. "Look, Inez. We've ridden down a lot of roads together, sat at game tables side by side and across from each other. Been through good times and bad. I can tell there's somethin' you're not tellin' me. Somethin' 'bout Flo's place. You've been duckin' and blowin' smoke ev'rytime I bring up the subject of buying the building. So, what is it? You got a card up your sleeve or a con you're pullin' that I don't know about?"

Inez swiveled side to side in the chair, making up her mind. "Okay, Abe. You're right. There's something I haven't been straight with you about. But, in my defense, I was asked to keep this confidential."

She swiveled to face the nearly wall-sized office window. Up here, on the second floor, it gave a view that ran all the way down State Street, including Flo's three-story building and the faint outline of mountains beyond. Flickering lamplight in the rooms of the bordello was further dimmed by roller shades half-covering windows like a flirtatious woman lowering her eyelids to shield too bold a stare.

Finally she spoke. "Flo asked me to go in partners on her business, and I said yes."

"You what?"

She turned back to look at him. "The business partnership is only temporary. It was a condition for buying the State Street building. As you know, she's planning a move to Fifth Street. Going uptown to join the other high-flying madams. Winnie Purdy, Sallie Purple, and the rest. She needs capital for the new place, but isn't ready to part with the one on State. So, by signing with her on the dotted line, I now own a portion of the State Street building, with the written understanding that I will eventually buy the rest when she's ready to sell."

Abe's affect was neutral. "You tangled up with her new business at Fifth?"

"Only temporarily." Inside, Inez squirmed. "And, well, since I'm telling all, there's an added complication. A third partner, I don't know who. Someone who is part of the Fifth Street

business. It could be another madam, a saloon owner, or someone running a legitimate business in town that doesn't want to
be exposed. But the State Street agreement is just between Flo
and me."

"Uh-huh. Sounds complicated." It was a flat statement, without inflection. Abe leaned back, his face blending even further
into the room's dark shadows. "Just wonderin', Inez. Where does
that leave me in your plans? Were you gonna bring me in? Or
sell me your half of the Silver Queen and vamoose? Or what?"

"Abe, honestly. I hadn't even thought it through that far. This
came up all of a sudden. It all happened so fast, right after I saw
the lawyer about getting a divorce." Inez took a deep breath.
"Well, you remember our earlier discussion. Without anything
written down on paper, except that Mark won the saloon title,
deed, and land, in a poker game, we—that's you and I—have no
legal claim. We have nothing. Mark holds all the aces, wherever
he damn well may be. It's his signature on the paper that went
with him the day he disappeared. All he has to do is come back
into town, waving that agreement and insisting that we were no
more than employees." She brought her hands up as if pushing
back from a table. "Game over. We walk away with nothing."

"So, you went in with Flo 'cause you figured it'd give you
somethin' apart from Mark? A backup plan?"

"Exactly." She rocked a little. The chair squeaked. "I used
the money that I've won and I've been saving on my own. The
money I thought would take me and little William to San
Francisco. The money I thought I could throw in my father's
face if I had to fight him. Money that would prove I could take
care of William. As if my paltry savings would mean anything
in the face of his millions."

The awareness was bitter. She could never best her father on
his own terms. She knew that now.

"So, I bought the next best thing. Insurance. By getting down
in writing that I am half-owner of the State Street building,
with a steel-clad option to buy it in its entirety, and a one-third
partnership in Flo's brothel on Fifth." She smoothed the front

of the velvet, feeling the nap through the thin silk of her gloves. "You know, Abe, now that this is out in the open, I'll ask you to consider this. We could go in together and buy the building entirely from Flo. Be partners. Even bring in Bridgette in some capacity as a partner. But we would do it all in writing. All legal."

Abe was silent. Then, "I gotta think about this, Inez. Truth told, I'm feelin', I dunno, shut out. Can I trust you? It's gotta run both ways. You talk about not trustin' Mark. Well, you see, it ain't just him. He always had my back. You, well, sometimes I get the feelin' that if it ain't convenient or not in your best interest, you might just take a powder and leave me wide open. It ain't a good feelin', Inez. I got my own concerns in this town. Think a colored man, just 'cause he's got money in his pocket and the bank, don't need t' worry? You know better than that. In some ways, I got more cause to carry a gun in my pocket than you do. But that don't stop me from bein' your partner, standin' up for you, and lookin' out for us as a team."

There was a knock on the door.

Abe stood up. "Guess your reverend's here. Kinda early, but way I figure, this conversation's over for now anyways. Sometime, if you got a notion, I'd like to see that agreement you signed with Flo. See what terms she set that you just signed with your eyes closed." He walked over to the door and pulled it open. "Well, howdy, Doc. We weren't expectin' you. How was the meetin' at the Veterans Hall?"

"Most satisfactory, most satisfactory indeed." Doc leaned on his cane, burnished top hat in hand. "But, more about that later. Mrs. Stannert, if you please?" He peered at her with a secret smile.

Curious as to what had Doc smiling like a child on Christmas morning, Inez joined Abe at the door, and stopped, stunned. A knot of gentlemen stood outside her new gaming room, murmuring amongst themselves. Closest to the office stood Lieutenant Governor Horace Tabor, looking around with bemusement, smoothing his distinctive walrus mustache and ex-Governor

Routt, deep in conversation with—her insides turned to ice—
Harry Gallagher. How dare he even set foot in here?

The figures shifted to reveal General Ulysses S. Grant, smiling and nodding at something Colorado Governor Pitkin said.
Much to her astonishment, she also saw John Wesley, standing to one side of Pitkin, nodding in tandem to whatever was being said. The inevitable Kavanagh stood back a few paces, halfway between Wesley and Tabor. He looked supremely bored. As Inez's gaze lingered on him, he smiled slightly and rolled his eyes heavenward in an expression of exasperation.

Grant unobtrusively pulled out a pocket watch, opened it, glanced at the time, and tucked it away.

Inez, glad of wearing her diamonds for this grand company, finally unstuck herself from the floor, and hurried to the group, accompanied by Doc and Abe.

"Gentlemen." She allowed her brightest hostess smile to light her face. "Welcome. This is an honor, indeed. Please, allow us."
She glanced back at Abe and pantomimed "key" with questioning eyebrows.

He nodded, pulled a ring of keys from his vest pocket, and stepped forward to unlock the door.

They all moved inside. Abe lit lamps while Inez set out a variety of liquor from the cabinet. The visitors wandered about the room, remarking on the view and the appurtenances. She silently thanked Sol for being so conscientious as to keep the cabinet well stocked, just in case of any eventuality. He had even, she noted, included a bottle of Old Crow, reputed to be Grant's favorite drink in the "old days." At least, according to Doc. She poured a shot of the sour mash bourbon, thinking to offer it personally to her guest of honor.

She felt a presence behind her and turned, offering of Old Crow at the ready, to meet Harry Gallagher's nearly colorless gaze. Silvered hair, dark mustache, impeccably groomed, there he stood. The man who had taken her affections a year ago, turned away from her, then tried to win her back when Reverend Sands entered the picture.

It took an iron act of will for her not to throw the shot glass, drink and all, in his face.

"You're looking well, Mrs. Stannert," he said. His gaze pinned her momentarily, butterfly to specimen paper. He pulled a cigar case from his pocket, chose one, closed it, and looked around the gaming room calculatingly. "Business must be good."

"Never better," she offered him a sub-zero smile, then turned her back to extract a small silver salver from the sideboard. "Mr. Jackson and I have made many improvements during your stay back East. Now, if you will excuse me."

She swept past him, holding the shot glass steady on the tray, stepped up to Abe, and whispered, "Come with me."

She could tell that this wasn't part of his game plan, but she was determined that he share the moment with her. They approached Grant, who stood by the mahogany gaming table with Tabor and Doc.

"General Grant," she made her voice as smooth and warm as a well-aged bourbon. "Allow us to welcome you to the Silver Queen and to Leadville. I and my business partner Mr. Jackson, who, by the way, is a Union veteran," she glanced significantly at Abe so there could be no confusion as to whom she was referring, "are so honored that you would visit. We have a special stock of Old Crow at hand. Doctor Cramer had advised us earlier that this was your drink of choice."

She held out the silver tray.

After a moment's hesitation, Grant accepted the drink with a gruff "Thank you."

Inez continued to the room at large, "Please, gentlemen, help yourselves. We have champagne, bourbon, whiskey, brandy, and wine. If you wish a particular libation you do not see, please tell us."

Doc had already helped himself to his favorite and stood to one side, beaming, brandy snifter in hand, looking much more like his old self. "Capital, Mrs. Stannert. And we should have time for one or two rounds of cards. As I mentioned to you all," he addressed the visitors, "sitting at the poker table with a player as lovely and accomplished as Mrs. Stannert is a Leadville experience that none should miss!"

"I concur," said Gallagher, who had lit a cigar and was now examining the view out the window. He turned to Tabor, eyebrows raised. "Mr. Tabor, have you had the pleasure of facing Mrs. Stannert across a table?"

Tabor shook his head. "I remember many a time playing against Mister Stannert, though. In the early days of the camp. He was one damn lucky fella when it came to cards and games of chance in general, as I discovered to my own personal sorrow, a'course."

Some general laughter at that.

"Why, I was at the table when he won this saloon on the turn of a card. Clever man, that Mark Stannert." Tabor turned his gaze away from the others to focus back on Inez. "Right sorry to hear of his passing on, Mrs. Stannert."

The glint in his eye was anything but sympathetic, though. In fact, she thought she detected a combination of calculation and common lechery that made her skin creep.

Inez murmured something that could be interpreted as a polite demurral and then inquired brightly, "Well, gentlemen, since I know that time is of the essence and, in circles such as yours and mine, time is money," some appreciative chuckles at this old chestnut, "shall we gather at the table? I shall ask our guest of honor to choose the game."

"I think the lady of the house should choose, as I'm but a visitor to your establishment. What do you usually play?" Grant set down the shot glass at the round gaming table and declined a refill from Abe with a polite wave of the hand.

Doc spoke up jovially before Inez could answer. "We have a regular poker game here most Saturday nights, sir, and I am honored to be a member of that chosen fraternity, as is Harry here. Well, when he is in town, that is. We indulge in fine liquor, pleasant conversation, and simple five card draw."

"It's good to see some things haven't changed," said Harry. Inez refused to look at him.

"Poker. The old soldier's game. Good enough for me," said Grant.

They all took their drinks and settled around the table. Harry took his customary seat to her right. Her irritation and unease increased. She tried to smooth the unwanted emotions from her mind as she might smooth out the wrinkles of a shirtwaist with a red-hot clothes iron.

Abe handed her a sealed deck, saying low, "I'm gonna go get Sol. He can help out up here an' I'll work the downstairs with Michael. And there's been a request for Taos Lightning from the lieutenant governor."

Inez glanced up at Horace Tabor, who was smoothing his extravagantly large mustache and grinning at her like a randy fool.

He winked broadly at her.

She tried to quell her disgust.

"Well, gentlemen." She looked around the table. All were in place, eyes fixed upon her. She made her voice tinkle with disarming feminine charm as she said, "Goodness, this is the first time in my life I've had the undivided attention of an eminent Civil War general and former president, two governors, two silver kings, a Congressional-hopeful, and the town's best physician, all at the same moment. I hope it doesn't go to my head."

She slit the seal with a fingernail, and opened the pack. "Gentlemen, let's play poker."

Chapter Thirty-six

"And where were you when these fine dignitaries made their appearances at the Silver Queen?" Inez asked Reverend Sands.

The company had departed but twenty minutes previous, with Doc, the good shepherd, clucking and herding them along so they wouldn't be late in arriving at the banquet at the Clarendon.

"There I was," she continued. "Having to play poker against Grant, who has to have the most granite poker face of all times. My God, he's good. I'd love to play him again, under different circumstances. Oh! And I had to jolly along a sulking John Quincy Adams Wesley, no wonder there. And fend off the oily advances of Horace Tabor, who appeared to be deep in his cups already. What's going on between Horace and Harry? Horace referred several times to that *Independent* piece, making jokes about Chinese immigration, Chinese workers, and so on. Most boorish of him. Threw in a couple of references to the Grants staying at *his* hotel, the Clarendon, rather than at Harry's hotel, the Clairmont. Horace must be ten times the fool I originally thought to push Harry like that."

"There was a problem."

At his tone, Inez paused in her assiduous extinguishing of the oil lamps. Only one remained lit in a wall sconce, casting long and wavering shadows about the room.

"A problem? What kind of problem?"

Sands, who had moved to gaze out the window at the pan-
orama that was State Street, turned and looked at her. He was
in deep shadow, his expression unreadable as he said softly, "You
are beautiful tonight, Inez."

He walked forward, into the light. Took her hand in his.
Lifted it to his lips and kissed the inside of her wrist, just above
the diamond bracelet.

Her heart full, she closed her hand about his. After a moment,
she said, "Don't change the subject, Reverend Justice B. Sands.
What problem kept you from accompanying everyone to the
Silver Queen? Doc could have used your subtle touch to help get
them out the door. They were having such a fine time drinking
my liquor and stripping me of funds that I believe they were
prepared to forego the banquet altogether. As it was, I had to
nearly shove them out myself and promise the lieutenant governor that I would certainly be most honored to sit on his left at the
banquet, should the seating arrangements be so construed."

As she'd hoped, her prattle caused the reverend's lined face
to relax into a smile. "Don't worry, Inez. God's representatives
have a certain power over even the head waiters and machinations of politicians."

"Good. Now, as to your problem?" She enclosed his hand
in both of hers.

He sighed and withdrew his hand. "One of Grant's stops
today was to be the Silver Mountain Mining works."

"Harry Gallagher's mine." It was no question. She knew
whose it was.

"By the time we arrived, he had but a little while to visit the
offices, examine the main head frame, and then depart. The plan
had been to have Grant and Gallagher descend the mine shaft
for a quick tour of the underground, but Grant declined at the
last moment, due to time constraints."

Silence.

"That was the problem?" she inquired.

"No. It's what happened later, after we left." He walked back
to the window, looked out into the night. "When the mine

returned to normal working order, the first time the bucket was lowered…"

"Yes?"

"The cable snapped." It was said with a flat finality. "Two men plunged to their deaths down the shaft."

Inez's hand crept up to cover her mouth. "Do you think someone tampered with the cable?" she finally managed to say.

"So the mine supervisor says. It's unknown who the intended victim was. Could have been Grant or Gallagher." He shook his head wearily. "Or even the governor. Pitkin was also supposed to be in the descending party."

Inez sank onto a nearby chair. "Who did it?"

"We may never know."

"I've heard talk," she said. "Long before Grant arrived, of course. But even in the last couple of days. And then, there was that attempt at the parade." She looked up at Sands. "Is it more, do you think, than just a few disgruntled souls? Is there something more organized going on?"

"At this point, Gallagher has ordered that not a word is to be said of the particulars of the mine incident. No further investigations. Anyone who says anything will be fired."

"Knowing Harry, he'd not stop at a mere firing if someone crossed him," Inez said under her breath.

Reverend Sands swung around. "What's that?" His voice was sharp.

Inez could almost see a wall of dissension slam down between them, as it often did when Harry was the subject.

Not that we've had occasion to discuss him for a long time. I swear, he's like the snake in the Garden. All is well until he appears and then all Hell breaks loose.

"Just talking to myself. This is such a terrible thing to happen. But, to not investigate, to order, for heaven's sake, that no one discuss the incident! Harry is not well loved at his company. I mean, look at the letter Jed printed in *The Independent* today. It says Harry has actually considered bringing in Chinese workers to man his mines. If *that* isn't fuel to the fire, I don't know what is. When the strike occurred in May, he was back East telegraphing brutal orders to his mine manager. Oh, I hear things, you know. I heard that he told his manager to spread the word that anyone attempting to stop the strikebreakers would never walk again. I know that you will defend Harry to the death. That you probably did just that in the War, when you were under his command. But does this mean no proper burial and mourning for the men? What of their families?"

"Inez, Harry is not as black-hearted as you make him out. Of course the men will be mourned and properly buried." His voice was sharp. "Harry is also providing a generous settlement to each family."

"Buying their silence no doubt," Inez said, louder than she intended.

There was a long, cold pause.

Finally, Reverend Sands turned to her desk, picked up her fan, and brought it to her. "We should go. They'll be opening the doors to the banquet room at eleven o'clock." He touched her cheek with a gloved hand. "What I wanted to say—before the conversation got derailed—is that I've been asked to accompany Grant and his party for the rest of their Colorado stay."

She forced herself not to jerk back from his touch. "Hasn't he bodyguards of his own? Or is he hoping you'll provide intervention of a more heavenly sort?"

Sands said nothing.

"How long will you be gone?"

"At least a week. Maybe two."

"I see." She lowered her eyes. The moonlight glinted off her fan's silver chasing. "Well, you are correct in one regard. We should be going if we are not to be the last in the banquet hall. I do hope that Tabor hasn't bribed someone to tinker with the seating."

Chapter Thirty-seven

The banquet and the speeches afterward were just as interminable as Inez had feared they'd be.

The only good, she reflected, as first one o'clock, then two o'clock in the morning ticked by, was that she had managed to dodge the disaster of being Horace Tabor's dining partner. It had taken some heavy "iron hand in velvet glove" ministerial persuasion on the part of Reverend Sands to undo the seating arrangements, but place cards were hastily moved around and the untenable conditions rectified to Inez's satisfaction. However, it did make her a little nervous that the lieutenant governor of the fair state of Colorado directed an occasional drunken and sulky glower her way, as if very much aware of her decision to give him the cold shoulder.

She was also gratified to see that Serena Clatchworthy was in attendance, particularly since the feminine sex was only lightly represented amongst the hundred or more attendees.

Despite her defiantly purple dress of differing hues and fabrics and a most becoming clutch of purple flowers in her upswept hair, Mrs. Clatchworthy seemed uncharacteristically subdued. It could be, Inez reflected, the tempering effect of her brother at her elbow. He chatted amicably with his dinner partners but, it seemed to Inez, kept a close attention whenever his sister opened her mouth to converse. As with the other attendees of a journalistic bent, once the speeches began, she pulled out her notepad, retrieved a pencil, and scribbled surreptitiously while the speakers went on. And on.

Inez hid a yawn behind her fan, as yet another speaker rose and began, "Owing to the lateness of the hour, and after there has been so much said, and so well said, I can scarcely think of anything that I can say that will add to the sentiments already expressed."

Oh, but you will come up with something, thought Inez, as the speaker launched into his speech with an enthusiasm that was a sight to behold at three in the morning. He had just begun a long and laborious passage about Colorado and her greatness and welcoming the general on behalf of the whole people of Colorado, except Utes and Chinamen, when one of Mrs. Clatchworthy's flowers fell from her hair and dropped onto the white tablecloth.

Mrs. Clatchworthy leaned toward her brother, said something in his ear. He nodded. She picked up the flower, set her napkin on the table and rose, heading toward the ladies' dressing room. Inez excused herself with a whisper to the reverend, who, focused on the speech, nodded absentmindedly, and hurried after Serena, hoping to catch her alone.

Luck was with her, for once. A servant sat in one corner, nodding precipitously with an occasional snore that sounded more like a sneeze. Serena, standing before one of the mirrors, was plucking the delicate flowers out of her hair, and attempting to re-tuck them back in so they would stay.

"Mrs. Clatchworthy, may I lend a hand? I know how hard it is to arrange the back of one's coiffure without help."

She started, then looked up at Inez's reflection in the mirror. "Oh, thank you, Mrs. Stannert. Yes, it is such a bother and I am all thumbs. I actually hired a neighbor to do my hair, never guessing it would begin to shed in such a way. But Willie, Mr. Casey that is, threatened to leave me at home if I didn't dress up properly and be on my best behavior. Bah! But what could I do? He is the veteran of the War, the one who received the invitation. To hear and observe for myself, it was necessary to acquiesce." She shrugged.

A purple flower poised over one ear let go and landed on her shoulder, clinging desperately to a bit of lavender lace.

"Allow me, then." Inez untangled the delicate bloom from her collar.

Serena surrendered the handful she'd collected. Inez set to work, carefully inserting the blooms in the complicated twisted plaits of Serena's dark brown hair and trying to decide how to broach the topic of Mrs. Wesley and the damning letters published in *The Independent*.

Serena, however, saved her from the difficulty of setting a devious conversational trap at three in the morning.

"Honestly, can you believe these speeches," Serena said conversationally. "'The whole of people of Colorado, excepting the Utes and the Chinamen, welcome you.' Are the Celestials and Indians not men, women, and children as well? Honestly. It just feeds into the fervor over the *The Independent* paper today. As if the Celestials are not even human."

"Ah yes, *The Independent*." Inez tucked one blossom between two thick ropes of hair. "And then, there was Mr. Wesley's views on women's suffrage."

"Oh yes indeed. I will say," her voice perked up, "I sold every single copy of the *Cloud City Clarion* today, due to the mention of that letter. I shall have to thank Mr. Elliston for the free advertisement."

"So, the letter was real?" Inez tried to sound casually interested, as if this was all just idle conversation to pass the time while she replanted the bouquet in Serena's hair.

Serena twisted around to look at Inez, causing the most recent of the replaced flowers to once again loosen and fall. "Why, I have no idea. I never received it. So, I didn't have the chance to view the contents myself." She twisted back to the mirror, the wings of her dark eyebrows drawn together. "But I tell you, I will be there at the duel tomorrow to see Mr. Elliston's proof. If he has a letter addressed to me, it is my property and should be returned. Stealing from the U.S. post is a most grievous offense."

"You think that it is not a hoax? Has Mr. Wesley written to you in the past?" Another bloom slid neatly into place.

"Well, really it's Lucretia Wesley and I who are likely to hold common correspondence." Serena touched her hair tentatively.

"No no, don't touch. That's what makes them loosen and fall out. So, you and Mrs. Wesley are comrades in arms in the fight for women's suffrage, and her son's views are…?"

She shrugged. "His own. But I would be surprised if he did not share his mother's opinions. She has been a strong influence on his life, and I certainly agree with him about the plight of the Chinese. Why shouldn't they be allowed to work? Why should we bar them from this country? Did we bar the Irish during the Great Famine? Did we bar the Dutch when they first came to New York? Did you know that during the famine, a group of Indians, Choctaws actually, put together a collection and sent it to Ireland to help the starving? Now, I ask you, why shouldn't Indians, Celestials, and yes, women of all races, be allowed to vote and take on honest work?"

"Why not indeed," said Inez, desperate to keep the conversation on track as she only had two more blossoms to position. "Speaking of women and honest work, did you know that Mr. Elliston hired a woman typesetter for *The Independent*?"

"No!" Definite, genuine surprise and disbelief. "Mr. Elliston? Well, I am speechless."

"So, you don't know this typesetter? A woman named Zel or Zelda…?" Inez watched Serena's open mobile face in the mirror closely.

"I'd no idea she even existed! I shall have to find her and hire her away from him. Imagine, a women's rights paper, created and designed solely by women. How wonderful that would be to put on the masthead."

"Well, she's disappeared," said Inez.

"Oh, I am so sorry to hear." Serena sounded genuinely, completely disappointed. "Zelda. Do you know her surname?"

"Thomas?" suggested Inez, injecting doubt, hoping to see perhaps a flicker of recognition at the last name.

Serena looked blank. Not a shred of recognition. "Ah, well. Such a shame. I shall keep an ear out in case she resurfaces."

She looked back at her reflection, twisting one way, then the other to view the flower arrangement, and broke into a sunny smile. "Why, it's beautifully done, Mrs. Stannert. Thank you! How can I ever repay you?"

Inez smiled back. *You already have, Serena. You already have.*

Chapter Thirty-eight

The banquet lasted until nearly dawn. Inez had the reverend drop her off at home.

Splashing water on her face, she noted the overcast nature of the lightening Sunday morning sky through the bedroom window. The banquet clothes and fine jewelry came off and she replaced her best corset with one that was worn and lightly-laced. Finally, she slid with a sigh into a well-worn walking dress and ancient boots. *If I'm heading to Chicken Hill, I need to be prepared to walk.*

It was just after daybreak when she tapped on the back door of the Silver Queen and called, "Bridgette? It's me, Mrs. Stannert. Don't shoot."

Inez knew that, when Bridgette was at the saloon alone in the early mornings, she tended to have the shotgun near to hand, just in case some drunk tried to jimmy a door, with an eye to obtaining shelter or additional liquid reinforcement.

The door creaked open. Bridgette, with a full apron, flour in her hair, and, sure enough, shotgun in one hand, stood aside and let Inez in.

"Why, ma'am. I wasn't sure I'd see you this morning. I understand the banqueting and speeches went on nearly 'til dawn. I thought you'd be catching a small nap before going to church." Bridgette paused, looking at Inez's ancient dress doubtfully. "You *are* going to church, aren't you, ma'am?"

"It all depends," hedged Inez. "Actually, I have a very important question to ask you. You know many of the folks who live on Chicken Hill, don't you?"

"Well, not all. Those in the parish, certainly, and those who have been there a while. After all Mister O'Malley was one of the first to stake a claim in California Gulch, God rest his soul." She dabbed at an eye with a corner of her apron, leaving a floury smudge behind. "And of course, I know those who want to make themselves known in one way or another."

"As I said, you know many, if not most, of the Chicken Hill folk." Inez perched on the edge of the table, careful to avoid the rolled out sheet of biscuit dough, exhibiting neat and systematic holes stamped out with the biscuit cutter.

"And I know I asked you once about a family named Thomas, with a girl named Zel," she continued. "I have more information now. Can you think of a family with no mother, a daughter supporting an invalid father and two young brothers, perhaps twins? The daughter would probably not be around much. Possibly nicknamed Zel or Zelda or some such."

Bridgette stared. "Why bless my soul, ma'am. It sounds like you're talking about Preacher Thatcher and his three children, Zelpha, Zeke, and Zed. But those boys aren't children. Why, they're in here all the time. They are muckers at Silver Mountain. They made that big strike late last year and sold out to Mr. Gallagher, remember? Oh my, they tore up the town right proper. Then, when all the money was gone, in comes the father and sister. Sad story. Why, I took pity on that poor family—those two boys are worse than useless, I always thought so—and would bring them supper on occasion. The girl, Zelpha, is such a pretty little thing. I thought for certain she'd find some handsome young man up on the hill or somewhere in town. But I think she found some position in town. She's seldom home, you're right. And when she is, well, they keep to themselves. You know Preacher Thatcher? Blind as can be, more's the pity. Tends to go on about politics and the Lord and so on. Not of the faith, but I can appreciate his sincerity."

"Zelpha, Zeke, Zed. Yes! I do believe you've hit it, Bridgette!" Inez cut her off, afraid that Bridgette would rattle all day if the least encouraged. "You're a wonder! Now, I don't want to take another moment of your time. We are so appreciative of you coming in today, I feel guilty for taking up so much time gabbling. Where do the Thatchers live?"

Bridgette bustled around and found a scrap of paper and a pencil. "Why, I'll draw you a map, ma'am. Chicken Hill is not laid out in streets and alleys, you know. But they're not far from where I live. Here, I'll show you."

<><><>

Inez stopped outside the disreputable-looking shack, eyeing it dubiously while she caught her breath. In the interest of speed, she had hailed a passing hack on Harrison and had paid the driver well to take her as far up Chicken Hill as possible. The Thatchers, it turned out, lived close to the top. Inez took a deep breath, thinking on what she knew about the twins. Since yesterday was payday, they'd probably been out drinking all night. So she would have the drop on them in terms of surprise. All she needed to do was ask them about their sister and observe their reactions closely. Inez felt certain they would tell her what she wanted to know, one way or another.

Inez knocked on the door. The rattle shook the flimsy porch. Silence.

She knocked again.

Finally there was some stumbling and swearing from inside. The door swung open. Zeke stood there, swaying slightly, holding a sawed-off shotgun and wearing pants paired with an under-vest.

"Zeke. I haven't much time. Where's Zelpha?" Inez had decided that the direct attack was best. If she could take him off guard, he was bound to give something away, through word or action.

Sure enough, his reddened eyes darted to the side before centering and fixing again, somewhat blearily, on Inez. "Mrs.

Stannert? What the hell you doin' here? What's this 'bout Zelpha?"

"I know she's been accused of Lizzie's murder," she said. "I know she was working as a typesetter before she disappeared. Listen, she's the only one who can untangle a whole mess of problems. I need to talk to her. She's still here, isn't she? She hasn't taken the train and left town, I hope?"

As she expected, Zeke's gaze shifted briefly to the right again and back. He took the bait she offered. "Hell, ya know the mess she's in, a'course she left town. We gave her the money and sent her out on the train to Denver."

He stared stubbornly at her.

She stared back. *Liar.*

"Well, then, do you know where she's staying? Can you get a message to her?"

Zeke tried to look crafty. "For a fee, I suppose so."

I should have known.

Inez dug in a pocket and extracted a gold dollar piece. "Tell her that I must talk to her. It has to do with the business at Flo's place. I believe she didn't kill Lizzie, and I think I know how the murderer got into the room. Finally, she has something of great importance that belongs to the newspaper. It needs to be returned. She'll understand."

"Zelpha's no thief!" Brotherly ire was aroused.

"I never said she was," said Inez gently. "I'm trying to help. That's all."

Zeke broke eye contact, hawked, and spat off to the side.

Recognizing signs that the conversation was over, Inez said, "I've got to get back to the saloon. Please, the sooner you get the message to her, the better for everyone. Zelpha included."

Inez turned and started picking her way down the slope, doing her best to avoid the offal and garbage strewn about. She turned the corner of a path that wound around one shabby residence, sheltered in a small pocket of scruffy pine, and stopped. She counted to five, crossed in front of the cabin, and made her way around the other side before peeking around the corner.

Sure enough, there stood Zeke, still in his pants and grey woolen top, staring at the path she'd taken down. After a minute longer, he disappeared inside. Inez settled herself down to wait, hoping that it wouldn't take long. She allowed her eyes to wander in the direction of Zeke's sidelong glances. A withered tree, no more than a stump. Another shack, residence or possible outbuilding, it was hard to say. Beyond that slumped an abandoned, half-dismantled headframe.

She didn't have to wait long.

Zeke reappeared. He carried a tin lunch bucket and what looked like a canteen slung over one shoulder. He paused in the increasing morning light, looking around. Then, with a furtive hitch to his shoulders, he headed to the right, just as Inez surmised he might. He passed her first guess, the outbuilding, and kept going to the second, the abandoned mine shaft. He whistled the first bars of "Closer to Thee," before climbing down the shaft on what must have been a ladder.

Inez nodded to herself. *Now I know the signal. So I just need to figure out a way to get down without arousing suspicion.* She glanced at the nearby clothesline. There hung a gigantic pair of overalls that, with the cuffs rolled, just might work. *The good Lord is smiling on me today.*

Inez tugged the worn overalls off the line and slipped them on, stuffing her long skirts into the ample torso and cinching the straps up tight.

Zeke was up and out of the shaft before she was finished with her toilet.

She watched as he returned to the homestead without lunch bucket or canteen.

After a few minutes, he reappeared, this time with the kind of floppy sombrero favored by prospectors, and headed down the hill at a fast clip.

Good. Looks like he's headed to town. That should give me some time.

It began to rain, large drops, widely spaced. But the dark lowering sky promised that this was just the beginning of a major downpour.

Inez scanned the back of the dwelling, hoping for another miracle. Sure enough, another hat—not exactly like Zeke's but wide-brimmed and nondescript enough—hung on a peg. She removed her old bonnet, set it on a stump, placed the floppy men's hat on her head, and immediately understood why it was relegated to outside: the odor of skunk hung unmistakably about it at those close quarters. Stifling an impulse to take it off and throw it to the ground, Inez hastened up to the shaft. There was no ladder. It looked, for all purposes, completely deserted. *But I saw him climb down.*

She took a deep breath and, trying for the same key as Zeke, whistled. The lyrics rose unbidden along with the tune. "Let me come closer to Thee, Lord Jesus. Oh, closer day by day…"

She waited, unsure whether there might be an answer. Sure enough, a soft whistle echoed from below. "Let me lean harder on Thee, Lord Jesus. Yes, harder, all the way."

A rickety ladder appeared up out of the shaft and settled against the dirt-packed wall. Inez turned inward and started down, gripping the rungs tightly, hoping the light from outside was dim enough to hide details and bright enough to cast her figure into deep shadow. She prayed that overalls and hat, along with the exchange of signals, would be enough to lull Zelpha into a sense of security. She also prayed that, if her disguise wasn't good enough to last until she could get to the bottom of the ladder, that Zelpha wasn't armed with a gun.

The shaft was only about fifteen feet deep, and Inez was about seven feet from the ground when she heard a young woman behind her say with sisterly impatience, "Okay Zeke, what'd'ya forget now? I knew I shoulda written down the message for Mrs. Stannert. Okay, like I said, go tell Mrs. Stannert that I'll talk to her, if'n—"

Inez jumped the last few feet to the ground and said, "You can tell me yourself, Zelpha," and removed her hat.

Zelda jumped back, out of the circle of light delivered by the shaft. "Shit! What're you doin' here?"

Inez caught the gleam of wide eyes, and something else. Something that looked like the blade of a knife. Inez held out her hands, open, empty, and unthreatening.

"Zelpha. Zel. Zelda. Miss Thatcher. Miss Thomas. I'm here to help. We must talk."

"I'm not gonna go to jail. I didn't kill Lizzie." The knife didn't waver.

"I know. But someone did. And I think I know how." She briefly described the tunnel that joined Lynch's saloon to the brothel and Doc's observations about the violence of Lizzie's death wound and the smell of chloroform. "So you see, someone could have gotten in, when you weren't looking. Someone who knew about the passage and frequents the saloon next door. Someone who could have set it up with Molly to put Lizzie in Flo's room, then snuck in, knocked you out with the chloroform, did what he meant to do, and left, leaving you with the knife in the locked room."

Zelda had set her knife down on the hard-packed dirt. She sat on a large rock and covered her eyes with her hands. Inez noticed that several blankets and a pillow were in a jumble in the deep shadows.

"What am I going t' do?" Zelda cried.

"Trust me." Inez said this as persuasively and gently as possible. "Is there anything you remember about that night? Anything you saw or heard that will help me help you?"

Zelda looked up. "The man came up behind me. I'm sure it was a man. He was strong, and his hands..." She shivered. "It was a man, I'd swear."

"Yes, go on."

"Well, he had a cloth with something sweet smelling on it. Made me dizzy, then knocked me out cold."

"That was the chloroform."

"There's one more thing." She hesitated. "But I gotta have you swear. Swear on the Bible. Swear on your mother's grave. If'n I give this to you, I want something in exchange."

"What? Money? A ticket out of town?"

"Two tickets out of town. For me an' my beau. Takin' us as far West as we can get. Out of Colorado, for sure. To Nevada or Californy."

"Done. My mother's still alive, but I give you my word."

"You kin give the tickets to Zeke this afternoon. Zeke seems like a fool and been known to act like one. But he's changed some, now that I'm in trouble. He's taking good care of me and Pa. He'll come after you and kill you if anything happens to me or you back out. And if'n you give him the tickets, he'll bring 'em right to me. He wants to see me safe, too."

"I promise."

Zelda held up something. A small necklace of delicate links interspersed with small, white beads, and a cross dangling from it.

"This came off the man who kilt Lizzie. It caught on the shawl while I was fightin' with him. Can't say exactly what it is, but it's his. Unless he stole it, of course."

Inez held out her hand, palm up, waiting.

After a moment's hesitation, Zelda draped it across her fingers. Inez squinted at it in the dim light. "Something religious, I'd say."

"I've seen some folk on Chicken Hill with these. But they carry them in their pockets, not around their necks. I can't rightly say what it is. Go look at the back, in the light."

Inez moved to the light, turned the small cross over, and read: "To Abigail, First Communion. 1877."

First Communion.

"Catholic?" Inez said aloud.

"I dunno." Zelda had crept up behind her. "Pa never let us talk with the mackerel snappers. But you know, Mrs. O'Malley, she's a papist. And she was so kind to us. Kinder than most of the other folks around here."

Inez's hand closed over the object. "Thank you, Zelpha. This may be what we need to bring the real killer to justice."

"Well, whatever you do, I hope I'm long gone by then. Oh!" She sat back on her heels. "And somethin' else."

She went over to her canvas bag and dug inside, returning with a bundle. "Could you please give this to Miss Flo?"

It was a beautiful dressing gown, covered with embroidered flowers and butterflies.

"When the fire started, I grabbed it, and it's hers. I didn't 'zactly mean to take it or steal it or anything."

"One more thing. You're the girl that Mr. Elliston hired to be a typesetter at the newspaper, right?"

She nodded despondently. "I liked that job. I liked Mr. Elliston. I sure wish I could've stayed and learnt the trade."

"Do you have a couple of things that you forgot to leave there that night?"

"Oh. Sure do." She moved to the bedclothes, lifted the pillow, and extracted a fat envelope. "I hope it didn't cause him any trouble. I meant to return them to him somehow. Couldn't have Zeke waltz up and give them to him, though."

Inez slid the letters and the carte de visite out of the envelope.

"Pretty nasty picture," Zelda commented. "A Celestial, too. Sounds like this Wesley is in a world of trouble."

"Thank you, Zelda. And if he's in a world of trouble, well, it's by his own design." Inez unbuttoned the top buttons of her dress, tucked the envelope into the top of her corset, and place the delicate white chain of beads around her own neck. She glanced down at the oversized overalls. "I'll need to return the clothes I've borrowed here."

A thought occurred to her.

She smiled to herself and turned to Zelda.

"I will get you your two tickets. Now, do you need clothes? A hat? Some kind of disguise, perhaps? It may take a while to clear all this up, and I'm sure you'd rather leave sooner rather than later."

Zelda stared down at her Sunday best, soiled beyond repair. "I hadn't thought of that. I don't have anything extra that's decent. I'll bet the police'll be lookin'. How are we gonna get to the train, much less get on it and gone without gettin' caught?" She sounded despairing.

Inez rested a comforting hand on her shoulder. "I have an idea. When Zeke comes to get the tickets, I'll also have a bundle of clothes for you. Now, let me explain…"

Chapter Thirty-nine

"Mrs. Stannert, where you been in this rain? You look like you just finished runnin' a race at the racetrack, mud'n all."

"Never mind, Abe! I've got to—" In a fever, Inez yanked off the hat she'd forgotten to return to the shanty. She'd remembered to restring the overalls on the clothes line, none the worse for wear, and unfortunately left her bonnet outside on the stump. *Now that will confuse the residents.*

"Weeeeeuuuuw. You run into a skunk?"

"It'll take too long to explain." The little religious necklace felt like it was burning a hole against her skin. More and more, as she thought about it, she thought it was Catholic in nature. She tossed the smelly old hat outside. It sailed through the air, buoyed by its wide brim, to finally settle on a pile of trash.

"Where's Bridgette?"

"Well, she finished the bakin' early this mornin', and I told her to get on down for the late Mass and come on back later. Figured she'd appreciate some time with the Lord today. Might make up for all she's doin' for us on what's supposed to be a day of rest."

"Abe. What do you make of this?" She pulled out the chain and crucifix and set it on the kitchen table. Abe bent over it, arms crossed, hands tucked in high in his armpits.

"Why, that there's a rosary. Seen enough of 'em in my time. 'Specially in N' Orleans, when I was growin' up."

"Do you know whose it might be?"

"Well now, Inez, them Catholics, they don't go just pulling these out and swingin' 'em around any old time. Most times, they're only taken out for special prayer times. Tellin' the rosary or such. Or at Mass."

"Bridgette might know." Inez said. "When is she coming back? "

"About three I reckon. Is there a problem?"

"No, no. Yes! Actually, yes. I just…What time is it, Abe?"

He pulled out his pocket watch. "Near noon. Say, Zeke Thatcher came on by. Said he had a message for you. Wouldn't leave any other word, and said he'd be back about two."

"Then I've got to hurry! Abe, I'll be back a bit later this afternoon. Oh! And Jed, his duel's at six. Look, if you see that boy around again, the one that's always hanging around the State Street door—"

"Yeah, the one you've got a soft spot for."

"—Tell him to track down Mr. Elliston and ask him stop by the saloon after two-thirty. He should tell Mr. Elliston that I've got something he's searching for. Elliston will know what I mean."

⟨⟩⟨⟩⟨⟩

Inez hurried home. She took off the rosary and set it on her nightstand.

What man would carry such a thing with him? Whoever he was, he either was still here or he was gone. And if he was still in town, he probably didn't feel in any danger. Anyone looking for Lizzie's killer would still be looking for Zelda, not him.

Inez splashed soap, water, and vinegar in her washbasin, swished her hairbrush through it, and pulled it viciously through her hair, trying to neutralize the pungent odor of skunk. Finally, in despair, she bent her head over the bowl and, using the pitcher, repeatedly poured the mixture over her head. Toweling vigorously, she thanked God silently for hair that was no longer waist length.

Yielding to a desire to clean up as much as possible from the filthy and lengthy hike down Chicken Hill, she poured fresh water in the basin and hurriedly washed, getting the worst of the mud and sweat off, and leaving puddles everywhere in the process. She dressed in a clean, dry skirt and bodice, swearing as her still-damp skin stubbornly resisted her efforts to pull, fasten, hook, lace, and button everything in place.

She hastened over to one of the trunks in the room and threw it open, releasing the scent of mothballs and the sight of her husband's everyday clothes, neatly folded.

Waiting.

She bundled up two complete ensembles, from handkerchiefs to hose, and hunted down an old pair of Mark's shoes and two men's hats, bowlers still lingering more than a year after his disappearance. She stuffed some newspaper—an old issue of *The Independent*, she noted—into the toes of the shoes and shoved all the clothes into a nondescript canvas satchel.

She attempted to pin her hair back—it was a straggly mess now—and finally jammed a bonnet on her head.

Now to rustle up the manager of the Denver and Rio Grande ticket office, wake him from his Sunday after-dinner nap, and make him an offer he can't refuse.

Chapter Forty

Inez made it back to the saloon by a quarter after two. Zeke was waiting, glowering through his beard and shoulder-length scraggly hair, a shot glass, uncharacteristically still full, at his elbow.

Sol sidled up to her. "Mr. Jackson told him you were coming back," he whispered. "Mr. Jackson even gave him a drink on the house, while he waited. But he's not touched it." Sol sounded alarmed, as if such unusual behavior might herald a new kind of epidemic in the hard-drinking fraternity.

"Mr. Thatcher, thank you for your patience. Please, let's go upstairs where we can talk," said Inez. Clutching the satchel, she proceeded up to the office without a backwards glance.

She knew he'd follow.

Once inside and behind closed doors, she wasted no time on niceties. "Here." She handed Zeke an envelope. "Two tickets to San Francisco. Zelpha and her traveling companion needn't go all the way through, of course. There are many stops along the way. Nevada City, Sacramento—"

"Yeah, I kin give her the picture," said Zeke. He reached down into his boot top and, right in front of Inez's shocked eyes, drew out a Bowie knife.

She stepped back a pace, snaked a hand into her pocket, and gripped her small revolver.

Zeke fastidiously slit the top of the envelope with the wicked knife, pulled out the tickets, and made as if to examine them.

Inez relaxed, but kept her hand curled around the grip. *Zeke can't even read. Those tickets could be to Timbuktu, for all he knows.*

Zeke tucked the tickets back in the envelope. He didn't have that unholy gleam in his eye anymore, but seemed more worried than anything else. "Zel said you'd have something else. What is it?"

She handed him the satchel. "My husband's old clothes."

To her satisfaction, he looked nonplussed.

Good. This will work.

She continued, "Now, I'll give you instructions as to what she and her traveling companion are to do. And don't leave anything out. If she follows my directions, I promise, this will work."

⟨⟩⟨⟩⟨⟩

After Zeke left, Inez had naught to do but return to daily business, while casting anxious looks at the two doors whenever one or the other swung open. In consequence, she spilled more liquor, broke more glasses, delivered more incorrect orders—

"Mrs. Stannert, you're jumpy as a cat too close to a dogfight. What's got into you?" Abe moved her aside to clean up a spill of Madeira wine and offer a clean bar towel and an apology to the dandy now swearing volubly over the red splash on his pale yellow waistcoat.

"You know about the duel? Jed Elliston and that whelp John Quincy Adams Wesley. Pistols at six. I need to reach Jed before then."

"Well, most like Jed's either off someplace practicin' with whatever gun he's got or writin' up his own obituary. Mebbe both."

"You have so little faith in his marksmanship?"

Abe sighed. "Mrs. Stannert. You ever seen him lift anything more dangerous than a pencil? If'n it was shotguns at six paces and he got to fire first, don't know that I'd place a bet on him even then."

"But just yesterday, he had any number of people in his corner, right here in the saloon, taking odds on him."

"Well, that was afore Mr. Wesley went out to the tracks with all those swells that follow him around, along with most of Leadville's writin' contingent and a good few of Leadville's population, and let 'em watch him practice."

Her heart sank.

"He's good?"

"Word is, he could probably outgun Doc Holliday in a shootout. That's probably stretchin' the truth, but folks swear he's plenty good enough to take on Jed Elliston."

Inez swore softly, and the urchin appeared as if by magic, a miniature genie summoned from the bottle. Dirty hands appeared first, hooking on the top of the bar, followed by a filthy cap over a pair of peeping eyes. "Sorry, Mrs. Stannert, ma'am. I've ast ever'where. Looked ever'where. No one's even seen him the whole day."

"Well, you tried." She fished a penny out of her pocket. "Just keep your eyes open. If you find him, there's still that nickel in it."

"Yes ma'am!"

He shot out the Harrison Avenue door, nearly bowling over Bridgette who was coming in. She caught one ear and said, "What would your mother say if she knew you were here, and on a Sunday no less. And running around like a hooligan! What do you say, young man?"

"Sorry, ma'am!"

She let him go.

"Bridgette! I'm so glad you're here. I need to talk to you." Inez hurried from around the bar and followed Bridgette into the kitchen.

"Why, surely ma'am, but I'll need to start setting up for supper. You still want to offer supper tonight?"

"Very limited choices. Cold, sliced chicken. Leftover stew. Cheese and pickles. That kind of thing. Now, this is quick. I want you to look at this. " She felt around her pockets and sighed in annoyance. "Oh! I left it at home! Well, I came across something that may point us to who killed that poor woman in the brothel the other night."

Bridgette paused, pickle jar in hand, eyes popping. "The girl who was found dead in the alley, then wasn't dead, and then had her throat cut? Poor thing. I heard she was murdered by one of the other fallen women."

"Well, anything's possible, but I think now it was someone from the outside. But listen: this is what was left behind afterwards." Inez described the rosary.

Bridgette set the pickle jar down with a thump and a frown. "A white rosary, you say. That's a child's rosary. Probably given to her on her first communion, poor child."

"I'm wondering if you might know who'd have something like this?"

"Well, it tickles my memory, it does, but nothing I can put my finger on. Oh dear. What if it belongs to someone in our parish?" Sh straightened up, looking anxious. "I should talk to the good father about this."

"No! Not yet. If I bring it in tomorrow, could you look at it? That might help you remember."

"Of course, of course. And I'll think on it now. What do you plan to do with it?"

"I'll turn it over to the police, of course. And tell them how I came about it. Tomorrow." *After Zelpha is safely out of town.* "But if you think of anything that could help me, please tell me, right away."

Bridgette hustled to the pie safe, began pulling out cherry pies and lining them up on the long kitchen table. "I certainly will, ma'am."

She sighed and returned to the bar, sidled up to Abe and motioned for him to pull out his pocket watch. She looked at the time, then up at Abe.

"I'd better get down there. He's certainly going to arrive before six. There's still time to stop this."

"And how do you figure on doin' that? You gonna stand as his second and then knock him on the head so's you can take his place?"

"No. Better than that. I've got the proof."

◇◇◇

Inez hurried down to the tracks, envelope safe in her reticule.

A large crowd had formed already and was milling about. She identified representatives from the local papers and several visiting pressmen from Denver who tended to congregate at the Silver Queen when in town. Wesley was there, with his usual group of sycophants and yes-men. She also noticed a large number of the local law about, including The Hatchet, his tall thin figure looming a head above the rest. There to keep order in the crowd, clean up after the bloodbath, or just to watch.

Wesley made a show of inspecting the sun's declination, pulling out his pocket watch with a flourish, and shaking his head.

Murmurs grew through the mob. "He's not coming." "That yellow-livered…" "Hell, he's a pencil-pusher. No sense of honor." "Guess all that talk was nothing but hot air and slander."

Then, everyone's attention shifted.

Jed Elliston.

Coming down Third Street, accompanied by two men.

Indefinable animal sounds of anticipation rolled in a hundred throats. Inez pushed out of the crowd and almost ran up the hill to meet him.

"Mr. Elliston! Jed!" She was breathless.

He looked at her. As near-dead from fear as anyone could be and still standing and walking. "Come to see the show, Mrs. Stannert?" He sounded bitter.

"Jed! For God's sake. I've got it."

Jed blinked, not seeming to understand.

"The letters and the…other thing."

She pulled the envelope, much crinkled and the worse for wear, from her purse. She hesitated, holding it up. "There's one more thing I need from you."

"What? Anything!" His gaze seized the envelope with desperate hope like a dying man might clutch a Bible to his breast.

"Not now. But later. Afterwards. You must promise."

"I promise. My firstborn, should I live to have such. Just… please, Mrs. Stannert."

She thrust the envelope into his hands.

Ignoring the shouts of the masses down the hill, Jed tore the envelope open with trembling hands. His two cronies—newsmen from Boulder, she thought—craned their necks to see what he held.

One whistled. "*Wesley* wrote *that*? He must have a death wish. Or at least, must've decided that politics wasn't the job for him. 'Cause this'll bury him."

The other pulled the photograph from Jed's hand, examined it with much attention, turned it over, and read aloud: "'To My John. Come Back. See Soon. Love.' Whoa. What else is there to see? Looks like it's all there for the viewing."

Jed snatched back the carte de visite. He held up photo and letters above his head and said in a voice that carried to the railroad tracks and beyond. "Wesley! You want proof? Here's proof of all I wrote. In your own hand. When I'm done with you, you'll want to use that gun on yourself!"

The reporters in the crowd were the first to break ranks, heading up the slope at a dead run, elbowing each other out of the way to be first in line to view the evidence.

Chapter Forty-one

"How d' I look?" Zelda waited anxiously for a word from her paramour.

"Zel, you're the prettiest thing in the world," said Reuben. "Even in pants and a derby hat."

She twisted the buttons on the maroon vest. Her legs felt so strange in the trousers. But she kind of liked that she didn't have to worry about skirts and petticoats and all that.

"So's, you don't mind about my hair?"

He lifted her hat and gently ran a hand over her cropped curly hair. "Who cares? It's just hair. It'll grow back. Like mine will."

She looked at him, all spiffed up, in the duds Mrs. Stannert had provided. With his stringy hair all cut off and slicked back, he looked like a right proper swell, and real handsome, too. Her heart felt near to bursting looking at him.

"You gotta remember to tip your hat to ladies and bow," said Reuben. "All the stuff the gentlemen do. Now, I gotta have a name t' call you."

"I got a new name, remember? It's right here in this letter that Mrs. Stannert had delivered up. Abel. Can't get much farther away in the alphabet from Zelpha or Zelda, that's for sure."

"Then, you kin call me Cain. We'll be like brothers. Leastwise 'til we hit San Francisco." He pulled her close and gave her a passionate kiss. "Guess that's the last time we kin do that for a while."

She pushed him away and glanced up at the circle of fading sky showing through the shaft's opening. "Time to go. We got a train to catch." She cleared her throat, looked over at Zeke, who had his eyes glued to a section of the adjoining drift, as if, by looking hard enough, that elusive flash of silver might suddenly materialize.

"Now Zeke, you gotta promise t' take good care of Pa."

"'S all right, Zel." His voice was gruff. "You kin count on me. Unlike Zed, who has no brains at all."

"I'll send you money when I get a job." She sniffed, wiped her nose, and smiled. "Mebbe I'll just keep this set of clothes. I could get a job as a typesetter someplace else. Could be as a feller or a girl, since I got two letters of recommendation here." She pulled out two crumpled, hastily composed letters written and signed by Jed Elliston. "This here's about Zelpha Thatcher. And this here one's about Abel Atcherson. 'To Whom It May Concern. Abel Atcherson has been in my employ as a typesetter for three months and shows great promise—'"

"Let's go, Zel. Can't miss that train."

Reuben hefted the carpetbag over his shoulder and ascended the ladder to the top of the shaft. Zelda followed. At the top, on real ground at last, she paused in the coming dusk and turned around once. She took in her shanty home, the peaks of Mount Massive and Elbert outlined by the last fading flash of sun, and the lights of Leadville coming on in a soft glow below. "Good-bye home," she said softly. "Good-bye mountains and Leadville. Good-bye Flo an' Mr. Elliston an' Mrs. Stannert. Good-bye Colorado. And hell-o Californy, here we come."

Chapter Forty-two

Down in the saloon, Inez watched the door anxiously even as her hands stayed busy pouring another line of drinks for Jed Elliston and his cadre of celebrating journalists. This round had been paid for by none other than the editor of the competing *Leadville Chronicle*.

The urchin appeared as he always did, as if from thin air, dirty hands clamped to the bar first, followed by the hat and eyes. "I did all you said, ma'am."

"To whom did you give the letters?"

"Zeke Thatcher, ma'am. Here's the piece of paper you ast me to bring back."

He let go of the bar and disappeared, dropping down to explore his pockets. Then, a small chubby hand appeared over the lip of the counter, pushing a crumpled piece of paper toward her.

She examined Zeke's hastily scribbled mark on it, and nodded, satisfied. And slid the nickel back to the waiting hand. "As promised."

"Thank y', ma'am!" The urchin shot out the door like a squirrel chased by hounds.

She leaned on the bar, thinking to give Jed a sign that he was now released from any obligations to her, but he was occupied with being the hero triumphant of the evening. His offer to buy drinks for the house had been roundly voted down by the sturdy few who'd bet long on him winning the duel and had come out big against the overwhelming odds.

"Well, Elliston did win the duel," pointed out one literal wag as he collected from the grumbling losers. "And I think you oughta pay us double, because he did it without even pulling his gun!"

The losers all groused good-naturedly and slapped Jed on the back. "So, Elliston, you going to share your sources with us next time?"

"A reporter never shares his sources," said Jed, then launched into a lengthy, somewhat slurred speech about the honor of the press.

Inez wondered if any of the fourth estate were out covering the former president's goings-on that Sunday evening. They all seemed to be present at the Silver Queen. And, she wondered if the streets of Leadville were unprotected tonight as most of Leadville's finest also seemed to be participating in the celebration and rounds of drinks. Except for The Hatchet, who was sticking to his usual coffee with cream. He stayed with the other officers, down at one end of the bar, listening, talking occasionally, but mostly, it seemed, watching Inez.

Every time she glanced his way, he was watching her.

It gave her the creeps.

She wondered if he were keeping track of her, just in case she decided to slip on down and question Flo at the jail or the girls in the parlor house.

"Well, that's that," said Inez, turning to Abe. "I suppose John Wesley will need to find a different line of work in a different city." She had a momentary pang for his mother.

"He's young," pointed out Abe. "He's got money. He'll survive."

"If his mother doesn't throw him out on his ear."

"Hey, Mrs. Stannert!" One of the officers waved an empty shot glass.

She sighed and said to Abe, "And if no one is buying right now, I'm sure he's going to want that on the house. I'd at least like to know I'm getting some protection for all the liquor we give to the boys in blue." She grabbed a whiskey bottle and headed toward them.

The kitchen door at the back flew open, and Bridgette came out, shawl wrapped around her.

"Ma'am, I'm leaving now, but I just thought of something… Oh, good evening officers, and Officer Ryan! Why, Officer Kelly, does your wife know you're here? For shame!…As I was saying, ma'am. Tomorrow night's Rosary. Why don't you bring that little rosary by the saloon tomorrow morning? Maybe I'll recognize it. Goodness knows, it's not common for a grown man to be carryin' a child's beads. It must have a story, and if there's a story, I'll find out, from the good father or from someone else in the parish. That way, when you take it to the police station, you can tell them about that tunnel and—"

"Thank you, Bridgette. I'll definitely bring it in tomorrow. Thanks so much." Inez cut her off, afraid what else she might blurt out in her enthusiasm.

Inez turned back to the policemen, whiskey bottle ready to pour for Officer Kelly and two others that suddenly had empty glasses to fill.

One of the State Street patrolmen said to his fellows, "Let's see if'n we can find an assembly of lewd wimmen on the boards, showin' off their ankles t' help sell beer! Oughta be good for a fine or two, whaddya say, City Collector Ryan? Shall we go enrich the city's coffers?"

The Hatchet said nothing. Only downed his coffee and left with the rest.

Chapter Forty-three

Later that night, Abe paused on Inez's doorstep, looking over her little house. "Well, that was some evenin'. I think we took in more than we did the whole week, and that's sayin' somethin'. Inez, what's all this Bridgette was sayin' about the rosary an' a tunnel an' police an' such?"

"Well, there's an underground passageway that connects Lynch's saloon to Flo's place. It's there from the days when Mrs. DuBois owned both places. I think Lizzie's killer used that tunnel, and that he's but a hair's breadth away. As soon as I show Bridgette the rosary, I'm taking it to the police. Or maybe the city marshal. I trust him more."

"Be careful, Inez. You don't know who might be behind this. Could even be the law."

Inez looked off to the distance. The mountains cupped the city like a pair of hands: Mosquito Range on one side, Sawatch Range on the other. In the vast night, made darker by clouds that covered the stars, Inez couldn't help but feel that the Almighty was watching the doings of Leadville. If He were, she thought, He'd be sick of all the greed, avarice, lust, lies that boiled in the town. It would be nothing for Him to bring those monolithic hands together and squeeze.

"It has occurred to me," she said quietly. "The officers have access to nearly everything. And the power. But, who would stoop to killing a prostitute? And why? Even a policeman wouldn't escape punishment, and censure."

"Hard to say." Abe scrubbed the back of his neck, contemplatively. "You want me to go talk t' Lynch tomorrow? Ask him 'bout that tunnel? You think Lynch might be part of this?"

"It's possible. But let's not alert any more folks to the fact that we're looking around. When Bridgette started talking this evening—" Inez winced.

"You want me to sit outside your place with a shotgun t'night, Inez?"

She laughed. "Abe. I'll be fine. It's, what, four hours to daylight? And besides, it's going to rain again. No need for you to sit out here getting soaked. Go home to your wife. I'll see you later this morning."

She searched her pocket for keys and her fingers brushed her pocket revolver. Just feeling its compact but deadly bulk gave her comfort. She unlocked the door, said good-night to Abe, went inside, and locked the door firmly. Then, thinking that she didn't hear the bolt slide, she unlocked and locked it again.

For a moment, she stood in the dark, listening. Only the usual sounds, the creaking and popping of a frame house settling. The wind moaning around the corners, whispering through invisible cracks and seams.

"It's all right," she said aloud. "This is my home."

Just to prove the point to herself, she went into the parlor room, pulled open the heavy curtain to let in what little light there was. She ran a hand over her parlor grand piano, riffled through a pile of music, and wished that Reverend Sands were there.

She placed the music in a neat stack on her piano and headed to her bedroom across the hall.

With a sigh, she lit the small crystal coal oil lamp by her bedside and repositioned the glass chimney. She pulled her pocket revolver from her pocket, lay it on the nightstand, and then picked up the small rosary, running the beads through her fingers and examining the small figure on the tiny cross. Wondering who and where its owner was, she let it snake back on the nightstand. Inez settled into the chair next to the stand, picked up her buttonhook, and began unfastening her shoes.

The house settled into a familiar symphony of pops and creaks as the wood floors and planks of the walls responded to the wind and the cold.

Inez heard a small patter of timpani on her rooftop: *Raining again. What a strange July this has been. No doubt General Grant must think Leadville as rainy and muddy as—*

Her bedroom door slammed open with such force that the glass doorknob hit the back wall and exploded. Inez gasped, prelude to a scream, and began to stand. An arm came around her neck from behind, brutally cutting off air, lifting her up and off the chair. Inez clawed, seeking just a little room to breathe.

A heavy clank boomed off the floor. The attacker leaned toward the nightstand, dragging Inez with him. A black-gloved hand grabbed the small rosary. Inez saw, from her bent-over position, a lantern on the floor. A bull's eye lantern, shuttered.

A policeman's lantern.

The chokehold eased slightly. Inez gulped air just before a damp cloth wrapped around her nose and mouth. She caught the sweet whiff of apples as the cloth descended.

No!

She held her breath. She tried to kick backwards with her one shoe to take him off balance, distract him. But her attacker seemed to expect this. Prepared to just stand and take it, until she had no choice but to inhale.

Near dizzy with fear, heart pounding, lungs shrieking, in desperation Inez hooked her stockinged foot around the spindle-legged nightstand, and yanked.

The delicate table lurched and tipped, the light from the coal oil lamp jumping crazily over walls.

The lamp hit the floor by Inez's bed with an explosive crash. Flames licked from the broken crystal base and lantern, kissed the bedclothes that draped from featherbed to floor.

The nascent fire leaped up in a triumphant roar.

Her assailant stumbled backwards. The cloth on her face loosened.

Inez tore the cloth off, ripping it from his hand, and took in a huge gulp of fire-seared smoky air.

A curse rasped from behind her.

His arm clamped around her throat again, his hand seized her wrist.

She wriggled desperately, kicked backwards again, more successfully, as he tried to push her toward the flames.

She still had one hand free.

The hand that gripped the buttonhook.

Inez wrenched violently side to side. She finally caught a glimpse of his face.

The Hatchet.

Heavy curtains covering her bedroom window burst into sudden flames. In the blindingly stark light, The Hatchet looked like a beast from Hell itself, lips drawn back in a snarl, eyes black pits.

She plunged her buttonhook into the nearest pit.

He screamed, and let go. His hands convulsively cupped his eye, the buttonhook hanging in the socket.

Inez shoved him away. Away from the door and her escape.

The Hatchet stumbled, his boot kicking the police lantern over. Like a can in a child's game, the lantern rolled toward the inferno that had been her bed and sanctuary.

Inez raced past The Hatchet, who was now bent over, hands cradling his face.

She was out of the bedroom. Sudden heat and flash bathed her back as the additional liquid fuel from the lantern fed the fury behind her.

Coughing, choking in smoke, feeling seared, Inez looked wildly to the front door.

Too late!

The thin wood walls of her home were no barrier to the fire's energy. Flames consumed the front door, lapped across the inner entryway wall, raced along the molding, and headed for her parlor.

My piano!

Then, the screaming began again, and didn't stop.

She looked, once, back at her bedroom. A curtain of fire filled the doorway and began working in the other direction. Flames licked hungrily along the wall, spreading to the floor, heading to the back of the house.

There was no choice.

She clapped her hands over her ears to block out the inhuman sound, and she ran. Ran toward the back of the house, trying to outrun the flames jumping down the hallway.

Despite her covered ears, she could still hear The Hatchet, getting weaker, his screams now drowned out by explosion after explosion rocketing behind her as lamp fuel exploded, drapes burst into spontaneous flames, varnish blistered and peeled, taking everything, everything, into oblivion.

A torrent of cold air flowed past her, rushing, tunneling into the hallway. Her shoulder flared in pain as she clipped the kitchen entryway. One of the panes in the back door was shattered, mute testimony to The Hatchet's entry.

Gripping the knob, her ticket out of the inferno, she twisted it, yanked the door open, and fell, gasping, into her back yard. She crawled away from the perdition that had been her home.

Through her own coughing and crying, she heard voices at the front of the house, alarmed voices raised in cries for help.

Then, she was aware of something more.

Rain.

Cold, cold rain, pattering on her skin and her clothes. Tapping on her splayed fingers, drumming on the flagstones that her husband had laid out so carefully to form a walkway to the privy, in what seemed another lifetime.

Inez leaned forward over her hands and vomited.

"Mrs. Stannert!" A voice, at first unfamiliar, but full of relief came from above her.

A warm jacket settled over her shivering shoulders. It was only then that she realized, in some distant way, that her clothes had been smoldering. Now, charred bits hung from her neck, the remains of a lace collar. She moved her fingers experimentally. They all were there, all working.

A hand pulled her up to sitting and snugged the jacket around her. She looked up into the worried face of Cecil Farnesworth, mapmaker.

"Mrs. Stannert! I saw the fire and I didn't dare to hope. I thought I was too late."

She buried her face in her hands. Cecil continued in a rush, as if with the opening of the leaden skies, the bonds that had held him had also eased. "It was Officer Ryan. I talked with Lynch, the saloonkeeper, but he wasn't nearly as forthcoming as his partner, McCarthy. You see, the entrance to the passage was in a room that Lynch rented out by the hour. He's got, well, a couple women working there."

She heard Cecil clear his throat, embarrassed.

"In any case, all this last week, McCarthy told me, since a few days before Grant's arrival, the room's been rented by Ryan." His face twisted. "McCarthy also said that Lynch was sweet on Lizzie. I guess he'd hoped she'd come work for him. But that's neither here nor there."

Inez finally spoke, the light of fire bringing out the truth. "The Hatchet knew about the tunnel. Where it connected. He killed Lizzie with Molly's help. She put Lizzie in Flo's room, most likely as insurance, just in case Flo was right and Lizzie wasn't dead from the cold, the liquor, the drugs."

"Most likely that was it. Yes." Cecil sat down on the ground, unaware or uncaring of the mud.

"And The Hatchet. He set the fires?"

"Probably."

"Why?" said Inez aloud. "Why would he bother with Flo's business? Why warn me to stay away? What business would he have—" She stopped.

Business.

Flo's third partner.

"Inez!" Another voice. Well-known. Beloved. Welcome.

Familiar arms came around her this time, offering sanctuary, and lifted her up in an all-encompassing embrace.

Reverend Sands voice ran over her like a lover's touch. "I saw the flames from Harrison. I thought…"

She clung to him, fingers wrapped in the overcoat. "I'm fine. But my house. My piano. All my things. The Hatchet. In there."

His arms around her tightened.

She rested her head wearily on his shoulder.

"The Hatchet? Officer Ryan?"

"Yes."

She felt him shake his head.

"Let's get you to someplace warm. Where do you want to go?"

"The Silver Queen."

My second home. The only one I now have.

Chapter Forty-four

By Monday mid-morning, Inez had steeled herself for the expected visitation from representatives of her church. She knew they would come, to offer clothes, food, and spare blankets to one of their own. Of course, the church women would not set foot in the saloon where she now lived, so they had harried their hapless husbands until three could be found to make the requisite call.

Inez, nursing her second cup of coffee of the day, rose when Sol brought them back to the kitchen area, and thanked them for their offerings. Bridgette interrupted their visit when she arrived breathlessly late that morning.

"Oh, ma'am! I'm sorry, but it took forever for me to get down the Hill and through town. The whole of the parish is buzzing with what happened last night." She looked askance at the baskets of food and small bundles of used clothing and blankets on the table.

"Goodness, ma'am," she said after the church members left. "Don't they know I'll be sure you eat well and proper and that you've plenty of clothes and such upstairs?"

Inez stacked the clothes on top of the blankets. "They're just trying to exhibit Christian charity, Bridgette. It's the thought that counts."

And thought was all that was left to her this morning.

She turned the coffee cup around and around, its revolutions echoing her spinning thoughts. There was one person who could help unravel the last mysteries behind Lizzie's murder. But she was, as far as Inez knew, still in jail. And Inez hadn't the energy yet to go and see her.

Bridgette, hovering as she did, also added her own stream of commentary and inadvertent information. "Well, ma'am, it's just so sad. Your home. And such a pity about Officer Ryan."

"Yes," said Inez, spinning the cup. She, the reverend, and Cecil Farnesworth had agreed. Until more was known, it seemed best to let people believe The Hatchet had died in the fire trying to rescue her. "I've no desire to pursue this further," Inez had said wearily to the two men, while unlocking her office door in the dark after-midnight hours of Monday morning. "Who will believe us? We have no proof. And those who know won't talk."

Bridgette kept up a steady stream of comfortable chatter in the face of Inez's silence. "On my way here, I was stopped by Mrs. Kelly. You know, Officer Kelly's wife? She says, it's just tragic, tragic, that Officer Ryan died in the flames trying to save you. Because, he told her once, soon after he came to town, about his little daughter. She had perished in a fire not two years ago."

Bridgette paused, wiped her eyes, and crossed herself. "The missus apparently just never got over it. That's why she and Officer Ryan...well, why she's not up in Leadville with him. But, Mrs. Kelly says, Officer Ryan nearly died himself in trying to save their little girl, and ended up burned all over, lungs and throat damaged from the smoke. It almost took his voice. Not that one would know, since the fire didn't reach his face. But it apparently caused him pain, every day. He hardly slept from the pain and the demons, I gather. And Mrs. Kelly's brother was Officer Ryan's physician, so she should know. I'm truly surprised that Officer Ryan never turned to drink, in the face of such an awful thing. He was a saint, a saint. Mrs. Kelly told me that he refused to take to the bottle, because her brother said that Officer Ryan found relief through chloroform. Chloroform, can you imagine? Thank goodness for miracles of modern medicine. Although Mrs. Kelly also whispered that Officer Ryan wasn't above taking a wee bit of something else when the pain was too severe, on occasion. *Opium*, she said. Humph. She said her brother swore on the holy cross this was so. But only after she'd nearly forced him to say so, I suspect. Or maybe she made it up. I don't know that I'd believe everything that Mrs. Kelly says. She tends to let her mouth run ahead of her thinking, if you know what I mean, ma'am."

"I do," said Inez, clutching her own aching head. "I do believe I know what you mean, Bridgette."

All in all, Inez wasn't surprised when, just before the saloon opened that afternoon, there was a light tapping at the back door, and when Bridgette opened it, Frisco Flo was there. The madam stood on the narrow back porch, outfitted in a severe and very proper walking suit, holding long skirts up with one hand to reveal mud-splashed galoshes, and gripping a wrapped bundle and an umbrella with the other.

"Excuse me, Mrs. O'Malley," Flo said with great dignity. "I'm here as a representative of the church to extend my sympathies to Mrs. Stannert, if I may."

"Well," sputtered Bridgette. "Well now. She's already had some church folk stop by—"

"Bridgette, it's quite all right." Inez rose. "Mrs. Sweet, please come in. Do you wish any coffee?"

Flo shook her head. "Thank you, but no need."

"If you have a moment, I have something that needs to be returned to you. It's upstairs in my office."

Flo's eyebrows went up a fraction. "I suppose I could take a minute, then."

Inez herself took the madam's umbrella from her and waited while Flo removed her galoshes. The two of them then left the kitchen and headed upstairs.

"I need to talk to you," Inez said under her breath, while unlocking the door.

Flo stared straight ahead, clutching the wrapped parcel to her suit jacket. "It's quite all right, Mrs. Stannert. I'd quite understand, if in the light of current events, you may wish to cancel our agreement."

"Shhhh. It's not that." Inez opened the door, gestured Flo inside and to the loveseat, entered and closed it behind her, and moved toward the safe, talking. "You see, after we signed our agreements and you were detained by the law, I returned to your house and locked your front door." She held up Flo's house key and set it on the table by the loveseat.

"Why, thank you, Mrs. Stannert." Flo picked up the key and dropped it into her purse.

"And one more thing." Inez rose, went into her dressing room, and returned with Flo's embroidered purple dressing gown. "Zelda asked me to return this to you." She handed Flo the neatly folded bundle.

Flo looked surprised. "Zelda had this? She must've grabbed it when the fire broke out. Last I saw it, Lizzie had it on." She smoothed the rich purple fabric on her lap, sadness sweeping across her face. "Lizzie and me, our last conversation, if you can call it that, we argued about this wrapper. I was so damn angry she'd stolen it from my room. She was always sneaking through my things." Flo looked up at Inez, eyes haunted. "A stupid dressing gown."

"I'm sorry for your loss." Inez sat in her office chair. "I, too, have a younger sister. When I tried to imagine what I would have done in your position…I would have hunted down and killed whoever did that to her. Or tried to." She rolled the chair back and forth, thinking how to phrase what she was about to say. "Flo, I have a question. Your third business partner. The Hatchet?"

Flo sighed. The release sounded like it came from her very soul.

"Why?"

Her mouth twisted. "It wasn't my decision. He knew I ran the most financially successful brothel in Leadville. He saw a business opportunity. When I decided to move, he came and…" She stopped. Then, "He didn't want anyone to know that he was part-owner of a whorehouse. Given his reputation in his church, his hopes for being elected city marshal, and who knows what-all."

"Well, it seems you held all the cards, Flo. You could have exposed him at any time."

"No." It was said harshly. "He knew that Lizzie was my sister. He was supplying her with opium, laudanum, liquor. He just laughed when I confronted him. He knew I'd not have my own sister thrown into the streets or jail."

Inez frowned. "Then why kill Lizzie? She was his guarantee. His insurance. I don't understand."

"While I was cooling my heels in the county clink, I had lots of time to think about Lizzie's death. I couldn't hardly think of anything else." Flo looked down at the dressing gown and traced one embroidered butterfly. "I think she knew about my deal with The Hatchet. I didn't tell her, of course. Lizzie could never keep a secret, even when she was little. So, maybe it was something I said, or something she found while sneaking through my stuff, or something The Hatchet said. Hell, it could've been Lynch next door that told her. He and The Hatchet were in cahoots in all sorts of schemes, and Lynch was soft on Lizzie. But however it happened, I think she found out, and then The Hatchet learned about it. He must've guessed she'd talk, sooner or later, and then his plans would be ruined."

"But once Lizzie died, what held you back?"

Flo's gaze slid to the photo of Inez's own son, on the desk.

Inez sat back, sure at last. "The child. The baby in the picture in your home. Yes, Flo, I'm sorry. I did snoop. I went back for my glove and to see if I could find out the identity of your other business partner. But then, I saw the photograph. The half-finished letter. Is she your daughter? Is that what The Hatchet held over you, so that you couldn't do anything about the deal or what he was doing to Lizzie? Did he threaten to tell your parents how you *really* make your money here in Leadville?"

Tears formed in Flo's eyes, but did not spill over. Still, she didn't look away from Inez. "Janie's not my daughter. Not mine. Lizzie's."

Inez closed her eyes. Not knowing what to say.

Flo cleared her throat. "But I'm the one who supports her, loves her. It was just easier to say she was mine. Well, what's one more little lie, after all?" She patted her blond curls absently. "I'm passing myself off back home as a successful Leadville dressmaker and laundress. Pretending to be Janie's mother is easy, compared to that. Because I do love her, as I would love my own."

She turned to the bundle beside her, saying, "Thank you for the key. Now, this is for you." She handed it to Inez and clasped her black-gloved hands together. "It's a small thing. But when I heard about your house, about The Hatchet…You saved me, Mrs. Stannert. It's a token of my thanks and gratitude."

Inez picked at the plain brown paper and string, finally revealing a neat stack of piano music. She leafed through it, amazement growing. "Chopin. Beethoven. Mozart. Oh, Mrs. Sweet, I don't know what to say."

"Well, you know, the gentlemen who come by for comfort and companionship, they really prefer the lighter variety of popular music," said Flo, busy rearranging her hatpins so that her small black hat sat at a jaunty angle. "I looked at all that this morning, after they released me and I returned to my girls. What a mess the house has become in my absence! And, of course, Molly has disappeared. Took my best clothes and some of my jewelry, damn her eyes. Thank goodness the jewelry was mostly paste. I keep the real diamonds hidden in my home. In any case, I thought, who better to put these to use than Mrs. Stannert?"

She cocked her head to the side, smiled brightly, and stood, holding the rolled-up dressing gown under one arm.

Inez rose with her, clutching the music close. "How can I thank you?"

"It's I who must thank you." Flo tweaked her gloves, lining up the buttons. "I really must be going now. So much to do. Don't trouble yourself, Mrs. Stannert. I'll see myself out." She fluttered her fingers at Inez. "Toodle-oo. Until later. Partner."

Chapter Forty-five

Inez begged off the opera that night, much to Bridgette's dismay. "But ma'am, he's the *president*. You'd get to see him, say hello."

"Bridgette, I played *poker* with General Grant, and he skinned me alive. Believe me, attending an opera and sitting somewhere in a distant box, listening to all that singing, would be very anticlimactic."

However, when Reverend Sands dropped in to see how she was doing, she insisted that he attend. She also asked that he stop by the Silver Queen in the early hours so she could accompany him to Malta, where Grant's party and the reverend were to catch the four-thirty morning train.

⟨⟩⟨⟩⟨⟩

The sky was still dark when Inez and Reverend Sands disembarked from the hired hack in Malta to say good-bye.

They stood on the outskirts of the group that had come to see General Grant off on the next leg of his Colorado tour—a much smaller group than had greeted him a mere five days ago.

Five days. An eternity. Five days in which lives were lost, reputations ruined. On the other hand, lives were also saved. Jed is still alive. Zelda and her beau are on their way to California and a new life.

There was the dark, and there was the light. There was water—she held out a gloved hand to catch a few new raindrops—and fire.

The private car attached to the D&RG train waited, door open to receive the travelers. The reverend gripped her hand tight. Inez could sense his reluctance to let go of her.

"I could stay another day. Help you get settled, and catch up with them later. This is a bad time for me to leave you."

"I'll be all right. You said yourself you'd be back in two weeks. Besides, you can hardly deny a direct request from the general himself. And I have Abe, Sol, goodness, Bridgette will be feeding me non-stop in the hopes that her cooking will mend not just my aches and pains but my sorrows as well. I'll be busy at the saloon, and busy seeing if there's anything salvageable from my home. I doubt it though. My piano is gone. William's baby things, my music, my books. Some of them I've had with me since I first left home. They cannot be replaced."

"Perhaps it's time for you to look forward and cease looking back."

Inez shook her head, not willing to admit how much the loss of her things—mere things—distressed her.

There was a time when I could fit everything I had in a carpetbag or two. When traveling light was the rule of the road for Mark, Abe, myself. Now, it appears I've set down roots, somehow, when I wasn't looking. Even with everything up in smoke, I could no more pick up and leave than I could chop off my right hand.

She looked at the departing party, her eyes automatically identifying now-familiar faces. General Grant. Mrs. Grant. Former Governor Routt. Horace Tabor, minus his wife. Kavanagh, off to the side.

"Where are the Wesleys?" she asked Reverend Sands.

"They left yesterday. Quietly. No fanfare. That's to be expected after the revelation about young Wesley. It's a shame that his appetites got out of hand. Although, for the voters' sake, I suppose that bringing his political beliefs out into the light for scrutiny is all for the best. I'd not fault him for pushing for women's rights. I think that will come eventually, when the times are right. As for Chinese immigration..." He turned to her and smiled. "Well, you don't care about politics as you've said many times, so I'll not bore you with my views. Particularly now."

"Another time. I'm thinking I shouldn't cut myself off so much from the machinations of politicians, suffragists, and so on. After all, so many of the men I know drive the engines of commerce and plot the future of Leadville and the state. I don't want to be cut short by a change in the political winds."

He smiled and released her hand. "I'd better board."

The various trunks, hatboxes, and cases were being loaded.

Inez glanced at the hack that waited patiently to take her back to town. "I'll stay until the train leaves. Send me a letter or two on your travels through the Gunnison country."

The reverend seized her hand and brought it to his lips.

She smiled. "God speed, Reverend."

She moved closer to the train as he boarded first.

No doubt looking for hidden explosives, assassins, who knows what. But it's the assassins without knives, who use words as weapons, who seem the most insidious. How does one guard against them?

Someone at her elbow discreetly cleared his throat.

She turned to meet Kavanagh's wide smile.

"Just wanted to bid you adieu, Mrs. Stannert." He removed his hat. "It's been a pleasure."

Below the courtesy, she sensed irony, beckoning, daring her to ask.

So she did. "What are you doing here? I heard the Wesleys left Sunday. I would have expected you to be with them."

"So you would." He glanced at the milling party by the train. The ladies were boarding, navigating the steps slowly with fashionably tight skirts. "But I've been instructed to thank you by my employer. And, as you know, I am forever the obedient, faithful servant."

More irony. This time, thick as snow in winter mountains.

She crossed her arms. "What earthly reason have the Wesleys to thank me? I was the one who resurrected the evidence that brought John Quincy Adams Wesley down in disgrace. Not that he didn't deserve it."

"Did he?" Kavanagh's smile broadened.

Inez narrowed her eyes, dissecting his enjoyment. "What do you mean?"

She felt that familiar drop in her stomach, the sense of dread. The certainty that she'd been played, bluffed from a winning hand. "Are you saying it isn't true? But, I talked with Mrs. Clatchworthy. Heard Lucretia Wesley with my own ears. Young Wesley and his mother were sympathetic to the suffragists."

"Mrs. Stannert." It was said in the tone of a tut-tutting school teacher scolding a star pupil for missing an easy question. "One third truth doesn't make the whole. Simple logic. But emotion, particularly when carried by an entire populace, can be a powerful thing. People see what they want to see. What they want to believe."

She stared at his grinning face. Understanding struck. "You? You wrote the immigration letter?"

"Among my many talents as a 'Pink' in the agency long ago, I found a knack for forgery very useful."

"You had access," she gritted through her teeth. "You took the stationery."

"Like taking candy from a baby."

"That photograph. Yours?"

"Money can buy anything. A scandalous picture. A few words dictated and scrawled on the back. Money buys silence."

"Whose money?" she demanded. "Lucretia paid you to keep charge over her son. Not that you did a very effective job of that! Her son paid you to look the other way."

He leaned toward her, appearing to enjoy every moment. "They paid me well. But someone else paid me better. Someone who saw a way to kill two birds with one stone. Politics. Money. C'mon, Mrs. Stannert. My employer says you are clever for a woman, although not so bright when it comes to treating powerful men right. I say that you'll figure it out. You'd probably have figured it out much earlier, except for the fire and all the rest of that State Street business. The train is leaving, Mrs. Stannert.

Don't force me to tell you. I'd be very disappointed. We've a small wager on this."

Politics and money. Who stands to profit by casting Wesley into political limbo? Who stands to profit by tarring Harry Gallagher with the brush of being on the side of Chinese immigration? Who is powerful enough, thinks he knows women, wants me to understand and see how he has maneuvered events, wants my attention, is someone I might have slighted…

She felt the color drain from her face. She turned toward the train, took two steps forward.

The women had boarded the train, as had all the men except for…

Horace Tabor stood on the steps, as if to take a last look around the area that held the silver mines that had made him millions. Mines he continued to accumulate, amassing enough power to, by all accounts, eventually propel him to Congress.

If none more qualified stands in his way.

His wandering gaze finally landed on Inez, before switching to Kavanagh. Kavanagh raised a hand, waved. Tabor shrugged and glanced at Inez once more, a small smile nearly hidden beneath his walrus mustache, then disappeared inside the train.

Kavanagh turned to Inez. "Thank you, Mrs. Stannert. I've won my bet. I'd better board and collect."

Like Tabor, he looked reflectively about, his gaze settling on the mountains. "Nice place, Leadville. Lots of opportunities for a fellow like me. Might be, you'll see me again sometime. Maybe you won't mind standing me a drink for old times' sake."

Chapter Forty-six

The hack creaked to a stop in front of the Silver Queen saloon, and Inez stirred in the seat, half-awake.

"This where you wanted to go, Mrs. Stannert, ma'am? Not back to your home?"

"I guess you haven't heard, Mr. Jones. This is my home now."

She pulled out her purse, but the hack driver stopped her. "It's okay, ma'am. The reverend's taken care of everything. We're square."

She nodded and climbed out of the hack, taking a deep breath of rain-washed air, holding it, then letting it out slowly. All during the creaky ride back, she had wondered, tried to divine, how she could have been played for such a fool.

Finally, she worked it out.

I wasn't. I just happened to be there. I snubbed Horace Tabor, true, but he'd set everything in motion long before he walked into the Silver Queen three days ago. It was a lucky chance for him that Zelda had the letters and photo, and that I was after Zelda for other reasons. And everyone knows, Tabor is a lucky man. Well, it was lucky for Jed as well. Too, would I trade the life of a friend for some young whelp's political ambitions? Luck runs like a river, toward some people and away from others. And there is just no telling who will profit and who will lose in the end.

The Wesleys' future was not her business nor her concern, really. They had money. They could move, start over somewhere else. New Mexico territory. The Dakotas. Back to San Francisco, Boston, or Nevada City. They had the world at their fingertips. Money did that. This was just one move in a much larger chess game, and she had no doubt that they would recover. *Unlike Jed, if I hadn't found the so-called proof. He'd be lying under a pile of dirt in the graveyard right now or dying of a gut wound, I'm sure of that.*

And—she glanced at the sunrise—there was so much ahead of her.

Seeing her son again. Deciding what to do with Flo's old building. Perhaps she and Abe could look into buying Lynch's place. Or maybe Abe could buy it straight out, and they could run two businesses, side by side. A respectable boarding house for gentlemen only, and another high-class saloon. Either way, they'd work it out, and swing the deal.

There was the divorce to pursue. *And, the good reverend. Where shall that lead?*

Musing, Inez unlocked the door to the saloon, and walked into the gloomy interior. The rising sun hadn't yet penetrated to the corners.

By the backmost table in the darkest shadows, a figure stirred, stood up.

Inez tensed, then relaxed, identifying a familiar black hat, pulled low, on a black-garbed figure. *Did the reverend change his mind? But, I saw him get on the train.*

Then, a voice.

A voice she hadn't heard in over a year.

"Hello, Darlin'."

Author's Note

Beware all who enter here, for spoilers lurk. So, if you haven't actually read *Leaden Skies* yet (preferring, as I often do, to flip to the back of the book first to see what the author has to say), you may want to reconsider.

Serendipity is a word that well describes the process of writing this particular story. For a long time now, I've wanted to do something with a mapmaker who comes to Leadville. I have copies of "Birds Eye View" maps of Leadville pinned to the walls of my writing room and, of course, have browsed the ever-fascinating Sanborn maps (earliest for Leadville is 1883, not quite early enough for me). But what fired my imagination was a small pamphlet that a coworker, Katie Walter, lent to me about a decade ago. *Fire Insurance Maps: Their History and Applications*, by Diane L. Oswald, introduced me to the backstory of fire insurance maps and mapmaking. Such maps began popping up in urban areas as early as the 1830s. It was in this booklet that I first learned about "trotters," "pacers," or "striders," that is, the itinerant surveyors for the fire insurance map industry. As Oswald notes, "Regardless of where the strider was stationed or how long he was there, he could be assured of taking away at least a few good stories to share with fellow pacers....Surveyors met more than their fair share of interesting characters. They were sometimes treated with suspicion and occasionally their travels led them into danger."

Danger, you say? Good stories? Interesting characters? I thought: I can use this.

Still, it took until *Leaden Skies* for me to finally work my way around to inventing Cecil Farnsworth, surveyor for the entirely fictional Johnson Fire Insurance Map Company. Serendipity insisted that Cecil's sojourn in Leadville should become irrevocably entwined with the national and local politics of the day.

My focus on politics can be blamed on a couple of "a-ha" moments that occurred during my random research and wanderings through the events of 1880. The first of these moments actually goes back to the genesis of *Iron Ties*, the Silver Rush mystery preceding *Leaden Skies*. *Iron Ties* explores the coming of the first railroad, the Denver and Rio Grande, to Leadville in the summer of 1880. That first D&RG train brought no less a celebrity than former U.S. president and Civil War general Ulysses S. Grant into Leadville (fact). At the end of *Iron Ties*, I knew there was more story to tell. *Iron Ties* brought Grant into Leadville; *Leaden Skies* covers the five days of his visit. While Grant's shadow looms large in the story, the twists and turns play out on entirely fictional John Quincy Adams Wesley, a young man with high political aspirations, who unfortunately draws the attention and ire of the very real Horace Austin Warner Tabor, Leadville's home-grown millionaire and Colorado's Lieutenant Governor from 1878 to 1884. Horace and his wife, Augusta Tabor, were very much present in Leadville for Grant's visit. From books such as *The Legend of Baby Doe* by John Burke, *My Search for Augusta Pierce Tabor* by Evelyn E. Livingston Furman, *Augusta Tabor: A Pioneering Woman* by Betty Moynihan, it's clear that Horace had political aspirations stretching to Washington, D.C., and the Senate.

How, I wondered, would Horace have reacted if faced with a personable, charming younger man, also quite wealthy, who was gunning for the same political ends and who appeared to have a spotless record in the bargain? Would he be tempted to arrange something to get this young whippersnapper out of the way? Perhaps. Maybe. Why not? But, what would he do and how would he accomplish this? I luckily (serendipity again) stumbled across the tale of the "Morey letter" while researching Grant's failed bid to win the 1880 Republican nomination in a convention that bests some of the worst political wheeling-dealings of today. With the Morey letter, Tabor's fictional path through *Leaden Skies* was clear.

What is this letter? Of course, you can search it out on the Internet, but I'll give you a summary here. October 20, 1880, just weeks before the presidential election between Republican nominee James Garfield and Democrat Winfield Scott Hancock, a letter purported to have been written by Garfield was published in the New York City newspaper, *Truth* (nice bit of irony, that). The letter, written on congressional stationery, implied that Garfield was in favor of increased Chinese immigration. Chinese immigration was a hot-button issue of the day, particularly in the West. Garfield refused to say anything until it was nearly too late. (Sources say he kept silent for so long because, without seeing the actual letter, he wasn't completely sure he hadn't written it.) The Democrats took full advantage of this and nearly sunk his presidential aspirations. Finally, Garfield allowed a real letter by him to be compared to the Morey letter, and the difference in handwriting cleared him.

The Morey letter was the genesis of the damning packet that fortuitously lands on the doorstep of my imaginary Leadville newspaper, *The Independent*. Of course, I couldn't just leave it as a letter supporting Chinese immigration, although I liked this angle a great deal: Leadville's 1880 census has no Chinese at all amongst its 15,000 souls (a number hotly contested at the time by local press and others who placed the total number closer to 40,000). So in marched the women's suffrage movement, circa 1880. I had been reading about the suffrage movement in Colorado and was particularly interested in Caroline Nickols Churchill, publisher of the *Colorado Antelope* (later renamed the *Queen Bee*), Denver's earliest women's rights newspaper. A fascinating woman, Churchill liked to brag that she "single handedly performed the duties of editor, publisher, reporter, printer, and hawker." Readers of *Leaden Skies* will find echoes of Churchill in my fictional suffragist Serena Clatchworthy.

And what about Leadville's local police and politics? The year of 1880 was a tumultuous one, according to Eugene Floyd Irey's PhD thesis (1951), *A Social History of Leadville, Colorado, During the Boom Days, 1877–1881*, and *History of Leadville & Lake County, Colorado*, by Don and Jean Griswold. Leadville's city government spent more than it had coming in and was in danger of becoming insolvent. The gathering of taxes, licenses, fees, and fines was pretty haphazard, to the point that much of the money never made it to the city's coffers. Early in 1880, the city council created the position of city collector and appointed a member of the police force to the position. The city collector was instructed to go forth and collect fees, particularly from the saloons. (The major source of the city's revenue, as it turns out, came from the licenses of billiard and gambling halls, saloons, and bawdy houses.) However—and here's the catch—it wasn't until October 1880 that the city council passed a resolution that "the several officers collecting moneys for the City be required to account for the same…and that they make a monthly report of the same." (Irey, pg. 219) The force had its own problems, including corruption. Leadville's *Daily Chronicle*, June 11, 1879, described the typical Leadville officer as "numbered and branded with a star and turned loose.…He is amenable to nobody nor nothing. Makes arrests when he feels like it, and sometimes tries and discharges his own prisoners. If there is one place in the city where he can find more comforts than another, that place will be well watched." This and more provided a very plausible door for the imaginary Hatchet to bully his way into my story.

To continue down the darker side of State Street…For information about drugs, drug use circa 1880s, and poor Lizzie's fate, I turned to *Chloroform: The Quest for Oblivion* by Linda Stratmann, *Ether Day* by Julie M. Fenster, *Menace in the West: Colorado and the American Experience with Drugs, 1873–1963* by Henry O. Whiteside, *Buried Alive* by Jan Bondeson, and the ever-responsive and genial D.P. Lyle (author of *Murder and*

Mayhem: A Doctor Answers Medical and Forensic Questions for Mystery Writers). As for prostitutes in the Old West, well, they are a slippery bunch when it comes to facts, despite all the books written about them. However, among those that continue to give me much food for thought are *Daughters of Joy, Sisters of Misery: Prostitutes in the American West 1865–90* by Anne M. Butler; *Hell's Belles: Denver's Brides of the Multitudes* by Clark Secrest, and *Gold Diggers & Silver Miners* by Marion S. Goldman. I particularly recommend the last, which has a succinct section exploring the relationship between lawmen and the prostitutes on the Comstock Lode from the mid-1860s through the 1880s. Much of what is said here applies to Leadville as well. I'll just quote one enticing bit from page 107: "Most of the local legislation regulating sexual traffic indirectly encouraged police corruption in their interaction with prostitutes....Police had the option of enforcing the law at their own discretion, and a friendship or a bribe could shut their eyes to misdeeds, while a rebuff might open them."

Now, as to what is real and what is fiction in *Leaden Skies*. One of the pleasures of writing historical fiction, I've discovered, is to slide my fictional characters and their doings into the "shadows" of actual historical events. First, Leadville is real. Two marvelous books about the city and its fascinating history are *Leadville: Colorado's Magic City* by Edward Blair and *History of Leadville and Lake County, Colorado* by Don and Jean Griswold. Second, the really bad weather that storms through *Leaden Skies,* making life generally miserable for my characters who must slosh through it all with or without galoshes, waterproofs, and bumbershoots, is no fiction. Leadville's *Evening Chronicle,* July 26, 1880, notes that during Grant's visit "the skies were a nasty medley of rain, hail, and fog nearly the whole time." Grant's Leadville itinerary is, for the most part, straight from the newspapers of the time. The midnight procession from train to downtown is real, but not the assassination attempt. A persistent "firebug" (the culprit was never found) did indeed torch the marshal's home while the fire companies were in the procession, and for a while, it was feared that State Street would go up in smoke. Of course, Frisco Flo's brothel is an invention of the mind. Grant and his associates indeed toured Leadville's mines, but not the Silver Mountain Mine as that, dear reader, is made up. Though the various banquets, dances, and speeches really happened, Grant never stopped in at the Silver Queen nor played poker with Inez Stannert as both saloon and saloon owner exist only in the fictional realm.

Finally, a word about the ending. I suspect some folks may want to throw the book against the wall for the last few sentences. However, after several futile attempts to write a different conclusion, I finally accepted what I knew all along in my heart: The book. Ends. Here. The tale of *Leaden Skies* is over, but Inez's story goes on.

To receive a free catalog of Poisoned Pen Press titles, please contact us in one of the following ways:

Phone: 1-800-421-3976
Facsimile: 1-480-949-1707
Email: info@poisonedpenpress.com
Website: www.poisonedpenpress.com

Poisoned Pen Press
6962 E. First Ave. Ste. 103
Scottsdale, AZ 85251